The Mists of Sorrow

The Mists of Sorrow

Book Seven
The Morcyth Saga

Brian S. Pratt

For information concerning books written by Brian S. Pratt, or where to obtain them in either paperback or eBook formats, visit the author's official website at:

www.briansprattbooks.com

ISBN-13: 978-0983338420

Books by Brian S. Pratt:

The Morcyth Saga

The Unsuspecting Mage
Fires of Prophecy
Warrior Priest of Dmon-Li
Trail of the Gods
The Star of Morcyth
Shades of the Past
The Mists of Sorrow*
*(Conclusion of The Morcyth Saga)

Travail of The Dark Mage
Sequel to The Morcyth Saga

Light in the Barren Lands
Book 2 *Forthcoming 2011*

The Broken Key

#1- Shepherd's Quest
#2-Hunter of the Hoard
#3-Quest's End

Qyaendri Adventures

Ring of the Or'tux

Dungeon Crawler Adventures

Underground
Portals

Non-fiction Works

Help! I don't Want to Live Here Anymore

For my children:

Joseph
Breanna
Abigayle

Prologue

The smell of corpses rotting in the summer heat reaches them long before they arrive. Over a dozen wagons trundle across the gray desert in search of treasure. Several days earlier a massive explosion had rocked their small village to the west, a tower of flame reached far into the heavens until finally returning back to earth.

Unsure what caused the explosion, they were curious but fearful. Then word came a day ago that what they witnessed had been part of a battle and the dead were lying all over the place. Knowing the worth of weapons and armor the dead may still possess, they immediately gathered their wagons and went toward where the tower of flame rose. Times are hard in the desert and the gold they can get from the sale of the items could well mean their continued survival.

A half day into the journey, they encounter the gray sand. Fear grows among the scavengers but the promise of wealth pushes them onward. The gray sand wasn't so much sand as it was a powdery substance which worked into every crease of their bodies, making the trek miserable. But these people are no strangers to adversity, life in the desert being what it is and all. Pushing onward they continued forward.

Finally, the dead begin to appear ahead of them. Zyrn, the leader of the scavengers, licks his lips in anticipation when he sees the armored bodies lying before them. Scanning to the left and right, he searches for any others who may already be here to gather the booty. But as far his eyes can see, there's nothing moving.

"What a haul!" exclaims Nyn, a goat herder by trade.

"Yes," nods Zyrn in agreement.

Continuing to draw closer to the dead, Zyrn suddenly comes to a stop and an odd expression comes over him.

Stopping beside him, Nyn asks, "What's wrong?"

Pointing to the area where the dead lie, he says, "The gray sands end where the bodies begin."

Nyn looks ahead and sees the almost perfect circular area wherein the dead lay. "What could it mean?" he asks. Indeed, in some places where the dead must have fallen across where the gray sand begins, the parts that would have extended out onto the gray area are gone. Sections of bodies lie all the way around the perimeter, all of them show signs of scorching from great heat.

Shaking his head, Zyrn replies, "I don't know." *What could have caused this?* Scanning the area once more he glances back to Nyn. "Looks okay now," he says with a touch of nervousness.

Others come abreast of Zyrn and Nyn as they too look upon the oddity. Mumbled fears pass between them until Zyrn raises his hand and the others fall silent. "Whatever happened here is past," he tells them. "Let's be about our work."

Once again rolling forward, the wagons move to the dead where the men and women begin stripping them of their weapons, armor and other valuables. What gold and jewels they find go into a communal pot so to speak, which will be distributed evenly among them upon their return to their village. The armor, weapons and anything else of bulk goes into the wagons.

While stripping the dead, Zyrn finds not only dead northerners, which he assumes once belonged to what people are saying was a band led by none other than Black Hawk, but also soldiers of the Empire. When he comes across a slain Parvati lying in the sand, his hand hesitates a fraction of a second before removing the swords from its dead hands. He knows what a Parvati would do should he see a non Parvati in possession of such.

As they continue about their work, the mood of the scavengers lightens from that of fear. When nothing immediate happens, they press forward with more vigor and enthusiasm. Wagon after wagon begin to fill with the booty from the dead, not only weapons and armor, but clothing as well. Anything that may be of use or sold is taken.

They work throughout the afternoon until the sun begins to reach the horizon. "We're not going to get it all before the sun goes down," Nyn says as he comes to where Zyrn is taking a knife from the chest of an Empire soldier.

Standing up, Zyrn flips the knife into the nearby wagon and gazes around the battlefield. Still a hundred or more of the dead have yet to be stripped. The wagons are all but full and none wish to remain in this area once night has fallen. There's just a bad feeling about the whole place.

Gazing to the sun to gauge the time, Zyrn turns to Nyn and says, "Another half hour and then we'll leave."

"That's cutting it kind of close don't you think?" he asks.

Greed and fear battle within him, but greed finally wins out. "By the time we return, someone else could have come and taken the rest," he explains. "I'm sure we'll be alright."

Nyn gazes at him for a moment then nods his head. Leaving Zyrn's side, he returns to where he had been working before coming to talk with Zyrn. He spreads the word that they will remain another half hour, most of the others are not entirely happy about it. Speeding up their efforts, they try to collect as much as they can before it's time to go.

A half hour later, the sun has reached the horizon. Everyone is packing the last few items away as Zyrn mounts his horse and takes position at the head of the wagons. Once all is ready, he hollers for them to roll and they begin leaving the dead behind. Dozens of the dead soldiers have yet to be stripped of their armor, though the rest of their valuables have been taken. Some look back longingly to the items left behind but none wish to stay any longer in such an area. The prospect of being here when the sunlight fades makes them very nervous.

They are still in the gray area when the sun completely drops below the horizon and dark begins to envelope the world. Pushing onward through the growing dark, they roll for a couple more hours until they finally reach the edge of the gray area. At least they think they do as the only light with which to see is that of the stars.

Zynn pauses and then dismounts. Picking up a handful of dirt, he confirms the fact that they are indeed past the gray area. The sand here once again feels like it's supposed to. "Make camp," he says. As the wagons gather together and the horses are taken from their traces, he gazes back to where the dead lie. In a way saddened by the loss of life, yet at the same time thankful for the opportunity his village will have to survive another year or two. Sighing, he turns back to the others and helps with setting up the camp.

The night continues to deepen as the hours fall away. When the world has slipped into the deepest part of the night, a figure moves among the dead. His passing brings cold, cold to the world and cold to the soul. Behind this figure move two others, both wearing dark armor with another four in robes following them.

Winding their way around the bodies of the dead soldiers, the one who leads searches for the place he desires. All his carefully laid plans are coming to fruition. When his dark lord set him upon this task so very long ago he knew it would take centuries until he arrived at this critical moment.

First he destroyed the priests of Morcyth. His lord told him how they would send for another, one not of this world. He would know of this one's coming when the Fire and Star walked together under the sky. Then, all that followed would culminate into what happened here.

When he sent Abula-Mazki to bring this mage to him, he wasn't sure if this was indeed the one told of in the prophecy. But when his warrior priest was defeated and said the Fire walked with the Star, he knew. For Ozgirath, High Priest of Dmon-Li, the waiting has come to an end.

His yellow eyes pierce the dark as if it was day, but it is not with his eyes is he searching. Magic of the darkest sort flows through him as he hunts for the exact spot he requires. He hardly gives the dead, both stripped and otherwise, any consideration as he walks among them.

Then, his senses come across a slight vibration. Pausing for a moment, he searches for its source. Once the location is found, he moves again and walks to where the vibration resonates the strongest. *This is the place*, he tells the others mentally.

They come to a halt and wait. One comes whom he requires for what is to happen next. He sensed her approaching since he first came here. That which is driving her leads her directly to him and it isn't long before she appears out of the dark and comes to stand before him.

A bedraggled woman with madness in her eyes, she doesn't know why she's here, simply that she must be. Haunted and driven by needs and desires since that fateful time in Willimet, Serenna gazes into the yellow eyes and trembles.

With a thought, Ozgirath has the two warrior priests take hold of the woman. A scream is ripped from her throat as her arms are taken. Despite her struggles, the grip of the two warrior priests is like iron. Incoherent gibberish issues forth from her as fear takes what little mind she has left.

The four priests of Dmon-Li move into a diamond formation around the source of the vibration. Once they are in position and have begun casting the required spells, Ozgirath removes a dagger from within his robe. The two warrior priests bring Serenna to the spot where the vibration is the strongest and hold her there.

Magic continues to build as the priests ready the area where James' explosion ripped the fabric of this plane. Not a hole mind you, rather a weakening in the boundary between this plane and the rest. Such a weakening can be manipulated to create a temporary gateway between this plane and another. For a permanent one, it requires something a bit more.

He holds the dagger in his hand for a full minute before sensing that the critical point in the creation of the spells has been reached. Then with a deft move, he plunges the dagger within Serenna's heart.

A soul wrenching cry and then she sags into lifelessness in the hands of the warrior priests. They lay her down on the ground, her blood aiding to weaken the barrier still further. But that alone was not why she was here. If that was all that was needed, he would have used those scavengers that were here earlier.

With her death, a dark spirit forms above her lifeless body. It has been waiting within her since that time in Willimet when she had used the globe to control her followers. When the globe was smashed, the spirit contained within took up residence inside of her. Yet again another part of his plan the mage unwittingly helped along.

It's a spirit from the plane upon which Dmon-Li resides. Centuries past it was brought to this world and put within the globe like a genie in a bottle to await the time when it will be needed.

Floating upon an unfelt breeze, it hovers above her body at the center of the vibration. The resonance of the vibration begins to change as it works to warp the resonance to match that of the plane the spirit originated from. Once the two resonances synchronize, the four priests unleash a wave of power that intersects the spirit.

With the waves of power pouring into it, the spirit begins sinking into the ground. As it comes into contact with the ground, the ground itself begins to glow a deep dark purple. The purplish glow expands until the spirit is completely within the ground. Now twenty feet across, the glowing area comes to within inches of each of the four priests.

Ozgirath sends forth his senses yet again and finds that the barrier between this plane and Dmon-Li's has been reduced to almost nothing. Satisfied, he then sends his senses up to the sky. It takes but a moment to find that which is required to punch through from this world to the other.

In seconds, it makes its appearance as it hits the atmosphere. A greenish ball of fire arcs through the sky on a trajectory to the purplish glowing area. It leaves a brilliant trail of bright green light across the sky as it hurtles toward the ground. In the blink of an eye, it strikes dead center to the glowing area.

The energy from the force of the impact is absorbed by the magic of the four priests. Taking the energy from his priests, Ozgirath opens the way.

Suddenly, from the purplish area a hand emerges. A mammoth hand which is followed by the rest of the creature and soon one of the monstrosities from the plane of Dmon-Li stands upon the sand next to Ozgirath.

As the next monstrosity makes its way to this world, several shadows pass through as well. Again and again more monstrosities pass through until six stand upon the sand, over a dozen shadows move about the area. With the number he requires, Ozgirath begins closing the way. Several more shadows slip through before he reaches the point where the void will close on its own.

At that point the magic from the priests stills, and the High Priest of Dmon-Li walks from the battlefield. Behind him come the two warrior priests, the four priests and the monstrosities summoned. Most of the shadows come with him but a few wander away into the desert.

Filled with a sense of triumph he returns to the portal which will take him and the others back to Ith-Zirul. When again the Shroud of Killian blinds the giant's eye, his lord will come.

Far away in the desert, Zyrn stands in fear. The greenish star hurtling through the sky sent a premonition of impending doom through him. Others gather near him as they ponder the ramifications of such an omen. It doesn't take them long to decide not to wait for the coming of dawn. As quickly as they can, they hitch up the horses to the wagons and hurry back to their village. All thoughts of returning to the battlefield for the rest of the booty are gone.

Chapter One

James stands on the battlements of Al-Ziron. Once the northern fortress of the Empire it now protects the southern border of Madoc. Stripped of all but a handful of men, it fell quickly when the forces of the Alliance led by Lord Pytherian arrived.

Illan's Black Hawk banner whips in the wind atop the highest spire of the fort signifying that Black Hawk has taken up residence here in Al-Ziron at the request of Lord Pytherian. He now bears the title 'Keeper of the Southern Reaches', which effectively makes him a nobleman. Aside from the new title and the nobility it confers, he has been given large tracts of land in the surrounding countryside for his own. Most of the land he plans to divide among those Raiders who have been with him since the War of Barrowman's Field.

Illan and the others arrived here shortly after the fort fell two days ago. Shortly after their arrival Lord Pytherian had asked Illan and his men to take over the southern defense. Madoc is woefully short of men and Black Hawk has the only sizeable force which could be spared for the duty.

James glances out over the battlements as he gazes at the long shadows stretching across the countryside with the approach of dusk. He's still not feeling his normal self. The backlashes of power he experienced during the final moments of the battle with the mages have left him weak and achy. About the only magical thing he can do now is his orb. Also with the insistence of Jiron, he uses his mirror to hunt for Tinok but that has yielded nothing. Every time he's tried, the mirror has remained blank.

After relating what transpired in his vision, Jiron has been most anxious to find his friend. Unfortunately all James has managed to determine is that Tinok lies somewhere to the south. How far or where exactly he couldn't pin down due to the fact the only magical location spell that works is the cloth to point his whereabouts.

Within the walls of Al-Ziron the wounded have been brought, both those of Madoc as well as the Empire. Miko, along with Brother Willim and the two remaining members of the Hand, have been among the wounded and ministering what aid they can since they entered the gate of Al-Ziron. Other healers work with them, but they use practical methods rather than magic.

As far as the Empire soldiery still out in the field, here around Al-Ziron there are no forces of any size. To the east, with help from the Kirkens, the Empire has been thrown back to the previous border. To the west the battle still rages but it's only a matter of time before the Empire is forced completely out of Madoc.

"You okay?" a woman's voice asks.

Turning around, he finds Tersa walking toward him.

"Better," he replies. "Still not great." He can see the weariness in her eyes, eyes that have witnessed too much battle. "How about you?"

Shrugging, she gazes over the battlements to the west. With the last rays of the setting sun shining upon her face she says, "I just want to go home."

He understands how she feels. However, the area between here and Kern is not safe. There are still roving bands of Empire forces on the move, not to mention one or two bands of mercenaries out looking for mischief. The southern route to Cardri is not safe at the moment.

The Merchant's Pass, according to all reports, has yet to reopen and probably won't until the hostilities further subside. So that leaves the northern route through Dragon's Pass. The area due north of Al-Ziron is firmly in the hands of Madoc and once at the Sea they could turn west and make it to the Pass with relative safety.

"Has Jiron talked with you yet?" he asks.

She shakes her head in reply.

"He wants to go in search of Tinok badly," he explains. "But his need for keeping you safe is more important to him." He pauses as she turns to look at him. "So in the morning we're going to ride north and escort you, Delia and anyone else who wishes to return home to Dragon's Pass."

"What about Tinok?" she asks. "This could take days or even weeks." In her eyes is the fear that because of her, Tinok might die.

"Illan's going to loan us spare horses," he explains. "If we ride hard, we should make it there and back in just over a week."

She looks at him skeptically. "That isn't going to leave you much time," she states.

"What good will Jiron be if we leave you here with Illan?" he asks. "His state of mind will be shot. Besides it's not just you but Delia too. She's a trader at heart, not a warrior. From what I understand she's managed to get Devin and the others to be guards for her caravan when she returns."

Smiling, she asks, "How did she do that?"

Shrugging, he replies, "I don't know. Maybe they finally got sick and tired of all the blood and guts. Caravan guard duty is less valorous, but you stand a good chance of surviving it."

Giving out with a slight chuckle, she says, "True."

Illan offered them all a position in the command structure he's creating to secure the southern border. Only Jorry, Uther and Yern took him up on it. The pit fighters, when they learned that James and Jiron were going in search of Tinok, turned him down. If Tinok is in trouble, they wanted to help. Illan informed them that the offer stands should they ever change their minds. There are few enough people that he feels he can completely trust, and those that have ridden with him the last year are among them.

Even at this late hour, riders continue to pass through the main gates. Most are scouts and messengers, though a few are civilian in nature though not many. Some of the freed slaves they brought out of the Empire decided to remain with Black Hawk and have taken service here at Al-Ziron. Those who wished to continue further into Madoc in search of home or loved ones have already done so.

At the gates the grizzled old timer Nerun, along with a squad of men, questions everyone who passes through. Their job is to see to it that no spies of the Empire enter the fortress.

"Illan's giving us a send-off tonight in the main hall," he tells her.

"I heard that," she replies. "Seems he even dug up several musicians."

"Probably just soldiers with some talent," he guesses.

"We should get ready, it's going to start soon," she says. "That's what I came up here to tell you."

"Very well," he says and then follows her down from the battlements.

Wounded are lying in rows across the courtyard. Fortunately for them, it hasn't begun to rain yet and it doesn't look as if it will for some time. James and Tersa are forced to make their way around pockets of wounded as they head for the main hall. Off to one side they see Miko with the Star healing a man with a bloody rag tied around his face. Brother Willim and the other two remaining members of the Hand are elsewhere in the courtyard helping others, green glows surround each of them.

"I'll meet you inside," he tells her.

"Okay," she replies and then continues on toward the main hall.

Angling over toward Miko, he sees him still kneeling next to the man with the head injury. Just as he draws close, the glow from the Star winks out and Miko sighs. A healer who has been assisting him removes the bandage from his face to reveal a pink line where a jagged cut had been moments before.

Miko looks up at him with weary eyes.

Offering a hand, James helps him to his feet. "How much longer are you going to be?" he asks.

"As long as it takes," he replies.

"You're dead on your feet now," states James. Glancing around at the wounded still waiting for Miko's attention he says, "None of these men will die if you get some rest."

"I know," he says. "But I can shorten their recovery time and perhaps some will be able to have better lives because of what I do."

James nods, he can understand where he's coming from. "We're leaving in the morning," he tells him. "A quick ride north to see Tersa and the others safely to the border of Madoc then we set out in search of Tinok."

Miko nods his head as he comes to a man who lost two fingers during the battle. The man's comrade sitting on the ground next to him holds a blood soaked rag containing the severed digits. "I'll be there," he assures him.

"Get some rest if you can," he suggests.

Taking the bloody rag containing the fingers, he turns to look at James and says, "No promises." Then he removes the digits and has the man's comrade hold them in place as the glow shines forth from the Star.

Leaving Miko to his healing, James heads toward the main hall. Jiron is standing on the steps having just witnessed him with Miko. "He's not coming to the dinner?" he asks.

Shaking his head, James replies, "No. I doubt if I would in his place." Glancing at Jiron he adds, "Some things are more important."

"You got that right," he agrees. Just like Miko, he's torn between what he wants to do and what he must. Tinok or Tersa? A hard choice but Tersa won out even though he still agonizes over the decision. He simply could not let her and the others brave the trip through war torn Madoc by themselves. If something should happen, he never would have forgiven himself.

Side by side, the two friends pass through the archway leading to the main hall. As they enter the short hallway that goes from the archway to the main hall, music begins to play. Not great music, but at least the musicians are all on the same beat. Walking down the hallway, they approach the doors leading into the festivities.

Not a great many people were invited to the feast; the old time Raiders, the crew from The Ranch and several others whom James doesn't know. He wishes Lord Pytherian had remained but he and his men had left shortly after Illan agreed to take over the southern defenses. He and his men were needed in the west to finish the job there.

Upon entering the hall, Illan who's dressed in regular clothes waves them over. Off to one side are the three musicians, though they look the part of scruffy old soldiers more, who fill the hall with music.

When they take their seats, he leans forward to better be heard over the musicians. "Word came that another force is on its way up from the south," he tells them. "Should be here in a day or two."

"How many?" asks Jiron.

"Not enough to cause us any problems," Illan assures him. "It may be a delegation to discuss the cessation of hostilities."

"That would be welcome news indeed," nods James. "Are they going to want their fort back?"

Illan laughs, "Probably. But they're not going to get it. Reports say that they stripped their southern territories of soldiers in anticipation of the summer's campaign in Madoc. Most of those have been slaughtered since our first attack at Lythylla."

Just then Delia comes in from one of the side entrances, with her hand resting on Shorty's arm. When they join them, Shorty has a big smile on his face and Jiron arcs an eyebrow at Delia.

"Oh stop what you're thinking right now," she says, a slight blush coming to her face. "It's nothing like that."

James glances questioningly to Shorty who grins and says, "I asked her if she would like an escort and she said yes."

"Escort," snorts Jiron.

Shorty pulls out her chair for her and holds it while she sits down.

"Thank you," she says to him.

"You are welcomed milady," he replies with a bow. Then he moves down the table and takes his seat.

"...I tell you it is true!" Potbelly's voice comes to them before he enters through the main doors. Scar, who's walking beside him nods in agreement.

"Oh lord now what?" James says.

Jorry and Uther walk with them and you can see they aren't buying whatever it is the other two are saying.

"I swear it! She had three breasts," continues Scar.

"In your dreams maybe," counters Jorry.

Uther crosses to their table and asks Jiron, "Have you ever heard of a three breasted woman?"

"Can't say as I have," he replies.

"Ha!" Jorry exclaims. "I thought not."

"He wouldn't have known her," insists Potbelly, "she only came to our fights. Once in awhile she would invite us back to her place for a little entertainment."

Under his breath Uther says, "I bet it was little."

"Ah, what do you know from anything?" blusters Scar.

"I know a lie when I hear one," retorts Jorry.

"Enough!" shouts Illan.

The entire hall falls quiet and the musicians abruptly stop as all eyes turn to them. Realizing they are now the center of attention, they glare at each other and take their seats at the table. When no further commotion happens, the musicians resume their play and the normal murmur of the guests returns.

Devin and the rest of the recruits arrive as a group and take their places at a nearby table. The last to enter is Aleya. When Jiron sees her he freezes in place. From somewhere in this fortress she's found a dazzling blue dress that fits her perfectly.

Delia reaches over and pushes up his chin to close his mouth. "Go over there and escort her to her chair," she urges.

Getting up, he hurries over and just as Shorty did with Delia, he offers her his arm. Placing her hand upon his forearm, she strolls with him back to their seats. James gets up and offers her his chair so she can sit next to Jiron.

"Thank you," she says as she takes the offered seat.

Jiron practically thrusts James out of the way so he can be the one to push her chair closer to the table once she's seated.

Rather than be angry at the rude way he was pushed, James grins at Jiron.

Once James and Jiron have taken their seats, Illan stands and takes his goblet in hand. Banging it three times on the table, he stands and waits until the hall has quieted. Nodding to the two guards at the other end of the hall, he signals for them to close the main doors.

With every eye on him, he raises his goblet and says, "For Madoc. May her future be better than her past."

Throughout the hall, glasses are raised as the guests cry out, "For Madoc!"

Once everyone has taken a drink and thus honored the toast, Illan sets his goblet down and says, "Friends and comrades. I for one never thought I would host a dinner here in the fortress of Al-Ziron." At that several chuckles sound out from various men in the hall.

"Tonight we honor one who more than any other made this happen," he says. Picking up his goblet once more, he turns to James and says, "To James. Mage and ally of Madoc, without whom Madoc would even now be grinding under the heel of the Empire."

"To James!" the cry resounds throughout the hall. Jiron glances to his friend and grins. He knows how James hates the spotlight and would rather just sit at the fringe observing.

"Now," announces Illan, "let the feast begin!"

From the sides of the hall, men bearing platters of food enter and begin sitting them on the tables. Not a great variety, nor are there any specialized treats, this is the best that can be had on short notice.

During the meal, the talk gravitates from the past, to the future then back to the present. All are hoping for a complete and quick halt to the war. Once the feast begins to wind down, Delia takes Shorty by the hand and soon has him out on the floor dancing. Aleya, not one to be outdone, drags Jiron out as well.

The night is spent with feasting, music and friendship. They all try to forget that their group will soon be splitting up as James and those going with him leave on the morrow. At one point the musicians fall silent and are given a break while Jorry and Uther regale those at the feast with a tale of how they got the better of an assassin who was trying to kill Jorry. Seems he besmirched the daughter of a well-to-do merchant who hired the assassin to take care of him. One thing led to another and the assassin was eventually handed over to the town guard and the matter was never again brought up.

When they finished their tale, the listeners responded with a vigorous applause. Scar and Potbelly were about to start in on one of their own when the musicians started up again. Scar glances over to the musicians and was about ready to tell them to stop when he sees Delia standing there next to them. Giving him a glare and shaking her head, she moves to Yern and drags him out to the dance floor. Apparently she wanted to dance more than hear another of his wild tales.

About this time, Miko makes an appearance. Blood soaked clothes and some serious bags under his eyes, he walks through the main doors. James notices in one hand he's holding a half-eaten tart. Where he managed to acquire one of those he has no idea.

Plopping into the seat next to him, Miko stuffs the remainder of the tart in his mouth.

"Where did you get that?" James asks him.

"The cook," he replies. "One of the men I healed was his brother. He asked me what my favorite food was and I replied 'Tarts, though I doubt if there are any to be had here.' Well, two hours later here he comes with a plate containing half a dozen steaming hot tarts."

"Don't suppose you have any left?" he inquires.

Looking somewhat guilty, Miko shakes his head. "Sorry, that was the last one."

James pats him on the shoulder and gives him a grin. "That's okay," he says. "After all you've done for everyone, you deserve them."

"Next time I'll save one for you," he assures him.

A few minutes later, Brother Willim and the other two priests of Asran enter the hall and make their way toward them. When Brother Willim draws close James indicates the chair recently vacated by Jiron while he's out dancing with Aleya.

Taking the seat, Brother Willim leans back in the chair and sighs. The other two priests join Derek and the others at their table.

"Tired?" asks James.

"Yes, very," he replies. Nodding to Miko he adds, "I think between Miko, my brothers, and I many lives were saved. What there is left can be readily dealt with by the healers." A server brings him a cup of ale and he downs it in one gulp. Giving out with a satisfied 'aah' he sets the cup on the table where another servant carrying a pitcher comes forward and refills it. "Thank you my son," he says to the server as he takes up his cup once more. The server nods and immediately withdraws back to the wall where he scans the assembled guests for anyone else in need of a refill.

"I heard you are leaving in the morning?" asks Brother Willim after taking one more swallow of ale.

"That's right," replies James. "We're going to escort several of our comrades to Cardri. Most of them aren't really suited for warfare."

"None of us really are," he states. After pausing for another drink he says, "I would still like to accompany you if you don't mind."

"What about your fallen brothers?" he asks. "Aren't you going to escort them back with the other two?"

"No," he answers. "My brethren can do that well enough, what I needed to do has already been done."

James is delighted to have such a man journey with him. But then a thought comes. "This wouldn't have anything to do with me being the 'Gardener' would it? If I remember right, you called me that during that last big battle in the desert."

Brother Willim gets a crooked grin and nods. "Somewhat, yes," he replies.

"Just what does it mean that I'm the Gardener?"

"There's an old prophecy handed down from old…," he begins.

"Isn't there always?" interrupts James with a sigh.

"What?" questions Illan who had been listening in on the conversation.

Not realizing he had spoken aloud, James turns to him and says, "Oh, nothing." Then to Brother Willim he says, "Sorry for interrupting you, please continue."

"Centuries ago, a man came to one of our lord Asran's temples," he continues. "Which one I'll not say. The man was wracked with fever and eventually slipped into the sleep of the dead. Not completely dead yet not completely alive either."

Must have been in a coma, reasons James.

"During the time when he lay in the sleep of the dead, there were times when he spoke. At first the priests attending him thought his words were gibberish until one old scholarly priest realized the man was speaking in a language long dead to the world of men. Only the most learned scholars still understood the language, some of the oldest surviving tomes we have are written in it."

"Immediately they had the priest begin writing down the words the man spoke. He wouldn't speak often so they had the priest stay with the man constantly, ever prepared to put to parchment the words of the man."

"And has anything the man spoke of come to pass?" James asks.

Nodding, Brother Willim says, "Yes, several." He takes a sip of ale and then continues. "After the first several months, he began speaking of the end of the world. Of fire and shadows consuming all life."

At that James and Illan glance to each other. They can see reflected in the eyes of the other the memory of the shadows they have encountered.

"There are many passages linking the Gardener to the end of the world. Some foretell of his coming, others speak of events that will transpire before he walks upon this earth." Glancing first to James then to Illan he adds, "At least five that I know of have come to pass in the last few years."

"Okay," says James. "What makes you believe that I am the Gardener of which he spoke?"

"I will tell you of two," he says. "Here is the first,"

> **When *evil arises, its neighbors to swallow,***
> ***A man shall come to lands gone fallow.***
> ***With might and right its tide to slow,***
> ***The Gardener walks the lands to sow.***

"We believe the arising evil is the Empire," he states. "'Swallowing its neighbors', that's exactly what it is doing. And since it mentions the Gardener, that would conclude he would appear at this time."

"But that's pretty vague," James says. Turning to Illan he asks, "Hasn't the Empire been 'swallowing its neighbors' for hundreds of years?"

Nodding, he replies, "Yes they have."

James turns back to Brother Willim.

"As I said there have been other prophecies the man spoke that foretells the time of the Gardener's coming," he says. "I and my brothers have no doubt that that time is now." He can see the doubt in James' eyes. "This next prophecy we have never been able to satisfactorily discern its meaning. However, it should have meaning for the Gardener."

> *Ships through air, a walk on the moon,*
> *Invisible death his kind has strewn.*
> *Box of pictures, music from stone,*
> *By these things the Gardener is known.*
>
> *Traveling far from a land apart,*
> *Lost and alone on the path he will start.*
> *The light of knowledge shall be at his side,*
> *Salvation or death, the edge he doth stride.*

When he finishes he looks to James for his reaction.

James sits back, his mind churning over the prophecy. The first stanza has to refer to Earth. *Ships through the air, a walk on the moon, Invisible death his kind has strewn.* Airplanes, Neil Armstrong and the invisible death could refer to radiation fallout. The rest of the first stanza is also referring to his home.

The next stanza, well he definitely comes from a land apart. And he did start lost and alone when he went through the door at the interview. He glances to Miko who has been listening to the whole conversation. "The Star must be the light of knowledge," he says. "Morcyth is a god of learning so that makes sense."

"But the last line, *Salvation or death, the edge he doth stride,*" Miko replies. "What can that mean?"

Shaking his head he says, "I don't know." He then arcs an eyebrow questioningly to Brother Willim.

"You are heading toward a time when you are going to be placed in a situation where your actions will determine the fate of this world," he explains. "Other prophecies refer to it, but none are clear as to when you will reach that moment or the decision that will be pivotal. I'm sorry I can't be of any more help than that."

Great, thinks James. *As if I don't already have enough to worry about.* "I think I would have just as soon not known all this."

"I understand," says Brother Willim. "Many of our brethren argued that foreknowledge could alter the outcome to our doom. Others of course argued that it could only help if you knew what was going on."

"What do you think?" Miko asks.

"I am not sure," he replies. "Before I left, I was instructed only to reveal this to you should you specifically ask."

"But I never would have asked if you hadn't mentioned it earlier," James says.

Nodding, Brother Willim says, "True. I can only believe that Asran wanted me to say it so you would know. I have prayed about why I said what I did and each time receive a feeling of peace."

"Whether it helps or not," James says with a yawn, "I'm to bed." Looking at the others near him he adds, "We got a long way to go and a short time to get there." As he stands up he breaks out into a chuckle as the phrase sparks a memory from home.

"We'll see you in the morning," Illan says. "I must remain until the feast winds to a close."

"See you then," says James. Leaving the table, he's joined by Miko who's all but dead on his feet. Jiron sees them leaving and waves to them from the dance floor. When he passes by Scar, Potbelly and the other pit fighters he asks, "You guys staying?"

"For a little while longer," Scar tells him.

"Don't stay up too long," he tells them and then heads for the exit leading to his room.

Miko walks with him until he reaches his room. Both remain quiet, the words Brother Willim spoke still running through their minds.

At James' door, Miko takes his leave and goes down to the next door which is his. Entering his room, James creates his orb and undresses before crawling into bed. Canceling the orb, he begins to drift into sleep.

Just before he completely succumbs to sleep, the tingling of magic comes to him. Alarmed, he grabs his slug belt and hurries out the door. The cry to Miko dies on his lips when he finds one of the members of the Hand of Asran outside his door, a soft green glow about him.

"Rest peacefully," the priest tells him. "I shall watch tonight."

"Uh," stammers James, slightly embarrassed for running out into the hallway in his small clothes, "thanks." Ducking back into his room, he closes the door and returns to bed. Chuckling at the mental picture of himself in the hallway, he's able to drift off to sleep.

Later in the night, a guard is walking the battlements when a green light appears in the sky and falls to a point to the east. He's seen many falling stars, but none of that color. Making the sign against evil he pulls his coat tighter around himself and continues his watch.

Chapter Two

The following morning James rises with the sun. Quickly getting dressed, he buckles on his slug belt and throws his pack over his shoulder. Leaving his room, he meets Miko in the hallway as he's leaving the room next to his.

"Ready?"

Closing the door, Miko nods. "Yes. The cook should have breakfast ready when we get there."

James grins at that, Miko had always been one who liked to eat. It's a marvel he's not fat. Walking side by side, they follow the aroma of fresh baked bread to the dining area where everyone else has already arrived and begun to eat.

Moving through the morning diners, James makes his way to the table where Illan sits. Ceadric is there as well and he takes the seat to his right.

"Good morning all," he says as he sits down. No more than a moment elapses before a server comes with a plate of tubers and boiled beef from the Empire's store of goods. This fortress had been well stocked with all the necessities by the Empire before it fell. Illan isn't going to have to worry about resupplying for at least a month.

Illan nods as he sits down and says, "Looks like you will have fair weather for travel."

"The road north is clear," adds Ceadric. "Reports say the only Empire forces in Madoc are those currently locked in battle with our armies."

"That's good to know," he says as he digs into the food.

"Be careful anyway," warns Ceadric. "You never know."

"We will," he replies.

It's a somber mood among the companions, each knowing that when the meal is over most will head north while others stay behind. Even Scar and Potbelly are subdued. They're going to miss the rivalry they have enjoyed with Jorry and Uther. The four of them sit off to the side and every once in awhile one or the other raises their voices in good natured scoffing. The fact that it is only once in awhile and not a constant series of outbursts reveals how melancholy they are about their impending separation.

The meal finally comes to a close and the companions make their way to the courtyard where several Raiders have already prepared horses for travel. As the others mount, Delia comes to Illan and gives him a hug. "Your Alaina would have been proud by the way things have turned out for you," she tells him.

A slight tear comes to his eye as he replies, "Yes. I think she would." He helps her into the saddle and then turns to James. "There will be fresh horses waiting for you on your return."

"I appreciate that," he says from the back of his horse. "Expect us in a week."

Illan grins. "If you make the trip in a week you will definitely need other steeds."

"Good luck to you all," Ceadric says. To the sides of the courtyard, all the Raiders stand at attention in respect for those who are leaving.

Once everyone is mounted and ready, James salutes Illan smartly and then turns toward the gate. Making their way out from the keep, he can't help but glance back one more time to the friend he's leaving behind. He seriously doubts that things would have turned out so well if Illan had not been with him. Not for the first time does he wonder if another had a hand in such a stroke of good fortune. It's been awhile since Igor's made an appearance and he wonders what he may be up to.

Behind him ride Miko, Jiron and Aleya, and then Brother Willim. The other two remaining members of the Hand of Asran are there to bid him farewell. They will leave later in the day to return their fallen brothers to the temple.

Next come Delia and Tersa, the pit fighters and then finally the recruits. As the last rider leaves the gate and they close, he gets them up to a fast gallop. The road ahead is deserted, which is what they were expecting. Who in their right mind would be traveling in a war zone anyway?

Keeping a fast pace, they make Saragon in two days. Along the way they encounter the occasional Madoc patrol which does little more than find out whom they are and where they are going before allowing them to continue.

They make camp at Saragon the second night. The last time they were here it was occupied by the Empire and gangs of slaves were reconstructing the city. That is until the slaves rose against their captors to give James and Jiron a chance to escape the city.

He remembers the old man Derrion, whose family had kept a secret given to them centuries past. That secret eventually led them to Ironhold and the Star of Morcyth. James has not forgotten his promise to tell the tale of the last fight when Derrion led the slaves in revolt here to allow them a chance to escape. He plans to when time and opportunity permits.

Tents of Madoc soldiers dot the landscape in front of the gates. The soldiers appear fairly lax. Now that the lines are far to the south once more, they can afford to drop their guard some.

"A bit different than the last time we were here isn't it?" asks Jiron as he comes to stand next to James. They didn't bring any tents with them, just bedrolls and gear for inclement weather. He plans to move fast and the added weight would only slow the horses down.

"You can say that again," replies James. "I thought for sure that they had planned to stay."

Scar and Potbelly make their way from the soldier's camp where they had been finding out the news of the local area. Coming straight to James, they stop just before him. "It's clear to the north," Scar states.

"Yeah, appears the reports Illan received back at the keep were accurate," adds Potbelly. "Except that the Merchant's Pass is now open. Looks like we won't have to make the added trip all the way to Dragon's Pass."

"Excellent," Jiron says, happy that there will be a few less days before they begin the search for Tinok. "We can escort them to the Pass and then head back south."

The sound of sparring comes from where Stig is drilling with Devin and Moyil. The recruits have become fighters of some skill, though nothing to the degree of the pit fighters. Against regular opponents, thieves and such, they should be able to hold their own. Devin, aside from the sword, puts in some practice with the spear James had given him so long ago. Why he still carries it is a mystery. Maybe it's due to the fact James had used magic to harden and sharpen it, it's really quite a good weapon.

"We'll be at the Pass in little over a day," Potbelly says.

"Good," James says as he glances over to where Delia and Tersa are talking with Aleya. He makes his way over to them and their conversation halts when he draws close.

"Excuse me," Aleya says. She then gets up and walks over to Jiron. Taking him by the hand they walk some distance from the camp.

James looks questioningly to Delia and Tersa but they don't offer any explanation. Shrugging, he sits down with them. "The Merchant's Pass is open," he tells them. "We'll be there day after tomorrow."

Tersa gets a sad look on her face and Delia pats her on the knee. "So we're not going all the way to Dragon's Pass?" she asks.

James shakes his head. "No, you should be safe once you're within Merchant's Pass," he says.

The sad and worried look comes to her face again as she glances over to her brother.

"He'll be okay," she assures him.

"I know," she replies sadly.

Delia glances to James and says, "She's worried for her brother."

"Hey," he says reassuringly, "We've been through some tough situations before. I'm sure everything will turn out alright."

"Besides," offers Delia, "Aleya will be with him." That brings a smile to Tersa's face. "How much of a risk will he take with her along?"

"You have a point," she admits.

At the mention of Aleya, they all turn to watch them sitting on Jiron's blanket together. Her head is lying on his shoulder and his arm holds her tight.

"I made her promise that if they were to marry to wait until they returned to The Ranch so I could be her maid of honor," she tells them.

"I doubt if that boy will ever ask her," Delia says. "It took Cassie to work on Tinok before he even thought to ask." Sadness comes over them at the mention of Cassie and Tinok. Both lives have taken a definite turn for the worse. Cassie died and Tinok is facing an unknown fate at the dark of the moon.

"We'll see," James says. Then to change the subject he asks Delia, "What do you plan to do once you're back?"

"Start up with trading again," she says. "I doubt if any trader over in Cardri knows half as much as I do about what it's like over here and what is needed. My wagons should still be with Roland and hopefully the horses too. I told him he could sell them if he needed to."

"I doubt very seriously if he'll need money that badly," replies James. When he left, a bag of gems still remained in the chest sitting in his room from the last expedition to the cave under the Merchant's Pass.

"We'll see," she says. "May have to hire more guards, though." She then nods over to where the seven recruits are congregating around the fire. "They may not be enough in an emergency."

Giving out with a yawn, James stands up and says, "This might be a good time to turn in. We still have a long way to go." He then turns and makes his way over to his bedroll. On his way he lets everyone know it's time for sleep. Lying down, he hears the sound of the rest beginning to turn in.

Next to him, Miko is already asleep. Still worn out from the extensive healings he did back at the keep, not to mention the grueling ride of the last two days, he turned in some time earlier. His now familiar snores disturb the quiet of the night.

He lays there for awhile, unable to sleep despite the fatigue he feels. Staring up at the night sky, he stills his thoughts and begins to breathe deeply. This method of calming his mind has at times aided him in falling asleep. Gradually he sinks further toward sleep. Just before he completely succumbs, Miko's arm suddenly begins thrashing and strikes him in the side.

Jerked back into wakefulness, he grabs Miko's arm before it has a chance to strike him again. He can hear him moaning and from the light of the campfire, sees his other arm thrashing slightly.

Sitting up, he takes his free hand and places it on his friend's chest. Shaking him slightly he says, "Miko, wake up." But he continues to thrash in whatever dream has hold of him.

Then from behind him a green glow suddenly springs to life and Brother Willim moves toward them. "Do you feel that?" the priest of Asran asks.

"What?" asks James.

"Something..." he says then trails off when he sees Miko there on the ground, thrashing around slightly.

Giving Miko a firmer shake James says a little louder, "Wake up."

With a gasp, Miko sits up and quickly looks around. Panting and sweating, his eyes finally settling on James. "Oh man," he says, voice trembling.

The light from Brother Willim disappears and James glances back at him. "It's gone now," the brother says. Looking around the camp, he finds they are the only ones awake.

"You okay?" he asks his friend.

"It was just a dream," he finally breathes. That's when he notices James has hold of his arm.

"Sorry," apologizes James as he releases his arm, "you were thrashing about."

"What was the dream?" asks Brother Willim. James can detect a slight seriousness in his voice.

Taking a deep breath he says, "I was running through a shattered city." Looking to James he says, "That's the best way I can describe it."

James nods and says, "Go on."

"Well, something was after me though I never saw it," he says. "I just knew. I raced through the broken buildings toward a bright shining light. When I finally got there I found that it was a temple, shining forth with a light that eased my fears."

"Then, my fear returned stronger than before. I looked around but couldn't find the cause of the feeling. Then, the light coming from the temple began to dim. Blackness started to ooze up from the ground, and where it touched the stones of the temple, the stones darkened until finally turning black." He looks at them, eyes wide with remembered fear.

"The further up the walls of the temple the darkness climbed, so rose my fear. Just before it completely consumed the entire temple, you woke me." He sits there a moment in silence then turns again to James. "It seemed so real."

"It may have been more than a normal dream," states Brother Willim. "There was something while you dreamt, something from elsewhere." When James looks at him questioningly, he adds, "I can't really explain it better than that. I feared it may have been a return of the shadows but it felt different."

"But what could it mean?" he asks glancing first to Brother Willim then back to James.

"I don't know," admits James. "But the way you were acting can't be good."

"Dreams are often sendings from the gods," Brother Willim says. Then to James, "The more closely you deal with them, the more likely they will touch you that way."

"Could my dream have been a message from Morcyth?" Miko asks. "From an actual god?"

Shrugging, Brother Willim says, "Perhaps. However, it's been suggested in theological circles that when you grow closer to one god, you also become closer to others." He can see the confusion on Miko's face at that. "Let me put it to you this way. In a city there are various districts, the rich, merchant's, poor sector, so forth. You follow me so far?"

Miko nods his head though still looks a bit lost.

"Okay, say you go to visit someone where the rich and affluent live. When you go there, you are also in closer proximity to the others that live there too. And thus, they are able to reach you better. Does that help?"

"Not really," he replies.

"I think I understand," says James. "The more you interact with one, the more likely you can be reached by another."

Nodding, Brother Willim says, "Yes. But it is only a theory, though a favored one."

"So who sent this dream to me?" asks Miko.

"We don't know," replies Brother Willim. "All we do know is that it is more than just a dream and thus should not be dismissed lightly."

James sits there in thought for a moment then says, "I would guess the temple you saw, the one emitting light represents Morcyth. Either a specific temple or the religion in general."

"That would make sense," agrees Brother Willim. "Seeing as how closely you are tied to Morcyth."

"Then the darkness…?" he asks.

"Is something threatening its very existence I would think," Brother Willim says. "Considering the way you reacted."

James can see the worry on his friends face. "We're not going to figure this out tonight," he says. "Let's all try to get some sleep. Maybe a night's sleep will help."

"Good idea," suggest Brother Willim.

Lying down, Miko says to James, "What if it comes again?"

"Brother Willim and I will be right here if it does," he replies. "Don't worry about it."

Chuckling, Miko says, "Yeah, right." Closing his eyes, he tries to return to sleep.

James glances to Brother Willim who only shrugs. They each return to their blankets and think on what Miko had told them. If James had trouble falling asleep before, it's nothing like now. Sometime later in the night, he does manage to sink into sleep.

Zyrn stands under the stars at the edge of his village, gazing to the west. Within his village of Abi Salim, there is much celebration. The loot that had been acquired two days ago will go a long way in seeing them through the coming years. Already, plans are being made to send the wagons to the south to sell the weapons and armor at the markets of the larger towns.

But for some, there is no celebration. When they had returned to Abi Salim that first day, a dozen of the younger men had decided to return and collect what had been left behind. They should have been back by this morning at the latest. The fact that they haven't worries him.

He's not alone in his vigil, several wives of the young men as well as various other family members stand with him. "What could have happened to them?" one woman asks to no one in particular.

Remembering the ill omen that had streaked through the sky, he has little hope of seeing them again. It was decided that in the morning if the young men haven't returned, he and several other men would ride out to see if they could find them. Some have supposed the men could have had a wagon wheel break on them, or maybe a horse took lame and they were returning slower than usual. Unwilling to dash their hopes, he keeps his opinions to himself.

Then from out of the desert a movement is seen in the starlight. From its shape it appears to be a man stumbling about. Zyrn and two of the other men rush out toward the approaching man, the women follow right behind.

"Khalim!" cries out one man in recognition. Khalim was one of the young men who had gone to the battlefield and happens to be the man's son.

Zyrn and the father reach him at the same time. Another man carrying a lantern joins them and they stop in shock at what they see. Eyes wide, a tinge of madness to them, his hair is disheveled and matted to his head. He hardly looks like the same man that left two days ago.

"Khalim!" exclaims one of the women. "Where are the others? Where is Ibala?"

Khalim's eyes dart around without recognition. A speck of white foam begins to ooze from the corner of his mouth.

"What's wrong with him?" his father asks.

"I don't know," Zyrn replies. "Take him home."

"Ibala!" cries the woman, and then others begin crying out the names of their loved ones.

"We can't wait until morning," one man says.

Zyrn turns to him and says, "No, we can't." Taking five of the men with him, they hurry back to their homes and saddle their horses. Once they are ready and each has several torches, Zyrn has each light one. Then with torches held aloft, they race into the desert to try to find out what happened.

Chapter Three

The next morning they are up and off with the dawn. Throughout the day they see the signs of the battles that have raged through here. Ever since the battle at Lythylla turned the tide in Madoc's favor, the enemy has been pushed further back toward the original border. In places the dead remain unburied though there are work details out collecting them as quickly as they can.

Travelers are still nonexistent, at least those of a civilian nature. The odd patrol, messenger or rider at times approaches them from the north but continues by without a word on their way to the south. None ever so much as says hello.

When they reach the town of Cerinet to the north of Saragon, there are more visible signs of battle. Mounds dot the countryside from where the dead have been buried in communal graves. The walls surrounding the city show extensive damage from the Madoc catapults which battered away in their attempt to breach the walls. One gaping hole in the wall shows where the attackers finally were able to bring down the defenses of the defenders.

A squad of men ride to intercept them when they approach but only delay them a moment. Once they find out who they are the soldiers allow them to proceed. Not bothering to linger any longer, they once more head up the road to the Merchant's Pass.

They push their horses relentlessly in their desire to reach the Pass quickly. When darkness begins to fall they are forced to stop and give the horses a break. Even with the spare horses, the unrelenting pace has worn them out.

A quick meal and then they're to bed. Out here on the road, they rotate a watch throughout the night. The recruits have the honor of pulling that particular duty. The barest sliver of moon rises to shed a small amount of light on the world. James looks at it with anxiety. For when it again passes to full and returns to dark, the knife will fall and Tinok will die.

He sees Jiron staring up at the moon too. Getting up, he goes over and takes a seat on the ground next to him. "Worried?" he asks.

Nodding, Jiron replies, "Everyday his doom approaches. And here we are, moving further away."

"I know," he says reassuringly. "Tomorrow we'll see the others safely to the Pass then we can return in search of him."

"Sometimes life can be hard," a voice says behind them. Turning around they see Shorty standing there. "There comes a time in everyone's life when he's faced with two choices at odds with each other. If it's any consolation, I think Tinok would be satisfied with the choice you made."

"Thanks," says Jiron. "Doesn't make me worry any less though."

"If the god's decide we are to find Tinok in time, we will" he says with conviction.

"But what if one god wants us to find him and another doesn't?" Scar asks as he and Potbelly join the conversation.

"Then we are left to our own devices," states James. He gives the pair an irritated gaze. They are doing nothing to alleviate Jiron's anxiety over Tinok.

"Which I find has been the case more often than not," says Jiron. Glancing at everyone he adds, "I appreciate your concern, I really do." Then his eyes flick to movement behind Scar and Potbelly and sees Aleya coming toward him.

As she makes her way between the pair, Potbelly clears his throat then says, "Maybe we all should make ourselves scarce."

With a grin and a wink to Jiron, Scar says, "An excellent idea."

They leave and allow Jiron and Aleya what privacy they can. As James returns to his blankets Aleya sits next to Jiron and as they've done so much of late. They sit and just hold each other as they talk quietly. The last sight he sees before falling to sleep is them sitting together, her head on his shoulder.

That night as he sleeps, dreams of Meliana run through his mind.

Miko had an uneventful sleep, no dream came to awaken him in the middle of the night much to his relief. He didn't mind it when James had the dreams that left him in a cold sweat, but he definitely doesn't care for them now that they are happening to him.

Up with the dawn, they're quickly riding hard down the road. The road has continued to run alongside the river throughout their journey and if James' memory is correct, they'll follow it all the way to the Pass.

Not long after they leave camp they approach what once was the town of Pleasant Meadows. Now little more than a demolished ruin, there's not much more to it than stone walls and chimneys which survived the flames that raged here. Throughout the ruins, people can be seen as they search through the rubble.

"I feel sorry for them," comments Delia.

"War is always hardest on regular folks," adds James.

A few people here and there take notice of their passing, only pausing in what they are doing to watch them ride by. Another road intersects the one they've been following and they turn onto it heading west toward the Pass.

The Silver Mountains begin to appear before them and it isn't long before Pleasant Meadows disappears behind them.

"Not much further now," states Jiron. Elated to deliver his sister to a place of safety, he's also saddened by the prospect of having to leave her once again.

Signs of the Empire encampment where they maintained a presence before the mouth of the Pass appear as the day progresses. They had constructed several buildings during their occupation and fire pits dot the area. At one point a Madoc patrol intercepts them, but as before, they are allowed to continue their journey.

When the mountains have risen high before them, a wooden wall appears ahead. It crosses the road and extends to the river on the right and far to the mountains on the left. Where the road passes through stands an open gate guarded by a squad of men. They see that the men are a mix of Cardri and Madoc soldiers.

One of the men wearing the uniform of a Cardri soldier steps forward as they draw close. Holding up his hand he signals for them to stop. "Good day to you all," he says when they come to a stop. "Are you planning on taking the Pass into Cardri?"

"Yes," replies James. "Some of our group plan to."

"There isn't a problem is there?" asks Jiron concerned.

"Not at all," replies the guard. "Seeing as how they put us out here in the middle of nowhere and all the action is down south, we must look like we are actually doing something." Giving them a smile he waves for them to continue through the gate and into the Pass.

Jiron moves his horse next to his sister's and says, "I guess this is where we part again."

"It looks like it dear brother," she says. A tear begins to well from her eyes and she adds, "I told myself I wasn't going to cry."

Leaning over to her he envelopes her in a big hug. "Everything will turn out fine," he assures her. "You keep working on those bears of yours and I'll be back as soon as I can."

Those who are leaving and moving on into Cardri begin to disengage themselves from the others. The pit fighters move to face the recruits as they gather near Delia.

"Now you be on your best behavior!" Scar tells them.

"If you aren't," says Potbelly, "we'll have to come and thump you."

"Leave them alone," Delia says to them, "they will be fine. A lot better than the last guards I had. They were a bunch of drunken layabouts!"

Shorty laughs and says, "You take care."

"I will," she says and moves to give him a hug.

Blushing, he sits there in the saddle and hugs her back. Behind him, barely heard jeers and inappropriate comments come from his friends.

Aleya gives Delia and Tersa both a big hug goodbye.

Turning to the pit fighters, Delia says, "You boys better be on your best behavior as well." Nodding to Aleya she adds, "If I hear of anyone being rude or belligerent around her I'll come back and do a little thumping of my own!"

"Yes ma'am," Stig says with a serious expression on his face which lasts all of a second before he breaks into a grin.

"We better go or we'll never get home," states Delia. To those not going with her she says, "You be careful and bring Tinok home." Then she turns her horse toward the Pass and begins the last leg of the journey back to The Ranch. Tersa and the recruits follow along behind.

Jiron sits there and waits until they disappear further into the Pass then turns to James. "Ready?" he asks.

Nodding, he says, "Let's go find Tinok."

They spread out in a search pattern not long after leaving Abi Salim. In the dark they went slow as they kept a close eye out for any of the others who might be lost in the dark. By the time dawn comes, none of the young men have yet been found.

"Zyrn, look," one of the men who accompanies him says. Pointing off to the south, he directs their attention to a dozen wagons moving on an almost parallel course with them.

"They're heading to the battlefield," Zyrn says. He knows those who are driving the wagons, they belong to a town south of theirs. Not known for their sociability, Zyrn decides to give them a wide berth. "If they are on the way to scavenge the dead, they won't act kindly to anyone who happens by."

"Maybe they would help us look for the others?" another suggests.

Shaking his head, Zyrn turns his attention to the man and replies, "Not these people. They would just as soon kill you as not."

Just then, the men driving the wagons take notice of Zyrn and his group. With a flick of the reins they race forward to be first to the battlefield, apparently not knowing the dead have been almost completely scavenged already.

Zyrn gauges the distance between them and figures the wagons will reach the battlefield first. "We'll keep our distance," he tells the others. "We have more important things to worry about right now."

Kicking his horse into motion, he moves quickly across the desert. He doesn't travel far before he sees a body lying in the dirt a little to the north. "Over here!" he hollers. The others move to join him and they soon reach the body of one of the missing young men.

Hoping down from his horse, he's quick to realize the young man is dead. Lying on his stomach the way he is, the man almost appears to be sleeping. Reaching out, Zyrn turns him over.

Jumping back in startlement, he almost loses the contents of his stomach. One of the men traveling with him does double over and begins vomiting. The skin of the young man is gray, gray like the sand surrounding the battlefield. Not only that, but his features seem to be sagging like wax held too close to heat. The young man's eyes are open, the pupils are gray as well.

"I think it is Hakim," one man says.

"He is," confirms Zyrn.

"What happened?" another man asks.

"I don't know but we better find the others quick," he says. Mounting he turns to the others and says, "We'll come back and get him on our return." With the rest following he continues toward the battlefield.

When they reach the beginning of the gray area he pauses. The face of the dead man they left behind comes to mind. The fact that his face was gray gives him pause in entering the gray sand.

"There's another!" cries out one of the men.

Further into the area of gray sand lies another of the missing young men. As one of the men makes to enter the grayness, Zyrn yells, "Stop!"

"But he may need our help, Zyrn," the man says.

Dismounting, Zyrn moves to the edge of the gray sand. Bending over, he hesitantly reaches down and touches it. The feel of it is the same as it was when they were here before. Turning to the man he stopped, he nods.

Kicking his horse in the sides, the man races over to the body lying in the sand. By the time Zyrn has remounted the man has stopped and is kneeling by the body. When Zyrn and the others approach, the man glances back to him and says, "It's Ibala."

His features mimic that of the other dead man; gray skin that looks like melted wax and pupils that have turned gray. "Do you think anyone is left alive?" one man asks.

Gazing out over the grey desert Zyrn shakes his head and replies, "I doubt it." Further toward the sight of the battle, he sees the wagons of the other scavengers. They have stopped before reaching the area where the dead soldiers lay.

"They stopped," he comments.

The others look to see what he's talking about. "What do you think made them do that?" one of his companions asks.

"I don't know," he replies. Putting his hand across his forehead to keep the sun off his eyes, he tries to get a clearer view. Then movement catches his eye. Six figures are running away from the wagons back the way they came. "They are running away," he says nervously.

"What should we do?" asks the man next to him. Despite his attempt to sound calm, fear has crept into his voice.

"I'm not sure but we better find out what's going on," he says. Kicking his horse in the sides he bolts toward the fleeing men. Before he has gone half the distance, three of the men fall and don't get up. Then another falls and then another.

He reaches the last man just as he hits the ground. "Stay back!" Zyrn orders the others. Moving closer he watches as the man writhes upon the ground. Not a sound does the man make other than that of his limbs moving in the dirt. A spasm rips through him and he flips onto his back.

Most of his skin has turned gray and is beginning to sag in the same manner as the young men they found. One pupil is gray and the other is almost there. The man's jaw opens and closes as if he's trying to say something. Then another spasm tears through him before his body becomes still.

"Zyrn," one man says with barely controlled fear evident in his voice, "let's get out of here."

"But we haven't found my son," another man argues.

"He's dead!" the scared man exclaims. "They all are!"

"I'm not leaving here until I find my son!" the man shouts.

They look to Zyrn for a decision.

He glances from one to the others and then says, "I'll stay here with Zaki. The rest of you return to the village and tell them what is going on."

The fearful man immediately turns his horse and heads in a straight line home. The others turn to follow him.

"Thanks Zyrn," Zaki says.

"Come on," he replies. Glancing to the wagons, he sees the horses are down even though they are still in their traces. Angling away from the wagons, they begin to creep further toward the battlefield.

Before they go very far Zaki sees another body further into the gray area. Recognizing the cloak upon the body he cries out, "My son!" Kicking his horse in the sides he bolts toward where his son lays.

Zyrn makes to follow him when he notices the ground ahead of them seems to shimmer and shift. A bad feeling comes over him and cries out for Zaki to stop but he doesn't heed the warning.

Pulling up to a quick halt, he watches as Zaki's horse passes into the area that shimmers and shifts. Where the horse's hooves touch the ground, the grayness seems to ripple but Zaki doesn't notice.

"Come back!" Zyrn yells one final time.

Then suddenly, Zaki's horse stumbles and he's thrown to the ground. Zyrn watches in horror as the grayness seems to ripple away from the spot where Zaki lands like ripples across a pond. The horse screams as it hits the ground.

Getting to his feet, Zaki takes a step toward his son before he notices his hands. The parts that had touched the ground now have gray flecks across them. He tries rubbing the gray off on his shirt and some of his skin comes off, leaving a gray trail across his front.

"Zaki!" Zyrn screams.

Zaki turns to look back and Zyrn can see where the gray is already beginning to spread across his skin. Turning back to his son again, he races across the ground until he reaches his side. By this time his horse has stopped its thrashing upon the ground and has grown still.

Kneeling beside the young man, Zaki tries to pick him up but lacks the strength. With a moan, he tips to the side and begins to writhe upon the ground before growing still.

"Zaki!" cries Zyrn. Lifelong friends, he and Zaki go way back. He looks in anguish at his friend who lies unmoving next to his son. "Damn!" he curses.

Just then, his horse rears backward and stumbles. Zyrn leaps from his horse as it falls and hits the ground hard. Glancing back to his horse, he sees its forelegs turning gray. Slowly the gray begins working its way to the rest of its body. Thrashing about, the horse neighs in fear until finally growing still and quiet.

Zyrn scrambles backward until he has put several yards between himself and his now dead horse. He tries to come to grips with what happened to his horse. He knew he stopped outside of the gray area and his horse hadn't moved the entire time he watched Zaki's ordeal.

Then he notices how the edge of the gray area seems to slowly be expanding. *Oh my god! It's growing!* Scooting backward another couple of feet, he pauses and stares at the edge to make sure his eyes weren't paying tricks on him. After a few moments, sure enough he sees the edge expand again.

It's not a constant growth, seems to grow in periodic spurts. Getting to his feet, he casts one last look back at his friend then turns around and runs for all he's worth. If this continues to grow, then his whole village is in danger. Leaving the grayness behind, he races across the desert.

Chapter Four

Four hours past Pleasant Meadows they stop for the night. A quick meal then right to sleep for they plan to make an early start in the morning.

Jiron has pulled the midnight watch tonight. During his watch he keeps a fire going for the comfort of the others, but primarily stays in the darkness surrounding the camp. His eyes remain better accustomed to the dark that way.

Walking the perimeter in a continuous loop, he keeps watch externally with only the occasional glance to those within the fire. He remembers well the shadows which paid a call that one night a couple weeks ago. They had come to attack James and only the quick thinking of Miko and Brother Willim saved him from death.

He is greatly relieved that Tersa is on her way back to The Ranch. If there's anywhere safe in this world it would be there. During their meal he asked James to use his mirror to check on them and had found them camped along the trail. From the way everyone was relaxed around the campfire listening to Moyil tell a story, he knew they were alright. It must have been a comical one from the way they were all smiling and laughing.

Every time one of the sleepers would make a noise, he would glance into the camp. After what James had told him of Miko's experience two nights ago, he's been worried Miko may have another episode.

It's drawing closer to the time for him to wake Stig for his turn. How they all miss the younger guys who use to pull this duty. Another noise from the camp and again he looks to where Miko is sleeping. This time he sees one of Miko's arms moving, if only slightly. Worried, he moves into the camp toward him.

When he reaches his side, he sees sweat beading on his forehead and his lips are moving in silent conversation. James is lying next to his friend and Jiron quietly wakes him. Once James' eyes open and he sees him kneeling beside him, he nods to Miko and whispers, "He's having another dream."

Instantly awake he looks over to where Miko has begun to thrash more animatedly. "Get Brother Willim," he says as he moves to Miko's side.

Jiron nods and goes to get him.

Just as before Miko thrashes, sweats, and his mouth works silently. James is about to awaken him again when a green glow springs to life and Brother Willim steps to his side. "Don't," he tells him.

James' hand stops bare inches away and he turns to glance up at the priest of Asran. "Shouldn't we do something?" he asks with a catch in his voice.

"Is it the same as before?" asks Jiron. He was told after the last time that Brother Willim had sensed another presence during the time Miko was affected by the dream.

Nodding, Brother Willim says, "Exactly the same."

"But," argues James, "we must do something."

By this time the rest of the camp has awakened and stands in a semicircle around them. "I heard about something like this before," Scar says. "It was back in…"

"Not now Scar!" exclaims James.

"Yes now!" he retorts back which draws everyone's attention. "I know you guys don't believe half the things we say but you need to listen now." Beside him Potbelly nods in agreement.

"What is it?" asks James in exasperation. He turns back to his friend on the ground all the while keeping an ear to what Scar is saying.

"There is a way for you to help him," he insists. "You need to understand what is being sent and why."

"How is he to do that?" asks Jiron.

"You must join him in his dream," replies Scar.

At that James turns and looks at him. "I can't do that."

"There is a way," he tells him. "When a person is within a dream or vision sent by a god or being of power, it is possible to join them in the dream."

"How?" James asks.

Scar glances around to the others before retuning his gaze to James. "Take hold of his hand and send magic without guidance into him," he explains. "Whatever power has hold of him will latch onto it. If at that instance you push your awareness into Miko along with the magic, you will be drawn in."

"How do you know this?" asks Jiron.

"Just believe me," Scar insists, ignoring Jiron's question. "You need to get in there."

James sees the sincerity in Scar's eyes. Turning to Brother Willim he asks, "Is it possible?"

"I don't know," he admits. "As part of the Hand of Asran, we were more into the practical use of Asran's power. We didn't spend much time on theory. It sounds plausible though."

James turns his attention back to Miko and sees him thrashing about. Stig has taken hold of his arms so he won't hurt himself. As James reaches out his hand to take Miko's, Jiron grabs his arm.

"What if he's wrong?" he asks.

"It feels right," is the only reply he can give. "Let go."

Jiron removes his hand from James' arm.

Now free of Jiron's grip, James takes Miko's hand. He takes a deep calming breath then sends magic through the connections of their hands and into Miko. Immediately it's grasped by whatever has hold of Miko and he thrusts his awareness along the magical stream.

"Catch him!" hollers Jiron as James suddenly stiffens and begins toppling to the side. Brother Willim reaches him before he can hit the ground and then carefully lays him down.

Indicating where James has hold of Miko's hand, Scar says, "Make sure the connection isn't broken."

"Why?" asks Jiron.

"It could be bad," he explains.

"Bad?" exclaims Jiron. Coming to stand in front of Scar he shouts, "What do you mean, bad?"

"It worked!" is all he can say when he all of a sudden is standing within a city. At a crossroads of intersecting streets, he looks first up one and down the other. Except for himself the place is deserted.

"Miko!" he yells. Listening for a moment he fails to hear a reply. Then from the far side of town a bright light pushes back the gloom. Neither night nor day, the city seems to be in a place of in-between.

He breaks into a run toward the light. After what seems a very long distance, the street he's on turns into a broad avenue. The bright light is coming from the end of the avenue. Hurrying toward it, he reaches the place where the street opens up onto a large courtyard. In the center of which stands a building, the building being the source of the light.

"Miko!" he cries out. Again no reply. The light coming from the building is blindingly bright but he's able to make out an open doorway at its base directly ahead of him. Shielding his eyes against the light, he crosses the courtyard quickly and passes through the doorway.

Once inside, the blinding light diminishes to a more comfortable level. Still no discernable source for the light, it seems as if the stones of the walls themselves are aglow.

"Miko! Where are you?" Still no reply. Moving forward down the hallway he has a feeling of urgency, of needing to find Miko and fast.

Quickening his pace, he flies down the hallway until it opens up onto a large room. In the center of the room is an opening revealing a stairway leading down. Feeling as if he's been here before, he approaches the opening and gazes down. A flight of fourteen steps descend down to what looks to be another level.

Taking the steps quickly, he finds himself in another hallway extending ahead. The glow which had pervaded the stones above is present here as well. "Miko?" he hollers into the hallway. When no answer is forthcoming, he moves down the hallway, a little more cautiously this time.

As he progresses down the hallway, he sees a figure standing with his back to him. Before the figure is a door standing ajar. "Miko?" James asks as he slows his pace even further. When he gets closer he sees that it is in fact Miko.

"Miko!" he hollers and rushes to his friend.

Miko turns his head and says, "I need to get in there."

"Why?" James asks as he comes to stop at his side.

"If I don't, something bad is going to happen," he replies.

"Something bad?" he asks. "I don't understand."

"Neither do I," he replies.

James reaches for the door to open it and Miko says, "Don't."

"How are we to get in if we don't open the door?" James asks.

Miko looks at him and shakes his head. "I have to get in there," he repeats.

Then all of a sudden, the light that had been constant since he first entered the building starts to dim. Glancing behind them back down the hallway, he sees the end of the hallway growing dark. And the darkness is moving toward them.

"We can't stay here," he says. The sight of the darkness sends a tremor of fear through him. Reaching for the door, he again hears Miko say, "Don't."

"There's no other place to go!" he hollers. Taking hold of the door, he pulls it open. For a brief moment he sees the interior of the room, octagonal in shape with a raised pedestal rising from the floor in the center of the room.

Then, a presence comes bringing fear and sapping their strength. The room grows dark as a wave of force lashes into them. Knocking them off their feet, it sends them flying backward down the hallway toward the approaching blackness.

James summons the magic and forms a protective barrier around them. Striking out with magic of his own, he attacks the presence within the room but has no effect. A ripple of laughter, more felt than heard, comes to him from the room as the blackness which has been drawing closer finally arrives.

The stones all around them grow dim and when the darkness touches them it burns like acid. Even the barrier surrounding them does little to keep the darkness from them. Pain, torturing pain erupts from every nerve ending on his body. The last thing James sees is the door to the room slamming shut before he blacks-out.

When James passed out after touching Miko's hand, they watched him closely for several minutes. Anxious that what Scar had suggested might in some way hurt him, they were relieved when he continued breathing and appeared as if he were asleep. Miko too seemed to quiet down shortly after James joined him.

"Keep an eye on them," Jiron says to Brother Willim.

Sitting down next to them, he gives Jiron a nod.

"Now," Jiron says as he turns back to Scar, "just where did you learn this little tidbit of information?"

Scar glances to Potbelly and licks his lips. Turning back to look into the intense gaze of Jiron, he says, "Back in the City of Light." When Jiron doesn't make any comment he licks his lips again and adds, "From Sorenta."

"Sorenta?" he asks incredulously. From the way he said the name it's obvious he knows of whom Scar is referring to.

"Who's Sorenta?" asks Shorty.

"She's a prostitute," replies Potbelly. "Worked over in Mother Chlia's place."

"You risked his life based on a story a prostitute told you?" Shorty asks in disbelief.

"You don't understand," explains Scar. "She wasn't just a prostitute. She had the 'gift'. At least that's what she called it."

"That's right," agrees Potbelly. "There were times when we would visit her when it happened. She said it rarely came while someone else was around, and that since it did, it must mean something."

"And when it happened, she told you to have James take Miko's hand?" asks Jiron.

"Not exactly, no," replies Potbelly.

"When I saw Miko there and heard what James and Brother Willim said to each other, I knew I had to tell you," Scar states. "At the time she told us, she wasn't sure why she felt she had to only that she did. Said the information could come in handy some day, though she was a bit vague about when."

"Things happen for a reason," Brother Willim says from where he sits next to James and Miko. "Who are we to judge their merits?"

"What should we do?" Stig asks.

"Wait," he says. "All we can do is wait."

"If something goes wrong," Jiron says to Scar, "I'm holding you personally responsible." He continues staring at Scar then flicks his eyes to Potbelly before returning to James' side.

Several minutes pass while both Miko and James lie there quietly. Then they all of a sudden begin spasming and with a gasp, James opens his eyes as he sits up. Releasing Miko's hand he gasps, "Oh my god."

A fraction of a second later a scream is torn from Miko as he snaps awake as well.

James looks around with eyes wide. When he realizes he's back in the camp with the others he visibly relaxes. Next to him Miko holds his arms around his chest and groans in pain.

Brother Willim arcs an eyebrow questioningly at James and he says, "Better check him out. I'm fine." The pain which was so excruciating while in the dream with Miko is now quickly beginning to fade.

Nodding, Brother Willim moves closer to Miko and says, "Let me have a look."

Miko removes his arms from his chest and Brother Willim pulls up his shirt. Beneath the shirt his chest is a mass of burns, boils have formed and some are oozing pus. "Get the Star," he says to Jiron.

As Jiron removes the Star from Miko's pouch, Scar asks, "What happened?"

Once the Star is in Jiron's hand he gives it to Miko. No sooner does the Star rest in his palm than a glow envelopes him. They watch in awe as his chest begins to return to normal. The boils recede and the burns turn brown, eventually flaking off to reveal the new skin that has formed underneath.

When the glow from the Star vanishes, Miko is breathing much better.

"Now, what happened?" Jiron asks.

James begins to relate to them his experiences within Miko's dream. When he's done Miko has little to add, the memory of the dream has already begun to grow cloudy. "All I can remember is that I needed to get into that room, but was unable to," he finally says.

"What was the room like?" Shorty asks. "Why did you need to get inside?"

Miko shakes his head. "I can't remember," he admits.

"I caught a quick glance within before the door slammed shut," announces James. "The room was of average size and a pedestal stood in its center."

Jiron has a thoughtful look on his face when he asks, "Did the room have eight sides?"

Shrugging, James says, "Maybe. I couldn't see it all but I suppose it could have. Why?"

Jiron doesn't answer his question, instead he turns to Brother Willim. "You said that the same force or presence was here both times Miko had these visions. Was the presence malign or good?"

"It didn't feel either way," he replies. "It just was."

"Hmmm..." he says as he resumes thinking.

"Let me get this out before I lose my train of thought," Jiron says. "Miko has the Star which is from the god Morcyth. Miko has now had two visions in which a temple is involved, both times the temple radiates bright light." Turning to Miko he asks, "Am I correct so far?"

Miko nods.

Turning to Brother Willim he says, "In one of the prophecy you mention that 'the light of knowledge will be at his side'." Then back to the others he adds, "I believe the temples he saw are the High Temple of Morcyth in the City of Light."

"What makes you so sure of that?" asks Scar.

"First, Miko holds the Star," he says. "Second, a temple of light. I hardly think an evil temple would have a white light associated with it." Turning back to Brother Willim he asks, "Would it?"

Shrugging, the brother says, "I really couldn't say one way or another. But since it was Miko's dream, everything in it would be based upon what he believes to be true."

"So the light would have to be good then," he says. When Brother Willim nods he continues. "Third…" Turning to James he says, "Remember just after we met and were trapped in my hideout, before we fled the City of Light?" When James nods he continues. "How did we get out?"

"Through a secret door my medallion opened up," he says. "A flight of stairs went down and we…" His eyes widen as he remembers.

"Exactly," continues Jiron with a nod, "we went into an eight sided room that had a pedestal sitting in the middle."

"I don't see the connection," Shorty says.

James turns to him and says, "At the time I figured the room with the pedestal to be located beneath the site of the previous High Temple to Morcyth."

"There are too many things here that point to that spot," Jiron concludes. "It has to mean something."

They look at each other until finally their eyes settle on Brother Willim. "If all you say is true," he begins, "then I would have to believe Miko needs to enter that room." He glances to James and says, "And soon."

"It has long been believed that dreams, especially dreams of such power, are sendings from the gods," he explains. "The fact that so many have come in so short a time cannot be dismissed as mere coincidence. James, you have had dreams of Cassie and Tinok in that place you call a carnival. Miko, your dreams are of a temple that is swallowed by blackness. Blackness that you are terrified of."

He glances around and says, "I myself have had dreams of late. Nothing compared to the power of the ones you two have experienced, but potent nonetheless."

"What were yours?" asks James.

"A garden," he replies. "None too surprising given whom I serve. I often have dreams about gardens and such. However, since I've accompanied you, they have become more intense. Lately they have begun differently, but all end at a withered garden. A blackened tree, wreathed in mist, rises high. The tree cracks open, a monstrous creature steps forth and consumes the garden."

"That's it?" Potbelly asks.

Nodding, Brother Willim replies, "Yes." He pauses a moment as the others assimilate what he told them. Then he turns to Miko and James. "I would guess that you, Miko, were sent that dream to tell you something. Possibly by Morcyth or one of his agents. The fact that you were prevented from going into the room seems to indicate that another force was working to stop you from discovering why."

To James he says, "Take your dreams. They start out nice, but when you are about to make contact with Cassie, shadows and other things work to stop you. Finally thrusting you from the dream altogether."

"That would explain a lot of things," agrees James.

"So what should we do about it?" Stig asks. "Wait for more dreams?"

James shakes his head. "No. In the morning we are going to head to the City of Light, find the room with the pedestal, and discover why Miko must go there." He glances at Jiron and says, "I know this will take more time before we can begin the search for Tinok. But with everything going on, I feel we must."

"Then tomorrow we make for the City," agrees Jiron. "You haven't steered us wrong yet. If you feel this is what we must do, then so be it." Behind his eyes the others can tell he wants nothing more than to head straight into the Empire to find his friend. Circumstances seem intent on keeping him from that goal.

James stands up and says, "We all need to get our sleep. It's a long way to the City from here."

Miko nods and lies back down on his blanket, the Star already having been returned to his pouch.

James makes sure everyone is returning to their blankets, everyone but Stig that is, it's his turn at watch. Once they are, he lies down and churns over the events in his mind. He's amazed by the fact that he was able to enter another's dream and wonders if he could do it again. He can't help but wonder if someone had a hand in supplying Scar with that information, wouldn't be the first time such a handy piece of information crossed his path at just the right time. Trying to still his troubled thoughts, it's a long time before he's finally able to fall back to sleep.

Chapter Five

_____

Up with the sun, they head cross country toward the northeast and the City of Light. They ride in silent contemplation. Miko is worried about what may await him in that room below what use to be the High Temple to Morcyth. Will there be a fearsome creature as in the dream? Or will it be something else.

James worries about what all their dreams can mean. In each, a terrible presence has manifested. Within his dreams it was the shadows and monstrosities, Miko had a powerful presence, and Brother Willim a dead, black tree from which a monstrous creature steps. Are they all interconnected, or does each deal with a different event? He doubts if he'll understand before it's too late.

Riding hard, they swap between their spare horses periodically to better able maintain the pace. Cutting cross country as they are, they don't encounter any other travelers, the few farmsteads they pass look deserted. A couple have been utterly destroyed, quite possibly when the Empire came through here last year.

Throughout the day and into the night, they ride. Only the fact their horses are on the brink of exhaustion do they even stop for the night. But it isn't for very long. No sooner does the sun rise than they are again in the saddle and racing across the countryside. A half hour after the sun rises they come to a road traveling east and west. Several wagons are on the road heading toward a town visible to the east.

"That's Reardon," Scar announces when the town comes into view. "Follow the north road leaving the city and it will take you directly to the City of Light."

"Excellent," says James.

They ride for the road and upon reaching it turn eastward toward Reardon. The men on the wagons glance their way but otherwise offer no greeting. The loads they are hauling are mainly comprised of lumber and stone, materials needed in rebuilding the city. As they draw closer to the walls surrounding Reardon, many people are seen moving in and out from the gate where the road passes through.

The walls look fairly intact, though there are places where it's evident the Empire's siege equipment came into play. Not wanting to get caught up with what's going on inside the city, they turn and pass along the outside of the walls as they circumvent the town.

When they reach the road moving northward, they turn onto it and again increase their speed to a fast gallop. Along the road between Reardon and the City of Light, they encounter many civilians. Families as well as merchants and the occasional group of soldiers are upon the road heading south to Reardon. Many have their belongings with them and their mood is one of hope for the future.

James remembers last year and the refugees who were fleeing the approach of the Empire. His heart is gladdened that the fear and hopelessness he had seen on the faces of many has been replaced with joy and hope. He fervently wishes that they will be able to continue having hope and joy for a very long time to come.

Before the walls of the City of Light come into view, camps are seen where they've sprung up along the sides of the road. Tents turned into makeshift taverns operated by smart tavern keepers supply ale and other essentials to those who are working to put their lives back together.

Few women and children are seen, though there are pockets of them here and there. The majority of those they encounter are men, workmen who are here to begin the rebuilding of their country.

When at last the walls of the City come into view, the pit fighters come to a stop. This is home for them. Where they were born and raised. James is actually surprised to see a tear come to the eyes of some of these hardened fighting men.

"There she is," breathes Potbelly.

"Never thought I'd ever be coming back here," Stig says.

"Let's go," urges Miko. When he first laid eyes on the walls his sense of urgency increased. Nudging their horses, they take a more moderate pace as they approach the gates to the City.

"James," Jiron says, "look over there." He directs their view over to an open area west of the road near the walls.

"What about it?" asks James.

"That's where you took out the majority of the enemy when we left," he replies.

James looks hard, but after the effect of several seasons, there's hardly any evidence left of what happened. A few blackened trees here and there are all that stands in testimony to the explosion that rocked the night so long ago.

The closer to the gates they go, the denser the tents and number of people become. The pit fighters scan the people they pass for any sign of those they knew, but so far haven't recognized anyone.

Soldiers stand guard at the city's gates, more for maintaining order than anything else. Jiron leads them through and into the city. Surprisingly enough, the streets are fairly clear of debris.

"They sure cleaned up this place," remarks Jiron. During their escape, James had played merry hell with several of the buildings, exploding them in the night in order to cover their escape.

Moving across the courtyard, they pass through the next gate into the city. Signs of reconstruction are going on everywhere. People, mainly shopkeepers working to get their business back in shape, are seen setting stones and hammering planks.

"If Delia hurries, she could make a killing selling these people building supplies," comments Shorty.

"I think she already has that idea," replies Stig.

"Didn't Lord Pytherian say the first building that would be rebuilt here would be that temple you wanted?" Jiron asks.

"Yes he did," answers James. "But I don't expect them to be able to arrange that until the hostilities subside." Glancing over to his friend, he adds, "Besides, it's not like we'll be around to tell them where to build it."

Nodding, he says, "That's true."

"Can you find your old hideout?" James asks.

"Shouldn't be a problem," he replies. "Even with the state the City is in now, I know my way around."

"Oh, man," Scar says sadly.

"What?" asks Jiron.

"Beggerman's is gone," he says, indicating a destroyed building that once sat on the corner ahead of them.

When James looks questioningly at Jiron he says, "It was a place where pit fighters hung out. A tavern and brothel all rolled into one."

"Yeah," agrees Shorty. "Beggerman had been a pit fighter in his younger days. Set it up when he had accumulated sufficient money to last him the rest of his life. He claimed he won the building in a card game, though no one's ever been able to verify that."

"Wonder if he's still alive?" Potbelly asks.

Just then three young teenage boys come running around the corner and Scar signals them to stop, that he wants to talk.

Slowing down, the three lads approach him. "What do you want?" one asks.

Scar reaches into his pouch and says, "I'll give you each a copper if you can answer me a question."

"Sure," says one. The other two nod as well.

"Beggerman," he says. "Do you know who I'm talking about?"

"Sure do," the first boy replies. Gesturing back to the destroyed establishment he says, "The guy with only one eye and missing half an ear, right?"

"That's him," nods Scar. "Do you know if he's still alive?"

The lead boy glances to the other two who only shrug. Turning back to Scar he says, "We haven't seen or heard about him since the City fell."

Removing three coppers, he flips on to each of the lads. "Thanks," he says.

"Sorry we couldn't be of more help," the lead boy says. Then they're off down the street on whatever errand they were about before being stopped.

"Remember that massive mace he use to keep behind the bar?" Stig says. "He always said anyone who caused problems would get real familiar with old 'Ironhead'."

The others laugh at that. "Never once saw him take it down," Potbelly states.

"I would think it came down when the City fell," Scar says more somberly. "He wasn't one to run off when trouble came calling." Several of the others nod at that.

They slowly continue to make their way through town. Jiron leads them unerringly from street to street toward the entrance of his hideout. Along the way, other places that once held meaning to them are passed and James learns more about the men who have chosen to travel with him.

Finally Jiron says, "It's not too much further."

A green glow springs to life around Brother Willim. James notices and asks, "Trouble?"

Shaking his head, he says, "I don't think so. I can feel something here."

"What?" asks James.

"I'm not sure," he replies. "I think what I'm feeling is the holiness of this place." Glancing to Miko he sees the odd look on his face. "You feel it too don't you?"

Nodding, Miko says, "I didn't know what it was."

The greenish glow disappears as Brother Willim's attention is turned back to James. "When a holy place stands for a long time, the rocks, stones and at times the ground itself resonate with the god's power. The more holy the place, the stronger it becomes." Glancing around he adds, "And the longer it remains."

"Why can't I sense anything?" James asks. Usually when magic is near his skin tingles.

"It's not active magic in the sense you are referring to," he explains. "More like a resonate signature that marks the place as holy. Having once been the location for the High Temple, I can understand why I can sense it even after the Temple has been gone for so long."

James nods his head. He remembers one of the early visits by Igor in which he took him to Disneyland. Igor referred to Disneyland as a focal point. That to those who are good, the place is like a beacon in the night. Perhaps it's the same principle.

Jiron turns after a severely fire damaged building and then enters a street with a large crater in the middle of it. He remembers when they had originally been sneaking out and Cassie had sneezed just when a column of enemy soldiers were passing by. The hole is where James blasted a group of them to give them time to return to the hideout.

Rounding the corner of the building, they enter what once use to be a park. When James first saw the place, it was an area with trees and grass. Not very large, simply a place where people could come to escape the bustle of the city for a time. Now, mounds of dirt and piles of rocks litter the area. Its former beauty almost completely lost.

"Looks like they dug out the collapsed tunnel," comments Jiron.

On the far side of the park where the entrance to Jiron's lair had been now gapes a large hole leading down into the ground. After escaping back down into the hideout they had to fight off enemy soldiers that followed after them. James had to collapse the passage leading to the surface to keep them from being inundated by soldiers.

Crossing the scarred ground to the entrance, Shorty says, "They must have wanted in here bad."

"This would definitely have taken some time to accomplish," states Scar. "From what you told me, they knew you were out of here shortly after you left the City."

Nodding, Jiron says, "That's right."

"So they wanted in here for another reason," reasons Brother Willim.

Dismounting, they pause momentarily at the gaping hole in the ground. "Could they have known about this being the place where the High Temple once stood?" asks Stig.

"Possibly," answers James. "Would make sense considering the amount of manpower they used to clear the way down."

Miko stands at the edge of the hole and gazes down into it. Jiron begins to move past when he reaches out and grabs his arm. "Wait," he says.

"What's wrong?" asks James, concerned.

"Remember the dream?" he asks. Turning his gaze to James he adds, "There could be something down there."

"Maybe," replies Brother Willim. "Maybe not." When Miko turns to look at him he continues. "The fearful presence in your dream could have been there simply to prevent you from understanding what the dream was trying to tell you. You still don't know if you learned everything you were supposed to."

"Do you feel something?" asks James.

"No," he says. "Nothing like that." Pulling out the Star, he sees that it's quiet. No glow of any kind is being emitted by it.

"That's a good sign," states James. "If there was trouble, it wouldn't be still like that."

Miko nods in agreement. "I think I should lead here," he says. He glances to Jiron and receives a nod in reply.

"We're right behind you," Jiron says. Stepping aside, he waits for Miko to move into the opening.

Hesitantly at first, Miko steps into the opening. The stairs that once had extended down are now worn and broken from the excavation that took place. Step by step he descends into the ground until coming to the bottom. Here, the passage extending away from the stairs is rough and uneven. Sections of the walls and floor they pass by reveal the stonework from the original corridor that once moved through here.

Then they come to the section where the ceiling must have collapsed and the stone was removed. Timbers line the sides of the passage as well as across the ceiling. Feels more like they are walking through a mine than a passage leading to what may very well be the inner sanctum of the old High Temple of Morcyth.

Debris lines the passage, evidence that others have been here since the tunnel was excavated. Old blankets and other forms of refuse litter the floor from one end to the other. From the looks of it, no one has been here for some time.

Jiron picks up a blanket and looks questioningly to James.

Shrugging, he creates his orb for more light and says, "Maybe people holed up in here after the Empire was through."

"Could be," he replies and drops the blanket to the ground.

James follows closely behind Miko with his orb in hand. Then comes Brother Willim, a soft glow can be seen emanating from him as well. Next comes Jiron and Aleya, then Stig, Potbelly and Scar bring up the rear. Shorty had been left topside to keep an eye on the horses.

"It won't be too much further," Jiron says.

And indeed the light from the orb soon reveals where the secret door had stood during their last visit. Now, the door is gone. Signs of chisels and hammers mar the wall where the Empire had taken it out.

Miko comes to a stop as the light enters the room. Memory of his dreams haunt him, fear rises at what may lay within the room.

"It's okay Miko," says James reassuringly. He glances to Brother Willim questioningly who shakes his head no. "There's nothing in there. We're right behind you."

He glances to where the Star rests in the palm of his hand. Not even the tiniest flicker of a glow can be seen in its depths. Gathering his courage, Miko steps forward and into the room...and nothing happens. Not even the soft glow that had appeared the last time James and the others were here. Releasing the breath he had been unconsciously holding, he looks around.

The pedestal from his dream stands in the center of the room. The crystal platform that had been sitting on top of it when James and the others fled down here is gone, no surprise there. The pedestal itself has been marred and defiled by hammers and chisels. Its surface shows many marks made by those who had come after James and the others had left. A sizeable chunk has even been broken off of one side, the missing piece resting on the floor by its base.

When the light from the orb reaches the far side, James isn't surprised to see the secret door that had concealed the way they left the room torn from the wall and lying on the ground.

Moving to the pedestal itself, he finds the indentation that had been the Star of Morcyth ruined beyond recognition. It looks as if the entire top several inches of the pedestal had been chiseled off. If he hadn't of known what it looked like before, he would never have been able to figure it out now.

Removing his medallion, James attempts to place it where the impression of the Star used to be to see what happens. After placing it there, he stands back and watches.

"What are you doing?" Scar asks.

Nodding over to the ruined secret door, he says, "The last time we were here, placing my medallion on the pedestal raised the secret door and allowed us to escape. Just seeing if anything would happen again."

They wait for a full minute before Potbelly says, "Maybe we weren't meant to come here. Could the dream have meant something else?"

When all eyes turn to Miko he shakes his head. "I know I am supposed to be here," he states with conviction. "I just don't know why."

Brother Willim comes to James and asks, "What did this place look like when you first entered?"

"Not much really different than it is now," replies James. "The two doors were still attached and the pedestal was perfectly formed. On top of it was a crystal platform that had an inverted pyramid indentation in the top where I believe the Star could have rested. Looks like the Empire took that when they were here." He glances around the room and adds, "Beneath the crystal platform was engraved the Star of Morcyth, and that's where I placed the medallion to open the secret door. The walls and floor are still pretty much the same."

Brother Willim takes in the room. The pedestal standing in the exact center and the octagonal shape to the room. How each wall is facing directly to the center, and the pedestal.

"Miko," he says. "Place the Star upon the pedestal."

"But it's broken," explains Miko.

"Be that as it may," replies Brother Willim, "put the Star upon the pedestal."

Miko looks to James who gives him an encouraging nod. Moving forward, he places the Star upon the pedestal's center. Letting go, he takes several steps back.

They stare in anticipation at the Star, unsure what may or may not happen. "I don't think…" begins Potbelly when the Star suddenly erupts into light, bathing the entire room with a strong, yet soothing radiance.

"Wow," Stig mumbles in awe.

So entranced by what the Star is doing, James fails to see what is happening with Miko until Brother Willim takes him by the shoulder and brings it to his attention. Enveloped by a white glow, more intense than any that ever appeared when he was using the Star's power to heal, Miko stands with his eyes closed and arms lax at his side.

"What's going on?" he asks Bother Willim.

"Wait and see," he says.

The sound of his voice causes James to glance toward him. Brother William stands there with a radiant expression on his face. Lips turned up in a smile, his eyes fixed upon Miko.

The others move back from Miko as they watch the event transpiring before their eyes. For a full five minutes they stand there in mute silence as the glow surrounds him. Then all of a sudden, it winks out. Miko opens his eyes as a grinding noise is heard coming from the pedestal.

Stepping forward, James asks, "Are you okay?"

"I am fine James," he says. "I now understand why it is I must be here." Stepping forward, he moves to the pedestal which is rising up out of the floor and removes the Star from its top.

Too astonished for words, the others stand there as the pedestal continues to rise from the floor. What they had took for a pedestal is in actuality the top section of a tall marble column. Before the top of the column comes to within a foot of the ceiling, it grinds to a halt.

Miko moves around the column and then comes to a stop. James follows him as do the others and they discover engraved at the base of the column, the Star of Morcyth. Bending down, Miko takes the Star in his hand and places it against the Star engraved upon the base.

An audible click is heard then a section of the base falls away revealing a hollow cavity. A bundle lies within the cavity and Miko reaches in and pulls it out. Wrapped in a velvet cloth bearing the sign of the Star, Miko holds the bundle reverently.

"What is it?" asks Stig.

"It's the Book of Morcyth," Miko replies. He places the Star once more in the pouch at his waist then picks up the section of the column that fell away and replaces it. Once it is pack in place, the column begins to slide back into the floor.

James glances at Brother Willim questioningly. Giving James a jubilant smile, he says, "Few outside the inner circle of the temples have ever witnessed what you just did."

"And what is that?" asks Jiron from where he stands beside James.

"The sanctifying of a High Priest," he replies.

"Miko?" Scar asks incredulously. "He's the new High Priest of Morcyth?" Beside him Potbelly looks on in disbelief.

"You can't be serious," exclaims Jiron. "He's...Miko!"

Brother Willim glances at the faces of the others and says, "Who are we to question the decision of a god?" He glances over to where Miko has the Book of Morcyth laid open on the pedestal and is turning the pages.

Stig comes up behind Miko and glances over his shoulder at the pages of the book. "Ah!" he cries out as his head rocks backward and his hands fly up, covering his eyes.

"Stig!" Potbelly cries out.

Stumbling backward he yells, "I'm blind!"

As Potbelly rushes to aid Stig, Miko closes the book and hurries to his side. "None but myself may look upon the holy pages," he says. Removing the Star, he silently prays to Morcyth and the glow suffuses him. Now stronger than it was before, it envelopes both Miko and Stig for a short time before going out.

"Open your eyes," he tells Stig once the glow dissipates.

Everyone holds their breath in anticipation as he opens his eyes. Squinting, he glances at the others and says, "I can see again."

Sighs of relief escape them as Potbelly helps Stig back to his feet.

Coming to Miko, James asks, "How do you feel?"

Laying a hand on James' shoulder he says, "I am fine. This is why I had to come here." Glancing around at the other he adds, "And why the malignant presence tried to keep me away."

"To become the High Priest?" asks Jiron.

Nodding, Miko replies, "Yes." Returning to the pedestal he lays his hand upon the Book of Morcyth and says, "And to retrieve this."

"Why?" asks Scar. When everyone turns their attention to him he says, "I mean, he already had the Star, why was there an urgency for him to come here. Wasn't he bound to come here at some point anyway?"

"It was time," explains Miko.

"Also, consider this," interjects Brother Willim. "Why did something work so hard to prevent him from understanding the dream? What did it have to gain for him to remain as plain Miko rather than the High Priest of Morcyth?"

The others shake their heads, not entirely understanding what he's trying to get at.

"As a High Priest, he will now wield significantly more power, have greater understanding, and with the Book of Morcyth and the Star now in his possession, will be a force to be reckoned with."

"So now what happens?" James asks. Turning to his friend, he asks, "Will you be continuing with us? Or are you to stay here?"

"Nothing has changed," replies Miko. Putting the Book of Morcyth under his arm, he says, "I still travel with you. You're my friend."

Smiling, James says, "I'm glad to hear it." Then he sees Miko's grin that has been so much a part of him. Returning it he asks, "Shall we leave now?"

"Yes," replies Miko with a nod. "We are finished here." Turning toward the way they came in, he leads them back to the surface.

Chapter Six

Once they've returned to where Shorty waits with the horses, Scar and Potbelly tell him of what happened within. Also that Miko is now the High Priest of Morcyth. Shorty's laugh bursts out when they tell him. But then he glances to the others and sees them nodding in agreement.

"You're not kidding," he says, his amusement dying. Turning to Miko he hesitates a moment and then bows his head respectfully.

Miko comes over to him and says, "None of that." Slightly embarrassed, he lays his hand upon Shorty's shoulder. "I am still the same person I was before I entered there."

Shorty raises his head and says hesitantly, "Uh, yeah. Sure."

"We still have a long way to go before we're back with Illan," Jiron says as he swings into the saddle. "Best if we don't tarry too long."

Miko takes the Book of Morcyth and slips it into a saddlebag, securing it tightly. The last into the saddle, he looks to Jiron and nods that he's ready.

Before they start to get underway, James asks him, "Shouldn't we hide the entrance or something?"

"It doesn't matter," Miko replies. "The place will be rebuilt, so whatever damage may happen in the interim won't make any difference."

With that, Jiron moves to take the lead and they return along the same route back to the gates that they took on their way in. The group is silent as each tries to come to grips with this new development, Miko as a High Priest. How are they to treat him? What should they call him? All this runs through their heads as they make their way through the streets of the City of Light.

"Father?" Scar asks Miko and is immediately cut off by the raising of Miko's hand.

"Please," Miko says, "don't call me Father. Or priest, or High Priest." He glances behind him where Scar rides and says, "I'm still Miko."

"Alright, Miko," replies Scar and then he goes silent.

"What were you going to ask me?" he asks.

"Oh, uh," he begins then seems to lose track of what he was going to say. "Oh yeah, right. What is in the Book of Morcyth?"

"From what I saw in the brief glimpse I was able to take," he begins, "it describes customs, rules and other things that makes the Priesthood of Morcyth a body."

"Every god has a set of rules that his priests must abide by," comments Brother Willim. "Each has certain mandates that those who follow him must adhere to in order for the god's interests on this world to be accurately reflected."

"Like what?" Potbelly asks.

"Take my lord Asran for instance," Brother Willim says. "As a priest of Asran, one of the mandates for me is to not harm another living person except under the most strictest of exceptions. And let me tell you, there are very few of those."

"I take it the Hand has more leeway than others in your order?" Jiron asks.

"Not as much as you would expect," he says. "Weeds must be pulled, branches at times must be pruned for the tree's ultimate health." Brother Willim sighs and then adds, "But that doesn't mean every blow we deal or death we cause won't have an accounting later on. At the end when we stand before Asran, we will have to justify every hurt that we gave others. Those who are found to have caused pain and suffering during their time as a priest for no good reason..." He trails off into silence, leaving the sentence incomplete.

"I think I get the idea," Potbelly says.

Turning to Miko, Brother Willim says, "You may find that having people call you 'Miko' will not be allowed. As High Priest, you now must cultivate the dignity and prestige that comes with the title."

Setting his face into a stern expression, Miko pats the saddlebag wherein lies the Book of Morcyth and says, "I have yet read in this book that that is so. And until I do, I wish to remain just Miko."

"But remember," Brother Willim says, "You are no longer 'just Miko'."

James turns in his saddle and looks back to Brother Willim and Miko. He can see the stubborn look on Miko's face and tries to hide a grin. "If the High Priest of Morcyth wants me to call him Miko, then I shall," he says much to Miko's relief.

"So will I," adds Jiron.

They proceed down two more blocks in silence until Miko suddenly breaks into laughter.

"What's so funny?" asks Shorty.

"I just got to thinking that Scar and Potbelly now have another fantastic story to tell that no one will believe," he explains, then breaks out into another fit of laughter. And with that, the uncertain mood of the group is shattered and everyone joins in with their own laughter.

"Yeah I can see it now, 'It's true! We were there when Miko the street brat became the High Priest of Morcyth!'" he says imitating Potbelly's voice which only makes everyone laugh all the harder.

"You got one now that Jorry and Uther aren't going to be able to top!" laughs Stig.

The few people they pass on the street pause in their work to watch the group of men riding down the street, laughing uproariously. A few of them simply shake their heads and return to their work.

Still scanning those they pass in the hopes of seeing an old friend that managed to survive the fall of the City, they continue working their way to the gates. Face after face go by, yet none that any of them recognize. As the gates come into view ahead of them, they have all but given up hope of finding anyone they know.

Then, when they reach the gates, a voice calls from the crowd congregating near the opening. "Shorty!" a woman's voice cries out.

Turning toward the sound of the voice, Shorty comes to a stop as he scans the crowd for the source of the voice. Then he sees auburn hair tied back with a green ribbon. "Millie!" he cries. Dismounting, he races through the crowd toward her.

The others have come to a stop and watch as he reaches her and envelopes her in a very friendly hug. James glances questioningly to Jiron who explains. "That's Millie. Shorty and her had a thing before she married some shopkeeper." Turning to Scar he asks, "Do you remember his name?"

Shaking his head, Scar replies, "No. All I remember is the binge Shorty went on after she told him she was to wed someone else."

Breaking off the embrace, Shorty asks, "Did what's his name make it too?"

She gives him playful pat on the shoulder and says, "You know his name is Rulen. And yes, he made it. When we heard the Empire was being pushed back, he wanted to be one of the first to return and get the business up and running again."

Slightly saddened that she isn't his, yet happy that she's alive and in good spirits, he says, "I'm glad for you."

Reaching out, she gives him another big hug and then asks, "Can I see you later? Rulen could use help in getting the business back up and running."

Shaking his head, he says, "No." Nodding back to where the others are waiting for him he adds, "We were about ready to leave town."

"I'm sorry," she says. "Shorty, I'm glad you made it."

"As I am for you," he replies. Emboldened by the fact that he's leaving, he grips her in his arms and kisses her smack dab on the lips. "May be back someday," he tells her as he releases his grip.

"Come see us when you do," she replies.

"I will," he assures her. Turning back to his friends, he says to her, "If I don't see you again, I wish you all the happiness."

She follows him to his horse and waits while he mounts. "Fare you well, Shorty," she tells him. "I missed you."

"Let's go," says Jiron as he begins moving once more toward the gates.

As Shorty's horse starts to follow the others, he turns in his saddle and waves goodbye. Millie stands there and waves back.

Finally, they reach the gates and pass through. Once past the crowd by the gate and on the road, Jiron quickly has them up to a gallop. Behind them, the walls of the City of Light quickly fall away in the distance, until finally disappearing altogether.

Throughout the rest of the day they ride hard until their horses, even with trading off with their spares, begin to show signs of exhaustion. They spend a night of relative quiet and are again off before first light.

The days of hard riding are beginning to show. Their horses are starting to weary faster so they're forced to slow the pace and add a couple more rest breaks throughout the day. Some time before noon they pass the city of Reardon, only slowing down to work their way through its streets and the people upon them. Then once past they again resume a pace as fast as the condition of their horses will allow.

There's no time to waste, the clock is ticking. They now must find Tinok!

After spending two more nights on the road, the walls of Al-Ziron appear before them in the late afternoon. Their horses are all but spent and they desperately need the replacements Illan promised them when they left just over a week ago.

Squads of riders patrol the countryside and they come across two with Raiders who had accompanied them to Korazan earlier in the summer. They report that the area is clear and the delegation from the Empire has arrived. Talks are already underway to halt the fighting permanently.

A cessation to the fighting is now in place until the conclusion of the talks. Whether it will become a permanent situation will depend on the skill of the representatives of the two sides. The last patrol they encountered sent a rider to inform Black Hawk of their approach. So when they draw close to the walls of Al-Ziron, they are met by Illan, and the two remaining brothers of the Hand of Asran.

Brother Willim is surprised to see the priests still here.

"I thought they were taking your fallen brethren back home?" asks Stig.

"They were," he replies. "The fact that they are here cannot bode well."

As the two groups meet, Illan says, "I didn't expect you for a couple more days." Then he takes in the thinness of the horses. "Rest assured, I have fresh mounts ready for you."

"Thank you," says James.

Just as he's about to continue, Illan holds up his hand. "We need to talk in private," he says quietly. Glancing to Brother Willim he adds, "You too."

"Very well," Brother Willim says.

"Trouble?" asks Jiron nodding over to the tents of the Ambassador's party.

"Not here," he says with a shake of his head. Turning his horse around, he leads them through the gates of Al-Ziron. "Are Delia and the others safely within Cardri?" he asks.

"Yes," replies James. "Then we had a side trip to the City of Light."

"Interesting?" he asks.

"Oh yes, very," says James.

"I'd say," adds Scar from where he's riding behind them.

Once inside the main courtyard, guards come and take their horses. "Follow me," Illan says as he leads them into the keep.

As they begin removing their things, Illan says, "Leave them. They'll be taken to your rooms."

Everyone but Miko takes his advice. Miko removes the saddlebag containing the Book of Morcyth and carries it with him. He plans on never letting it out of his possession.

Within the fortress they move down the somewhat familiar halls. As they pass down one of the hallways, Ceadric makes his appearance from out of a doorway and holds it open for them. Nodding to Illan, he stands there as they pass through.

On the other side of the door they find themselves in a large room with many tables and chairs. Once they are all in, Ceadric closes the door and stations himself outside to prevent them from being disturbed.

Illan moves to the far side of the room and takes a seat at one of the tables. The others take seats in the other chairs close to him. Brother Willim and the other two priests of Morcyth sit together at the table adjacent to his.

"Now," says Jiron, "why all the secrecy?"

"Is the Empire up to something?" asks Stig.

He sits back a moment, then says, "I'm not sure." Pausing for only a moment, Illan continues. "The day you left, one of my Raiders was found dead in one of the hallways. There was no discernable cause of death. No wounds from weapons," then he gestures to the two priests of Asran, "and they said it wasn't poison."

Brother Willim and his brothers begin whispering together as the others assimilate what he just said. "They were kind enough to postpone their journey to return their fallen comrades until the following day. Unfortunately, by then two more had died, again within the keep and no discernable cause of death."

"After the first death, a thorough search was made and the keep was locked down, no one allowed in or out. The brothers joined the search that first day but nothing was found. By this time the Ambassador from the Empire arrived."

"Were they somehow involved do you think?" Potbelly asks.

"Nothing points in their direction, but you can't dismiss the coincidence of my people being killed and their presence here," he replies.

"Have you spoken to the Ambassador about the situation?" Jiron asks.

Shaking his head, Illan says, "No, it could possibly be taken as an implied accusation. At this stage in the negotiations, we can't afford to do anything that would adversely affect the talks."

"But people are dying," insists Brother Willim. "Surely you could talk to him about aiding you in ferreting out the killer?"

Again Illan shakes his head. "Our negotiator, who by the way is Councilman Tethias and one of the members of Madoc's ruling Council, says that we should not mention it in any way." Seeing the suspicion arise in James' eyes he adds, "Don't worry, his House is currently at odds with that of the former Councilman Rillian."

"That's good to know," states James.

"We do have the Ambassador and his people under constant surveillance," Illan tells them. "We know that he has been informed of the deaths, though he has yet to comment upon them."

Just then the door opens and Ceadric sticks his head in. Illan gives him a nod and servants come in bearing food and drink. "Thought you might be hungry," he says.

"Yes, thank you," affirms Scar.

The servants hurry about their work and platters of beef, bread and cheese are sitting before them. Pitchers of ale arrive too. Once everything has been placed upon the tables the servants quickly leave the room and Illan relates to them the rest of the events while they eat.

"The morning of the second day, another died but this time there was a witness," he explains. "One of Hedry's archers, Galin, was on his way to meet with him when one of the new additions to the Raiders entered the hallway further down. The man waved to Galin and took three steps when what looked like an arm reached from the wall and touched him."

"Staggering, the man gave out with a groan and remained there with the hand on his shoulder for no more than a second before the hand let go. Then he sagged and hit the floor. When Galin reached him, he was already dead."

"And there was no one else in the hallway?" asks Jiron.

"No, there was not," states Illan matter-of-factly.

"Did Galin get a good look at the arm?" James asks.

"He said the hallway was dark with but a single candle at either end," he replies. "Said he didn't really pay much attention to it, that at first he thought his eyes were playing tricks on him. Possibly a trick with the shadows."

"Shadows?" asks James. He looks to Illan and who nods his head. "Could it be one of those shadows that tried to kill me on the way to Korazan?"

"There have been three other deaths since," he says. "Another attack was witnessed. The witness said that the wall came forth and enveloped the servant."

James sits back and thinks while whispered murmurs pass between the others in the room.

"My brothers say they have not sensed the presence of evil or anything magical the entire time we were gone," Brother Willim states. "They have searched the keep from one side to the other but thus far have been unable to locate it."

"We'll be able to find it," bursts out Scar. Patting Miko on the shoulder he says, "We have the High Priest of Morcyth here."

Illan's eyes widen as Miko blushes slightly. He glances to James who nods his head then launches into a brief description of what happened in the City of Light. When he's done, he looks to Miko with a grin, "So what do I call you now?"

"Miko will do nicely," he replies.

"We'll need to…" begins James when Miko suddenly stands erect.

The Star of Morcyth suddenly bright in his hands he turns for the door. "Someone has died," he announces.

"How do you know?" Jiron asks.

"I felt his passing," he replies.

Green auras spring to life around the brothers as Miko reaches the door. Pushing it open, he strides into the hallway. Pausing only a moment, he moves to the right past a startled Ceadric with the others right behind and hurries down the hallway.

"Another has been killed," Illan tells Ceadric as he leaves the room. Nodding, Ceadric draws his sword and falls in with the others.

The light emanating from the Star fills the hallway with brilliant light. "Can you sense the shadow?" James asks.

"Yes," he replies. "It's above us and on the move." Quickening his pace, Miko passes stunned servants and guards as he hunts the shadow. One guard of the keep had to practically jump out of his way to prevent from being run over.

Reaching a flight of steps going upward, he turns into the stairwell and proceeds to the next floor.

"Can you sense anything yet?" James asks Brother Willim.

Nodding, he says, "We do now."

Hurrying along the hallway, Miko comes to a stop before a closed door and opens it. "We're near," he says. "Its pace has quickened."

"Could have sensed our magic approaching," suggests James and Brother Willim nods in agreement.

The door opens up onto a storage room filled with boxes, crates and barrels. Moving into the room, the light from the Star blazes forth revealing every nook and cranny. Across the room from them stands another closed door.

"We must hurry," Miko says as he runs to the other door.

"Can't be much further until we reach the outer wall of the keep," Illan says as he enters the storage room.

Jiron beats him to the door and has it open for Miko to pass through. The light from the Star reveals another storage room that's practically empty. A dark shape is moving across the floor and is almost at the far wall.

"There it is!" exclaims Miko.

With a shriek, the shadow races from the burning light of the Star. Passing through the wall, it seeks to escape.

The glow surrounding the priests of Asran suddenly intensifies tenfold. "Got it," says Brother Willim.

Moving to a small narrow window in the wall, James and the others look out to see the shadow enveloped by a green glow hovering far above the ground. As the brothers work to send the shadow back to whatever hell it came from, it lets out with an ear shattering scream. Inch by inch the green glow surrounding the shadow shrinks until finally it winks out.

"Great," breathes Illan in a less than happy tone.

"What?" asks James.

Indicating out the window to the ground below, he says, "That's the Empire's Ambassador's camp."

Everyone in the camp below is staring up at where the shadow had been held by the brothers. All of a sudden, a group of men break from the crowd and make for the gates to the keep.

"He's coming," comments Jiron.

Illan immediately moves from the window and says, "Ceadric, take them somewhere out of sight until the Ambassador returns to his camp."

"Right," he says.

"Why?" asks Shorty.

Gesturing to James he says, "James here is the most wanted man in their Empire. According to what our agents have discovered, they've issued a hundred thousand gold piece reward for your death. It appears they don't even want you alive."

Leaving the room, Illan begins to return the way they came while Ceadric takes the others the rest of the way. Coming to a stop Illan says to Brother Willim, "I'll need to borrow your brothers."

"Why?" he asks as everyone pauses in the hallway.

"The Ambassador knows something happened," he replies. "He already knows these two have been here for a while. If we put forth that they were the ones that destroyed the shadow, it might quell any further questions."

Brother Willim nods to his two fellow priests who then move to stand with Illan.

"When he's gone I'll send word," Illan tells them. "Until then, stay low and get what rest you can. I know you must be exhausted."

"That's an understatement," jokes Shorty.

To Ceadric he says, "Meet me in the Hall when you have them stashed away."

Nodding, Ceadric resumes leading them down the hallway. He hurries along until coming to another hallway branching off to the right. Moving into it, he leads them all the way to the far end where they come to a flight of stairs going up. The stairwell is dark so James creates his orb to light the way.

"You are putting us in the tower?" Scar asks.

"That's right," replies Ceadric. "At least until the Ambassador returns to his camp."

Ascending the flight of stairs, they pass one level and leave the stairwell on the next. A short hallway extends from the stairwell with but one door on either side. Coming to a stop at the doors, he turns and faces the others. Indicating the two doors, he says, "These must have been designed for visiting dignitaries. Beyond each door is a suite of rooms with sufficient beds for all of you."

"Thank you," James tells him.

Nodding, Ceadric says, "I must return. It would be good if you could stay within your rooms until morning."

"I don't think that will be a problem," he says with a yawn. "We're all about dead on our feet."

"Then I shall leave you to your rest." And with that Ceadric moves to the stairs and begins making his way back down.

James, Miko, Brother Willim, Jiron and Aleya take one set of suites while the rest take the other. As it turns out, they are identical in the way they are laid out. A large room designed for entertaining guests lies beyond the door from the hallway. Three other doors lead to rooms containing beds, tables, and dressers. Two of the rooms have two beds each while the third is much larger. Most likely for the prominent member of the guests staying here, it has but a single bed larger than the others as well as the addition of a walk-in closet.

"Nice," comments Miko after checking out the rooms.

"Have the others come in here for a moment," James says to Jiron. While he waits for Jiron to go across the hall and bring in the others, he takes a seat on the long couch in the front visiting room.

"Better than any inn we've stayed in," Miko says as he sits in one of the padded chairs next to him. Brother Willim sits at the other end of the couch from James.

James nods agreement then gazes at his friend. "When did you start being able to tell when people died?" he asks.

"Since the City of Light," he replies. "I've only felt it three times before now. The first time took me by surprise, let me tell you. But there was no fear or apprehension involved. When the person died here tonight, it felt different and I knew it was no normal passing."

"The benefits of having a High Priest travel with us are already coming into play," James says.

To Miko, Brother Willim says, "It was the fear of the person who was killed this night that you felt. When a normal death occurs, there's no fear, maybe just a little apprehension of the unknown fate that awaits them."

Miko nods his head, "I think you're right." Then he gets a contemplative look as he and the others wait for Jiron's return.

They haven't long to wait until Jiron returns with the others. The fading light coming from outside doesn't give sufficient light with which to see so James continues to leave his orb active.

Scar and Potbelly have to pull chairs from the adjoining room for everyone to be able to sit down. Once everyone is seated, James says, "This business of the shadow being here has me worried."

"It didn't seem as if it was after anything or anyone in particular," Brother Willim states. "As far as we can tell its attacks were entirely random."

"I know," replies James. "Up until this point, every time we have encountered shadows there was a reason behind it. So there must be one now."

"Stands to reason," nods Jiron. "But what can it be?"

"I don't know and that's what is bothering me," admits James.

"Other than keeping our eyes out for signs of others, there isn't a whole lot we can do about it," Stig says. "With Miko and the priests of Asran here, I can't see how they can give us much trouble."

"If we know they are there, that's true," agrees Brother Willim.

They sit there a moment and discuss the shadows, finally coming to the conclusion there's not much that they can do about it.

"Are we leaving to find Tinok soon?" asks Jiron.

"We all need a rest," replies James. "I thought we would leave tomorrow night after it gets dark. It wouldn't do to have the Ambassador's men see us leave."

"True," he agrees.

James takes out a strip of cloth and casts his seeking spell. The cloth rises in his hand and points straight toward the south. "Tinok's there somewhere," he explains, "we just have to find him." Canceling his spell, he replaces the strip of cloth in his pocket. "Now, everyone get some rest, stay in your rooms, and we'll leave as soon as the sun goes down tomorrow night."

As the meeting breaks up and those who are staying in the room across the hall leave, James glances out the window at the crescent moon rising in the sky. Knowing time is slipping away, he makes his way to bed, cancels the orb and tries to go to sleep.

Chapter Seven

_____

Early the next morning, Ceadric shows up with a dozen servants carrying trays of food and pitchers of ale. "With Lord Black Hawk's compliments," he says as the servants set the trays down upon the tables. Once the food is in place, he has them return back downstairs.

"I've been meaning to ask you," begins James as he starts to load his plate with food. "Where did you get the servants?"

"Some are relatives of the Raiders who are now living here," he explains. "They started arriving two days after we took over. How they learned of it so fast is anyone's guess."

"I suppose," agrees James.

"The rest are the people we freed from slavery. Some didn't have anywhere else to go so remained with us." He glances from James to Jiron then adds, "Couldn't very well say no."

Shaking his head, James says, "No, you couldn't."

"What happened with the Ambassador last night?" Jiron asks.

"Not much," he says. "Black Hawk explained what happened, how the priests of Asran caught a wayward spirit that was causing the deaths. He didn't look too convinced, but what could he do but take him at his word?"

Laughing, Scar adds, "Must have scared them something awful when that shadow was hovering above them surrounded by a green glow." Several of the others chuckle at that.

"It didn't do anything for the negotiations I'll tell you that," explains Ceadric. "I think Councilman Tethias plans to talk to you sometime today before you leave."

"What about?" asks James.

Shrugging, Ceadric answers, "Not sure." He removes a piece of pork from a platter and takes a bite.

"We plan to leave after the sun goes down tonight," James informs him.

"Thought that might be the plan," he says. "Lord Black Hawk wanted you to know that there are several Raiders here who are fluent in the Empire's language if you think you might need one." He glances at James a moment before adding, "Just be more careful than you were with the last one."

"Hey," counters James, "if Jared hadn't panicked, he would be alive today."

"Be that as it may, should you desire one let us know." Finishing the piece of pork, Ceadric takes his leave.

When he's left the suite and the door is shut, Jiron exclaims, "What nerve!"

"Yeah," exclaims Miko. "The way he said it, you would think you killed Jared yourself."

The others chime in with their opinions before Scar says, "Jared was a cousin of his."

"Oh, that would explain it," says James with a nod.

"Still no cause to say what he did," insists Jiron.

After finishing the meal, James says to Stig, "I want you to see about the horses Illan plans to give us. Make sure his people give us good ones."

Nodding, Stig says, "Will do."

"And see what you can learn about the Ambassador," he adds. "His men may not readily recognize you as they would Jiron, Miko, or me."

"See what I can find out," he replies. Getting up from the table, he heads for the door and leaves the suite.

Once Stig is gone, Miko asks, "Don't you trust Illan's people?"

"Sure I do," he affirms. "It's just that I hate sitting here and doing nothing. This way it feels like we are doing something."

Rest of the morning goes by uneventfully, everyone is glad for this brief time to rest before returning to the road. When Stig returns, he states that the horses are superb. As for the Ambassador, he couldn't ferret out any more information than what they were already told.

"I did find out one thing though," he tells them. "They want this keep back in a bad way."

"Doubt if they'll get it," remarks Potbelly. "After all they've done to Madoc, Councilman Tethias would be a fool to hand it back over."

"If they did it would take Madoc a year or two to rebuild theirs," figures Shorty. "From what I've heard, it's all but a pile of rubble somewhere to the north."

"I talked with Hedry for a bit," Stig says. "He was out at the stables when I stopped by. Seems the reports coming from agents within the Empire tell of the Empire still having a large standing army."

"But if they committed them to retake this keep, wouldn't that leave their southern states open for rebellion?" asks James.

"Who knows?" replies Stig. "That's what I heard."

When the others begin to argue about the stupidity of certain leaders, James raises his hand. "It's not our concern right now what Madoc does or doesn't do with this keep." Turning back to Stig he asks, "Anything else?"

"Actually yes," he replies with a grin. "The Raiders have begun calling the keep, 'Hawk's Aerie'. Of course they mainly do it when those of the

Empire are near to hear it, seems it's bothering the Ambassador something awful."

"Hawk's Aerie," mumbles James. Nodding he grins and says "I like it." The others add their agreements.

It was sometime after the noon meal when Councilman Tethias decides to pay them a call. Ceadric was able to give them all of a minute's warning before the councilman's footsteps could be heard coming up the stairs. Ceadric asked them to assemble in James' suite for the Councilman's visit.

A rather short man, Councilman Tethias stands only five foot six. His brown hair, salted with a smattering of gray, is combed to rigid perfection. Not a single hair is out of place. He's accompanied by two aides who follow a step behind.

Ceadric is waiting in the hallway for him and they can hear him greet the councilman. Opening the door, he allows the councilman and his aides to enter first.

They come to their feet in respect as he enters the room. "Councilman," Ceadric says after he enters the room and closes the door, "may I present James, a mage of some power, and those who travel with him."

James and the councilman stand there and eye each other for a moment. James is decidedly uncomfortable, he feels likes he's a bug under a microscope. Extending his hand, he says, "Nice to meet you, Councilman."

Taking James' hand, the councilman gives it a firm shake and replies, "I've heard a lot about you. Even before I arrived here for the talks, tales of your exploits had reached me."

Giving the councilman a disarming grin, he says, "Nothing too terrible I hope."

Shaking his head, he releases James' hand. "On the contrary," he begins, "what I've heard can only be called miraculous."

"Would you care for a seat?" Jiron asks, indicating the finest seat in the suite.

"Thank you, I would like that," replies the councilman. Crossing over to the chair, he sits down and his aides position themselves behind him.

"To what do I owe this visit?" asks James.

"Nothing more than curiosity I'm afraid," admits the councilman. "When Lord Black Hawk informed me you were here, I asked him if he thought you would mind a visit. I do appreciate you seeing me."

James gazes at the councilman questioningly. This hardly seems a man who is one of the Patriarchal Council of Madoc, and who is use to his word being law. Before he can stop himself he says, "You aren't what I would expect of a Councilman."

Arching an eyebrow at him, he grins and says, "You mean I'm more cordial than others in positions of power?" When James nods he continues. "Just the way I am I'm afraid. Also what makes me a good negotiator. They considered sending a hardliner down here but that would have been a grave mistake."

"I understand that the Empire is demanding the return of this keep," Jiron says.

"It's true," the councilman replies.

"You don't plan to give it back do you?" asks Scar.

"Hardly," he assures them. "That would be the surest form of stupidity. No, this keep will be a sore spot between our two lands for some time to come I'm afraid."

Shorty comes forward with a mug of ale and offers it to the councilman. "It's the best we have," he apologizes.

Taking the offered cup, the councilman gives him a nod and says, "Thank you." He takes a sip while the others remain silent. Then he returns his gaze back to James. "You know, they believe you are still in the Empire."

Surprised, James asks, "Why?"

"I'm not entirely sure," he replies. "But rumors are surfacing of someone in the Empire causing massive destruction. Bridges, army encampments, even one report of an entire city collapsing, though I give that last one little credence."

James glances at Jiron for a second and sees that he came to the same conclusion that he did. Those seeds of destruction he sowed in wagons earlier this summer are still active. At one point he tried to recall just how many he planted, but couldn't quite remember exactly. The number had to have been over two dozen, possibly as high as forty. If they are still active, then they're still gathering power. The longer it takes for them to go off, the more powerful the explosion.

"A whole city you say?" he asks.

"Supposedly," he replies with a nod. The councilman notices the expression of anguish that comes over James' face. Though he doesn't comment, he realizes that James does know something about it.

"When are you planning on leaving?" he asks.

"As soon as d…" Stig begins before he's cut off by Jiron.

"We haven't decided yet," James says quickly. He casts a quick glance to Jiron and gives him a brief nod. James has always been one who hated someone else knowing his business.

"Ah," the councilman says as he comes to his feet. The rest of the room comes to their feet as well. "I'm sorry I must make my visit brief," he says. "The meeting will begin shortly."

James extends his hand for a goodbye shake which the councilman takes. "It was good to meet you," says James.

"You too my boy," he replies. To Ceadric the councilman says, "Tell Lord Black Hawk I would like to meet with him later this afternoon after the talks have ended for the day."

"Yes, milord," assures Ceadric.

"Very good." Moving for the door, he pauses but a moment to give one of his aides time to open it for him then exits into the hallway.

When the door shuts behind him James turns to Ceadric. "He seems nice enough."

"He is," agrees Ceadric. "I have yet to meet anyone who can say an unkind word about him."

"Surprised he's able to survive on the Council," states Potbelly. "I hear they are a bunch of cutthroats."

Laughing, Ceadric nods, "They can be at times. Despite his amicable manner, he can be hard as nails when he must. Always kind, but hard."

"I think I could like a man like that," observes James.

"I must be off," Ceadric tells him.

"Will everything be ready for this evening?" asks James just as Ceadric reaches the door.

Nodding, Ceadric opens the door and turns back toward him. "Everything's set," he assures him. "Just after dark."

"Thank you," James says.

Passing through the door, Cedric enters the hallway and closes it behind him.

The rest of the afternoon is spent getting what rest they can for when they leave. Miko spends the time not sleeping lying on his bed with the Book of Morcyth propped open on his stomach reading.

At one point Jiron comes over to him and asks, "I thought you still couldn't read that well?"

Taking his eyes from the pages, he glances to Jiron and shrugs. "I can now," he says.

"Is it interesting?" he asks indicating the book.

"Some parts are," he explains. "Others not so much."

Jiron indicates the foot of his bed and looks questioningly to Miko.

Nodding, Miko says, "Sure." He closes the book and sets in on the bed next to him. Scooting into a sitting position, he props his back against the wall as Jiron sits on the bed.

"How is all this going?" asks Jiron.

"You mean being the High Priest and all?"

"Yeah," he replies.

"For the most part, I don't feel any different," Miko admits. "All the priests I've known have all been kind of stuffy. You know what I mean?"

"Oh yes," agrees Jiron. "In fact, back when Tersa and I were still living in the City, there was this Father Corwyn. He was a priest of Vyll." Vyll is the god of luck, gambler and thieves. "He was very full of himself, and despite following the god of thieves he was a very upright fellow. As bad as it makes me feel now, I and a few of my buddies would make fun of him behind his back. He was fat and it bothers me now that we use to laugh at him for it. If I ever see him again I plan to make it up somehow."

Nodding, Miko says, "There were a few like that back home too." He falls quiet for a moment. "I don't think I know how to be a priest, let alone a High Priest." His gaze is one of almost panic when he finally brings his eyes to bear on Jiron. "I mean look at me! I am not refined, I know nothing about anything."

Jiron reaches out and pats him on the leg. "Relax," he says. "A god wants you to be his representative on this world. Doesn't that make you feel good?"

"Of course it does," admits Miko. "I simply fear that I will not live up to the trust Morcyth is putting in me."

"I think you are worrying too much about nothing," Jiron tells him. When he sees he's not getting through to him he continues. "You have used the power of the Star to heal, to bring people back from the brink of death. You have battled shadows, wielded a sword in battle against a warrior priest, and *prevailed!* You've seen things that the majority of those living on this world have not. Now I ask you, don't you think you are a little more than a street brat off the streets of Bearn?"

Miko looks at him thoughtfully for a time. Then he nods and gives him a grin. "Maybe you are right, my son," he says.

"*My son?*" asks Jiron with a grin. "Okay, *Father.*" Together they break into laughter at the same time.

"Thanks Jiron," Miko tells him when the laughter finally subsides.

"Anytime, Miko," replies Jiron. Getting up off the bed, he leaves Miko to continue reading the Book of Morcyth.

An hour before nightfall, Ceadric brings them another meal, complete with tarts, and tells them their horses are ready and waiting for them. "There's only one problem," he says.

"Isn't there always?" asks Scar.

"Ever since the shadow incident, the Empire's Ambassador has had someone stationed near the gates to keep an eye on who goes in and out," he explains.

"Do they know I'm here?" James asks.

Ceadric indicates the tarts that came along with the meal. "The cook said to tell Miko these are for him," he says. "I don't know who informed the cook that you were here, but if it has made it to him, it's only a matter of time before word makes it to the Ambassador."

"If it hasn't already," finishes James.

"How are we going to get out the gates?" asks Shorty.

"Hedry is scheduled to lead a patrol this evening," he explains. "I figure if you were to leave with him then your leaving may go unnoticed." He glances to where Brother Willim sits eating in his brown robe, the emblem of the Hand of Asran upon his breast. "We are going to have to do something about your robe."

"I can easily take it off," assures Brother Willim. "Maybe slip an ordinary cloak on instead?"

"I was thinking more along the lines of some armor," counters Ceadric. "You are going to need to blend in with the others."

"I'll not wear armor," he states. "Our order forbids it."

"But they will realize you are not one of our men," objects Ceadric.

Seeing Ceadric clearly getting irritated and Brother Willim balking, James gets to his feet. "If the rest of us are wearing breastplates and helms, and we put him in the center, then in the dark we might be able to get away with it."

Ceadric nods his head. "That might work," he says.

"Why sneak out at all?" Stig asks. "There isn't anyone around here who could effectively stop us."

"Two reasons," James says as he turns to him. "One, if we are seen leaving and then moving into the Empire, war could erupt all over again and a lot of people are going to die."

"Second, we are trying to rescue Tinok. Our effort would only be hampered should the Empire learn we are on the move again."

"Oh," says Stig slightly embarrassed, "that makes sense."

"Alright," Ceadric says, "there's an hour or so until sunset. Once it begins growing dark I will return and escort you through the back ways down to the stables. Then those of you who have no armor will be fitted with a breastplate and helm. When you are away from the keep, you can return the armor to Hedry and he and his men will bring it back once their patrol is over."

"In your horses' saddlebags, you will find clothes that will enable you to blend in with the citizens of the Empire." Turning to James he asks, "Did you wish a translator?"

"I think that would be best," he says.

"Very well, I'll have him meet you there." Before he leaves he asks, "Is there anything else?"

Shaking his head, James says, "Not that I can think of."

"Then I will return when it is dark." With that, he heads for the door and exits to the hallway. Closing the door behind him, they can hear his footsteps as he makes his way toward the stairs.

James commences to fill his plate and then stops when his eyes catch something. He stares at Miko until Miko asks, "What?"

Smiling, he says, "I never saw a high priest before with tart jelly smeared across his cheek." Laughter fills the room as Miko wipes the jelly off his reddening face.

Now, almost two hours later, James stands at the window in the darkened room looking out into the night. A knock at the door breaks the stillness and when Jiron opens it, light comes in from where Ceadric stands in the hallway with a lantern.

"It's time," he says.

Coming from the window, James along with the others pick up their things. Leaving the dark room behind, they follow Ceadric down the hallway to the stairs where they descend all the way down to the bottom.

Once they leave the stairwell, Ceadric takes them through hallways other than those they used to initially reach the tower. Few servants are about, those they encounter pay them little attention.

They finally arrive at a locked door where Ceadric pauses a moment and produces a key that unlocks it. Pushing the door open, the unmistakable odor of straw and horse manure comes to them.

Hedry along with a dozen other Raiders whom they recognize turn toward them when they hear the door open.

"Everything set?" asks Ceadric as he moves into the stable.

"Yes sir," replies Hedry. He and his men begin equipping those who need it with armor they brought. All that is except Brother Willim who dons a plain dark cloak which is as far as he's willing to go.

Ceadric waves over a soldier who comes and joins him while he helps James into his armor. "This is Reilin," he says. "He's willing to accompany you and be your interpreter."

"Welcome aboard, Reilin," James says in greeting.

Reilin merely nods in reply. Standing a hair over six feet, he makes an imposing figure with his jet black hair.

"Are the gates still being watched?" Jiron asks.

"Last we checked they were," Ceadric replies. "Don't worry, I doubt if they'll suspect anything."

"Let's hope not," says James.

When at last they are all suitably attired in armor, they mount their horses. James and Miko need help, the additional weight of the armor making it difficult for them to make it up. With the aid of two Raiders, they manage to get into the saddle.

Hedry mounts and looks back. "Form it up back there," he commands. James and the rest tighten their formation with Brother Willim in the middle. "We leave the barn and head straight for the gates. No talking or stopping." After receiving acknowledgement for the plan, he turns back toward the stable's exit and nudges his horse into motion.

They leave the stable and begin crossing the open courtyard toward the gate. As they draw near, a clank is heard and the portcullis begins to be drawn up. On the other side of the wall is a group of four men dressed in Empire attire not more than ten feet from the gate. Standing around a fire, they turn at the raising of the portcullis.

One of the men comes forward and asks good naturedly, "Out for no good again Hedry?"

"You know it, Ezzin," he replies. "You'll have to wait to win your gold back for a few days I'm afraid."

Laughing, Ezzin says, "See you when you return."

As James and the rest pass by the area where Ezzin and his comrades take their ease by the fire, his anxiety rises with fear of being discovered. But he has little to worry about as Ezzin and the others hardly give them more than a cursory glance. Still, he doesn't relax until they are swallowed by the night and the light from Ezzin's fire disappears in the dark.

"You know him?" asks Potbelly.

"Ezzin?" asks Hedry. "Oh sure. He likes to lose at cards and I'm quite happy to oblige him." Several men chuckle at that. "You would be surprised what one can learn during a friendly game of cards."

They ride to the southeast in the dark with only the stars and the moon above to light their way for an hour before Hedry brings them to a halt. "Here's where we part ways," he tells them.

Removing the armor they used to disguise themselves, they return it to Hedry and his men who pack it away behind their saddles. "I appreciate this," James tells him once the heavy weight of the armor is gone.

"Not a problem," he replies. "Just hope you find what you're looking for."

"So do I," James tells him.

With farewells passing from one group to the other, Hedry gets his men moving and soon James and the others are left alone in the night.

"Which way?" asks Jiron. Now that they are finally on their way to find Tinok, his impatience is getting the better of him.

"Better head south until daylight," says James. "When it's light I'll try to get a better idea of where he is."

"South it is," Jiron says and they get underway.

James glances with foreboding at the moon shining above them. Now less than three weeks before the Shroud of Killian once again blinds the Giant's Eye, he fervently hopes they can find Tinok before it's too late.

Chapter Eight

After their initial grief over losing the members of their village to the grayness in the desert, Zyrn sent a rider south. He hoped that when the rider reaches the temple he'll be able to convince someone to come and deal with this. The rider was none too happy about the fact that the only temple close was that of Dmon-Li. After all, their priests were none too helpful to the ordinary man.

The day following Zyrn's return to the village, he along with several others returns to the gray area. He makes sure to keep his distance, the memory of his friend's death within the grayness still very much on his mind. When they finally reach the border of the gray area, Zyrn has the feeling it didn't take him nearly as long to reach it as it did last time.

Only one of those who accompanied him this time had been with him last time. Kabu, one of the ones who are seeing the grayness for the first time, sits there on his horse with eyes wide and mouth open. It seems as if the grayness extends all the way to the horizon. "I can't believe this," he says.

"Believe it," asserts Zyrn. "Don't go near it or it may kill you."

"Why are we here?" another asks.

Coming to a stop well back from the edge of the grayness, Zyrn removes a bundle from behind his saddle. Laying it on the ground, he unrolls the cloth to reveal six Parvati longswords. Picking up one of the swords acquired during their initial scavenging expedition, he begins walking toward the edge of the grayness.

"The last time I was here…" he explains then stops and glances back to where the others remain with the horses. "It's safe enough to come a little closer," he assures them.

"If it's all the same," Kabu says, "we'll stay right here."

Sighing with a shake of his head, Zyrn resumes his trek to the edge of the grayness. "As I was saying," he begins again, this time raising his voice so the others can hear him better, "the last time I was here, I saw it expand."

Stopping three feet from the edge of the shimmering grayness, he eyes it warily. Grasping the hilt of the sword, he holds it point downward. Raising the hilt as high as he can, he thrusts it into the ground. The blade sinks half a foot before coming to a stop. Making sure it is securely in the ground, he then turns back and hurries to rejoin the others.

"What I want to do is see how fast it is growing," he explains as he reaches the others. "By placing these swords along its edge every fifty feet or so, we'll get a good idea of what it's doing."

"Why?" asks one of the men as Zyrn takes another sword.

Zyrn stops and looks the man in the eye. "I don't want to wake up one night to find it at our village," he says. "Or worse yet, not waking up because it is encompassing our village."

Striding off to the right of the spot where he placed the first sword, he goes approximately fifty feet from where the first blade is in the ground before coming to a stop. Trying to place the sword exactly the same distance from the edge of the grayness as the other, he thrusts it into the ground. Again making sure the sword will remain standing upright, he returns for another.

Again and again he takes the swords and thrusts them into the ground at the edge of the grayness. When all six swords are firmly fixed into the ground, he stands back and looks at them.

"Now what?" asks one of the men.

Gesturing to the swords he says, "Look at where the swords stand."

After they look for a few seconds one of them asks, "So?"

"Can't you see?" he asks. "They do not mark the edge of a circle."

Taking another look the men see what he is trying to explain. Instead of a smooth circular line, the swords mark areas that extend further out than others.

"It isn't growing consistently," Zyrn summarizes. "Rather different areas are pushing out at different rates."

"Guess your time at the School paid off," Kabu says.

"The High Lord Magus would know what to do," he explains. "Though by the time word reached him it might be too late for our village."

"What now?" asks one of the men.

"Now we wait," he says. "Learn as much as we can about it so when the priest gets here we can give him some idea of what he's facing."

"Look!" one of the men says as he points to the first sword Zyrn placed in the ground. Already the edge of the grayness has reached the blade and is creeping past. Glancing to the others, they see that the grayness in those areas has not moved forward at all.

"Let's return home and come back tomorrow," he says. "Then we will know how fast it is spreading."

Mounting their horses, they turn around and race back to their village.

Day after day they return, Zyrn continues bringing six swords to mark the new edge of the grayness. Though it is spreading, it isn't spreading very fast. As near as Zyrn can figure, the grayness is advancing around six feet per day. Some areas advance faster while others not so much. Overall, it is keeping a somewhat consistent shape. Should one area advance six or more feet one day, the next day it may only advance a foot or two allowing the rest to catch up.

The mood of the village is gradually worsening. Talk is beginning to spread that they are cursed because they stole from the dead, that the gods are angry with them. Some believe the grayness is their punishment.

After the third day, others from various villages in the area can be seen as they too keep an eye on the advancing carpet of gray. Zyrn confers with other learned men from the different villages but this is beyond them. Still no word from the rider he sent to the south, he can only watch and wait.

By the fifth day, no one bothers coming out with Zyrn. Talk of the area being cursed by the gods and other such nonsense has kept anyone else from even thinking about going out there.

In the late afternoon of the fifth day, he again goes out and marks the edge of the shimmering gray area. Four rings of swords now stand within its boundary, every ring marking a different day. Zyrn shakes his head, worried over where this might lead if nothing is done to curb its growth. But what can be done about it?

On his way back home, he tries to think about what could possibly halt the spreading of the grayness. Halfway back to his village, he encounters a score of people from his village coming his way. Among them are the ones who have been most vocal about the gray sand being a punishment of the gods.

As he approaches them, he takes note of Khalim, the only young man to have survived the ill-fated second expedition to the battlefield. That is if you can call having lost his mind and constantly gibbering incoherently surviving. Nothing they've attempted has done anything to restore his mind back to him.

A feeling of dread comes over Zyrn when he sees Khalim's arms are bound behind him. The grim set of the men's faces does nothing to alleviate the feeling. Kicking his horse faster, he rushes to meet the approaching group.

"What are you doing with him?" he asks, gesturing to Khalim.

"We go to appease the gods," replies Maki, the one who has most fervently purported the theory of the gods being angry.

"Khalim has brought this doom upon us," another states. "Had he died with the others, the grayness would not be seeking him."

"Is that what you think?" asks Zyrn in disbelief.

"Yes," asserts Maki. "Only his death at the hands of the grayness will appease the gods."

"You are wrong!" Zyrn exclaims. "He is blameless for this!" Bringing his horse before Maki he says, "I will not allow you to do this."

"Stand aside Zyrn," Maki says. The others with him are unsure of themselves, but Maki glances back and hardens their resolve. "We do this for the survival of our village."

Another of the men says, "You yourself said that if the grayness isn't stopped, it will come to the village and destroy us all."

"We will satisfy the gods with our piety and devotion," Jatta asserts. Jatta, one of the elders of the village, is hardly someone Zyrn would believe to be party to something like this.

"All you will do is kill an innocent man!" he yells. "Will the blood of an innocent appease the gods? Do not fool yourself into a course of action that will damn you for all eternity." He meets the eyes of each of them and sees his words are having little effect. Fear, fear of the unknown has robbed them of their senses.

Knowing he will be unable to sway them with words, he reaches out and takes hold of Khalim's arm. Just before he pulled the mad young man onto his horse, he hears a whisk of a sword leaving its sheath.

"Take your hands off him," Maki says. The point of his sword is but inches away from Zyrn's throat.

Zyrn's gaze bores into that of Maki's. Releasing Khalim's arm, he stares at the men before him.

"Go home Zyrn," says Jatta.

"Let us do what must be done to save our village," Maki tells him. Still holding his sword, the threat of bodily harm hangs between the two men should Zyrn continue in his attempt to stop them.

"Don't do this," he again pleads with them.

Ignoring his plea, they begin moving again. Walking around Zyrn's horse, they head out toward the grayness.

Zyrn watches them go, a tear in his eye. *What madness!* Khalim will die because they are afraid. Turning his horse toward his village, he races across the desert. If he can get there in time, he might be able to convince others to go with him to rescue Khalim.

When his village comes into view, Zyrn knows he will not be too late if they can return quickly. Wailing comes to him as he draws closer. He finds the family of Khalim grief stricken.

As he approaches the outlying buildings, the people take note of his arrival. None are able to meet his eyes.

"Maki plans to sacrifice Khalim!" he cries out to a group of men standing together. "We must stop him. If we leave now we may be able to get there in time!" None of the men make a move or even raise their eyes to look at him. Then Zyrn understands, they all made the decision to sacrifice Khalim and are too ashamed to meet his eyes.

Off to one side he sees Khalim's father. Riding over to him he says, "Surely you will seek to save the life of your son?"

With downcast eyes Khalim's father replies, "I have three other children Zyrn. We have to think what is best for the village."

"How can you say that?" he yells. "Khalim's death will not stop the approach of the grayness. All it will accomplish is the death of an innocent man." The father remains quiet, eyes downcast in shame.

Looking around at the assembled villagers, men and women he's known all his life, he cries out, "Will no one come with me?" Not one person answers. He sits there on his horse in disbelief, amazed at the lengths good people will go when fear rules them. Saddened by what his village has become, he slowly passes among those he thought he knew until he comes to his home. Dismounting, he leaves his horse out front and enters through his front door.

Despondent, he sits alone and grieves.

Hours later, Maki and the others return without Khalim. There is little rejoicing as they make their way through the buildings, faces peer out from windows but none come to greet them. When they reach the lane outside his home, Zyrn remains within and simply stares at them through the window as they go by.

A few glance his way but when they see him staring, quickly lower their eyes to the ground. "Fools!" whispers Zyrn to himself. When they at last move out of his line of sight, he heads off to bed.

The following morning, he again takes six swords and readies to return to the grayness. Jatta makes to approach him while he's securing the bundle behind his saddle and stops when he sees Zyrn shake his head. Swinging up into the saddle, he turns his back on his longtime friend and rides out of the village without a word.

Out at the fringe of the gray area he finds the dead body of Khalim. Lying next to one of the swords he placed there the day before, his body shimmers with the grayness that has continued to advance. *What a waste!*

Dismounting a dozen yards from the fringe, he removes his bundle and begins marking the boundary once more. When he's done, he takes his horse by the reins and begins walking back home. Not in any hurry to return there, he wonders if he can even live among people who are capable of such an act.

No matter what may happen, his home will never be the same. Not after something like this. Deep in his thoughts, he fails to see the approaching riders before they're almost upon him.

"Zyrn!" one of the riders cries. It's the man whom he had sent for the priest, and riding at his side is the priest himself. Wearing the robes of a priest of Dmon-Li, the man looks at him rather haughtily.

"Thank goodness you came Father," Zyrn says as the priest approaches.

"Yes, yes, yes," the priest says rather impatiently. "This young man here was most insistent about some sort of problem. He harangued us until the temple gave in and sent me." Looking as if he feels this is going to be a complete waste of time and is only doing it because he has to, he adds, "So where is this 'thing'?"

Swinging into the saddle, Zyrn turns his horse back toward where he's been marking the fringe and says, "It's this way, about a mile."

Sighing, the priest says, "Lead on. Let's get this over with."

Kicking his horse into a fast trot, Zyrn leads the priest and the rider back to the grayness. When it comes into view, he says, "There it is."

At first it looks nothing more than the haze you would see from the heat rising off the ground. "Is this some sort of joke?" he priest asks, not amused.

Zyrn remains quiet as they continue to close the distance. Soon the rows of swords he has placed there over the past few days become visible where they are sticking out of the ground. He turns back to the priest and says, "I used the swords to mark the edge. It's growing."

The priest finally realizes the shimmer is not due to the heat as he at first thought. "What is it?" he asks, a nervous catch to his voice.

"I don't know," replies Zyrn. "But it's deadly. Whatever it touches, dies."

Then the priest gasps when he sees the body of Khalim lying within the shimmering field of gray.

"That's Khalim," explains Zyrn. "Last night, several men from my village brought him out here as a sacrifice thinking it would appease the gods."

"Why did they do that?" the priest asks.

Launching into the tale, Zyrn relates everything to the priest. From the first scavenging expedition, the second ill-fated one when all but Khalim had fallen to the grayness, and ending at the senseless sacrifice of Khalim.

Dismounting, the priest advances toward the carpet of gray. "Don't get too close," warns Zyrn, "it can advance pretty fast at times."

Nodding, the priest continues to draw closer to the fringe until he stands three yards away. Reaching down, he picks up a scorpion that was crawling across the dirt and tosses it into the shimmering gray. He watches as the scorpion lands within the grayness, takes two steps then stops. Its body gradually grows to be the same color as the grayness.

"Fascinating," he says.

"Is there anything you can do about it?" Zyrn asks.

The priest waves away the question. Summoning the magic of his god, he sends it out to the grayness in an attempt to discover what it is.

Zyrn watches as the priest closes his eyes and concentrates. At first nothing happens. Then a ripple seems to roll across the surface of the deadly grayness toward the priest, like a wave across the surface of a placid pond.

"Uh," begins Zyrn in warning to the priest as the wave rolls toward him. Backing up, he and the other man put some distance between themselves and the priest.

Then all of a sudden, the priest cries out as the grayness surges outwards. His cry is cut short as he and his horse become completely enveloped by the mass of shimmering gray.

Zyrn turns and runs as the grayness continues to sweep forward. Another horse cries in pain and fear as the gray comes in contact with its hoof. Glancing backward, he sees the horse stumble then collapse as the wave of gray seems to wash over it.

"Run!" he yells as the gray continues to sweep toward them. Running for their lives, Zyrn and the other man race across the sand. Glancing back to see how close it is, he slows then comes to a stop when he discovers it is no longer advancing toward them.

"Lord help us," he says as he sees the edge of the grayness now over a hundred yards further out from where it had been this morning. The body of the horse and the priest are now just lumps far within it.

"What are we to do now?" the man asks him.

Shaking his head in reply, Zyrn remains silent. It had reacted to the magic of the priest. He and others have been in as close proximity to it before and it had never reacted as it did just now. Could it be alive? If so he has no idea what that could mean.

He stands there thinking for several minutes as he contemplates the situation. The sound of the man leading the remaining horse over to him snaps him out of his reverie. "We better get back home," Zyrn says.

Climbing into the saddle, he reaches down and helps the man to swing onto the horse behind him. Riding double, they begin the trek back to the village.

Chapter Nine

_____

Since parting with Hedry, James and the others rode throughout the night with hardly any breaks. At one point during the night they came across a major road running east and west. Wishing that it ran more north and south so they could follow it, they crossed it and left it behind. Now hours later, the sun is beginning to peek over the horizon. James calls a halt. "Let's give the horses a break and I'll see what I can find out about Tinok," he tells the others.

Dismounting, he and Jiron move away from where the others are getting a quick bite to eat. Removing his mirror from his belt pouch, he holds it in his hands as he concentrates on Tinok.

Jiron watches the mirror with keen interest but after several minutes of trying, its surface fails to do anything. "What's wrong?" he asks.

"I don't know," replies James. "It could be he's too far away, the drain of magic for the spell continued to increase which is an indicator that what I'm looking for is nowhere close." Giving up, he puts the mirror back in his pouch and pulls out the piece of cloth. "I wish I had my compass back," he says. The compass in question is the one he made way back when he first arrived in Trendle after coming to this world. Fashioned from wood, it would turn and indicate the desired direction when he used it in conjunction with magic to try to find something. Not for the first time he wishes he would have had the good sense to have another built while he was at The Ranch all last winter.

Jiron nods. He remembers how well it had worked. But the cloth works fairly well, though it will most likely attract the attention of anyone close by when he uses it. After all, a cloth that all of a sudden rises and moves to point in a certain direction, who wouldn't do a double-take if they saw that.

Sighing, James holds one end of the cloth in his hand and concentrates on which way Tinok lies. Letting the magic flow, he opens his eyes and watches as the cloth rises until it's pointing in a rigid line. Based on the position of the sun, it's pointing off to the south.

"We figured that," says Jiron, James nods his head in agreement.

Stopping the spell, James returns the strip of cloth to his pouch.

"Wish it would tell us how far away he is," Jiron says, and not for the first time.

"Maybe in a day or two I'll get a better idea where he is," James says hopefully. "Eventually we will be close enough for the mirror to pick him up."

The others have finished their meal of dried beef and water. Brother Willim brings James and Jiron over a portion. "Did you find him?" he asks.

Shaking his head, Jiron replies, "No. He's to the south, but James is unable to determine how far."

"We'll find him," Brother Willim says matter-of-factly.

They eat their less than appetizing breakfast and then return to the saddle. In no time they are once again racing across the desert.

This section of the desert is uninhabited, its proximity to the border of Madoc probably accounts for most of the reason. Whatever the reason, James is glad they are able to move into the Empire without being noticed.

They ride for awhile when Shorty hollers out, "Rider to the east!"

Slowing down, they see a lone rider moving at a leisurely pace. The direction in which he's moving will cause him to cross their path further to the south. "Should we see what he's about?" asks Stig.

"No," replies James. "The less who knows we're here the better. Still, keep an eye on him." It takes the rider several minutes before he's even aware they are there. When he does, he immediately alters course to intercept. No longer moving at his leisurely pace, the rider is practically flying across the desert toward them.

"Damn," curses James. "Reilin!" he hollers to the Raider who is there to translate for them. When he has his attention, he says, "Go see what he wants before he gets here."

"Yes sir," Reilin replies. Kicking his horse into a gallop, he moves to intercept the rider.

The rest of them continue along their original course while they keep an eye on Reilin and the other rider. By the time Reilin reaches the rider and they stop, the rider has come to within a hundred feet of the rest of them.

Before Reilin has a chance to say anything, the rider begins talking quickly. What's being said is lost to the others but the rider is obviously agitated about something. Finally quieting down, the rider listens to Reilin for a moment before once again launching into another animated speech.

When it doesn't look as if Reilin is getting rid of the man, James says, "Jiron, go see what's taking so long."

"Right." Nudging his horse in the sides, he makes his way over and joins them. Reilin turns at his approach and the other rider grows silent again as Reilin talks to Jiron. Jiron asks a question and waits for the translation and then again for the rider's answer.

By this time James has brought the others to a stop. Surprised it has taken this long, he pulls out a strip of dried beef and chews on it absentmindedly while he waits. He doesn't have to wait long before Jiron leaves Reilin and the rider where they are and returns to the group.

"What's going on?" James asks as he nears. The look on Jiron's face says it's anything but something simple.

"The man's name is Zyrn," he begins. "He's a leader of a nearby village. He wanted to warn us not to go west."

"Why?" asks Potbelly.

"I didn't get the whole tale, but the gist of it is that it's death for anyone to go there," he explains. "Also, he says there was a big battle there not too long ago."

"A battle?" asks Miko. "As in the battle we barely survived?"

"I think so," he replies with a nod.

They all remember the mammoth explosion and then the fire that coated the outside of the barrier for a time. "What is it that's killing them?" James asks. Visions of radiation fallout run through his mind.

"Now this is where it gets kind of strange," admits Jiron. "In fact, if it wasn't for all I've seen and been through since I first met you, I would discount it as the man has lost his mind." He glances around at the others a moment before continuing. "He says the sand is killing them. That the sand is turning into a shimmering carpet of gray and whatever it touches, dies. He says it's growing."

Everyone but James and Miko, who had been unconscious at the time, remember the gray sand they traveled through when they left the battlefield. Which only lends credence to what the man is saying.

James has never heard of anything like this. Though he wasn't conscious when the bubble exploded at the end of the battle, he's heard plenty of accounts from various people as to its effect. Could he have caused this? In a world with magic, gods and other planes of existence, it's possible.

Nodding over to where Zyrn waits with Reilin, Jiron asks, "What should I tell him?"

Sighing, James knows what he's going to have to do. If nothing else at least go and see for himself what this man is talking about. "Go and ask him if he'll take us there," he says.

Turning his horse back toward where the man waits, Jiron hurries back over to him. As soon as he reaches the man and tells him what James said, Zyrn begins shaking his head. Then he kicks his horse and rides toward James and the others with Reilin and Jiron right behind.

"No, no, no!" he cries out. "You must not go there!" He waits for Reilin to come and translate. "It is a cursed place. Too dangerous!"

James waits for the translation then says, "Regardless, we are going to see this thing for ourselves." The pain on Zyrn's face is evident when Reilin translates for him. "Where can we find it?"

"Hey, aren't those Parvati swords?" Scar suddenly asks, indicating the handles of the swords sticking out of the bundle behind Zyrn's saddle.

"Yes," replies Zyrn. "After the battle I and many from my village came and scavenged what we could." He can see their disapproval stares directed at him and adds, "Our lives are hard. This is the only way we can survive." Lowering his eyes, he says, "Of course, there may soon be nothing left anyway."

"We'll see about that," James states. "Now, will you lead us there?"

Realizing they plan to go despite his warning, he nods his head. "Yes," he says, "I will show you. But be warned, it has already claimed the lives of many." Turning his horse in the direction of the grayness, he leads them toward it.

James rides directly behind Zyrn with Jiron and Brother Willim. "Do you think we caused this?" Brother Willim asks.

Shrugging, James replies, "I don't know. We'll know more when we get there." He raises his voice and asks Zyrn, "How far is it?"

Reilin, who is riding next to Zyrn, translates then replies "A little over an hour."

James rides in silence, mulling over what Zyrn has told them.

When the shimmering grayness appears on the horizon, Zyrn stops. "There it is," he says. As James begins to continue forward, he stops him. "Do not approach too closely, it sometimes advances rapidly."

"Thanks," replies James, "I'll remember that." Moving forward with Zyrn and Reilin beside him he's awed by the sheer size of the thing. It's immense! He notices the rings of swords standing upright far within the gray mass. Pointing to them, he asks Zyrn, "Marking the edge to see how fast it was expanding?"

Surprised that he would have realized that Zyrn says, "Yes. It's been growing about six feet a day." He points to where two rows have a large gap in one area. "Though it isn't consistent, some areas grow faster than others."

Nodding, James assimilates that as he continues riding toward it. A hundred yards from the fringe, he brings them to a stop. Dismounting, he says to the others, "You stay here. I'm going to get a closer look."

When Zyrn hears that he rushes to James' side and says, "You cannot!" Taking hold of James by the arms he stares into his eyes, "This is nothing to trifle with."

Jiron comes and disengages Zyrn from James. "Don't worry," he tells him, "we can take care of ourselves." With James go Brother Willim and Jiron. Zyrn tries to go with them too but Scar and Potbelly stop him.

"What do you make of it?" asks Jiron.

"I don't know," he replies. "Kind of reminds me of the Blob."

"The Blob?" Brother Willim asks.

"Sorry, it's a story from my world about a gelatinous ooze that eats everything it comes into contact with," he explains. "Of course the thing I never understood about it was, if its touch would dissolve metal, what kept it from just sinking into the ground?" He gives them a grin when he sees the lost looks on their faces. "But that wouldn't make for a good story now would it?"

"Uh, I guess not," agrees Brother Willim though not quite understanding what James is talking about.

Out within the shimmering gray there are several distinct lumps, though what they once were is no longer discernable. "Must be the people he said the grayness has already claimed," he guesses.

"Must be," agrees Brother Willim.

"Nobody do anything until I tell you to," James tells them. They continue to advance until ten feet from the edge. Coming to a stop, James stares at the edge for a moment and can see it gradually advancing toward them. "It's still growing," he says.

Picking up a handful of sand, he throws it onto the shimmering mass. When the sand particles fall and hit the surface, nothing happens other than they gradually turn gray. To Jiron he says, "See if you can find me an insect or something. Make sure it's alive."

A minute later Jiron returns with a large beetle. Tossing it into the grayness, he watches as it hits the surface. It jerks twice then becomes still as it gradually turns gray just as the sand had. "Interesting," he says.

"What are you doing?" asks Brother Willim.

"Just being systematical," he explains. Next, he closes his eyes and summons the magic to try to get a better look.

Zyrn watches as the three men move toward the edge of the grayness. Held by two of them, he watches helplessly as the three men move closer. First the sand, then the beetle, the one man tests it to see what it will do. Then, he sees the ripple form across its surface, the same as had appeared when the priest summoned his magic.

"Get them out of there!" he cries out. Pulling against the grip of Scar and Potbelly, he yells, "It's going to kill them!"

"Settle down!" Scar tells him.

Pointing to the ripples coursing toward the edge where James and the others stand, he yells "Look!"

That's when Miko finally takes note of what it is he's talking about. "James!" he cries out as he rushes forward.

As his senses move outward, he can feel...something. It's nothing like he's ever encountered before. Then, he hears a commotion from where the others are waiting. Keeping the power going, he glances back over to them. He sees a struggling Zyrn held between Scar and Potbelly. "Wonder what that's about?" he asks, turning his attention to Jiron.

Shrugging, Jiron says, "Who knows?"

Then, he hears Miko yell, "James!" Glancing once again back to them, he sees Miko racing toward him and pointing wildly to the grayness. Looking back just as the grayness surges toward him, he reacts with reflexes honed over a year of magical fighting. Without thought, a barrier springs into being surrounding him, Jiron and Brother Willim.

"Asran's Branch!" cries out Brother Willim as the grayness washes over the barrier and covers it completely.

"It's coming in underneath!" exclaims Jiron.

Looking to the bottom edge of the barrier, James sees the ground beginning to turn gray. Adding a bottom section to the barrier, he soon has them completely encased within it.

"What's going on?" asks Jiron. Gazing in apprehension at the gray, shimmering mass covering the barrier he stands there as a shiver runs through him.

"It's trying to get in," replies James.

"Can you hold it?" Jiron asks.

"Oh yes," he replies. "As odd as it may sound, it's hardly causing me any problems. It's almost as if it isn't even there."

"How are we to get out of this?" Brother Willim asks. A green glow has sprung up around him after the onslaught of the grayness.

"Not sure to tell you the truth," admits James. Staring at the solid mass of gray coating the barrier, he wonders just how they will get out of this.

When the gray mass surged over James, Jiron and Brother Willim, Miko came to a screeching halt and abruptly turned around and raced back to the others. The 'tide' of gray enveloped the barrier and continued on for another twenty feet before coming to a stop. Then, it began moving backward to the barrier. Ripples continue to form as more of the grayness seems to move toward where James and the others are trapped.

Aleya shoots an arrow at it but it simply embeds itself in the ground and has no effect on the grayness.

"Is one of them a mage of some sort?" asks Zyrn.

After Reilin translates Stig says, "Yes."

"Thought so," nods Zyrn. "It reacted the same way when a priest came to try to deal with it."

"Why didn't you tell us?" Shorty yells.

"How was I to know one of you was a mage?" Zyrn replies defensively.

"So how do we get them out?" asks Aleya, fear for Jiron in her eyes.

"I have no idea my dear," replies Zyrn. "I would have thought they'd be dead by now." Indeed, the gray covered barrier surprises him. Whoever is within there must be a mage of some power.

"Do you feel that?" asks Brother Willim.

"What?" questions James.

"It feels like sap running through a tree," he replies.

James sends his senses out again and after several minutes begins to understand what the brother is talking about. Small traces of energy are surging through the grayness covering the barrier.

"What do you make of it?" Brother Willim asks him.

He concentrates on the surges for another minute before turning to Brother Willim and Jiron. "It isn't magic," he says. "If it were, I would feel it." When he first saw the shimmering grayness, he thought that at first it might be a magical construct of some kind. But the familiar tingling that always comes with the workings of magic had been absent. "I think what you are feeling are electrical pulses," he explains. "Not entirely sure about that but that's what comes to mind."

"Electrical?" asks Jiron.

"Yeah," nods James. "Like lightning but on a much smaller scale."

Jiron glances to Brother Willim for confirmation but he just shrugs.

Closing his eyes again, James once more sends forth his senses to try to figure this thing out.

The grayness outside the barrier is constant and unchanging. Like a carpet of somewhat transparent gray, it diffuses the light coming through. Jiron gazes at it and a shiver runs through him again.

"The pulses of electricity seem to be originating from one place," James suddenly says, breaking the silence.

"So?" asks Jiron.

"So…" begins James, "that might be where the source of this is coming from."

"How far away is it?" Brother Willim asks.

"It's not close," he replies. Opening his eyes, he turns to them and says, "Can't be sure how far it is. Maybe a mile." He stands there and thinks for a moment, gazing at the bubble surrounding them and the grayness covering it. "Somehow we are going to have to reach the source of the electrical pulses."

"How are we to do that?" Jiron asks. "Shouldn't we first worry about how we are going to get out of here?"

Gesturing to the barrier Brother Willim asks, "Can you move this while we walk?"

"You mean push it under the grayness?" he asks. When Brother Willim nods yes, he thinks but a moment before he says, "Yes, I think I can."

"They've been in there a while now," says Scar.

They have done nothing but stare at the dome in the grayness where James, Jiron and Brother Willim are trapped since it first covered them. Miko had begun to try to use the Star in some way to rescue them, but Zyrn cautioned against it. He said that it was magic that it reacts to.

Frustrated, all they can do is watch. "If anyone can get out of this it's James," says Stig.

"You got that right," replies Potbelly. "In fact, I remember Jiron telling us about the time they were in this swamp…" He then goes into the story about the complex in the swamp with the skull pyramids and the headless torsos.

"Look!" exclaims Shorty.

Cutting off his story at the point James had found the hidden entrance to the complex, he again turns his gaze to the shimmering field of gray.

"What does he think he's doing?" Stig asks.

The dome in which their trapped comrades lie begins to move. Not toward them and safety, but deeper into the grayness. "Do you think he knows which way to go?" asks Scar.

"Could be moving blindly in order to find the way out," suggests Potbelly.

Shaking his head, Miko says, "I don't think so." He's been through too many things with James to believe he would engage in a course of action blindly. "He knows what he's doing," he states with conviction. *I hope you know what you're doing!*

Moving the barrier while still maintaining an air tight seal to prevent the grayness from coming in, at first was pretty hard. He had to keep the barrier beneath where they are walking stable so as not to trip them. At the same time, he needed to extend the forward area while retracting the rear.

Originally he thought to treat it like a hamster ball, and just have it roll along. But he soon realized that was not going to be feasible, not with the three of them in here. Going slowly at first, he moves the barrier along the ground at a crawl. Though as he continually does it, he finds that it's growing easier to do and soon doesn't have to work as hard to keep it going.

Another thing that's been bothering him that he has yet to mention to the others is their air supply. There's no way for the air within the barrier to be refreshed. The barrier itself is sizable so if this doesn't take too long, they may be alright.

As they move through the grayness, he had thought there would be more of a resistance. The rate of the electrical pulses had increased as soon as they got underway which is why he thought something was about to happen. But nothing manifested. The way it reacted to magic, how it moves, he can't help but think that it is somehow alive. Maybe not intelligent, but definitely alive. It almost feels like an episode of Star Trek where they meet an unknown life form. He wonders what Captain Kirk would do in this situation.

Thinking about Star Trek makes him melancholy. He misses home and the things that he can no longer have or do. What he would give for a pack of M&M's right now! Always a chocolate junky, he can almost taste the chocolate melting in his mouth.

"James!" cries out Jiron.

Snapping out of his reverie, he discovers the grayness has once again begun to seep through the edge where the barrier over their heads meets the barrier beneath them. With a thought he reconstructs the barrier sealing off the grayness that had seeped in, then pushes it out and away from the barrier.

"Sorry," he says slightly embarrassed.

One last errant thought crosses his mind as he wonders if there is anything similar to the cocoa bean here on this world. Getting back to the task at hand, he puts his idle curiosity to the back of his mind as he concentrates on more immediate concerns.

There's no way to tell how far they've progressed within the gray coated bubble. As near as he can tell they've crossed at least half a mile. At one point they passed one of the swords with which Zyrn had marked the edge of the gray area, but that was some time ago.

Grayness above them, grayness below them, it almost feels as if they are afloat on a sea of gray. If it wasn't for the firmness of the ground beneath them, he could almost imagine being in a gray storm cloud.

"Do you sense anything?" he finally asks Brother Willim.

Shaking his head, he replies, "Only what I originally felt." Nodding, James returns to the task at hand and they continue on.

The continuous concentration on the grayness has built sort of a picture in his mind of the paths the electrical bursts take as they course through the creature. *Creature?* he asks himself. Actually he has begun to think of it as something alive. The pulses always follow the same paths, almost like blood being pumped through arteries. There is a definite rhythm to it and maybe it's just his imagination, but he can almost feel a heartbeat.

"This thing's alive," he says.

"Alive?" questions Brother Willim.

"I think so, yes," replies James. "Nothing like we understand to be sure, but alive none the less." Stopping, he turns to Brother Willim and asks, "Wouldn't that mean this creature falls within Asran's domain?"

"I...I don't know," he stammers. Such a thought had never even occurred to him. Closing his eyes, he prays to his god for guidance and wisdom. After several minutes, his eyes open again. "You are correct in that it is alive. Now that you pointed it out, I can easily see it. But as to it falling within Asran's domain, it does not." He glances from one to the other then adds, "There are many living beings that do not fall within Asran's domain. His charge is that of all things that live in nature. Whatever this is, it doesn't live in nature or at least nature as I understand it."

"Well," says Jiron, all nervousness due to their circumstances vanishing. "If it's alive, we can kill it." Now that he understands it's a living creature, his confidence is returned. James gives him a grin and a nod before continuing on.

Another ten minutes or so of walking brings them to a point where their skin begins to crawl. Not due to the workings of magic, but something else. "What is that?" asks Jiron as he rubs his arm in a fruitless attempt to still the sensation.

"I don't know," replies James. Sending his senses out further toward the source of the electrical pulses he encounters what can only be called a void. "Oh man," he breathes.

"What?" asks Brother Willim.

"I'm not sure if I can explain it," he replies. "Give me a second." The others fall quiet as he continues his inspection of the void. Maybe void isn't the most apt term to use but it's the best he can come up with. In his mind's eye it appears to be an opening, a rip if you will. The electrical pulses are originating from the other side.

"I think we found where this is coming from," he tells them. "It looks like a hole, not a hole as you would understand the term. More like a way that is open between this plane and another. It's through this hole in our plane that the creature has entered."

"Can we close it somehow?" asks Brother Willim.

"Maybe," he says, "though it might take some time for me to figure it out."

Jiron waits there with Brother Willim while James works on the problem. Then a thought comes to him. "Could this be the spot where that explosion happened?" he asks.

"Maybe," replies James. *Could it be? Could I have ripped a hole in this plane of existence?* He seriously doubts that. Back home on Earth they have had larger explosions than the one that the others said happened here and no such thing happened. Yet, magic doesn't work there, nor do gods meddle in the affairs of men.

Brother Willim clears his throat and then says, "There is something one of my brothers told me that may have some bearing on this."

Turning toward him, James asks, "What?"

"Well, the night before we left to take your friends back to Cardri," he explains, "a green star fell from the sky. He didn't think anything of it, stars do fall from the sky at times. But it was the color of it that intrigued him, he had never seen one quite that green."

"That's saying something, coming from a priest of Asran as it does," remarks Jiron.

"Indeed," agrees Brother Willim. "He told me of it just before we left, said it fell somewhere to the south of the keep."

"Which is where we are," concludes James. "There's more to this than we know." A star falls from the sky, one that is a color that even a priest of Asran thinks is odd. And it just happens to fall in the vicinity where the magic bubble detonated with dramatic effect? Hardly a coincidence, but what can it mean?

"Think it has anything to do with what's going on here?" Jiron asks.

"Hard to tell," replies James. "It does seem just a bit too coincidental to me though." Closing his eyes again, he once more sends his senses to the void. It could have been possible that he weakened the boundary and the meteorite punched its way through. Realizing he doesn't know enough about how it came to be, he puts that train of thought aside for now and tries to come up with a way to close or mend the void.

After studying the void for several minutes, he comes to realize that there are a multitude of micro bursts of power directed at the edge of the void. Excited by the discovery, he narrows the scope of his examination to one small section of the void's edge. Then understanding dawns on him.

Coming out of it, he glances to Jiron and Brother Willim. "The void is working to close itself but the creature is somehow preventing it," he explains. "I can feel pulses of electricity that it is sending toward the edges of the void which I believe is preventing it from opening."

"Then if we can somehow interrupt the pulses," concludes Jiron, "the void will close?"

Nodding, James says, "I think so."

"How do you plan to bring this about?" asks Brother Willim.

"I'm going to short circuit it!" he exclaims.

"Do you think they're still alive?" asks Stig.

"Of course they are!" asserts Aleya.

Stig has the good grace to look embarrassed. He had forgotten her feelings for Jiron before he spoke.

After the dome in the grayness had begun to move, it continued along at a steady pace away from them. Gradually it grew smaller in the distance until they could no longer see it. Now, almost an hour later their worry for their comrades is steadily increasing. Surely something should have happened by now!

A rumble in the distance brings them to their feet. From every direction clouds begin moving across the sky toward the area where the dome disappeared. The rumble they heard was that of lightning moving between the converging storms.

"James!" Miko cries out jubilantly.

"Are you sure?" asks Aleya hopefully.

"Absolutely," he says. "He did the same thing after we fled Cardri."

As the sun is blotted from the sky by the thickening cloud layer, the wind that had been but a faint breeze all morning long now steadily grows stronger.

Then from their right they see a dozen people walking toward them. "They're from a nearby village," Zyrn tells them as the people come closer. Running across the sand, he quickly reaches their side.

"Zyrn?" asks Bokka, a man he's had dealings with before and a village elder too.

"Bokka!" exclaims Zyrn as he greets him.

Returning the greeting, Bokka looks up at the converging clouds with apprehension. "Something strange is afoot," he says.

"A mage is here," Zyrn tells him. Indicating where Miko and the others are waiting, he adds, "Those are his comrades."

"Is this mage causing the clouds to move across the sky?" another asks.

Nodding, Zyrn says, "Yes. He's working to destroy the grayness."

"How?" Bokka asks.

"That I do not know," replies Zyrn. Pointing off toward the center of the gray area he says, "The mage is out there right now."

Above the area where he's pointing is where the clouds are converging. Dark and black, the clouds are now darker than any this area has ever seen.

It's been a struggle to draw enough moisture to this dry area to form the storm clouds he's going to require. Beginning to feel the strain of holding the barrier for so long, and now having pulled clouds from miles away, he holds the clouds steady as he removes the water flask from his belt and drains it.

Brother Willim removes his and offers it to him. "I still have plenty if you need more," he says.

Shaking his head, James says, "Not right now, thanks." Replacing his now empty water flask back onto his belt, he returns to the matter at hand. He can feel the charged air in the sky above him. When the moment is right, he increases the polarity in an area away from the void to see what effect a lightning strike will have on the grayness before attempting it on the void itself.

He continues to increase the polarity to the opposite of that which is in the clouds. Then all of a sudden…

Flash! Boom!

…lightning strikes the grayness in the exact spot where he had increased the polarity.

James sends his senses out to pay close attention to that area. During the next couple pulses that come through the void, the ones that would ordinarily have passed in close proximity to the impact point of the bolt of lightning, fail to do so.

"Yes!" he exclaims.

"You killed it?" asks Jiron hopefully.

Bringing his senses back, he glances to Jiron and says, "No. But I think I will be able to close the void."

"Good," he says as James closes his eyes yet again.

Sending his senses back to the point of impact, he sees that the pulses are once again passing through the area. *So it's only 'paralyzed' for a few moments.* But a few moments may be all that will be required.

Now, he sends his senses to where the void lies. Picking a spot as dead center to it as possible, he begins increasing the polarity to attract a bolt of lightning.

Flash! Boom!

Lightning strikes the void dead center. However, unlike the earlier strike, this one has less of an effect. It did 'stun' the creature for a very brief moment and the void began to close. But then it recovered and pushed the void back to its original size. If he's going to do this it's going to take a lot more power.

Coming back to himself, he sits down on the bottom of the barrier and takes several deep breaths to settle himself. The air is beginning to grow stale, but not lethally so as yet. He sees Jiron gazing at him with concern. "I need a breather for a second," he says. "This is going to take more than I anticipated."

"Take your time," he says. "We aren't going anywhere."

James chuckles and gives him a grin. Closing his eyes, he again reaches his senses out to the storm clouds above. Using his magic, he tries to hold back the lightning from striking while at the same time causing the opposite polarity to increase at the void.

As the polarity increases, James can feel the static charge in the clouds fighting to form and strike. Finally unable to hold it off any longer, he lets it go.

Flash! Boom!

A mammoth explosion knocks Jiron and Brother Willim off their feet as the lightning strikes the void.

Sending his senses to the void, he sees that it has shrunk to half its original size while the pulses were nullified. Then, just as before, the pulses resume and it is again pushed back to its former size.

"Almost had it that time," he says. Opening his eyes, he glances to where Jiron is returning to his feet. "You better stay down there," he tells them. "The next time could be a little rocky."

Seeing the warning in his eyes, Jiron nods and takes a seat next to Brother Willim. "Rocky he says," Jiron mumbles to Brother Willim.

Ignoring them, James again closes his eyes and sends his senses up to the clouds. Working the same as before, he holds back the lightning for as long as he can then lets it go.

Flash! Boom!

Again the ground rolls from the impact. Not waiting to see what happens, he again begins to form the polarity to attract the lightning.

Flash! Boom!

Then again.

Flash! Boom!

Then one more time.

Flash! Boom!

Though deafened by the blasts, he sends his senses to the void and finds it all but closed. Then, the pulses once again begin to come and start pushing the void back. *What is it going to take?*

Flash! Boom! Flash! Boom! Flash! Boom! Flash! Boom!

Four more times he causes the lightning to strike the void in an attempt to keep the pulses from rematerializing and pushing the void wider. On the fourth strike, a spasming ripple runs through the grayness as the void finally closes.

Chapter Ten

Zyrn stands there in awe as the crack of thunder rolls over them from the massive bolt of lightning. There had been two lesser strikes before that one but neither had come close to the power of that last one.

"Such power," says Bokka. Several of the other villagers with him nod in agreement.

They hold their breath for a moment longer before another two bolts flash from the clouds and strike the ground with massive cracks of thunder. Then a few seconds later, three more bolts arc from the clouds to strike the ground. The grayness begins to rapidly draw back toward the area where the lightning is striking, already it's past the lines of swords Zyrn had set in the ground over the last few days.

"What's it doing?" asks one of the villagers.

Shaking his head, Zyrn says, "I don't know."

Then four bolts strike from the clouds. This time, a spasming ripple courses from one side of the grayness to the other then back again. "That hurt it," one villager says in satisfaction.

"Yes, but it isn't gone yet," observes Zyrn.

"It's still there," Jiron says.

"I can see that," replies James a bit testily. He was sure that when the void closed, the grayness would die. But it still covers the barrier and he can detect minor pulses running through it. There is no longer a set point from which the pulses are now originating, rather they come from all over.

"It must be like a giant amoeba," states James. When he sees the question about to be asked, he continues. "An amoeba is a single celled organism. As such, it could split off from its host and still survive."

"Right," nods Jiron still totally lost.

James sighs and shakes his head. What he wouldn't give for someone to understand him. Most of the time when he tries to explain things all he gets is that lost look that says they have no idea what he's talking about. Trying to make it so they can at least understand it a little he says, "In the broadest sense, consider it a worm."

"Ah!" says Brother Willim. "I understand. Cut off from the main body, it still survives."

"Something like that," nods James. Moving to the edge of the barrier, he peers closely at the grayness. "Come here and look at it more closely," he says, waving them over.

When Brother Willim and Jiron come over, Jiron says, "It seems to have the texture of sand."

"Yes, it does," agrees James. "When it came through, the first thing it must have come into contact with was the gray sand that remained after the explosion. And for whatever reason it took on that aspect." He sees them not entirely following. "Ever heard of a chameleon? It's a lizard that is able to change its color to match that of whatever environment it's in."

"Not by that name," replies Brother Willim. "But there is this bug over in Cardri that they say does the same thing though I've never actually seen it."

"Maybe this creature," he says as he taps the side of the barrier, "lives on another plane, between the planes, whatever and when it moves to another takes on the aspects of that plane to better blend in and survive."

Brother Willim nods, "I follow you."

"That's all well and good," states Jiron, "but we are still faced with the problem of what to do with this 'amoeba' I think you called it."

"You're right of course," he says as he moves back away from the barrier. He allows the winds and clouds to begin moving on their own, the strain of holding them was beginning to be too much to maintain.

Lightning is out. Though it did affect it, it didn't do so to any great degree. Fire? Possibly but he'll need a nearby source from which to draw upon and a tremendous amount of power.

"Wish Miko was here with us," he abruptly states.

"What?" asks Brother Willim.

"Oh, just thinking the power of the Star would come in handy right about now," he explains.

"You have an idea?" Jiron asks.

Nodding, he says, "Yes I do." Pulling out his mirror, he glances to them and says, "First though, I need to send a message."

Miko and the others have been keeping a constant eye on the grayness ever since the lightning bolts stopped and the cloud cover began to dissipate. They expected the grayness to die, go away, or something. But it remaining unchanged seemed to not bode well for James and the others.

"Could it have beaten them?" asks Scar.

"Would you shut up!" roars Stig. "It did not beat them." He moves over to where Aleya is off by herself. "I'm sure they're all right," he tells them.

Looking up at him with a tear in her eye, she says, "I hope so. After losing everyone when the Empire took my home, I was afraid to latch onto someone else. I feared going through that again."

He puts his arm comfortingly around her shoulders. She gives him a short laugh and says, "And look who I decided to latch onto. A man who always seems to be in the middle of whatever is going on, most of it life threatening. I must be out of my mind."

"Jiron's a good man," assures Stig. "I know he cares for you. Besides, your heart will love who your heart will love. There's not much you can do about it."

"I suppose not," she agrees.

"He and James have been in worse situations before and always managed to get out of them," he says. "So relax. They're probably just taking a moment to consider their options."

"I hope so," she says. She sits there with Stig for a minute before her eye catches sight of a dust devil swirling atop the ground not ten feet from where they sit. "Isn't that odd," she suddenly says.

"What?" Stig asks.

Pointing to the swirling dust devil she says, "It sits in one spot. I've never known one to do that before."

"Either have I," he replies. As they continue watching it, the feeling that something is odd about it grows stronger by the second. It's not moving, not growing smaller or larger, it just continues to twirl.

Just then Miko comes to stand beside them, his attention too is fixed upon the dust devil. "Strangest thing I've ever seen," he says.

All of a sudden, it moves in an erratic pattern then dissipates. Miko's eyes widen when he sees upon the ground where the dust devil had just been, a design roughly similar to the Star of Morcyth.

Grabbing a stick off the ground, he moves over to it and writes 'James?' in the dirt. Then as if an invisible finger is writing in the dirt, letters form. B...u...i...l...d."

"They're alive!" Aleya exclaims.

"Hey!" Miko calls to the others. "You better get over here."

Scar, Potbelly and the others come over quickly and watch as the letters continue to form.

Zyrn and those he's with see the commotion and come over as well to find out what's going on.

Letter by letter, the message appears in the dirt:

Build fire, then get far, far away!

"What do you suppose that means?" Reilin asks.

"Just what it says," Miko replies. To the others he says, "Gather what material you can. We're going to make a fire." Then he bends over and uses his stick to write once more in the sand.

When James sees Miko write, 'Ok' in the sand, he relaxes. Getting what rest he can, he continues to watch Miko and the others in the mirror. They scramble about gathering what combustible items as can be found. Dead bushes, roots and a few sticks are all that's readily available.

He watches as they pile those items together and then Scar kneels down beside it. Taking out his flint stone, he begins striking sparks then bends close to where a spark has fallen on a dried leaf and starts blowing softly across the red spark. After a moment a little bit of smoke appears, then a flame.

Once the fire has caught and doesn't look as if it's about to go out anytime soon, those who have horses mount while the others who are on foot begin moving away as fast as they can. James waits for them to put some distance between themselves and the fire before he begins.

Putting away his mirror, he looks to Jiron.

"Over the top magic again?" he says with a grin.

Returning the grin, he says "Something like that." Brother Willim looks from one to the other wondering what they are talking about.

This time, he lies down on the ground before beginning. "Hope this works," he says then closes his eyes. Sending out his senses, he first checks where the void had been and is happy to discover no evidence of it. Next he sends his senses over to the fire Scar had made to make sure it won't go out anytime soon. Satisfied that it will last a sufficient amount of time, he begins.

Using the magic, he forms a second barrier that completely encompasses the creature. Not nearly as strong as the one he created to protect them from the grayness, just strong enough to keep the air within from passing to the outside. Never has he created something so massive. The creature must cover over six square miles radiating out in every direction. Just creating the barrier took longer than he anticipated. The hardest thing was checking the perimeter to make sure the barrier extended several inches past the creature so that not even the slightest part of it was outside the barrier.

Next, he works to remove everything from the air within the barrier but the oxygen molecules. A hard enough job to do when you aren't trying to maintain two barriers at the same time, but with what he's already doing, it's incredibly difficult. Slowly, the concentration of oxygen within the barrier increases. At one point he allows additional air to seep in to augment the supply of oxygen.

Keeping an eye on the fire Scar built, he continues to intensify the concentration of oxygen. When the fire is on the verge of going out, he determines that he's done all he's going to be able to do with increasing the oxygen content within the barrier. He's not entirely sure but the air within the large barrier has to be pretty close to almost pure oxygen.

In a voice tight with strain, he says, "Get ready." Sweat is now beading down his face and his teeth are grit together in response to the great strain he's under.

"For what," Brother Willim asks.

Unable to respond, James puts as much magic as he can into the protective barrier surrounding them to strengthen it. Then, while maintaining both barriers, he extends the larger one to encompass the fire. And when the fire hits the almost pure oxygen within...

Ke-Pow!

...it ignites the oxygen in a massive fireball.

The blast hits the larger barrier with such force that he's unable to maintain it. Letting it go, he puts everything he has into maintaining the protective one around them.

The grayness that covered their barrier is burnt away as fire completely consumes it. Even the ground beneath their barrier turns red as the heat from the blast melts it into a smoldering slag. James' back is scorched, his hair begins to smoke as the heat from the blast enters through the barrier.

"James!" exclaims Jiron. The heat burning and scorching his flesh brings intense agony, then soothing comfort comes as the green glow surrounding Brother Willim moves to envelope him. Easing his pain and soothing his burns, Brother Willim works to protect them both against the heat of the fire. For James, Brother Willim is unable to offer much help, it takes all he can do just to protect him and Jiron.

The ground starts to settle down and the heat subsides as the fire begins to diminish. James continues to lay there in agony, trying with his last ounce of strength to hold onto the barrier. When at last he can no longer hold onto it, he releases his hold on the magic and passes out.

"My lord!" exclaims Shorty when the fire ignites the oxygen. Even as far away as they had managed to reach the heat could be felt, then the concussion wave hits and almost bowls them over. Rising into the air, a gigantic cloud of fire reaches to the sky.

"Nothing could have survived that," breathes Scar.

When it's observed that the flames are subsiding, Miko turns his horse back and says, "Let's get back there. They may need us." Kicking his horse in the sides, he leaps into a gallop as he flies back to the scene of the explosion. The others are soon racing to follow. Zyrn and the villagers follow at a slower pace as they are on foot.

The area where the shimmering gray area had been still shimmers under the summer sun. "The explosion didn't do anything," remarks Stig.

"They may be out there in need of help," Aleya says. "We have to go to them."

At the edge of the shimmering field, Miko comes to a halt. Heat still radiates toward him from the blast, in some areas the shimmering has made way for red, glowing areas that give off tremendous heat. To their right and left, it looks as if the blast radius had begun a few inches past where the gray area had been. Somehow James had managed to encompass it completely.

"We don't dare enter until we know if it's safe," Miko says. He wants to use the Star to locate James and the others, but the memory of how the grayness reacted when James used his magic causes him to refrain.

"Then what should we do?" Shorty asks.

While they sit there in indecision, Zyrn and the rest of the villagers run to join them. Zyrn comes to stand at the edge of the shimmering area and looks out upon it. Something is different but he can't quite put his finger on it. Then he concentrates on the fringe to see if it's still advancing. After a full minute he fails to see any sign that it is.

He looks around the ground near him until he finds a medium sized stone. Picking it up, he turns to face the shimmering area. Cocking his arm back, he throws it. The rock arcs through the air and lands fifteen feet past the edge of the shimmering area.

Crack!

When the stone hits the shimmering area, the area shatters as the stone passes right through it. Cracks spider along its surface away from the impact point for several feet. That was as far from what he expected than anything he could have imagined.

Shorty bends over and hesitantly touches the edge of the grayness then pulls back his fingers quickly. When nothing happens, he touches it again. Running his fingers along its surface he says, "It's glass."

"What?" asks Potbelly, surprised at what Shorty said.

"It's glass I tell you," asserts Shorty. Standing up, he steps out upon the shimmering area and the surface cracks under the pressure.

"He did it!" cries Potbelly.

"We must go to them!" exclaims Aleya and makes to ride forward.

"Whoa there," Stig says, grabbing her reins near the horse's head and stopping her.

"But they may need us," she says, about ready to ride over him if he doesn't get out her way.

"Our boots will afford us protection against the glass," he tells her. "But the horses' hooves will get shredded." When she glares at him, he adds, "We must walk."

Realizing he's not trying to stop her, only protecting her horse, she nods her head and dismounts. Taking her bow she makes to head into the shimmering area.

Stig quickly instructs Reilin to explain that they intend to go in search of their companions to Zyrn, and to wait here to keep an eye on their horses. Then he hurries after Scar, Shorty and Potbelly as they move to follow Aleya into the field of glass.

They are forced to step slowly as they make their way onto the glass surface. Each step shatters the sheet of glass covering the ground. "You could make a fortune off of this," comments Shorty. "Delia would love this."

"Yeah," agrees Stig. "Come out here and carefully cut out sections and sell them, it would definitely bring a tidy sum.

Crack! Pop!

Ahead of them the glass shatters and they can see bands of heat radiating out of the newly formed opening.

Crack! Pop! Crack! Pop!

More openings form as the heat trapped beneath the sheet of glass finds an outlet. "This could get bad," says Miko. Already, they feel the heat rising every time their feet break through the glass.

Crack! Pop! Crack! Pop!

Most of the heat eruptions are coming from further into the glass covered area, the area closest to the center of the blast.

"Jiron!" hollers Aleya. They pause for a moment, but the only sound they hear is that of heat breaking through the glass. Turning to Miko she asks, "Can you tell if they are alive?"

Shaking his head, he replies, "No, I'm sorry. However, I may be able to tell where they are." Taking out the Star, he concentrates on the whereabouts of James, Jiron and Brother Willim.

The others wait there for a moment before a light flares from the Star and points a little to the left of the direction they were originally traveling. "I believe they lie in that direction," he says.

"Thank you," she says and he nods in reply.

As they continue to progress toward the location of their comrades, their feet grow hotter by the minute. "Make for the areas where the heat broke the glass," suggests Shorty. When the others look questioningly at him, he explains. "If the heat has had a chance to escape, it may also have had a chance to cool."

"Good thinking," Stig says. He taps Aleya on the shoulder and says, "Let me lead here."

About ready to argue the point, she finally relents and nods her head.

Moving past her, Stig studies the area before them and plans a route that will take advantage of the sections of broken glass. Deciding on his route, he begins to move. A thought comes to him about the broken areas of glass. It could be that those areas are actually hotter than the rest and that's why the glass broke over them. If so, they aren't going to have any better time of it.

"Looks like that guy Zyrn and his buddies have figured out that the glass could be valuable," Shorty says from the rear. Glancing back, the others see Zyrn and two others holding a large piece of glass up while the rest inspect it.

"They should give James a percentage," states Scar.

"That's right," agrees Potbelly. "If it weren't for him, this glass wouldn't even be here!"

"Not to mention they would still have a deadly problem on their hands," offers Stig. As he reaches the first of the shattered areas where the heat escaped, he steps carefully. Finding it not any hotter than the areas of glass that have remained intact, he continues on.

At one point Scar leans on Potbelly as he inspects the bottom of his boot. Sections of the sole have melted away, though not so far as to expose the foot within. "If this keeps up," he says quietly to Potbelly, "we'll be walking barefoot."

"Let's hope they aren't too much further then," replies Potbelly.

With a knowing nod, Scar resumes to follow behind Aleya.

Crack! Pop!

Two feet away from Shorty, heat blasts its way through the glass. The steam that ensued from the new opening shoots upward until the pressure has been released. "I don't think this was such a good idea," he says loud enough to be heard by all.

No one replies as they continue on. A solid hour has elapsed already since they entered the glass covered area and the eruptions from escaping heat have all but subsided. Occasionally one can still be heard, but they are now few and far between.

At the head of the party, Stig comes to a stop. Shielding his eyes to see through the glare of the sun being reflected off the glass, he stares far ahead of them. "I think I see them," he says pointing almost directly ahead of them.

Aleya comes to stand beside him and scans the area he indicates. Like a bubble, a shiny dome rises out of the glass. "Think they're still inside?" she asks.

From beside her, Miko says, "They have to be."

"Then why don't they come out?" Stig asks.

"They may think the grayness is still active and it would be dangerous," supposes Scar.

Nodding, Stig says, "That would make sense."

Now with them in sight, Stig moves at a quicker pace until a section of glass slips along the ground under his foot, causing him to stumble. If it weren't for the quick reflexes of Aleya grabbing his arm and steadying him, he would have fallen. With the ground covered in broken glass from his passing, a fall could likely have been disastrous.

"Thanks," he says to her after regaining his balance.

"Be more careful next time," she says.

Once again stepping carefully, he leads the way toward the dome.

Once the fires had subsided, it was much easier for Brother Willim's magic to effectively protect all three of them from the heat. Still horribly hot within the barrier, at least they are no longer at risk of burning.

He moves over to where James is lying unconscious and turns him over onto his stomach. When he sees the extent of the burns he says to Jiron, "Help me get his shirt off. I need to take care of this." Moving to help Brother Willim, Jiron soon has the shirt off.

Jiron holds James steady as Brother Willim removes a jar from within his robe. "This will ease the pain should he awaken," he tells him. Dipping two fingers into the jar, he removes a large glob of salve and begins rubbing it over the burns.

"Miko is going to need to take a look at this," Jiron states as he watches Brother William apply the ointment.

"Yes," he agrees. "With the Star he can do a much better job of it."

"Do you think it's safe?" Jiron asks. "I mean, do you think he killed the grayness?"

"Possibly," he replies. "I can no longer feel what he called the pulses of electricity which were evident earlier."

Once Brother Willim finishes with James' back, he begins on the other parts of his skin that had been in contact with the bottom of the barrier. Back of his arms, legs and even his head all bear burns. The hair where he was burned at the back of his head is all but gone, a small red bald spot is visible where the hair once had been.

When the slave within the jar runs out, Brother Willim replaces it back in the pocket within his robe. He and Jiron put James' shirt back on him before they lay him down. Brother Willim then settles next to James and says, "He's sleeping."

Jiron gets up and inspects the barrier. "His barrier is down," Brother Willim tells him. "It went down shortly after he lapsed into unconsciousness."

Moving his finger toward the dome that surrounds them he hesitates an inch away from touching it. "Then what is this?" he asks.

"I'm not sure," Brother Willim replies. "This might sound funny but I think it's glass."

"Glass?" asks Jiron incredulously. Placing his finger upon it, he rubs its surface. "It does feel like glass."

"Not sure if it is though," Brother Willim tells him. When he sees Jiron remove his knife to poke at it, he says, "I wouldn't do that."

Turning back toward Brother Willim, Jiron asks, "Why?"

"We still don't know if it's safe outside of here," he replies. "Though I can't sense it, I think it would be wise to wait until he wakes up."

Taking a breath, Jiron says, "The air is getting pretty stale in here."

"I know," replies Brother Willim. "But we should wait."

Trusting to the brother's judgment, he returns his knife to its scabbard and comes to sit next to him. He then takes out his water bottle and upends it for a long drink while he waits for James to awaken, which from past experiences could be some time.

Crack! Pop!

From outside the dome the sound of heat escaping by breaking through the glass covering the ground comes to them. Not knowing what it is they can only sit and wonder.

Over time the sound of the heat escaping gradually becomes less frequent. Then another sound comes to them, this one sounds like someone walking through eggshells. "Jiron!" Aleya's voice comes to him from outside the barrier. Then, movement can be seen through the opaque glass that is the dome.

"James!" Miko's voice hollers as one of the shadows presses its face against the side.

"We're here!" shouts Jiron.

"He's alive!" exclaims Aleya in glee.

"Are all three of you alright?" Miko asks.

"Brother Willim and I are," replies Jiron. "James got burned pretty badly."

From the other side of the dome, Stig says, "We'll have you out in a second." Then a shadow raises its arm, the unmistakable outline of a mace clutched in its hand.

"Stop!" cries Brother Willim and the mace stops before smashing into the dome. "If you smash it, it's going to shatter and cut us."

The mace is lowered as Stig's voice asks, "Then what should we do?"

Everyone is silent for a moment then Shorty says, "We can chip around the base and lift if off of them."

"Good idea," agrees Jiron. Taking out one of his knives, he moves to the edge as the shadows on the other side do the same. As they chip carefully at the bottom edge of the dome, holes begin to form on all sides. As they work to elongate the holes and separate the dome from the rest of the glass, fresh air makes its way within. Jiron takes a deep breath and feels much better.

When they have chipped all the way around the bottom, those on the outside space themselves evenly around its outer perimeter. Then Stig says, "On three. We lift it off them and carry it my way." Once the others have indicated they understand, he says. "Alright, one...two...three." Then they begin to lift and the dome comes away from the ground.

They raise it until the bottom of the dome is above the heads of those who are within it, then very carefully begin carrying it sideways. Step by step they scoot along the glass covered ground until Jiron and the others are no longer under it. Then they set it down carefully back on the ground.

Aleya rushes forward and takes Jiron in her arms. "I thought I had lost you," she says as she buries her head in the side of his neck.

Patting her on the back he says, "It'll take more than this to keep me from you." Lifting her face up to his, he gives her a kiss.

Brother Willim remains by James. As Miko comes toward him he says, "He's okay. Just sleeping."

Miko stops less than a foot away and stares at the burns covering James' body. Reaching into his pouch, he removes the Star. The glow immediately surrounds him as he kneels next to his friend, then moves to envelope James.

As the others look on, the burns on James' back gradually heal. The dead skin flakes off and new pink skin takes its place. The patch on the back of his head heals as well, though hair does not regrow right away.

When the glow disappears, James opens his eyes and rolls onto his side. Looking up, he sees everyone staring at him. "What?" he asks.

Miko gives him a smile and says, "Nothing." Putting the Star away, he helps James to his feet and lends him a shoulder for support. A bit unsteady, he looks around at the landscape. "Wow," he says.

"You can say that again," Scar says.

Smash!

Everyone turns at the sound just in time to see the dome smashed into a million pieces by Stig's mace. He glances toward them with a grin. "I just had to," he says as the glass shards hit the ground with a tinkle.

"Maybe we should think about getting out of here," James suggests.

"Yes," agrees Brother Willim. "That would be a good idea."

Leaning upon Miko's shoulder, James nods to the others to lead the way out, though their path through the glass is easily identified by the two foot wide swath of broken glass they made on their way in.

Chapter Eleven

Once back where they left Reilin with the horses, they find Zyrn and the others already in deep discussion about what to do with the glass. In a world like this, it could turn out to be worth quite a bit.

Reilin waves at them from the edge of the glass field as they come into view. He has the horses staked out twenty yards further away where they are merrily grazing on what little there is.

Zyrn and Reilin greet them as they near the edge of the glass. "Thank you," Zyrn says with great enthusiasm.

James gives him a nod but doesn't reply, the trek through the glass has left him quite weakened and tired.

"Is he alright?" asks Reilin.

"He will be after he gets some rest," Jiron assures him. Glancing to his friend, he grins. Ever since they told him about his bald spot, he hasn't been able to keep himself from rubbing it. When he first touched it he promptly announced, "Guess I'll have to wear a hat for a while."

Miko helps him to move several feet away from the glass where he assists him to the ground. "You rest," he tells him. "The rest of us will get camp set up."

"Camp?" replies James. "I don't think so. Give me a few minutes and we'll be on our way."

"But you can barely stand as it is," Miko argues.

"I know," James says tiredly. "But after what I just did, any mage in the area will be coming to investigate. In ten minutes I want us ready to ride."

"What about that?" asks Stig indicating the glass. He understands the value of what lies out there.

Shrugging, James gazes back at him. At Stig's words, Zyrn's attention becomes fully focused on him to see what his reply will be. "We have more important things to worry about than that," he states much to the relief of Zyrn.

Stig glances at him then at the sea of glass and says, "Very well then." Turning his attention back to James he asks, "Where are we to go from here?"

James sits there and thinks for a minute while he eats a bite of dried beef and has a drink. "We'll skirt the edge of the glass to the east," he finally announces. "We know there's a main road moving north and south to the west. From the maps I went over back at Al-Ziron there doesn't look like there is too much east of us to cause us much trouble. Just a few villages here and there."

"We shouldn't go too far," joins in Miko. "You are quite tired and need to rest."

"Let's put distance between us and that before we stop," he says as he gestures to the field of glass behind him. "Then we'll rest through the night."

"Very well," agrees Miko. Getting up, he goes to make sure his horse and things are ready for travel.

While the others are busy with getting something to eat and seeing to their horses, Jiron comes and sits next to James.

"Don't you want to see to your horse as well?" James asks.

Shaking his head, Jiron says, "Shorty said he'd do it for me." Biting off a piece of dried beef, he remains silent for a second before he asks, "What do you think happened here?"

"I'm not entirely sure," he admits. "That I played a part in it is without question." He gazes at Jiron while he bites off and chews another piece of dried beef. "However, I do think there is more to this than just what I did at the end of the battle. A meteorite falls from the sky and happens to strike at the precise spot that would cause a rip and let in the creature? I hardly think it's mere coincidence."

"Then what?" Jiron asks.

"I don't know," he replies, "and that's what is bothering me. Something else is going on. That discussion we had earlier where Brother Willim was saying that the gods are becoming more involved worries me." Gesturing to the glass behind him he continues. "Something like that could hardly have just happened."

"You think it has anything to do with Tinok?" he asks.

Shrugging, he replies, "I doubt it. Maybe if Tinok were someone like Miko who has a god interested in him, maybe."

"So what should we do?" Aleya asks as she comes to join them.

"Listening in were you?" James asks.

Nodding, she gives him a grin. "Couldn't help it," she admits. "You two talk pretty loud."

James returns her grin and says, "Continue on as we have been. We'll keep our eyes and ears open for whatever else may be developing, but we'll keep looking for Tinok."

Jiron sighs. "That's good," he says.

Finishing up with their meal, James allows Jiron and Aleya to help him to his feet and then onto his horse. From behind him he can hear where Scar is explaining to Reilin why the creature turned to glass. "You see," he explains, "since it wasn't from our world, it couldn't survive long. When James torched it with fire, it died. What you see there is simply its bones that were left behind."

"Bones?" asks Reilin incredulously.

"Of course!" states Potbelly as he backs up his partner's explanation. "You can't expect something from another world to have the same kind of bones as we do."

"I suppose not," agrees Reilin, though he doesn't sound entirely convinced.

James smiles to himself and doesn't say anything.

"Is that right?" asks Miko from beside him.

"What?" asks James. "You mean what Scar said?"

Miko gives him a nod.

"I've been thinking about that," he says, keeping his voice low. "When the creature entered our world, it took on the characteristics of the first thing it came into contact with."

"The sand," interjects Miko.

"That's right, the sand," agrees James. "Where I come from it's long been known that heat will turn sand into glass. In fact, lightning striking a sandy beach can leave glass behind."

"Interesting," comments Miko. "So Scar is wrong?"

Grinning, James nods his head. "Of course he is, but I think we should keep that to ourselves."

Miko turns back with a grin and glances at where Reilin is hanging onto Scar's every word. "I suppose it would spoil it." Then he looks back to James and they both laugh.

Scar breaks off in the middle of a sentence and turns toward them. "What?" he asks.

Shaking his head, James says, "Nothing." Then both he and Miko laugh again.

When the rest are ready and are about to head out, Zyrn comes forward. "Thank you all again," he says with sincerity.

"You're welcome," replies James. "Take care." With that he kicks his horse and soon they are galloping across the sand on their way east.

Zyrn watches them go. Elated at the demise of the deadly grayness, yet at the same time filled with sadness over what his village has done. Can he ever go back and have things return to normal? That's the question that has weighed on his mind ever since Khalim was sacrificed.

But, they are his people, misguided though they were. Deciding to return and try to cope, he turns back to the other villagers and with them begins working out a way to harvest the glass quickly before someone else comes and takes it. With it, his people will not have to worry for a very, very long time.

When at last the mage and his companions disappear out of sight, he returns to the work at hand.

For the next several hours James and the rest ride quickly as they circumvent the perimeter of the glass field. Upon reaching the eastern edge, they angle more to the southeast to put distance between it and them.

When the sun at last reaches the horizon and is on the verge of sinking into night, James calls a halt. Fatigued and tired, the trials of the last twenty four hours have left him on the brink of passing out. Leaving the details of camp to the others, he quickly gets his bedroll and lays it out. In no time at all, he falls asleep.

The following morning it again dawns clear and sunny, heralding another hot summer day. James is the last to get up. The others had allowed him to sleep himself out, so he woke up several hours after sunrise. A quick meal and they're once again in the saddle.

James takes out his cloth and finds that Tinok still lies in the same general direction as the day before, to the southwest. Replacing the cloth back in his pouch, they get underway.

Cutting cross-country, they don't make the best time but they don't encounter anyone either. Late in the morning a village appears before them. On the eastern side of the village lies an orchard of date palms such as they've encountered before in the different oasis.

"Could use some dates," suggests Potbelly.

James glances to Jiron who nods in agreement. "Very well," he says. Angling his horse toward the orchard, he leads them there.

A farmhouse stands amidst the orchard. The farmer sees them coming and makes his way from the orchard on a course to intercept them before they reach the house. He calls out to those in the house and several lads who are obviously his sons appear and move to join him. In their hands are clutched a variety of weapons including a crossbow. Seems they've had problems with strangers before.

As his sons hurry to join him, the farmer holds up his hand and asks, "How can I help you sirs?" After translating for the others Reilin comes forward and begins haggling for a couple small casks of dates.

The sons visibly relax once they learn they are here to purchase dates. However, they remain where they are just in case.

As the others wait for the haggling to come to an end, Brother Willim gazes around at the date trees. "They're quite healthy," he says quietly to James. "This farmer is good for the land."

"Some are bad?" he asks.

"Oh yes," he replies. "Just because a man's a farmer doesn't make him a good one." He continues to gaze around the orchard then his eyes widen and a slight gasp escapes him.

James notices his reaction and asks, "What?"

Nodding his head to indicate an area on the edge of the orchard, he says, "Look there."

James looks but only sees a pile of leaves and dates lying on the ground. "I don't see anything," he tells him.

"It's a *Vyrilyzk*," he replies.

"I never heard of that," James says.

"It's an offering to the earth spirits," he says. Glancing to James he says, "It's an old custom. Farmers take the first of the harvest, surround it with leaves, and leave it for the earth spirits. It's supposed to give them a better harvest for the following year."

"Does it?" he asks.

"Oh yes," he replies. "The little brothers appreciate one who lays out the *Vyrilyzk*. Being earth spirits, they can help the farmer's trees produce more. You don't see it much anymore. The earth spirits are shy and are rarely seen so the farmers begin to forget."

"Little brothers?" he asks.

"Yes," he says. "They are of Asran and I have seen them many times."

"So have I," states James.

Looking in surprise at James, Brother Willim says, "That is a very rare thing indeed."

"It was last year," he explains. Then goes on to tell about his visit on Lyria's Island and of seeing the spirits while they sat and listened to her song.

"Yes, they were earth spirits," he states after he has him describe them.

About this time the negotiations between Reilin and the farmer have concluded. Two of his sons make their way to the farmhouse and are soon returning, each with two small casks tucked under their arms.

James hands over the required sum and the casks of dates are secured behind the saddles of four of them. "Thank you," James tells the farmer with a grin. The farmer nods his head in reply. Then he and his sons return to the farmhouse.

Leaving the farm behind, James glances back at the *Vyrilyzk*. "Do you think they worship Asran?" he asks Brother Willim.

Shrugging, he says, "I doubt it. Mainly the laying out of the *Vyrilyzk* has become a tradition. There are few who even remember when it started or why. All they know is that if they do it, they tend to have a good crop of whatever they grow the following year."

The rest of the day they continue their way southwest. Once they had to angle more to the east to avoid a column of troops heading north. "Think they're heading to Al-Ziron?" asks Stig.

"I would think so," replies Scar. "They would want to maintain a presence there strong enough to project strength. It's always better to barter from a position of strength."

"True enough," agrees Stig.

Later in the day they see people and wagons passing across the horizon ahead of them. "I figure that would be the road that runs north out of Korazan," observes Shorty.

"Do you think it wise for us to be anywhere near here?" asks Jiron. "After all, Illan came through here not too long ago and caused major damage."

"With everyone's focus on the talks going on further north," reasons James, "who will think twice about us?"

"Maybe those riders coming straight for us?" Everyone turns to see the half a dozen riders coming from the east. There's no doubt that they mean to intercept their party. From their armor and the Empire's emblem on their uniforms, there's little question about who they are.

"Everyone stay cool," says James. "Be on your guard in case things go bad."

"Look bored," suggests Scar. "It will just give them cause to inspect us closely if we appear like we are up to something."

"Good idea," agrees Miko.

They come to a halt and wait for the arrival of the riders. Reilin, whose outward visage projects calm and nonchalance, puts himself between the approaching riders and the others. Once the riders are close enough, he offers them a greeting.

The lead soldier replies. Looking to be the officer in charge of the group, he scans those behind Reilin. He and Reilin exchange words several times before the officer and his men ride off.

Everyone breathes a sigh of relief when the riders have left. "What was that about?" asks Jiron.

"They were looking for escaped slaves," he explains.

"Could it have been Tinok?" Jiron asks.

"He didn't say who or what they were," Reilin replies. "Just that they were loose and if we were to see them to notify the nearest garrison as to their location."

Jiron looks to James. "It could be," he says.

Nodding, James takes out his mirror and once again tries to get a view of Tinok to appear. But just as last time, the mirror remains quiet. "I don't think it would be him," James tells the others. "If he was this close, I would get something."

"Unless there was magic blocking him from being found," offers Potbelly. "Sort of like what you did that one time."

"First of all, why would anyone go to the trouble of hiding Tinok from magical searches?" asks James. "I don't think that would even be a possibility. Second, if he was to be hidden in such a way, I would never even be able to use the cloth to find him either."

"Oh yeah," Potbelly says. "I forgot about that."

"But, just to put everyone's mind at ease…" he pulls out the cloth and once again, it rises to point the way to where Tinok lies. It still indicates Tinok is somewhere to the southwest.

"So, are we going to take the road?" asks Jiron again.

"Yes," James replies. "Just keep Reilin out front in case we need to deal with someone." Indicating the native garb they are all wearing, "And we'll blend in."

"It did work with the riders," chimes in Shorty.

"Exactly," states James. He sees the way Jiron is looking and him curiously. "What?" he asks.

Shrugging, Jiron says, "This seems a bit bold on your part. Usually you like to stay away and avoid everyone."

"No one's out looking for us," he replies. "We're not here to cause mischief so I think this time, boldness will be the better way to go. Besides, if we tried to avoid everyone, our search for Tinok could take longer than we have." So moving like they belong here, they head over to the road and turn to follow it south.

The people traveling upon the road barely even glance at them as they gain the roadway, those going north give them a cursory glance, more to break up the monotony of travel than really caring who they are. The people they pass heading south at times give them a greeting that Reilin returns, but for the most part they keep to themselves.

"Sure looks different than when we came through here earlier this summer," observes Shorty.

Scar chuckles and says, "Yeah, everyone was running for their lives."

James isn't amused at all. Fear. Any kind of fear is a bad thing and to have been one to instigate it is nothing to be proud of. They did what they had to for the Empire to be pushed out of Madoc. He isn't proud of the effect it had on the common man, but at least it wasn't as bad as the effect the Empire had on the common man during their push into Madoc.

They keep a good pace throughout the day. Twice more they are stopped momentarily by patrols on the hunt for the missing slaves. From what Reilin gathered from the two meetings, the slaves are vicious, armed and likely to kill you as look at you. Numbering fourteen, they have supposedly killed dozens of unwary travelers on the road.

"Think we should be concerned?" Miko asks.

"They would have to be pretty desperate to take us on," Jiron states. "There are other more tempting targets they could choose."

"Just keep our eyes and ears open for trouble," James announces. "Keep a double watch at night just in case."

They fall silent as they ride, each thinking about the significance of the escaped slaves. Some think it could possibly be people taken from Madoc during the war trying to get home. Others are of the belief they are criminals out for vengeance.

From where Scar and Potbelly ride, James can hear them talking.

"...probably some old people who got lost..." Scar says.

"...rumors get, as it goes from person to person it continuously gets blown all out of..." adds Scar.

James grins. If there is anyone who blows things out of proportion, it's those two.

By sundown they reach a town. They recognize it as the last town Illan's force took before heading out into the desert to avoid the fortress of Al-Ziron. It looks pretty much as they had left it. The few buildings which took damage during the assault are even now being repaired.

"Best if we don't stay here," suggests James.

Nodding, Jiron replies, "That would be a good idea. Never know if someone may recognize us."

"Not to mention they are going to be extra leery of strangers," pipes up Shorty.

"If memory serves," Stig says, "we passed by an inn not too far south of here on our way north."

"That's right," agrees Scar. "Three of our freed slaves made off with several casks of ale. That is before Illan found out. After returning the ale, he gave the men five lashes for 'thieving without authorization' or something like that."

"I remember," says Shorty. "He gave them the option of keeping the casks and sending them off on their own, or they could return them and receive five lashes."

Laughing, Potbelly bursts out, "You should have seen their faces! I think one was actually contemplating keeping his cask but the other two talked him out of it. They didn't relish the idea of being made slaves again for a single cask of ale each."

"You guys didn't interact with the innkeeper did you?" he asks. They all reply that they hadn't. "Good," continues James. "Then let's stop there."

With Reilin out front, they move to enter the town. The rest of them pull their hoods closer about them to better hide their faces. The town has no protective wall surrounding it, the road simply passes through the outlying buildings.

Evidence of their recent occupation is evident. The sight of slaves walking the street is practically nonexistent. On his way out of the Empire, Illan stripped the towns of their slaves, both to bolster his own army and that James had asked it of him.

As they make their way through the city, the people appear to have gotten over the effects of the occupation and have returned to business as usual. A few glance at them as they ride by but none give them more than a cursory glance. At one spot they come to a building that must have been torched during the occupation, the smell of char is still in the air even after so long.

Out front of the burned out building is an old man dressed poorly sitting cross-legged with a bowl on the ground before him. A couple coppers rest in the bottom of the bowl. Feeling the need to help, James removes a silver from his pouch and flips it toward the beggar as he rides by. When the coin sails through the air and comes close to the old man, his arm shoots up and snatches the coin. Putting the coin quickly within his meager clothes, he nods a thank you to James.

James returns the nod with a slight smile and continues on his way. Before the rest of the others pass by the old man, other coins are flipped to him as well. All toll, they must have given the old man over two silver's worth of coins.

"It might not help him get off the streets," James comments to Jiron, "but it might make his life more bearable for a while."

"True," nods Jiron. He's come to realize that ever since he first met James, he's developed an appreciation for the world and his place in it that he hadn't had before. When he was still in the City of Light and fighting in the Pits, he didn't care much for others or how they may feel. But since joining with James and having him do 'good things' for no other reason than to do them, he's come to understand that there is more to life than simply surviving.

Another way that James has affected him is in the way he no longer sees killing as a solution. If the circumstances warrant it, he will end someone's life in the blink of an eye. But now, he questions more closely whether he must resort to that or not.

Continuing on their way, they finally make it past the last of the buildings on the south side of town. "The inn's about an hour away," Shorty states.

Nodding, James casts a quick look at the setting sun. It'll be getting dark about the time they get there, which suits him nicely.

The sun sets and twilight begins setting in by the time the group of buildings of which the inn is a part appears ahead of them. Within the cluster of buildings, they see a sign of a tankard of ale which must indicate a tavern as well as another bearing a sign of a wagon with a load full of goods. Obviously, this place caters to those traveling upon the road.

Stopping before the only three story building here, they see a sign of a flowing river passing underneath a bed. This must be the inn. They send Reilin inside to get their rooms, who returns several minutes later.

He got five rooms with enough beds for all of them. Around back they find the stables and after getting their horses settled in, they head up to their rooms. As they pass through the common room, the sound of a bard comes to them and they see a rather young balladeer entertaining a full common room. The song the bard is playing is one James has heard Perrilin playing on a different occasion oh so long ago.

Moving to the stairs, they pass up to the second floor and turn down the hallway. Two lanterns hang from hooks in the ceiling to light their way as Reilin takes them all the way to the end. "Thought being on the end might afford us a little more quiet," he says.

"Probably will," agrees James. He and Jiron take one room while the others divide themselves among the others. Brother Willim and Miko take a room for themselves. Seems Miko has taken to having discussions with Brother Willim about being a priest as well as other things dealing with the priesthood. Aleya's room, which she gets all to herself, is situated in between the one James and Jiron are in and the one Miko shares with Brother Willim. The others are on the opposite side of the hallway.

Once settled in, Reilin goes down and has a meal of roast goat, bread and a variety of vegetables sent up to their rooms. After the meal they are soon to bed for they plan an early start in the morning. James hits the bed, glad not to have to sleep again on the ground. No matter how many times he does, he will never find it even remotely comfortable. Jiron blows out the candle before getting to bed and they are soon asleep.

Chapter Twelve

The opening of the door awakens him. Sitting up in bed he sees a shadow standing in the hall outside his door. A floorboard creaks as Jiron makes his way from his bed toward the door, the glint of reflected moonlight from outside says he has a knife in hand.

"James," whispers Miko urgently.

His orb suddenly springs to life and they see Miko there at the door, Brother Willim's face peers over his shoulder. From where Jiron stands halfway to the door, James hears him mumble under his breath as he replaces his knife back in its sheath. Sitting up on his bed, James waves them inside.

"What's up?" he asks.

"Trouble," says Miko. "There's been a death here in the inn." He glances from James to Jiron then back again. "It wasn't a normal one."

"Normal?" questions Jiron. "What do you mean by that?"

"I think someone's been murdered," he explains.

"When?" James asks.

"A few minutes ago," he explains. "Remember how I told you that ever since what happened in the City of Light I've been able to feel when people near me pass on?" When James nods he continues. "Thankfully there haven't been many, it still unnerves me when it happens. But this time, it felt...wrong."

"Like the one back at Al-Ziron?" he asks.

Miko nods affirmatively. "Yes," he replies. "Just as wrong."

James can see the worry behind his friend's eyes. He turns to Jiron and says, "Go get the others."

"Right," he replies then moves to the door and passes through into the hallway. Shortly, the sound of a door opening and closing can be heard.

"Could you tell where it happened?" James asks.

"I'm pretty sure it was above us on the third floor," he states. They grow quiet as each listens for any noise that may indicate someone is moving around above them. Just as Scar and Potbelly arrive looking quite tired, they hear the creak of a floorboard in the room directly above James'.

"They must still be there," concludes James as Jiron and the rest finally join them. He quickly fills them in on what Miko believes happened.

"Maybe we shouldn't get involved," Stig says. "Could lead to complications." He looks to James for his reaction.

"We have to," James says. "There could be more people up there in danger."

"Alright then," Jiron says. To Scar, Potbelly and Shorty he says, "Whoever it is, is above us. You three go outside and keep a lookout for anyone leaving or acting suspiciously."

As they leave to do as requested, he turns to Stig and Reilin. "You two stay at the stairs here on the second floor in case they get by us," he says. "We're going up."

"Right," replies Stig with a nod.

Jiron turns to where Aleya stands and says, "You stay here. It'll be safer."

Giving him an annoyed look she shakes her head and says, "I don't think so."

Rolling his eyes, Jiron pulls a knife before moving to the door and passing into the hallway. Moving silently, he makes his way to the stairs and begins climbing up. James, Miko, and Brother Willim follow close behind. Turning back to James he indicates the orb and says, "Get rid of the light."

With a thought James cancels the orb and they are once again plunged into darkness. A floorboard creaks revealing Jiron is already moving up the stairs. Following, James keeps a hand in contact with the wall to guide himself until he reaches the stairwell. The blackness is gradually making way for indistinct shadows as his night vision returns. Moving quickly, he takes the steps up to the third level. When he makes the top, he sees the shadow that is Jiron standing outside the closed door of the room that lies directly above theirs. Stepping quietly, he comes to Jiron's side.

"Someone's in there moving around," he says. Then they hear another floorboard creak inside the room. He glances to James and nods to the door. When he receives a nod in reply, he steps backward and kicks the door hard with his foot.

Waaaaaaaaaaa!

A baby's cry rips through the night as the slamming of the door against the wall frightens it. Its mother turns in fear toward the door and clutches her baby tight to her bosom. The person they had been hearing moving around was a woman trying to get her child back to sleep. She screams as a man bolts up out of the bed that's sitting against the far wall. He looks in alarm at Jiron standing framed in the doorway, the light of the candle on the table glinting off the knife in his hand. Drawing a sword, the man moves to stand between his wife and child, and the intruders.

"Not this one," Jiron says. Then to the couple he says, "Sorry."

"Reilin get up here now!" cries out James.

Backing out of the room, Jiron moves to the next door and hits it hard with his shoulder, bursting it open. The smell that hits him tells him he's got the right room this time. "This is it!" he cries out as he enters.

Then Reilin appears at the top of the stairs. James turns to him and says, "We barged in and frightened these people." Indicating the man ready to defend his family, he says. "Give them our apologies and explain the situation to them."

"Alright," he says, then moves to the doorway and begins explaining things to the couple.

Doors along the hallway crack open as the other guests look out to see what's going on. When they see them in the hallway, they quickly shut their doors and throw the bolt.

"Miko," says Jiron from the other room, "you better get in here."

Leaving Reilin to deal with the family, they hurry over to the open doorway. Within they see Jiron moving over toward the open window, beneath which lies a woman bleeding to death. On the bed against the far wall is the murdered man whose passing Miko must have sensed. Bound and gagged, he lies face down on the bed with a knife still sticking out his back. On the floor next to the bed is an open chest. Whatever had been contained within is gone.

The light from the Star fills the room as Miko enters and rushes toward the woman. Soon, the glow surrounds him and then moves to envelope the woman. Aleya comes to his side to help in whatever way she can.

Snaking out the window is a rope that's anchored to the bed. Sticking his head out the window he looks down to see Shorty staring back up at him. "Did you see whoever it was that came down here?" he shouts.

"No!" he hollers back up.

"Look around, he can't have gone far," he says. "Take Scar and Potbelly and search the area."

Nodding, Shorty races away to get the other two.

A commotion is developing in the hallway. The raised voice of a man grows louder as he approaches. Jiron casts one look around outside and then returns his head back into the room. Just then, Reilin appears at the doorway with a rather irate innkeeper.

"He demands to know what is going on here," Reilin explains.

"Tell him a man's been robbed, his woman stabbed, and all their money is gone," he says.

Reilin turns back to the innkeeper who by this time has seen the dead body bound on the bed and the glow surrounding Miko as he works to save the life of the woman. Several exchanges later, Reilin turns back to those in the room and says, "He says there was a small girl too."

"What?" asks Jiron and James at the same time.

"They had a girl of about two or three with them is what he said," clarifies Reilin.

Glancing around the room, they see where a pallet had been laid out in the corner for a small child. "She may be hiding," says James. "Search the room." He moves to the bed where the dead man lays while the others search the rest of the room. Bending over, he pulls up the covers that are draped over the side and looks beneath. Nothing. Standing back up, he looks around and the others shake their heads. She's not here!

"Could he have taken her with him down the rope?" James asks Jiron.

"Possibly," he says. "If she was drugged or knocked out." After a moment he adds, "She would bring a large sum on the slave blocks."

"She would wouldn't she?" states James.

The room suddenly dims as the glow surrounding Miko and the woman winks out. James looks hopefully at him and receives a reassuring nod. "She'll live," he tells him. "May not wake up for a while though."

"Take her to our room," James says. Then he catches sight of Stig out in the hallway with the crowd that has gathered. "Stig!" he hollers. When he sees Stig looking his way he says, "You and Brother Willim help Miko with taking the woman and her things to our room." Then to Brother Willim he says, "It's bad enough to have lost your man, worse yet to wake and see him dead."

Brother Willim nods. "You intend to go after the child?" he asks.

"I can't let her be made a slave," he replies. The thought of that sends a shiver down his spine.

"Good," he says. "Miko and I will watch over the woman until your return."

"Keep Stig and Reilin with you just in case," James tells him.

"Very well," he says.

James glances to Jiron. "You ready?" he asks.

Jiron nods, "Let's go find her."

As they make to leave the room, they are blocked by the innkeeper and half a dozen other men, some with swords drawn. The innkeeper says something in a demanding way. He looks to Reilin who says, "He says you are not going anywhere until he knows what went on here."

"Didn't you explain it to him?" he asks.

Nodding, Reilin says, "Yes. But I don't think he entirely believes me."

"Tell him this," states James. "The girl is missing. I intend to go after her before something bad happens."

Turning to the innkeeper, Reilin translates. When the innkeeper replies, he says, "He thinks you took her and that you just want to get away."

Sighing over the fools in the world, James turns to the innkeeper and with Reilin translating says, "We came in here to save them. We were too late for the man but managed to save the woman. Right now their child is being taken away to a life I don't even want to imagine." He glares a moment while Reilin finishes translating then continues. "Some of our comrades will remain here until our return to look after the woman. Two of them are priests. If it makes you feel any better, you can consider them as hostages until our return. But time is running out and we are going!"

When Reilin finishes the translation, the innkeeper glances at James, then to Miko who is carrying the unconscious woman. Nodding his head, he steps aside to allow James and Jiron to pass. As James steps forward with Jiron right behind, the others in the hallway move aside for them too.

Hitting the stairs at a run, they return to their rooms and take only a moment for them to put their boots on. Then they are back at the stairs and hit the common room at a run. Once out the front door, James pauses a moment and removes the cloth from his pouch and begins seeking the girl. He's not sure that it will work, what with him never having seen her and all, but the cloth rises and becomes rigid as it points off to the right.

"This way," he says. As they move to follow the direction indicated by the cloth, Shorty appears and reports no one is in the vicinity. About that time Scar and Potbelly come running around the corner of the inn to report the same.

"Stay close," he says as he moves away from the inn, the others fall in behind.

Walking briskly, they pass by the rest of the buildings surrounding the inn and are soon out in the desert. The half moon above gives them sufficient light with which to see their immediate surroundings.

It isn't long before they can hear the crying of a small child ahead of them. "That's her," says Scar.

"Jiron, go take a look," suggests James.

Nodding in the dark, he moves toward the sound of the child's crying. While James and the others wait for him, they hear a man yelling in anger and then the sound of someone being slapped hard. It must have been the child that was slapped for her cries increase tenfold.

"I can't wait for Jiron," says Shorty and moves to follow. James, Scar and Potbelly trail along behind.

From out of the distance ahead of them, a structure rises from the desert. From one window the light of a single candle shines dimly out. The sound of crying is coming from that direction. Suddenly, a form passes in front of the window and they see Jiron moving to look in.

Off to one side of the structure, which as it turns out is a farmhouse, a dozen horses stand in the dark. Beside them sits a covered wagon. From the back of the farmhouse, the sound of a goat can be heard as it calls out.

The sound of them moving to join Jiron causes him to turn from the window. "They have the child in the other room," he whispers to them. "I saw two boys tied up in there with her."

"Okay," James says. He then squats on the ground under the window and signals for the others to do the same. "Jiron and I will go in and deal with their captors," he says. Turning to Scar and Potbelly he adds, "You two get into the room with the children and protect them with your lives."

"No problem," Scar says. Potbelly nods.

"Shorty, you stay out here and keep anyone from leaving," he replies. He then looks from one to the others and adds, "I don't care if any of these child stealers survives or not."

"That'll make things simpler," Shorty says as he draws one of his throwing knives.

To Scar and Potbelly he says, "We'll give you a minute to maneuver around to the window of the room in which the children are being held. Don't take too long getting in."

"We won't," assures Scar.

As they leave to move around into position outside the children's room, James and Jiron move to the front door. When he thinks Scar and Potbelly has had ample time to get set, a shield flashes into being around him and he glances to Jiron. Receiving an affirmative nod, he moves to the door and tries the handle. Surprised to find it unlocked, he readies a slug, opens the door and walks in.

Ten heads turn to see him enter through the door. Immediate pandemonium erupts as the men leap to their feet and draw swords. His slug flies to the nearest man and blasts its way through his chest.

Jiron flies around him, knives in hand as he moves to engage. A quick strike takes one through the side, dropping the man to the floor. His other knife flashes lightning quick and leaves a thin line spurting blood from where it severed the jugular of another.

From the back of the house, a crash can be heard as Scar and Potbelly gain the room with the children. Slugs fly and knives strike as the men in the front room fall quickly. When all but three men have been taken out, Scar appears in the doorway leading to the room with the children, bloody sword in hand. He gives James a nod saying all is well with the children. Seeing Jiron still facing off with three men, he exits the room and draws his second sword.

The three remaining men, after having seen their companions taken out so fast, lose heart for the battle. Throwing down their swords, they surrender. Jiron looks to James who nods that he should take their surrender. Wiping the blood off his knives on the shirt of a dead man, he then replaces them in their sheathes.

"Tie them up," James says and then moves to the front door. "Shorty!" he hollers as he sticks his head out. No longer needed, he cancels his shield.

"Yeah?" comes the reply from the dark.

"It's over," he hollers. As Shorty approaches, James asks, "Did any make it outside?"

"Two were out with the horses," he says. Then he points to two forms lying on the ground a little distance from the door. "They came running when you entered through the door."

James nods then notices Scar beginning to go through the pockets of the dead men for anything of value. Leaving him to his work, he crosses the room and passes through the door leading into the room with the children.

Potbelly is there, already having untied them. Two bodies lie on the floor of the men who had been here when Scar and Potbelly made their appearance. Potbelly has bits and pieces of glass and wood in his hair, testament that he had been the one to smash through the window first. Most likely jumped through.

Turning to the children, he sees their eyes wide with fear. He gives them a big smile in an attempt to put them at ease but fails miserable. "Are you okay?" he asks them slowly.

None understand what he's saying, they simply stare at him with fear. To Potbelly he says, "Stay here with them. Try to make them understand that we mean them no harm."

"I'll try," he replies, though he's dubious about his ability to do that when they don't even speak his language.

"At least keep them in here until we're ready to leave," says James before he turns and makes his way back out to the front room.

"What should we do with them?" Shorty asks about their three prisoners when he returns.

"We'll take them back to stand justice," James tells him.

Jiron is at a table over in the corner, several dead bodies lie on the floor before it. "Hey look at what I found!" he exclaims. Turning around to the others with a grin, he holds up a bulging sack. Jingling it, they hear the unmistakable jingling of coins.

"Must be the stuff they stole from the people at the inn," suggests James.

"Probably," agrees Scar.

Jiron takes it over to the large dining table and upends the sack, spilling out coins, gems and other valuables onto its surface. He picks up several gems and tucks them into his pocket. When he sees James giving him a disapproving look he says, "For our trouble."

"No," says James. "Put them back with the others."

Jiron frowns but does as bidden.

"That is going to go to the lady that was recently widowed," James says with conviction. "Small enough consolation for losing a husband."

"Perhaps," pipes up Scar. "Unless he was a real piece of filth like my old man was." Taking the items gleaned from the dead men, he adds them to the pile on the table.

"Whatever the case may be, it's time we took the girl back to her mother." James has Potbelly and Shorty begin getting the prisoners tied across the backs of horses in preparation for the trip back. Grabbing one off the floor, they take him outside to the waiting horses.

He then goes over to Jiron where he about has all the coins and such put back in the sack. Glancing at the table, his eyes briefly examine the coins and jewels still awaiting their turn to be returned to the sack. Several gold coins and others of a lesser value, half a dozen jewels of varying sizes and colors, and two necklaces.

Just about to turn away and cross over to the room where Potbelly has the children, he pauses and turns back toward the items on the table. When Jiron reaches to pick up another handful, he holds out his hand. "Hang on a minute," he says. Something, a whisper of memory comes to him.

Then realization strikes. Reaching out, he picks up one of the necklaces. It bears a heart shaped gold medallion with two small diamonds in the middle. The heart with two small diamonds is what drew him to the necklace, in his dreams they had been two lights.

Each time in his dream when he had entered the Tunnel of Love, there on the wall just inside was a large heart with two lights blazing forth. In each subsequent dream, one of the lights had continued to grow dim until at the last, it was all but out. The two stones, Cassie and Tinok. The one growing dim had to represent Tinok and the situation he is in.

Jiron halts putting the items back in the sack as James stands there motionless with the necklace in his hand. "You okay?" he asks.

Snapping out of it, James' eyes meet Jiron's. "This is the necklace Tinok gave Cassie," he says in a hushed whisper. "The one he took with him when he left us after her death."

"Can't be," he says then takes a closer look. Though only having a good look at it a couple times over a year ago, he comes to realize that James is correct, this is indeed that necklace.

Eyes narrowing, he pulls a knife and moves to the remaining two captives. Pointing to the necklace he shouts, "Where did you get that necklace?" Holding the knife close to the face of one of the captives, he yells, "Where!" The man's eyes stare at the knife before him, ready for the blow he's sure is to come.

"He can't understand you," James tells him. "We're going to have to wait until we get back to the inn so Reilin can interrogate them."

Jiron stands there with knife still before the man for several more seconds before turning away. As he does, he sees Potbelly in the doorway to the bedroom and then glances over to the front door where Scar and Shorty stare at him too.

Pointing to the necklace James is holding he says, "They have Cassie's necklace!"

Scar actually gasps. Shorty asks, "The one Tinok took with him when he left?"

Nodding, Jiron replies, "The very one."

"But how did they get it?" Potbelly asks.

"I don't know," Jiron says. Then turning to the men on the floor, he adds, "But I'm going to find out." To Scar he says, "Bring that other man back in here." Then with a glance back to James he adds, "I'm not about ready to hand them over to the authorities for justice until I have a chance to ask them some questions."

James meets his gaze and nods. Turning to Scar he says, "Go ahead and bring him back in."

Once the man is brought back inside, James says, "Potbelly and I will take the children back while you three remain here with them." When he receives Jiron's nod, he continues. "Then I'll return with the others and we'll see if we can learn anything."

"Good," states Jiron. He holds his hand out obviously wishing to have the necklace.

"Oh," James says as he turns to Jiron and sees his hand out. "I should take the necklace with me. It may have been that they stole it from the family at the inn. If so, then the woman may know where it came from."

Nodding, Jiron lowers his hand. "I want it when you return," he says.

"Don't worry," replies James, "You will have it." Turning to Potbelly he says. "It's time to bring the children out." Crossing over to the doorway, James follows Potbelly in. The three children have managed to relax a little bit, maybe they realized that he and the others are not there to hurt them. After all, they did kill the 'bad men'.

The older boy says something to them in the Empire's tongue but they fail to understand. In as soothing a voice as he can manage, James says, "It'll be okay. We're taking you home." The tone, if not the words, further relaxes them. When he motions for them to follow him from the room, they hop off the bed to follow.

He leads them through the front room where Jiron, Scar, and Shorty are working to remove the men killed in the fighting. They shy away from the three men sitting bound against the wall and hurry to follow him outside.

Potbelly helps the girl onto one horse while James assists the younger boy to mount another. The older boy is able to make it into the saddle of a third horse on his own. Once they are settled and not in any immediate danger of falling off, he swings up behind the younger boy just as Potbelly mounts behind the girl.

Giving the kids an encouraging grin, he leads the way with the older boy in the middle and Potbelly bringing up the rear. The return trip to the inn takes less time than the trip out and soon its lights appear in the dark.

Chapter Thirteen

Several people are milling around outside the inn as they draw close. One takes notice of their approach and runs inside. As they come to a stop, Stig emerges through the door with Brother Willim. "You did it!" exclaims Stig.

Brother Willim comes and reaches up to help the girl down from the horse. She gives a glance back to Potbelly who nods that it's alright, then allows Brother Willim to help her down.

From out of the inn another couple emerges and immediately takes possession of the two boys. The calls and cries of the boys tell James they must be their parents. He can see the tracks of tears down the woman's face from where she's been crying over the loss of her boys.

Once the father helps the younger child down from where he sits before James, he extends his hand in gratitude. Words rush out from the man as James takes his hand. The older boy has dismounted and wrapped his arms around his mother in a hug that's likely going to last awhile.

"He's saying thank you," Reilin's voice comes from where he just exited the inn.

"I figured as much," replies James. "Tell him that I am glad I was able to bring his boys back to him." When Reilin translates, the boys' father again shakes his hand vigorously as the mother gathers the children to her. He then takes his family and they move off to where a wagon sits next to the inn. Climbing aboard, the father takes the reins and with a last wave and salutation to James and the others, he gets the team of horses moving.

As James dismounts, Reilin comes to him and says, "The boys disappeared two days ago. When word spread that another child was taken and that someone had gone to get her back, they came in hopes you would return with their boys."

"I'm glad it worked out well," replies James. "How's the woman?"

"She's better," he says. "The loss of her husband was a brutal blow and she went into hysterics when told of what happened to her daughter." Glancing over to where Brother Willim is just entering the inn with the girl he adds, "But now that her daughter's back, I think things will be okay."

"Where is everyone else?" asks Stig.

James quickly fills them in on what happed at the farmhouse and of finding Cassie's necklace. When he's through, he tells Stig, "Get our horses ready. We're going out to the farmhouse once I ask the mother about this." He holds up the necklace to show them.

"She may not be in much condition to answer questions," explains Reilin.

"We'll see," he says. "Make sure our things are out of the rooms too."

"I'll take care of it," he assures him and moves off to get it done.

Reilin follows James as he heads toward the front door of the inn. The people he passes pat him on the shoulder as well as other forms of congratulations on bringing back the children.

Inside, he finds Miko and Brother Willim sitting at a table with the woman they found upstairs. Next to the woman sits Aleya with a smile on her face as she watches the mother and daughter. The girl is wrapped tightly in her mother's arms and they are crying together, both for happiness at being reunited and sadness at the loss of the father. The innkeeper meets him just within the foyer. Reilin translates.

"I'm sorry," he says. "I was mistaken about you."

James gives him a reassuring nod. "Don't worry about it, I understand," he assures the innkeeper. "By the way, we'll be leaving just as soon as I talk with the mother."

A pained look comes to his face. "If I've given you offense…" he begins.

James waves off the coming apology and says, "It is nothing you have done or didn't do. Something else has arisen that we must see to right away."

Somewhat relieved at that, the innkeeper says, "If you need anything, just let me know."

"I shall do that," James assures him. Leaving the innkeeper behind, he moves across the common room and makes for the woman and her daughter.

At his approach, the girl says something to her mother. The mother glances up to him with tears in her eye. "Thank you," she says in his language.

"You speak my language?" he asks amazed.

"Yes," she replies. "My husband and I spent many years in Cardri before our daughter was born."

"I'm sorry for your loss," he says. Pulling out a chair from the table he sits down.

"So am I," she says with a catch in her voice as her emotions get the better of her.

James waits patiently until the tears stop flowing. "There's something I would like to ask you if you don't mind," he tells her.

Using a kerchief to wipe away her tears, she takes a deep breath to calm herself then nods. "What would you like to know?" she asks.

He pulls forth Cassie's necklace from his pouch. "This was found in the possession of the men who took your daughter," he explains. "Did this come from you or your husband?"

She takes the necklace and looks intently at the heart with the two diamonds. After a moment she shakes her head. "I don't think so," she says as she hands the necklace back to him. "It's lovely though."

Just then Potbelly comes to the table and sets the sack containing the loot liberated from the captors. "Here you go ma'am," he says.

"What's this?" she asks as the sack is placed before her.

"Gold and jewels we found with your daughter's captors," James explains. "It's for you and your daughter."

"I can't take all of this," she says. "You keep some for yourselves. It's the least you deserve for what you did for my daughter."

Shaking his head, he says, "No. We don't need it and it will help you along now that your husband is gone." He nods to her daughter. "It will also provide a nice dowry for your daughter when the time comes."

Another round of tears comes as she says, "Thank you."

"There is no need for thanks ma'am," James says. Then to Miko and Brother Willim he says, "We need to get going." Standing up, he turns his attention again to the mother and says, "I would wish you happiness, but that may take some time to come again. Instead, I shall wish you long life and good health. That when happiness once more comes, you will be able to enjoy it for a very long time."

"May your travels be safe ones," she tells him. The little girl gets off her mother's lap and at first looks to be moving to give James a hug. Instead, she moves around him to where Potbelly has come to stand behind him. Wrapping her arms around his legs, she gives him a hug.

Standing there a little embarrassed, he reaches down and pats her on the head. Looking at a loss at what further he should do, he simply stands there until her hug comes to an end. Then she quickly returns to her mother.

James gives him a smile and nods toward the door indicating they should be going. With the others following, he crosses the room and leaves the inn. Outside, he finds that Reilin and Stig already have their horses ready with their belongings secured behind the saddles. Moving to his horse, James quickly mounts.

Several of the people standing nearby come to Miko and give him coins. Surprised, he at first makes to refuse them, but a quick shake of the head by Brother Willim convinces him to take them.

"Let's go," says James and then turns to head back to where Jiron is waiting at the farmhouse with the prisoners.

"It's an offering," he hears Brother Willim say to Miko.

"An offering?" he asks.

"Some people hold to the belief that if you give coins to a priest after he saves the life of someone," he explains, "that you will be blessed for your generosity."

Holding the coins in his hand, he asks, "What should I do with this?"

"Keep it and use it how you will," he replies. "If you had an actual temple, I would say to put it in the temple's coffers. But right now, you are the temple. So use it as you see fit."

Nodding, he puts the coins in his pocket.

James grins as he thinks of how the coins will most likely be used should they run across a bakery selling tarts any time soon.

They ride in silence on their return to the farmhouse. The light coming from its window soon appears in the distance ahead of them. As they draw close, a shadow disengages itself from the night and comes forward. "Everything go okay," Shorty asks them.

"Yes," James replies. "The girl is once again reunited with her mother. The parents of the two boys were there as well."

"Good," he says. "Find out anything about the necklace? Jiron's been climbing the walls ever since you left."

"She never saw it before," he says.

"Too bad for those three we have tied up inside," Shorty says as he walks with them back to the farmhouse. "Jiron's not going to be satisfied if they can't tell him something."

Sighing, James says, "I know." Moving to the farmhouse he sees Jiron framed in the doorway.

"Well?" he asks.

James holds out the necklace to him and says, "She didn't know anything."

Taking it, Jiron nods. Looking past James' shoulder he hollers, "Reilin! I need you."

"Be right there," he replies.

Jiron then turns and goes back in the farmhouse. James follows him in.

The three men still sit in the same place where they were when he had left to return the children. Even though the dead bodies have been removed, the blood that was spilled during the fight remains.

"What do you need?" asks Reilin when he enters the room.

Jiron waves him over to where he stands before the three prisoners and shows Reilin the necklace. "I want you to ask them where they got this," he explains.

"Why?" he asks.

"The last time I saw it was when Tinok left," he replies.

"The same Tinok we are trying to find?" he questions.

Nodding, Jiron says, "That's right."

Taking the necklace from Jiron, he turns to the prisoners. Holding up in front of them, he asks, "Where did you get this?" Three sets of eyes stare back at him silently. "Tell me!" he insists. When they still refuse to answer, he turns back to Jiron. "They're being stubborn."

Jiron removes one of the knives that the Renlon's gave him back in Illion. He grabs the hair of the closest man and puts the knife's point an inch away from the man's left eye. Then he says to Reilin, "Ask them again." The man whose eye is being threatened begins to sweat. His eyes flick from the point of the knife, to Jiron, and then to Reilin.

"Now, my friend is real anxious to find out about how you came to be in possession of this necklace," he explains to the man with the knife before his eye. "It once belonged to a friend of his, and the fact that you had it causes him great concern. Things will go much smoother if you would cooperate."

"It isn't ours," the man being threatened states. When he speaks, Jiron backs the knife a few inches away from in front of his eye.

"That's right," another of the prisoners adds. "If we tell you what we know will you let us go?"

Reilin translates for the others who have gathered to watch the proceedings. James says, "If they convince us they are telling the truth and have told everything they know, we won't kill them."

When Reilin explains that to them, the man says, "Very well." Eyes moving from James then to the others, he says "It was Gryll's."

Another of the men adds, "He claimed he bought if from some prostitute in Inziala before we came north. Said he paid her four gold pieces for it."

"What prostitute?" asks Jiron after Reilin translated for them.

A few moments' discussion with the captives and Reilin says, "They don't know her name. Supposedly she works down by the river at a place called The Split Navel."

"Can we trust them?" asks Shorty.

"I can't believe they would lie about something as trivial as where a necklace came from," suggests Scar. "I mean, what's the point?"

James glances to Brother Willim and asks, "What do you think?"

"I don't sense any attempt at deception," he replies. "I would tend to believe they are telling the truth." Beside him Miko nods in agreement.

"So then, what to do with them?" Stig asks.

"I gave them my word not to kill them," he says, "but I said nothing about releasing them." He glances to Jiron and says, "We leave them bound and gagged when we go."

"And then notify someone at the next town where they are?" asks Shorty.

Shaking his head, James says, "No. The people at the inn know that something happened here. More than likely someone will come out here to investigate."

"They will execute them when they find them," Miko says.

"If so, it's no more than they deserve," he says. "Let's get out of here, I don't want to stay is this place any longer." The blood soaked floor and rugs are beginning to make him a bit nauseous. Indicating the three men he says, "Make sure they are secure and won't go anywhere."

"You got it," says Scar. With Potbelly's aid, they make sure the men will not escape their bonds on their own.

James walks with Jiron and Aleya to the door. "Does anyone know how far Inziala is from here?" he asks.

"Not exactly," replies Jiron. "But if you remember, we did go through it during our search for Miko."

"Seems like we are always hunting for someone that the Empire has taken," James says.

"With luck this will be our last time," Jiron states.

"I hope so," admits James. "You know, I would love to simply sit by a river under a warm sun and do nothing for the rest of my life."

Laughing, Jiron says, "Don't we all." Aleya snakes her arm around his middle as they move through the door to where the horses are tied.

Off to the east the sky is beginning to lighten with the coming of dawn. As James swings into the saddle, still weary due to lack of sufficient sleep, he can't help but revel in the peace this time of day brings. Still and quiet, it's almost as if the world stops in anticipation of the sun's rise.

When Scar and Potbelly exit the farmhouse, they report that the men aren't likely to get free. Then they mount and James leads them back toward the road. He angles in a slightly more southerly direction to avoid encountering the inn and the people there. Things should be okay, but you never know.

By the time the road comes into view the sun has crested the horizon and is already warming the day. Jiron pulls alongside James and asks him if he can check to be sure Tinok still lies to the southwest.

Pulling out the cloth, he lets the magic flow and they both watch as the cloth once more rises toward the southwest. "Still there," James observes.

"Good," he replies.

"Plan to check on this prostitute should our path lead through Inziala?" James asks.

"Yes," he says. "But if our road should lead elsewhere, I won't worry about it." He rides in silence for about a minute before adding, "Though I worry what it could mean that he no longer has it." Glancing over to where James is riding he says, "He wouldn't have parted with it easily."

"No, I wouldn't think so," replies James. Considering how much he cared for Cassie and the degree in which he reacted to her death, James can't imagine anything parting him from that necklace except imminent death.

They continue following the road all morning long as it winds its way alongside the river. Twice they've come across ruined bridges that Illan had destroyed on his march north. One of them was already in the process of being repaired, workers on both sides were working to smooth the ragged edges. They observe a gang of slaves who are clearing the broken stone of the old bridge away and taking it to waiting wagons for transportation.

Close to the area where they work to repair the bridge, a makeshift wooden bridge spans the river allowing those on foot and wagons to cross. The make-up of the bridge is reminiscent of the bridges Delia and Hedry's force took out back at Lythylla.

"That didn't last too long," comments Jiron. When James glances to him he says, "I would have thought it would take longer to get trade going again across the river."

"They can't afford to have their routes impaired for too long," replies James. "I suspect we'll see this all along the river."

Then all of a sudden as a wagon was crossing over the makeshift bridge, the section it's on breaks off from the main body and begins floating down the river. Jiron guffaws and says, "I suppose they still don't have a handle on it."

James returns the smile with, "It doesn't look like it."

Men on both sides of the river run along its banks as they try to help the stranded wagon. The bridge section begins to spin with the current and the horses attached to the wagon start to panic. For reasons unknown, the horses suddenly bolt and drag the wagon into the river. The driver dives off into the current just before the wagon is pulled into the water.

Screams of the horses are heard as they struggle against the traces which drag them beneath the waters. Soon, it grows quiet as the river wins out and drags them under completely.

"Too bad for the horses," Aleya says. The others nod agreement. The section of bridge floating upon the river continues to slowly spin as it flows downstream until it finally disappears in the distance. An hour later they come to where the bridge section was stopped in its southward voyage when it got snagged on a sandbar in a bend of the river.

"Think they'll come get it?" asks Stig.

"Who knows," replies Scar. Keeping a steady pace, they soon leave the broken section of bridge behind them.

Once the sun is high in the sky, they pull off the road to allow the horses a chance to rest and for them to get a quick bite to eat. Off in the distance to the south on the far side of the river lies the outline of a town.

"A day or so south of that town lies Korazan," announces Stig. "Should be interesting to see what they've done to the place since we left."

"Could your friend be there?" asks Reilin.

Jiron stops dead in his tracks. He never even thought of that. If something had happened to Tinok, he could very well be sitting in a slave pen at Korazan. Glancing to James he asks, "If he is, could you see him in your mirror?"

"A day away?" he muses. "Possibly." Taking out his mirror, he concentrates on Tinok. Again, the mirror remains placid, the only thing he sees in it is his own reflection. "Nothing," he says. "Still, it could be that we're still too far away. I'll look again before it gets dark tonight."

"Okay," Jiron says.

After the break, they return to the road and continue their way south. The city on the opposite side of the river they saw during the break continues to grow until they reach where a branching of the road moves toward the river.

A wide bridge once spanned the river where the road crosses over, but now it's just two broken ends jutting from the ground on either side. Wagons and people have formed a bottleneck while they wait for their turn to cross. Two of the makeshift bridges span the water similar in nature to the one they encountered earlier. One of the bridges is used for traffic coming from the town and the other for those going the other way. A single wagon is making the crossing toward the town while a dozen people use the other on their way to the road James and the others are on.

"Wonder what would have happened if that bridge that broke loose further up had made it this far," supposes Scar.

"I doubt if those two bridges there would have survived the impact," James says.

"How long do you suppose it is going to take them to get the bridges we destroyed rebuilt?" asks Jiron.

"Years, I would think," replies James.

As they move on past, they keep watching those who are there at the bridge waiting to cross. It's obvious those in line are not happy about the speed with which the crossings are taking place. After several single wagons cross, one at a time, James tells the others that it's probably due to the unstable nature of the makeshift bridge. Too much weight at one time could cause them to break away like the other one did earlier.

The bridge and the people waiting to cross soon disappear behind them. Not much further after that they come to where a road from the east joins with theirs. At the junction, the river bends sharply to the east and the road moves to follow it.

"I remember this place," Potbelly suddenly announces. "I figure Korazan is only another day and a half's ride away."

"You sure?" asks James.

"Oh yes," he replies. "A sharp turn in the river followed by a town on the other side. Last time we came through here I was commenting to Scar how this would be a good defensible spot if someone was trying to cross over to the west."

"That's right," Scar says. "You brought it up because of the time up in Rycklin..." For the next half hour, he and Potbelly regale everyone with a tale of daring-do that, aside from being the usual unbelievable fare, is quite interesting. At least it helps to pass the time.

They're able to maintain a quick pace throughout the day and have covered many miles before the sun begins to set. With no inn or other suitable locale available, they pull off the road and make camp next to the river.

While the others are collecting firewood and preparing the meal, James removes his mirror and tries to locate Tinok. Still no luck. He glances back at Jiron who was watching the mirror over his shoulder. "I don't think he's in Korazan," he says. "I should have been able to find him by now if he were."

Crestfallen, Jiron sighs and goes over to where Aleya has laid out their bedrolls off to one side. James watches as he sits next to her and leans his head against her shoulder. Memories of Meliana come to him as he watches her put a comforting arm around him.

Putting away his mirror, he wonders what she's doing right now. He sure misses the way she felt when they were in each other's arms. It seems so long ago that he last held her, could she have found someone else by now? A woman isn't going to wait around forever. When this business with Tinok is over he's going to find a way to either go and see her or have her come to him.

Not for the first time he wonders how his grandparents would react if they knew he was in love. He really believes they would have taken to Meliana, she's a real nice woman.

"You okay?"

Snapping out of his reverie, he looks up to see Miko approaching with two plates of food. "I'm fine," he replies. "Just thinking of home."

"Me too," he admits. Handing James his plate, Miko sits on the ground next to him. "The guys back in Bearn wouldn't know it was me now."

"Not likely," James agrees. The fare this evening is a simple stew made of dried beef and some old tubers that Brother Willim had produced. Where he got them no one knows and none felt like asking.

They sit and eat in silence for awhile. James glances at his friend and can see there's something on his mind. "So," he begins, "how is being a High Priest?"

Miko finishes off a piece of tough beef as he thinks of his reply. "Frankly," he says after swallowing, "it scares me to death."

"You seem to be handling it well so far," James says encouragingly.

"It's not what I'm doing now that bothers me," he admits. Then he turns to face his friend and in a hushed voice he says, "I am responsible for increasing Morcyth's presence on this world. How am I to do that?"

"Does the Book of Morcyth tell you anything?" he asks.

"I haven't had much time to read it at any great length," he explains. "I sort of skip around to see what's in there."

"And?" prompts James.

"And it's full of rules, rituals and some other stuff I have no clue as to what it's trying to tell me." He takes half a tuber and sticks it into his mouth whole while he watches James for his response.

Trying to keep the smile from breaking out at seeing Miko work that tuber from one side of his mouth to the other in an attempt to reduce its size, he says, "Relax. Rather than being scared, be happy. Maybe even excited." At Miko's scoffing expression, he adds, "Think of it this way. Out of the millions of people on this world, *you* were chosen to be Morcyth's representative. That's got to make you feel pretty special, at least a little."

Finally managing to get the tuber down to a reasonable size, he finishes it off quickly. "It does," he admits. "I just don't want to let anyone down."

"Can't," James tells him. "Do what the book tells you, never go against what you think is right, and you'll do fine."

"I will," he says.

"Then you'll have no problems," James states matter-of-factly.

Then the grin that James remembers from before Miko began to be changed by the Fire makes an appearance. "Well, there is one problem I've been having lately," he says, the grin getting wider.

"And what would that be?" asks James.

"I have an unbelievable craving for tarts," he says then breaks out into laughter. James joins in and they finish the rest of their meal while rehashing old adventures, both fun and otherwise.

Chapter Fourteen

The following morning they hit the road before the sun crests the horizon. Traffic upon the road gradually increases with the rising of the sun. By the time noon has come, the level of travelers reaches those they encountered the day before.

Small villages become more frequent the further they go. Most are little more than clusters of buildings that cater to travelers. Usually consisting of an inn, a tavern and a dozen or so other buildings that are quite likely the houses they live in. Less than half of these areas have a chandler's shop of one kind or another. At one such spot, they take their noon meal and resupply their depleting stock of trail rations.

Once seated within the inn's common room and have placed their order, Reilin asks their server how much further is Korazan. "You should arrive there before nightfall," she explains. Then she takes a moment to give them a closer look. "You're not from the Empire are you?"

After a brief confab with the others Reilin replies, "No. We are from Cardri looking for trading opportunities."

"I thought so," she states with a knowing nod. "You might want to stay clear of Korazan."

"Why?" Reilin asks her.

"Earlier this summer, they had a bad time when Black Hawk's army came through," she explains.

"Bad?" he asks.

She nods her head in reply. "They say he and his men pillaged and burned down half the town," she goes on to explain. "One man from Korazan who came through here afterward said that Black Hawk left so many dead that the streets were literally flowing with blood."

"But why should that have anything to do with us?" he asks.

"You're from the north," she says, as if that should explain everything.

"Right," he says. When their server leaves he relays everything she said to the others.

"We can't bypass Korazan," insists Jiron, "no matter the risk. Tinok might be there!"

"I don't think he is," replies James. "If he were, I should have been able to find him by now."

"I say we go to Korazan," Jiron says, his gaze turning to meet the eyes of everyone. As if to dare them to say no.

James thinks a moment then says, "How about this." When he has Jiron's attention again he continues. "We have been trusting my cloth trick to lead the way, correct?"

"Correct," concedes Jiron.

"Then let's do this," he explains. "We bypass Korazan. If, when we are on the south side and the cloth points back toward Korazan, then we go. Otherwise we continue to follow wherever it may lead."

Jiron mulls that over in his mind. He knows James' magic is seldom, if ever, wrong. Nodding, he says, "Very well. If once we are on the far side it still points south, then I will forget about Korazan."

Everyone breathes a sigh of relief. The last thing anyone wanted was to return and spend any amount of time there. If there was any place where they may be recognized, it would be at Korazan.

"Then I suggest when we come close, we leave the road at that time," Stig says. "If we go to the city and skirt around its walls, it could seem suspicious."

"I agree," nods James.

When their meal of goat, bread and a root reminiscent of a carrot arrives, they dig in with gusto. At one point in the meal Shorty mumbles under his breath, "...flowing with blood."

"What?" James asks.

Looking up from his plate, Shorty didn't realize he had spoken aloud. "Sorry," he says. "It's just that we barely even went into town. The way they make it sound, we killed half the people and left their bodies rotting in the streets."

Scar laughs at that. "Pay it no mind," he replies. "In a few years the story will grow to that we killed half the town and bathed in their blood."

"Probably," agrees Potbelly. "Remember that time with Oofa?" Scar nods.

"Oofa?" asks Jiron. "I don't think I heard that one."

"Oofa was a man who often came to the Pits to watch me fight," he explains. "He was a self proclaimed aficionado of the Pits. Claimed he knew everything about everybody."

James and Miko give each other a knowing glance and grin. Potbelly may not realize it, but he and Scar come off as just that type every now and then.

"One night, he took me out to dinner," he continues. "Said he wanted to get to know me better so he would be able to make more informed wagers." Shrugging, he looks around at the others and says, "A meal's a meal."

"Was this guy about five foot six with a bad comb-over?" asks Stig.

Smiling, Scar says, "That's the guy."

"I remember him now," he says. "Always managed to get a spot right in front."

"Back to my story," Potbelly interjects. "While we were eating, he made some comment about how he's bleeding this one lord dry. Apparently he and this lord bet often and Oofa always won. Anyway, the next day, he's arrested."

Scar begins laughing and says, "Someone must have overheard their conversation. By the time the rumor mill churned it out, he was an assassin bent on killing this lord."

Potbelly starts laughing now and others join in. "It took him three days to straighten the misunderstanding out," explains Potbelly. "The lord, too proud to admit that he spent time at the Pits, claimed he didn't know the guy." Tears coming from his eyes, he concludes with, "The day after Oofa was released, the lord showed up at the Pits sporting two black eyes and a split lip!" Unable to contain himself anymore, Potbelly slaps the table and almost chokes to death on a piece of carrot. Scar slaps him on the back and dislodges it for him.

Laughing with the rest of them, James is suddenly aware that the entire room is quiet and the other guests are staring at them. Sobering up quickly, he works to quiet the others down a bit. "Everyone's staring at us," he says quietly. "We don't want to attract attention." One by one they calm down. When the laughter finally stops, the other patrons return to their meal and the buzz of conversation resumes.

They hurry through their meal and are soon back on the road. Taking out his mirror while he rides, he brings Korazan's image into focus. He sees the gaping wall where they made their way into the slaver compound. A mile out of town lies a mound of dirt that wasn't there the last time. Probably the mass grave where they buried the dead after the battles.

Workers have already begun to rebuild the destroyed section of the wall, a flurry of activity is taking place in and around the base of the opening. Wagonloads of stone blocks sit awaiting their turn to be set into the wall. It didn't take them long to begin the rebuilding.

Satisfied with what he's seen, he cancels the image of Korazan and again tries to find Tinok. After several minutes of fruitless searching, he gives up and puts away the mirror. Glancing over to where Jiron rides beside him, he can see the unspoken question. Shaking his head, James says, "Nothing. I can bring up Korazan, but not Tinok. I'm sure he's not there."

"We'll see," he says.

James continues to periodically check on the distance to Korazan. When he figures them to be less than an hour away, they leave the road. He feels rather conspicuous as they are the only ones not using the road. But, keeping a steady pace without appearing to rush, should alleviate any thoughts or concerns the other travelers may have about them.

Once away from the road, he uses his mirror to maintain a good distance from the city as they circumvent it. Also, he keeps an eye out for any roving patrols which may be in the area. They were forced to come to a stop at one point when he sights in his mirror a score of riders that would have intersected their path at an inopportune time. When the riders were past and there was no danger of running into them, they resumed their journey.

It's not only patrols that they work to avoid, but those living in the area as well. While unable to completely avoid all the farmstead in the area, James is at least able to have them thread their way through so they won't come in close proximity to them. They see some of the farmers out with herds of goats, occasionally one would wave a greeting as they ride by.

Due to the meandering path he leads them on through the farmsteads, it takes them close to two hours to reach the road on the south side of Korazan. At which time he takes out his cloth to see where Tinok lies, whether it will be north to Korazan or still to the south. Everyone holds their breath and when the cloth rises to point south, they collectively breathe a sigh of relief. They had been dreading having to return to Korazan.

"That settles it," announces Stig when the cloth rises.

"Yes it does," agrees James. Turning to Jiron he says, "He's not there."

Disappointed, Jiron nods. "Let's get going," he says.

Putting the cloth back in his pouch, James indicates for Reilin to take the lead as they continue along the road to the south. To their right sits the lake, Tears of the Empress. A beautiful lake, its water glistens in the sun. Many boats of varying shapes and sizes are out upon her waters.

They follow the road south along the shore of the lake for an hour until they reach a crossroad. Taking the right fork, they continue to follow the shoreline until they reach its southernmost point. There the road turns and for a brief distance goes due west until it comes to where the waters flow from the lake into a sizeable river. At that point, the road turns from due west and follows the river on a more southwesterly course.

Not too far from where the road begins to follow the river, they come to another bridge that has been destroyed. Again as in the previous ones they came across on their way down, this one too is in the midst of reconstruction. Two of the makeshift wooden bridges span the river here.

"We didn't come this far south," states Stig.

"No, you didn't," affirms James.

"One of your wagons?" asks Jiron in a whisper.

"It had to have been," he replies. Other than Jiron, he hadn't told anyone else about what he did with the wagon and wanted to keep it that way. After splitting off with Illan, he had planted seeds of magic in the beds of various wagons in many caravans they had passed. The seeds were to accumulate magic and then explode when they crossed over bridges. It looked as if one had.

"Then how did this happen?" Stig asks. Glancing to James he adds, "You do this?"

"Yes and that's all I will say about it," he replies. The last thing he wants is to have word spread about what he does with magic. An idea of what is possible could lead others in the magic business into embarking upon acts that could have serious repercussions.

The others take his lack of explanation with equanimity. They have been with him long enough to trust that what he does is for a reason and usually a good one.

Not too far past the ruined bridge they decide to stop for the night. It's been a long day and the time spent on the road is beginning to wear on them. Before the light fades completely, James again tries to get Tinok in his mirror but to the extreme frustration of Jiron, comes up with nothing. "How far away is he?" he asks when James tells him of the results.

"I don't know," replies James as he puts away his mirror. "I'll try again in the morning."

Practically stomping in frustration back to where he and Aleya have their blankets laid out, he fumes over James' inability to find him.

Sighing, James feels bad for his friend and would do more if he could. Though he's been able to do some pretty amazing things, he's not all powerful. He goes over to where Shorty has pulled cooking duty and gets a plate of what he calls stew. Not very good but at least it's hot and filling.

Once they finish eating, they turn in for the night. As James lays there under the stars he gazes up at the full moon above them. He can't help but think that time is running out and running out fast. Trying to put his worries aside, he eventually calms his mind sufficiently to fall asleep.

No sooner does James awaken the next morning than Jiron is bugging him to look for Tinok. Making him wait until he answers nature's call, he then gets settled on the ground with the mirror held in his lap. Concentrating hard, he visualizes Tinok and sends forth the magic. Nothing. Giving more magic to the endeavor, he sends forth a burst and for the briefest moment, the image in the mirror flickered then disappeared.

"Did you see that?" asks Jiron excitedly.

"Yeah," says James, "I saw." The image flickered for a moment when he used more magic.

"Something happen?" asks Scar as he and the others come over to investigate Jiron's outburst.

"He almost had him!" exclaims Jiron. Almost dancing with glee, he turns back to James and asks, "Can you do it again?"

"Possibly," he says. Returning his gaze to the mirror, he opens the gate so to speak, and the magic pours from him. The image in the mirror shifts and Tinok appears.

"That's him!" Jiron cries out.

The image is hazy, possibly due to the distance it's coming from. Tinok is sitting in the back of a wagon with hands and feet manacled. It's very hard to tell but it looks like the wagon is in motion.

"Where is he?" Miko asks. "Can you expand the image any?"

He tries but the drain of power is too great. Shaking his head he says, "It would require more magic than I have."

Suddenly, he feels Miko's hand on his shoulder. Glancing up he sees him there with the Star in his hand. "Maybe this will help?" he asks with a crooked grin and the Star flares brightly.

"Yes it will," he replies. Casting a leech line to him, James suddenly feels the power of the Star flowing into him via Miko. As he returns his gaze to the mirror he hears Jiron say to Miko, "Thanks."

With the added magic of the Star, the image clarifies some but the haziness remains. Expanding the image, they see that Tinok's wagon is one of several. One man in armor on a horse rides in front of the lead wagon while a dozen others ride alongside the rest.

The haziness gradually increases despite the amount of magic he's using. Then all of a sudden they come to the side of a large, black surface. It could possibly be a wall. A section of the wall slides open and the man in armor leading them rides inside. The wagons follow along behind, and when the last wagon passes through the wall, the mirror returns to normal.

"What happened?" asks Jiron.

"I don't know," admits James. Staring perplexed at the mirror, all he can see are the reflections of himself and the others as they stare down at it. The magic is still flowing, but there is no image. Stepping up the magic flow, he draws more from Miko. Steadily increasing the flow of magic he concentrates on Tinok but the mirror remains blank. With a sigh, he gradually reduces the magic flow until he stops it altogether.

"I can't reach him anymore," he says. When Jiron is about to argue, he adds, "I was using more magic than ever before in searching with the mirror. There's nothing more I can do."

"At least we know he's alive," offers Stig. "That's more than we knew before."

"That's right," agrees Scar.

"He's in trouble," Jiron says as he gets to his feet. Looking at the others he says, "What are we waiting for?" They quickly make ready for travel. Once they're mounted, Jiron leads them back to the road and maintains a quick pace.

After they've been on the road for an hour, James pulls out his cloth to see if they are still going in the right direction. When he casts the spell that he's cast every time he's done this, the cloth remains still. A shiver runs through him as he stops the magic. Attempting to home in on Tinok, he again releases the magic and says under his breath, "Come on!" But the cloth remains still and doesn't even twitch.

He glances over to where Jiron is watching him. "It's not working," he says.

"What's not working?" he asks.

"My cloth trick," he explains. "It isn't pointing to where Tinok is."

"Why not?" he asks.

Shrugging, James says, "I don't know."

Bringing them to a stop there in the middle of the road, Jiron moves his horse to his side and says, "Do it again."

"I've already tried twice and it isn't working," he tells him.

"Do it again," he insists. By this time the others have gathered around to observe what's going on.

Holding up the hand with the cloth once more, he concentrates on Tinok then releases the magic. Just as happened the two times before, the cloth remains down. Bringing his gaze to Jiron he sees the worry and fear for his friend that he's feeling.

"What can it mean?" he asks.

"Something is blocking my search," James explains.

"Or someone," adds Brother Willim from his position next to him.

"Or someone," agrees James.

"But who or what would do that?" asks Aleya.

"I don't know," James admits. Casting his eyes around the group, he looks questioningly for any ideas but they all shake their heads. Then he remembers the image in the mirror before he lost sight of Tinok. They had entered some building. Whoever is inside has to be blocking him. Glancing to Jiron, he decides to not add more worry to his mind and keeps the thought to himself.

"What about that prostitute in Inziala?" asks Stig. "Maybe she could shed some light on this."

"Yes!" exclaims Jiron. "Maybe she can."

"I doubt if she would be the one to have done this to Tinok," Shorty says.

"No," agrees Jiron. "But maybe she would have a good idea who did."

"If nothing else, we could find out where she got the necklace," offers Scar.

Nodding, Jiron asks, "Anyone know how far Inziala is from here?"

"I think it's south of here," Reilin finally answers, "but I don't know where."

Just then from the south they see a single wagon approaching with two men sitting on the driving seat. "Reilin," James says. "Go ask them if they know where Inziala is."

"Alright," he acknowledges and moves to intercept them.

Jiron waits with the others while Reilin rides ahead to meet with the men on the wagon.

The men on the wagon are wary of his approach. One actually pulls out a crossbow when he realizes Reilin intends to approach them. Reilin stops ten feet away, holds up his hand in greeting and talks. He and the two men exchange words for several minutes then Reilin turns his horse around and rejoins them. The two men on the wagon keep an eye on them as their wagon rolls closer.

"They said that Inziala is only about a day away," he explains. As the wagon passes them on its way north, James gives the two men a nod of thanks. The men only stare at them as they pass, their weapons at the ready.

"Friendly pair weren't they," comments Scar after they've resumed their trek south.

"You could say that," agrees Potbelly. Glancing back to the wagon, he sees the man with the crossbow turned in his seat and is keeping an eye on them. "Wonder if travelers run into trouble out here?"

"Who knows?" replies Jiron. "I want to make Inziala before the sun goes down if we can." Nudging his horse into motion, he gets up to a quick gallop.

The rest of the day they maintain a furious pace. They all understand that time is running out and now without James' ability to point the way, it could take them longer to pick up Tinok's trail. With only short breaks to answer the call of nature and to water the horses, they practically fly down the road.

When the sun begins to draw close to the horizon, still Jiron continues the fast pace. Three hours later when the horses are on the verge of exhaustion, the lights of a city appear out of the dark before them. Coming across a party of four men and two ladies, they ask them if the town is Inziala. James breathes a sigh of relief when they say it is. His butt was beginning to get sore from the hard pace Jiron had set.

With thanks and wishes for good fortune, they leave the party behind and continue on toward the city.

Chapter Fifteen

As they approach the city of Inziala, they see dozens of fires off to the east of town. It's a large caravansary with scores of wagons comprising many different caravans. Jiron leads them to the gates of the city where the two guards on duty give them a cursory once over as they pass through.

From behind him, James says, "Let's get a room first. Then you can go to The Split Navel and find this prostitute." He sees Jiron nod his head.

They don't go very far past the gate before they come to a two story building that looks fairly well kept. A sign depicting a man walking a road through the hills hangs outside near the entrance. "Could be one," Jiron says as he comes to a stop in front. Turning back to the others he says, "Reilin, go see about some rooms."

Pulling up next to Jiron, Reilin comes to a stop and dismounts. Instead of moving to the door he walks over to James. "I need more coins," he says. "The last place wiped me out."

James reaches into his pouch and removes a handful of coins, the glint of silver and gold can be seen among them. "Here," he says, "this should last you for awhile."

Taking the coins, Reilin grins and says, "I would think so," then pockets them before heading to the door.

While Reilin is inside acquiring accommodations, the others wait outside. It doesn't take long before Miko notices someone across the street paying rather close interest in them. Barely above a whisper, he says to Jiron, "There's someone across the street watching us."

Jiron turns his head just far enough to see the man there. Dressed in raggedy clothes, the man looks like someone who lives in the gutter. "I wouldn't worry too much about him," he says. "Probably wants a handout and is nervous about approaching us."

Thinking back to his times on the streets, Miko can't ever remember a time when he was nervous about approaching someone for anything. Nor anyone else who lived on the streets for that matter. "I don't think so," he says.

They continue to cast discreet glances to the man until Reilin returns with the room keys. As they move to take the horses around back, Miko glances over to where the man was standing and finds him gone. Casting a quick glance up and down the street, he fails to see him. Shrugging, he follows the others around back to the stables.

This time Reilin has managed to obtain five rooms, the last rooms at the inn as it turns out. Aleya gets her own room of course, being the only lady and all. James and Jiron again take a room together, Brother Willim and Miko take another. Which leaves the last two to be divided among the rest.

No sooner has James entered and set his pack on the floor by his bed than Jiron states his ready to go and that he intends to take Reilin with him. "Have him arrange for meals to be sent up before you go," James tells him.

About to protest the delay, Jiron realizes Reilin is the only one who can and nods. Moving from the room, he finds Reilin where he's bunking with Stig and Shorty. "I want to leave soon," he tells him, "and you're coming with me. But before we go you need to arrange for food to be sent up here for the others."

"You two going by yourselves?" asks Scar from the doorway.

"Might be better if you had a few others," suggests Stig.

Looking from face to face, he can see their desire to come with him and perhaps have an ale and some fun. "We shouldn't leave James here by himself," he says.

"Oh, come on!" objects Scar. "With Brother Willim and Miko here, not to mention Aleya, it would take an army to take him."

As if the stating of her name magically summons her, Aleya appears at the door. "I'm coming too," she states.

"No you aren't," counters Jiron. "It would look out of place and might call unwanted attention."

"I'm not about to let you go to some brothel by yourself," she states.

"Don't worry," assures Scar, "we won't let him do anything he'll regret in the morning."

"Or that you might take offense at," adds Potbelly.

"Besides," says Shorty, "not many guys bring girls along to visit prostitutes."

She eyes Jiron intensely. "Promise me you won't do anything," she says.

He gives her a disarming smile, comes to her and gives her a big hug. "I promise," he whispers in her ear then gives her a peck on the cheek.

"Alright then," she says. "But if I find out something happened…" she trails off, leaving his own mind to come up with the possible consequences.

"Good," he says. Then to Reilin, "Now go down and have meals sent up for James and the others. Then we'll leave."

"Alright!" exclaims Shorty jubilantly.

Once Reilin has left Jiron turns to the rest of them. "This is not some pleasure excursion with drinking and debauchery," he insists. "We are after information and that is all!"

"Hey, calm down," Scar says.

"Yeah," adds Potbelly, "we understand."

He gives them another stern gaze then has them go to his and James' room to wait for Reilin's return. Once he's returned and says the food will be up shortly, Jiron indicates the pit fighters and says to James, "They want to come too." When he receives James' nod that he's okay with it, he adds, "Be back as soon as possible."

As he is about to leave, James says, "Don't make me come and save your butt this time." Jiron pauses and glances back with a grin, "You won't." He remembers the ill-fated trip he and the others took where a tavern wench had tricked them and wound up hog-tied in her basement. If it wasn't for James and Roland rescuing them, they would have been sold off to slavers.

Turning back to the door, he leads the others out into the hallway and downstairs to the common room. There he makes a beeline for the exit and they soon find themselves out on the partially crowded streets. He makes a quick scan to see which way is the quickest to the river. When he catches a glimpse of moonlight reflected off water from down the street he immediately heads in that direction.

Jiron keeps a brisk pace as they make their way down the street to the river. According to the child abductor they question about the necklace, they will find The Split Navel down by the river. As they draw closer to the river, the density of people on the street thins and the buildings begin to show more signs of wear, tear, and lack of upkeep that those more toward the center of town hadn't. Definitely moving into the poorer quarter of the city.

The street they're on finally comes to an end at a cross street running alongside the river. On the far side of the street are shanties built almost all the way to the water's edge. "They don't leave themselves much leeway for floods," states Scar. One of the buildings looks to actually overhang the flow of the river.

"Not very smart that's for sure," offers Stig.

Jiron brings them to a halt at the intersection and looks up this new street first in one direction then in another. Neither direction reveals anything that would indicate a brothel or something similar.

"Do you think that guy lied to us?" asks Shorty.

"Brother Willim seemed pretty confident that he hadn't," Jiron says. Then to Reilin he nods over to several young men hanging out on the corner. "Go over there and see if they can tell us where it is."

Reilin nods then moves over and begins talking with the men. At one point Reilin reaches into his pocket and pulls out a couple coins and hands them over. After that the men are much more talkative and helpful.

The others wait and soon see him turn around and make his way back to join them. "It's down this way," he says as he points to the section of the street heading off to their left.

"Is it a brothel then?" asks Jiron. Moving out, the others follow right behind him.

"Not exactly," explains Reilin. "It's more a tavern than a brothel. When I asked them about it, they said there are a few girls that work there, but mostly it's a tavern."

"Great!" exclaims Potbelly.

"Don't be getting any ideas," Jiron says with a quick glance back. "We are not getting drunk tonight."

"Aw, come on," Scar says. "A couple ales won't hurt anything."

"I'll skin any one of you who gets drunk," he says. Then he comes to a stop and turns back toward them. "Do I make myself clear?"

"Absolutely," affirms Shorty.

Turning back to continue down the street, he glances at the buildings lining the sides and asks Reilin, "Which one is it?"

"They said to look for a doorway with two dark lanterns hanging next to it," he replies.

Moving down the darkened street, they leave the light coming from the hanging lantern on the street corner behind. Jiron searches the fronts of the buildings he passes for any sign of two lanterns, dark or otherwise.

"Be a good place for a murder," comments Scar. They are beginning to feel on edge.

Then, "There it is," Jiron announces. A rather dilapidated looking, double story structure standing on their right has a doorway flanked by two unlit lanterns. No light can be seen coming from any of the building's windows and the area is quiet as a tomb.

"That can't be the place," Stig says. "It looks deserted."

"Could be intentional," Shorty suggests.

"We'll find out," Jiron says as he moves toward the door. Pausing at the foot of the three steps leading up to the door, he glances back and says, "Stay alert." Indicating for Reilin to accompany him, he turns back and takes the steps up to the door where he knocks three times. When nothing happens he knocks again, this time louder.

The sound of a floorboard creaking comes through the door. "Someone's in there," whispers Reilin.

Jiron nods. He places his ear against the door just as the sound of the deadbolt being pulled back comes through to them. Then, the door opens a crack and a voice from the dark within asks, "Yes?"

Reilin looks at Jiron who nods toward the crack and mouths 'Go ahead'. "We were told this is The Split Navel," he says.

The voice from within the darkness remains silent for a moment then says, "I think you have the wrong place."

As the door begins to shut, Reilin exclaims, "Gryll sent us!"

The door pauses and the darkness remains quiet. "Gryll you say?" the voice asks after a moment.

"That's right," affirms Reilin. "He said this was a good place to go for women."

"How do you know Gryll?" the voice asks.

Reilin glances over to Jiron who's beginning to look impatient. Returning his attention back to the voice he says, "We helped him with a job up north."

"Indeed," the voice says. "One minute." Then the door closes.

"What did he say?" Jiron asks.

Reilin relates in a quiet whisper what they said to one another. By the time he's done, steps can be heard coming from within moving toward the door. This time when the door opens, a small amount of light escapes.

"Welcome gentlemen," a man no more than three feet tall says as the door opens all the way. A hallway leads twenty feet into the building where it ends at another door that's closed. The light is coming from a candle sitting in a wall recess midway down on the left. There are no doors other than the ones at either end of the hallway.

"So this is The Split Navel?" asks Reilin.

"Yes," replies the short man. Once all the others have entered, the short man again closes the door and throws the bolt. Turning, the man begins walking toward the other door.

"Creepy," whispers Shorty.

Scar gives him a nod in reply.

As they move down the hallway, they begin to hear the sound of voices coming from behind the other door. A bark of laughter followed by several curses being shouted in anger does nothing to put them at ease. Just before they reach the door a man cries out in pain.

Smoke billows out from beyond the door as the short man opens it, acrid smoke that smells quite foul. As the door opens completely, they see a fair sized room with many tables spaced about the room. Two men are dragging the body of a man from the table closest to the door toward a door on the far side of the room. A telltale red streak left by the man being dragged reveals that he must have been the one who cried out.

Jiron follows the short man into the room and is led over to a table near the middle. The eyes of many of the other patrons follow them as they cross over to it and take their seats. Without a word, the short man turns and moves toward the door through which they entered.

A lone serving woman makes her way through the tables, and places two tankards of ale before two men at a table against the wall. Easily in her forties or above, she has the look of one whose life has been anything but easy. A massive woman, her unkempt brown hair streaked with gray is tied back in a ponytail. Her face may have been comely at one time, but now it shows rigid lines and seems to be set in a permanent grimace.

She casts her eyes toward Jiron and the others, takes notice that they are there, then without a hint of acknowledgment, returns to the bar. Four more tankards are waiting for her. Picking them up, she makes her way through the middle of the room, past their table without a word and sets them before a small group of men two tables away.

"Lousy service," comments Stig.

On her way back to the bar, Scar waves her down and with a smile asks, "How about some ale?"

She stops in her tracks and locks eyes with him. After a moment of meeting her steely gaze, his smile gradually disappears. "You all want ale?" she asks in a voice more a man's than a woman's.

"Uh…" he says, "yeah, that would be great." With a barely perceptible nod, she returns to the bar.

"I've been in some dives before, but this place has to rank among the worst," comments Potbelly quietly.

"This place is a Den of Hollow Eyes," remarks Jiron. "Did you smell the smoke when we entered?" When the others nod he adds, "They're doing biloci." Biloci is a weed and a highly addictive narcotic. The user smokes it and is visited by hallucinations while they're under the direct influence of the drug. Once the drug begins to wear off, it leaves them with a feeling of euphoria which can last for hours. The downside is that when the euphoria wears off, the user tends to spiral into deep depression lasting days.

Dens of Hollow Eyes are illegal in most places and the Empire being no exception. Some places tend to go lenient on those caught within one, but the Empire has a more stringent approach. Death.

Glancing around, they can see many of the men sitting at the tables are not entirely there. Their vacant eyes stare at imagined visions the drug induces. Every once in awhile, one would grunt, burst out with noise, or exhibit some other indication of the drug's influence.

At the bar, the woman is loading a tray with six mugs. Picking it up, she sloshes some of their contents onto the tray as she turns and heads toward Jiron and the others. As she makes her way through the tables, one man in the throes of biloci touches her posterior as she passes. Without hesitation, she takes her left hand and strikes him across the face with a blow hard enough to send him to the floor. Men at other tables pause in their conversations and glance at the man on the floor for a second, then the talking resumes when nothing further looks to be happening.

"It'll be two silvers," she says as she sets the tray down. When it doesn't look as if she's going to remove the mugs, they quickly snatch them off. Jiron hands her the silvers and before she can depart, nods to Reilin.

"Uh, we were wondering…" he begins and then trails off as she turns her face toward him.

"What?" she asks.

Clearing his throat, he begins again. "We were wondering if there was a chance to have some female company?"

She eyes him a moment and says, "I don't get off for a couple hours. But if you hang around I'll be available then."

Reilin's eyes widen at the misunderstanding and he stammers, "Uh we don't have that much time. Gryll said there was a certain girl that works here that always took care of him."

"He did, did he?" she asks.

"Yes, he did," he replies. "I don't suppose she would be available."

"Hmmm," she says as she mulls it over, "the only one I can think of who he might mean is my sister." Then her face creases into a frown and a moment later anger begins to work its way across her face. "So, he dallied with my sister did he?"

Reilin is astounded by what she said. He can't for the life of him imagine anyone would wish to spend time with this woman's sister. The others glance at him, wondering what he might have said to elicit such a response.

With a roar she yells, "I'll kill him!" Picking up the tray she flings it across the room with such force as to embed it in the wall. Smashing her right fist onto their table in anger, Reilin's amazed to hear the wood crack beneath her blow. When she raises her fist, the edge of the table is drooping slightly.

Then she turns her attention back to Reilin. "So you would think to dally with my sister too?" she asks. The eyes of the entire room are now directed at their table.

"What's going on?" asks Jiron.

Reilin turns to him and says, "It's all a misunderstanding. She thinks…" He's forced to leave his sentence unfinished when she grabs him by the front of his tunic and yanks him to his feet by her left hand. Cocking back her right to strike him, she's knocked to the floor as Scar leaps from his seat and tackles her before she can complete the blow.

Twisting as she falls, she takes him by the shoulders and once her back slams into the floor, knees him between the legs. With an 'oof' he rolls off her. Then she grabs Reilin's leg and trips him to the floor. Getting up on one knee, she strikes out at Reilin and hits him in the side.

"Reilin, what did you say to her?" yells Jiron as he comes to his feet. Just then, a hand grabs him by the shoulder and spins him around where he's struck on the chin. Knocked off his feet, his back slams into the table and smashes it on his way to the floor.

Stig jumps up and connects with the jaw of the man who struck Jiron, sending him stumbling backward into another table. Reaching down a hand to help Jiron up, he gets jumped by yet another man who kidney punches him hard. Striking out behind him with his elbow, he has the satisfaction of feeling it connect solidly with the man's midriff. "Come on man," he says to Jiron with a grin. "Don't just lie there!" Turning, he lashes out at the man as he comes back for another attack.

The place erupts into a full scale brawl. Chairs fly, mugs and tankards are used as projectiles. Jiron and the others hold the center of the tavern and the perimeter surrounding them is strewn with broken chairs, tables and unconscious bodies.

Reilin is still engaged with the woman and looks to be getting the worse of it. Blood drips from his nose and a goose egg sized lump is forming on the side of his head where one of the flying mugs connected with him when he tried to stand and get away from the woman.

The pit fighters are in their element. None are able to close with them without being pummeled hard. All the frustration Jiron has kept bottled up during the search for Tinok has been released and he feels better than he has in a long time.

Suddenly from the right, Shorty jumps back and cries out as a knife leaves a three inch long shallow cut across his forearm. A lull develops in the brawl as both sides size the other up. What once was a friendly fight has evolved into something more.

Weapons are now held in the hands of many of those who stand against them. One, the man who had been behind the bar, holds a crossbow leveled directly at them. He shouts something at the woman who now has Reilin in a strangle hold. When she doesn't respond, he nods for two of the men to come and drag her out of there.

When they get her off of Reilin, Jiron asks him, "You okay?"

"I'll live," he says then takes in the situation. "If we get out of here that is."

The barman with the crossbow begins talking to them and Reilin translates. "You picked the wrong place to mess around in," he says. "We don't take kindly to troublemakers."

"We'll pay for the damages and just go," Jiron says. Any chance of learning more about the necklace here is gone.

"No, I don't think so," he replies.

Jiron sees Shorty standing next to him and nods to the innkeeper. "You got him?" he asks.

"No problem," he replies in a barely heard whisper.

The barman raises his crossbow and aims it directly at Jiron.

"Kill them!" screams the woman who's being restrained from attacking them by two men.

"Now," Jiron says.

Before the barman has a chance to release the crossbow bolt, one of Shorty's throwing knives embeds itself in his chest. Looking down at the handle sticking out of his chest as if wondering how it got there, he staggers and then topples over.

Without hesitating, Jiron draws both knives and leaps at the man across from him. Even though the man's sword is out of its scabbard and in his hand, the unexpected move by Jiron catches him totally off guard. Bringing his sword up too late, he fails to block the thrust that takes him through the throat. Kicking out, Jiron knocks the man off his knife as he moves to the next. With a cry, the other pit fighters draw their weapons and the battle is joined.

Leaping up atop a table, Shorty pulls forth a throwing knife, takes aim and releases. The knife sails through the air and penetrates a man's chest to the hilt. By the time the man begins to fall, another knife has already left Shorty's hand with deadly results.

Two men with swords and another with a knife rush Scar and Potbelly. The first one falls to Scar's swords before he even realizes what he's facing. Potbelly then takes the one on the right and Scar the one on the left. With his knife, Potbelly deflects aside his opponent's thrust while striking out with a slash of his own. He feels his blade connect with the man's thigh. As the man's leg gives way due to the severed muscles, Potbelly kicks out with his foot and connects with his face, sending him stumbling backward.

Reilin blocks a downward thrust and sees the sword of another man coming at him when Stig's mace strikes the blade, breaking it in half. "Thanks," Reilin says as he blocks another strike by his opponent. Stig nods his head and engages another.

Faced with the deadly skill of the pit fighters, not to mention the fact that they have already mowed down half the people there, the rest of the patrons of the tavern begin to flee. Once the first person breaks off and races for the door, the rest of them quickly follow.

Reilin sees the woman running out the back door of the tavern. "Jiron!" he yells getting Jiron's attention. Indicating the open door where the woman fled, he says, "Her sister is the one we need to talk to."

With a nod, Jiron hollers, "After her!" Kicking out with his foot, he sends his opponent reeling backward then races to follow her. One man stands between him and the door. When he sees Jiron coming toward him, he dives out of the way rather than face his knives.

Jiron hits the doorway with the others right behind. As Shorty is about to pass through, he glances back at the grisly scene behind them. Fifteen men lay either dead or wounded, ten tables lie broken and tipped over, blood is everywhere. Then he runs to catch up with the others.

Racing down the hallway on the other side of the door, Jiron sees her flee out the door at the end of the hall. Lining the hallway are doors, most are closed but a few are open. Within are people in the throes of biloci. Either lying on beds or on top of blankets laid out across the floor, they are oblivious to the carnage in the other room.

Jiron reaches the door and flies out into the alley on the other side. Glancing to the left and right, he sees her fleeing form running down the alley to the right. "This way," he says to the others as he races to follow. "Stop!" he yells to her but his words have little effect.

She ducks into a doorway to the left and it slams shut. He hits the door running and bursts through after her. A small room lies on the other side of the door, another closed door sits in the opposite wall. He runs to it and tries to open it but find it's locked.

The others are quick to join him as he pulls a knife to work on the lock. "Stig, you stay here in case she doubles back," he says. "The rest of you fan out around the building in case she gets out. Reilin, you come with me."

As the others race back out into the alley, Jiron feels the lock click open. Replacing his knife in its sheath, he opens the door to find another hallway stretching further into the distance. On his right is a narrow spiraling staircase going up to the second floor.

He motions for Reilin to be still as he listens for any indication of where she might be. Then above them a floorboard creaks heavily as if a person of weight is moving around up there. *That has to be her!*

"Up the stairs," he says and takes them two at a time. Upon reaching the second level, he finds another hallway extending in the same direction as the one below had. The sound of the creaking floorboard had sounded like it was right above them when they were still on the first floor. So whoever is up here must be in one of the rooms near the stairwell.

Moving to the door to his right, Jiron kicks out with his foot and bursts the door open. A young woman stares at him with wide, fearful eyes from her bed. "Not this one," he says and moves to the next. Reilin tells the woman, "Sorry," then closes her door.

Making his way quickly over to the door on his left, he kicks it open. The woman from the bar is there with her back to a wall, in her hand she holds a knife out threateningly.

Jiron sees that she's all alone. Holding up his hands, he says to Reilin, "Explain to her that we mean her no harm. That I have no intention of hurting her." Reilin translates for the woman.

His words do little to convince her of his sincerity. Jiron steps into the room and the woman raises her knife a little bit higher. Reaching slowly into his pocket, he holds up a gold coin. Her eyes widen at the sight of it and the point of the knife drops slightly.

"Tell her that I'll give this to her for some information," he tells Reilin. When Reilin translates his message, her knife drops even further.

Footsteps are heard coming up the stairs and Scar makes his appearance. He quickly scans down both directions of the hallway and sees Reilin in the doorway to the woman's room. Coming over, he enters the room and brings his mouth close to Jiron's ear. "Make this fast, the city watch has shown up," he tells him.

Jiron nods and says, "Go get the others." Scar then races back downstairs to do as bidden. To Reilin he says, "Tell her I just want to ask her sister a question."

When Reilin translates, the woman's eyes get a calculating look and the knife falls even further. Finally, the woman puts the knife back in its sheath though her hand still rests upon its pommel. Then she asks something and Jiron looks to Reilin.

"She's asking what you wanted to ask her?" he explains.

He holds up the necklace so she can get a good look at it. Her eyes widen slightly in recognition as he asks, "Where did her sister get this?"

Then from below they hear many feet running along the floor. Then at the bottom of the stairs up to their level they hear a voice with the air of command shouting orders. "They're searching the building," Reilin says.

Then from the stairs they hear the sound of several people on their way up. "We got to get out of here!"

The woman just stares at him as Reilin takes him by the shoulder and urges him back into the hallway. With one last look at the woman, Jiron curses and puts the necklace back in his pouch. Racing down the hallway away from the stairs, they come to an open doorway on their right. Without hesitation, Jiron runs through the doorway just as the guards reach the top of the stairs.

From behind them, they can hear the woman's voice screaming. He looks to Reilin who says, "She's telling them where we are."

"Damn!" swears Jiron. Closing the door, he throws the bar. Not very large, the bar won't hold long if they really want to come in. And he's pretty sure they will.

A single window is the only other exit from the room. Moving over to it, he shoves it open and looks down. In the street below several people are milling about, none of them bear the uniforms of the city watch.

"Come on Reilin," Jiron says as he puts a leg through the window.

Bam!

The door is struck hard from the other side. A voice hollers to them through the door and Jiron doesn't need Reilin's translation to understand what it's saying. Taking hold of the window ledge, he swings himself out and then hangs briefly by his hands before letting go. He lands right next to someone and scares him to death. After jumping almost a foot in the air in shock, the man races off into the night.

Jiron scans the area for approaching trouble, but other than a few bystanders looking in his direction, everything is calm. Looking up, he sees one of Reilin's legs emerge through the window followed shortly by the other. As the rest of his body follows his legs out the window, a group of four men turn the corner of the building.

His heart skips a beat before he realizes that it's Scar and the others. "Over here!" he hollers to them.

Reilin lets go and drops from the window as the other four join them. Then all of a sudden, around the corner the others had just emerged from come a dozen guards. "Let's get the heck out of here!" Jiron says and bolts down the street. The guards see them run, and with a holler to stop, give chase.

Up ahead lies an opening of an alley and Jiron quickly ducks inside. Within the opening is a pile of old broken crates and other refuse. Jiron comes to a quick stop and grabs Shorty by the arm. "I want you to stay here and keep an eye on that serving woman," he explains quickly. "She's back in that building on the second floor, maybe she'll lead you to her sister."

Just then the guards round the corner and practically run into them. Scar and Potbelly knock the first two to the ground with well placed blows.

Shorty dives to the side of the alley near the pile of boxes and Jiron knocks them down on top of him. "Let's go!" he yells then races down the alley.

Stig takes one of the crates and throws it at the guards as he and the others high tail it out of there. The flying crate causes the guards to halt a brief moment before resuming the chase.

Jiron races through the alley and into the street on the other side with the others right on his tail. Hoping Shorty isn't discovered, they run and then quickly duck within a doorway that's half open. Stig's the last one through and shuts the door a second after the guards exit the alley.

They find themselves inside an herbalist's shop and the herbalist is sitting behind a counter with a surprised look on his face. Jiron pulls a knife and puts his finger to his lips indicating for the man to remain quiet. "Get behind the counter," he tells the others. Moving quickly, they pile in behind the counter.

No sooner Does Jiron duck back there after them than the door opens and two guards come in with swords drawn. The herbalist glances down at the men hiding under his counter and Jiron menaces him with his knife and again puts his finger to his lips.

Licking his lips and beginning to perspire with fear, the herbalist greets the guards. They exchange words several times and then the guards leave. Jiron looks to Reilin who says, "He didn't say anything about us being here."

Jiron gives the herbalist a grin and says "Good." Removing three silvers from his pocket, he lays them on the counter. "Tell him they are for his trouble." When Reilin translates, the herbalist nods but remains where he is and doesn't reach for the coins.

"Out the back gentlemen," Jiron says. As they leave, Jiron again turns toward the herbalist and pantomimes running his knife across his throat in warning. When he sees the herbalist nod his head, he follows the others out the back door.

In the alley behind the herbalist's shop, they pause a moment and listen for where the searching is going on. Determining that the street the alley exits out onto on their left is quieter, Jiron takes them that way.

For the next hour, they steadily work their way back to the inn where they left the others. Patrols of guards are out combing the streets and at times they're forced to wait in hiding for them to past. Finally, they see the inn down the road.

The street running in front of the inn is quiet. They watch for half a minute from the darkness of a nearby alley until they're sure no one is about. Then they race down the street toward the inn. When they get there, they duck down the side alley and enter the inn through the courtyard entrance.

Moving steadily but not seeming in too much of a hurry, they pass through the back half of the common room and up the stairs to their rooms. Outside of the room he's sharing with James, he places his ear against the door and can hear Miko inside talking in a normal tone. Relieved, he opens the door and enters.

At the opening of the door, James turns and sees him there in the doorway. Blood from the fight at the Split Navel stains his clothes, as it does all of them. Coming to his feet, he puts his hands on his hips and with an expression bordering on anger, he asks, "Just what have you done now?"

Chapter Sixteen

Standing there under James' withering glare, Jiron and the others tell him everything that happened. Hardly pleased with the situation, James has Reilin change out of his bloody clothes and then go down to the common room to keep an eye and ear out.

Once they all are in a fresh change of clothes, James pulls out his mirror and brings an aerial view of the inn into focus. Finding everything calm, he then concentrates on Shorty to see how he's making out. Casting a quick glance to Jiron he asks, "Do you really think that woman's sister will help you now? After everything you did?"

Shrugging, he says, "I can but try. It's the only thing that we have to go on now that your magic can no longer locate him."

Turning his gaze back to the mirror, he finds Shorty shrouded by darkness. It looks like he's just within some alley and is staring out across the street to a well-to-do building.

"She must be in there," observes Jiron from where he's looking over James' shoulder at the mirror.

"Must be," agrees James. Expanding the image to include a much wider area, he checks for any squads of guards that may be searching for them. The streets are quiet. Scrolling the image first in one direction then another, he fails to see any concerted search being conducted. "Doesn't appear as if they are continuing the search."

"A whole group of people dead, and they do nothing?" asks Brother Willim.

"Maybe the death of a bunch of potheads doesn't really concern them too much," James says. "Also consider this. The penalty of using or distributing biloci is death in the Empire. Who is going to come forward and say anything? Any who do will also have to admit their guilt."

"That's a good point," nods Scar. "They'd be sticking their own neck out for the executioner."

James abruptly stands up and says, "I don't care if they are looking for you guys or not. We're leaving Inziala right now." To Scar and Potbelly he says, "Go take our things down to the stables and get the horses ready to ride."

"What about that woman's sister?" objects Jiron. "I'm not leaving until I talk to her."

"Relax," James tells him. "You and I are going to go find Shorty and this woman, talk to her and then get the heck out of here. The rest of you stay here. Better yet, go down to the stables and wait there so we won't have to spend the time to come back up here for you."

"As you will," Brother Willim says.

"Let's go," urges Jiron.

James nods his head and indicates for him to leave the room. Following him into the hallway, he puts his mirror back in his belt pouch. Once down in the common room, they flag down Reilin who has taken a seat at a table near the door. He gets up and comes over to James who then quietly explains what they intend to do.

Jiron then leads James and Reilin out to the street through the front door and heads down in the general direction of the tavern. James pulls out his cloth and concentrates on Shorty. The cloth quickly rises and becomes rigid as it points to somewhere off to their right. He shows it to Jiron who allows him to take the lead. Following the direction indicated by the cloth, they are soon at the alley wherein Shorty watches.

As they come close, Shorty disengages from the shadows and steps forward. Waving for them to join him in the alleyway, he retreats back into its darkness. When they are there with him, he tells them what's going on. "I followed that woman when she left the building," he explains. "She came straight here and went in through that door." Pointing across the street, he indicates a door in the building directly across from them.

"How do we know she's still in there?" asks Jiron. "She could have left through a back door."

"That's always a possibility," replies Reilin.

"Now what?" asks Shorty.

"We wait," James says.

"Wait?" asks Jiron. "I say we go in there and find out what we need to know."

"Look," counters James, "We don't need more trouble. I doubt if she would leave by a back door, unless she knew she had been followed." Turning to Shorty he gives him a questioning look.

"She didn't," Shorty tells him. "Besides, if you start knocking on doors, you may alert her that we are here and she will flee."

James can see the warring desires within Jiron. Finally he comes to see the logic in what Shorty said and nods his head.

They wait there a half hour before the door they are keeping an eye on opens. Two figures leave the building and begin walking down the street. "Is that them?" James asks.

Both are cloaked with hoods over their heads. One is rather bulky and the other is slightly shorter and looks thinner. "It could be," Jiron says. Taking a step from the alley, he says, "Only one way to find out." Moving quickly, he crosses the street to confront them.

Before he has a chance to close half the distance, the larger of the two quickly glances in his direction. Seeing him approaching, the cloaked figure grabs the shoulder of the smaller and together begin running down the street.

"I guess that clinches it," Shorty says as he runs to help Jiron catch them. James and Reilin hurry to keep up.

The larger of the two begins slowing down while the smaller starts to pull ahead. Finally, the larger one shouts something to the other and comes to an abrupt halt. Pulling a large club from out of her cloak, the large woman from the tavern turns to face Jiron. So unexpected and quick was the maneuver, that Jiron fails to see the club in time and is forced to dive to the side in order to avoid the blow.

Hitting the street, he comes up with knives at the ready. "Get the other one!" he hollers to the others as they speed by. Turning to face the large woman, he draws his knives.

"Don't kill her!" James insists as he flies past with the other two in pursuit of the second cloaked figure.

Jiron makes no reply as he and the large woman stand there, each sizing up the other. "I don't want to kill you," Jiron says in a mild tone.

"I know," the woman tells him in heavily accented northern. "But you are going to hurt my sister."

Surprised, Jiron exclaims, "You understand me?"

"Yes," she replies.

"All I want is information," he tells her.

She looks at him like he's lying. "You are a killer," she says. "You come and kill and destroy." Stepping forward, she swings the club at Jiron's head.

Ready for the blow this time, he easily sidesteps the descending club. Moving in close, he strikes her on the side of the head with the pommel of one of his knives and then jumps back to avoid another blow. But another blow fails to materialize.

The woman staggers backward from the blow to her head, the club falls from her hand and she slams backward onto the street. Jiron cautiously moves forward and finds her eyes closed. Worried that he might have killed her, he's relieved when he sees her chest rise and fall as she draws in a breath. He's glad she is alive, he didn't really want to hurt her.

Getting to his feet, he turns and races after the others. The street ahead of him is deserted and quiet, he hopes he'll be able to find them.

Leaving Jiron behind to deal with the club wielding woman, Shorty races after the other fleeing figure. Suddenly, the hood of the cloak falls back and reveals a much younger and prettier woman than the one facing off against

Jiron. When she passes through light spilling from a window, Shorty is shocked to see just how lovely she is. *This can't be that woman's sister!*

She ducks down a side alley and Shorty follows. He casts a quick glance back to see James and Reilin not too far behind before he enters after her. The woman ahead of him shouts something into the dark as she runs and then all of a sudden several forms detach themselves from the shadows. He sees the moonlight glint off the weapon in one of their hands.

Before he's even conscious of the decision to draw one of his throwing knives, one is in his hand. The four forms ahead of him move to block his way and call out to him. Even though he can't understand what they are saying, he knows they want him to stop. But if he lets that woman get away, they may never find her again.

Letting fly his knife, he draws another quickly as the first one strikes home and sends one of the forms to the ground. No sooner does the first one hit the ground than another begins to fall with a knife embedded in his chest.

Suddenly, light fills the alley as an orb springs to life in James' hand. The two remaining men stand blocking the way with swords drawn. Shorty draws his fighting knives and advances, Reilin comes up behind him to give support.

As they engage the two men, James looks further into the alley and sees a face framed by yellow hair watch the fighting from a doorway. She locks eyes with James for a brief moment then ducks into the building, slamming the door shut.

Reilin blocks his opponents thrust and then lashes out with his fist, connecting with the man's face. Blood bursting from his nose, the man reels backward. Beside him, Shorty has managed to get within the defense of his opponent and sinks a knife to the hilt just below the man's sternum.

Shorty shoves his man to the right and Reilin bowls over his man to the left just as James races between them toward the door where the girl had looked out. Following along behind, Reilin and Shorty keep a look out for any others who may try to impede them.

At the door, James finds it's barred from the inside. Placing his hand against the door, he sends his senses to the other side. Finding the sliding bar that's holding the door closed, he gives out with a micro burst of magic and splinters the bar in two. Pulling on the handle, the door now swings open and the light from the orb reveals a room on the other side.

Small and dirty, this room looks to have been the living quarters of vagrants. Possibly even that of the men they left in the alley behind them. Another door stands ajar on the far side of the room. Crossing the filthy room, James opens the door and enters the hallway extending into the building.

Dark and quiet, the hallway reveals no clues as to the whereabouts of the woman. He pulls out his cloth and with the hope that the brief glimpse he had of her will be enough, sends forth the magic to find her. Concentrating on the face he saw, he directs the magic and the cloth rises to show the way. It points down the hallway and slightly to the right.

Moving slowly with Shorty and Reilin right behind, he makes his way down the hallway. As he progresses, the cloth at first moves slowly to the right. Then as they approach the fourth door on the right, it begins to move quicker until they come abreast of the doorway and it points directly to the door.

Putting away the cloth he turns to the others and whispers, "She's in there."

Shorty nods and moves to the door. Placing his hand upon handle, he slowly turns it. With a knife in his other hand, he opens the door into the room. The interior of the room is dark, and when he has the door half a foot into the room, a hand wielding a knife strikes out at him.

Dodging backward, he avoids the blow and grabs the attacker's arm. Pulling hard, he kicks the door open at the same time and the yellow haired girl is dragged from the room. With a cry, the woman loses her balance and falls to the floor. From within the room, a small child begins crying.

Shorty and Reilin wrestle with the woman and pin the arm with the knife behind her back. "Drop it!" Reilin tells her. Shorty pulls her arm up, increasing the pain until her fingers let go and the knife drops to the floor.

From up and down the hall, doors open and faces peer out only to slam shut once again when they see what's going on.

James opens the door and says, "Bring her inside." Keeping an eye out for any other possible attacks from within, he enters the room.

Sitting on the floor in the corner is a small boy who is the source of the crying they heard. Arms outstretched to the woman, his cries intensify when she doesn't immediately go to him.

To Reilin James says, "Tell her that we'll let her go to the boy if she promises not to try to run or attack us again."

Reilin talks to the woman and receives an answer. "She says she won't cause any trouble," he tells them.

"Then let her go to the boy," James says.

Shorty and Reilin release her. Running over to her son, as that is who it must be, she takes him in her arms. Putting her back to the corner, she looks at them with fear in her eyes as she talks softly to him. His cries begin to settle down now that he's in her arms.

"Go find Jiron and bring him here," James tells Shorty.

"Be right back," he replies then leaves the room quickly.

Once he's gone and the door closes, James turns back to the woman. He feels bad to have scared her and the boy. Unfortunately, the world being what it is, there is little trust in strangers. "Tell her that we don't plan to harm her or the child," he tells Reilin.

When he tells her that, she relaxes only a fraction. Then she says something to him. "She says she knows why we are here," Reilin relays to him.

Turning to look at the woman he asks, "And what would that be?"

After asking and receiving her reply, he says, "She says that her sister told her of what transpired at The Split Navel. Also Jiron's visit at her home."

"Ask her if she knows anything about the necklace that Gryll had," he says. When he spoke Gryll's name, she visibly perked up.

"You know Gryll?" Reilin asks her.

"Yes," she replies with eyes downcast.

"Do you know anything about the necklace bearing a heart and two stones?" he asks.

A tear wells in her eye as she nods her head.

Turning to James, Reilin says, "She knows. But something about this has her very upset." After a second he adds, "And I don't think it's us."

Then she starts speaking and the words just gush forth, as do her emotions. It takes her several minutes but when she's done, she cuddles very closely with her son as sobs wrack through her. His tiny hand pats her head as if he's trying to reassure her.

"She got pregnant with the boy before being married," he says. "Around here that means no man can honorably marry her. She is considered 'soiled'. The lives of such can be very bad at times, many don't survive or wind up in brothels."

"Then she and her sister came up with a plan. They figured that considering how beautiful she is, she might be able to win the heart of a man before he found out about the boy. While her sister kept the boy, she began frequenting places the affluent go. She met a man and worked her charms on him. Their plan had been working off and on for some weeks. During this time, the man had given her the necklace as a present, he never said where he had gotten it."

"Deciding she couldn't put off telling him any longer, she told the man about her son. He became enraged at her for deceiving him. He demanded the necklace back but she new it had to be worth many coins that she and her son would need. Saying that she would bring it to him, she then went and hid until her sister said the man had left town."

"Then about a month ago she was at The Split Navel with her sister, sometimes she picks up work there to help feed herself and her son. Well anyway, she happened to be going through a rough time and needed coins. So she asked around and finally Gryll had agreed to purchase it for far lower than its value. But she didn't argue, she desperately needed the coins. That was the last and only time she had met Gryll."

As Reilin draws his narrative to a close, James looks at the girl huddling with her child. By this time her sobs have subsided and she sits there just holding her son protectively. Sadness for her situation prompts him to reach into his money pouch and remove a fistful of coins. He moves across the room toward her and she cringes back away from him. Stopping halfway, he sets the coins down upon the floor then returns to where he was.

In amongst the copper the glint of silver and gold can be seen. James had even managed to scoop up one of his few remaining gems, for a green sparkle can be seen lying at the edge of the coins.

Her eyes widen at the sight of what for her must be an absolute treasure. Just then, the door behind them opens and Shorty walks in with Jiron right behind.

"I found him several streets over," Shorty says.

"So have you found out anything?" Jiron asks.

Not wishing to have her story rehashed again, he gives them the gist of it. Jiron starts to move toward her, but James puts a hand on his shoulder and says, "Let me. I think she's beginning to trust me."

Jiron looks to see the panic that has returned to her eyes when he began to approach and nods. "Alright," he says and then backs up.

"Tell her the coins are for her and her child," he says. When Reilin translates and her eyes light up, James nods for her to go ahead and get them.

She started to set the boy down until he began to start fussing. So with him in one arm, she goes over and scoops the coins into her tattered dress then returns back to her position with her back in the corner.

"Now, ask her if she could tell us the name of the man who gave her this necklace and where we might find him," he tells Reilin.

Nodding, Reilin asks her and then waits for her reply. After she's through, he turns back to James and says, "His name is Azku and the only city he ever mentioned was Morac. That was where he was going when he left here."

"Morac," says James. "That place sounds familiar."

"It should," Jiron tells him. "We went through it during our search for Miko."

Nodding his head, he says, "Right. It's further south of here."

"Everything is leading us south," observes Shorty.

"It does seem that way doesn't it," agrees Jiron.

"What can you tell us about him?" James asks her through Reilin.

"Not much," she admits. "He's slightly shorter than you, dark hair. I think he is a merchant of some kind though he was never very specific about it."

"Did he say anything else that might help us in finding him?" Jiron asks.

"There was one thing," she says. "He mentioned having to meet someone there when he arrived. I think the name of the place was The Cracked Ladle or something like that."

Turning to Reilin, James says, "Tell her that we thank her for her help." As Reilin starts talking to her, he adds, "And tell her that if she ever makes it Al-Ziron, to speak to the lord there and tell him that James would consider it a favor if he were to find her work." It's not much and she may not be able to make it that far, but he can't just leave her in her present situation.

He adds the final message and her face lights up and she nods. "Now," James says, "Let's get out of here."

Shorty opens the door and they file into the hallway. Just as James exits the room, a roar comes from the end of the hallway they originally entered from. Turning toward the noise, he sees the girl's sister charging them with club in hand. "Forget her," he hollers when he sees Jiron moving to intercept.

Racing down the other way, they flee the oncoming woman. When the roaring stops, James glances back to find the other sister standing in the hallway with her son, blocking the woman's path.

The door at the other end of the hallway opens onto one of the streets of Inziala. "Which way is the inn?" James asks. Completely turned around, he has no idea which way to go.

"It's this way," Shorty says as he indicates they should move down the street to their right.

"You sure?" James asks.

"Pretty sure," he replies.

Gesturing for him to take the lead James says, "Lead on." With Shorty in the lead, they make their way through the dark, deserted streets until the inn finally appears before them.

Once there, they go to the stables where they find everyone but Stig asleep in the stalls. James hadn't thought they were gone all that long.

"About time you guys showed up," Stig says as they enter. "I was getting worried."

The sound of his voice awakens the others and Potbelly asks, "Did you find out anything?"

"Yes we did," replies Jiron. "I'll tell you on the way out of town." Even though no apparent search is going on over the incident at The Split Navel, they have no desire to tempt fate by remaining in Inziala any longer than they have to.

It takes but a minute for everyone to mount their horses. Then with Jiron in the lead, they leave the stables and make their way onto the street. The clip-clop of their horses' hooves echo through the night. Moving quickly they reach the outskirts of town and have soon left Inziala behind as they take the road to the south.

Once past the last building, Jiron gets them up to a quick canter where they stay for an hour and then pull off the road for a brief rest stop until morning.

Chapter Seventeen

As the sun makes its way above the horizon, they break camp and make ready to ride. Jiron takes the lead with Reilin close behind in case they are approached along the road. The day goes by rather uneventfully. They pass through many small towns and when the sun begins its descent back to the horizon, the town of Jihara appears in the distance ahead of them.

"Should we stop there for the night?" asks Reilin.

Jiron gazes at the position of the sun and shakes his head. "There are still a couple hours of daylight left," he says.

Pushing on, they reach the walls of Jihara and work their way through its streets. Once on the south side, they resume their quick pace and leave it behind. Jiron keeps the pace quick until well after the sun has set and the stars have come out. When the horses begin to droop from the steady pace he's kept, he leads them off the road and they make camp. In the morning, they are again on the road before the sun even rises.

During the hour after they leave camp, James has Reilin ask a fellow traveler on the road how much further they have until they reach Morac. The traveler tells them they should reach it before late afternoon which greatly boosts Jiron's moral. The sooner he gets to the bottom of what happened to Tinok, the quicker he'll be able to track him down.

Anticipating that they will reach Morac before the end of the day, Jiron keeps them at their speedy pace. Hour after hour the miles fly by until two hours after noon when a city appears out of the horizon ahead of them. "That has to be it," asserts Jiron.

As they draw closer to the walls, James all of a sudden starts chuckling to himself.

"What's so funny?" asks Miko.

James glances at him and then over to Jiron. He can see Jiron's ears burning slightly with the memory of their last visit to Morac. "Should I tell him or do you want to?" he asks.

"You can," he replies. "This is the one story you love to tell."

"I do don't I," he states with a grin. "On our way to rescue you from the mines, we passed through here. This was just after Cassie died and Jiron's friend Tinok left. Yes," he says, "the same one we're searching for. Anyway, Scar, Potbelly and several others took Jiron into town to get the recent events off his mind. To make a long story short, Roland and I had to go and find them when they didn't return. Seems they ran afoul of a woman and her old mother who somehow managed to get them into the basement of their house and tied them up."

He pauses a moment and then looks to Jiron. "You never actually told me how you got down there," he says.

"Frankly James," he says, "I don't remember." The blush that comes to his cheeks tells him that he probably does.

"Right," replies James with a little sarcastic tone to his voice.

Miko grins and Reilin actually breaks out into laughter at Jiron's and the other's expense. Jiron casts him a dirty look and he brings his amusement under control.

By this time they've come close to the gates of the city. The traffic moving in and out is quite heavy for this time of the day. They make their way closer to the gate and take their place in line. Somewhere behind the walls is a man named Azku and Jiron intends to find this man before the sun rises the following morning.

The line entering the city continues to move forward until they are but a few people away from the gate. When it's their turn to pass through, a squad of guards exits from within the city. All of a sudden they are surrounded by guards and James is about ready to panic. Then Jiron shakes his head telling him not to worry. The guards are merely there to relieve the ones who were on duty. Paying those in line little attention, the new arrivals take position while the ones being relieved form up to march back inside. James and the others pass through the gate quickly and into the city before the changing of the guard can be completed.

"Better find an inn first so the rest of us can be out of sight while you go in search of this Azku," suggests James.

"Very well," he says and starts scanning the streets for any sign of an inn. When he comes across a three story building bearing a sign depicting a winged bird in flight, he comes to a stop out front. He and the others wait while Reilin enters to see about getting the rooms.

They don't have long to wait before Reilin makes his appearance back out the front door. He holds up the keys showing them he got the rooms. Then they take the horses around back to the stables and are soon up in their rooms.

Dinner is still a couple hours away so Jiron suggests that he take Reilin and see about locating The Cracked Ladle. James tells him to take Stig along just in case and the three of them leave on their hunt.

Jiron hits the stairs down to the common room almost at a run in his impatience. "Hey," Stig cautions, "not so fast. We don't want to draw any attention."

Jiron holds back several choice words about unwanted attention, but heeds Stig's warning and slows down. Once in the common room they make their way through the tables toward the door. Several of the tables have men and women taking their ease during the heat of early evening. One of the ladies gives Jiron a slight grin and a wink. If he wasn't so intent on finding out what this man knows about Tinok, he might have paused. But then thoughts of Aleya come to mind and any errant thought he has about the woman in the common room vanishes like a breeze.

They exit through the door and come to a stop in the street. Unsure where the Cracked Ladle lies, Jiron has Reilin ask one of the passersby. Luck is with them and the man is able to give them directions. He points down the street they are currently on and tells them to continue for six blocks, then to take a right. And that's where his memory gets a little hazy. "It borders on a plaza that has a three tiered fountain," he says. "You can't miss it, it's the only public fountain here in Morac. Also, atop the uppermost tier of the fountain lies a statue of Aziki."

"Aziki?" asks Reilin. The man looks at him odd that he wouldn't know who Aziki is. "Oh yeah, right," he says to the man then thanks him for his help. He indicates to Jiron and Stig that he's got the directions and leaves the man standing there as he rejoins the others. Glancing back, he sees the man still standing there looking at him oddly. *Wonder who this Aziki is?*

Leading the others, he takes them down six blocks and then turns right down a cross street. "Somewhere in this area is a fountain with a statue of someone on top of it," he tells them. "The Cracked Ladle borders the plaza."

"Excellent," says Jiron. They continue down a few more blocks and at each intersection of streets they come to they scan down the cross streets for the fountain. The first two intersections yield nothing, but at the third when they look down to the left, they see over the heads of the crowds on the streets, a statue of a warrior.

"That must be it," Reilin observes.

"Let's hope so," Stig says.

Moving down the street to their left, they work their way through the crowds until the street opens onto the plaza the man had described. The splash of water can be heard as it cascades over the tiers of the fountain. It's actually quite large and children, some of them naked, are playing in the water.

The buildings bordering the plaza all look fairly identical. Most appear to be open markets where many people are currently looking over goods or sitting at tables having a drink or a meal.

"Which one is it?" Stig asks.

"The name indicates an eatery," Jiron replies. "Let's make our way around the plaza and see if there's a sign hanging out front of one of them that may tell us."

Moving through the crowds, they work their way from one shop to the next. By the time they have made a complete circle and come back to where they started, no sign indicating a Cracked Ladle could be seen.

"Go ask someone," Jiron finally tells Reilin.

Nodding, Reilin goes to one of the men passing by and asks, "Excuse me sir, could you tell me which one of these establishments is the Cracked Ladle?"

The man stops and peers at him through squinted eyes as if he's unable to see well. "The Cracked Ladle you say?" he asks. Casting his eyes around the plaza, they finally stop at one with a red tapestry bearing the design of a sword hanging next to the door. "I believe that is the one there."

"Thank you good sir," Reilin says before the man walks away. Returning to the others, he indicates the door with the red banner and says, "It's that one."

"Doesn't look like an eatery," Stig says.

"No, it doesn't," agrees Jiron. Turning to Reilin he asks, "Are you sure that's the one the man told you?"

Nodding, Reilin replies, "Absolutely."

"Very well then," Jiron says. Moving out, he crosses the plaza toward the door next to the red banner. Coming up to it, he takes hold of the handle and pushes it open.

On the other side they find a wide hallway extending further back. Lining the hallway are six suits of armor three to a side, each one from a different nation or era. "I don't think this place is an eatery," whispers Reilin when he sees the armor.

"I wouldn't think so," Jiron says as he passes through the doorway. His feet echo off the hardwood floor. Gazing down at it, he suddenly realizes whatever this place is, it has money. A floor like this, especially in this part of the world, had to have cost a fortune.

Just after the six suits of armor, the hallway ends at an open archway. On the other side is a large room, richly furnished. Couches, chairs and tables are spaced in such a way as to afford at least a small amount of privacy to those using them. Rugs line the floor and tapestries hang along the walls. Not cheap ones, these look to be made of fine cloth by master artisans. A few statues sprinkled here and there give the room an even added touch of elegance.

The room is empty but for a lone gentleman sitting at one of the tables reading a book. As they enter the room the man looks up from his reading, his expression is one of irritation. His eyes never leave them as Jiron comes to a stop just within the room.

He looks at the man then glances around the room in the hopes of someone else making an appearance that they could deal with. When after a minute of fruitless waiting, he sighs and begins walking over to the man.

Reilin walks at his side and notices the man's mood turns darker when he realizes they mean to approach him. "Good day," Reilin greets the man as they reach the table. Coming to a stop, they give the man a slight, respectful bow in the hopes of mellowing out his mood.

Unresponsive, the man continues to glare at them.

"We were hoping you could tell us if this is in fact the Cracked Ladle?" Reilin asks.

The man's eyes flick from one to the other. He closes his book and sets it on the table before him. "It is," he replies.

Reilin turns to the others and translates, "He said it is."

"Good," says Jiron.

Jiron was just about to tell Reilin to ask about Azku when the man says in perfect northern, "I can understand you."

"Thank goodness," he says turning to the man. "This doesn't look like an eatery."

"That's because it isn't," the man explains. Remaining ramrod straight in his chair, the man's expression hasn't softened in the least.

"Oh?" asks Stig. "What kind of place is this?"

"One where those who are not invited are not welcome," he states. "You are intruding where you don't belong. Please leave."

"But we have come a very long way," objects Jiron. "We very much need to find a man by the name of Azku. We've been told he comes here."

The man's eyes react slightly when Jiron said the name 'Azku', then returns to the same perturbed expression once more. "Please leave," the man says again. "I don't wish to tell you a third time."

Jiron locks gazes with the man and begins contemplating the ramifications if he were to force the man to talk to them.

"Oh, hello," a voice says from behind them, also in northern.

They turn to see another man, this one wearing a more jovial expression. "I see you've met Kozal," the jovial man says with a smile. Then he glances to the man in the chair and says, "Being your usual unpleasant self?"

"They've got no right to be in here," Kozal says.

"I suppose in the strictest sense that is true," the jovial man states. "But you can be my guests and that will settle that."

The man in the chair picks up the book and grumbles something as he returns his eyes back to its pages.

"Don't let Kozal's unpleasantness give you the wrong impression of us here at the Order of the Scarlet Sword," the jovial man says. He glances again at the man at the table and whispers to them, "We better find another place where we can talk so we won't bother him any longer."

"How about outside in the street," mumbles Kozal.

Shaking his head at Kozal's rudeness, the jovial man indicates for them to follow him. "We don't get many visitors here," he explains.

"I never heard of the Order of the Scarlet Sword," Jiron says.

"Not too surprising," the man replies. "Even here in the Empire it's not too well known. Being from the north, I would have been surprised if you had heard of it."

"What is it?" Stig asks.

"It's kind of like a guild," he replies. "Those of us who belong to the Order of the Scarlet Sword are mainly comprised of soldiers, fighters, weapon smiths and a few others whose profession has to do with such things. I believe we even have a couple Empire Commanders and Commanders of Ten counted as members." As he talks he takes them through the room and opens a door on the far side.

The hallway they find themselves in has a very fine carpet lining the floor. The walls are adorned with many fine works of art. "There's a room down here where we can have some peace and quiet while we talk."

"Are you a swordsman then?" asks Jiron. From the man's manner and build, he would hardly consider him a formidable opponent if he were.

"No," he replies. "I've never been one for the actual use of weapons. Rather, I teach those willing to learn."

He stops before a door on the left side of the hallway and removes a key. Using the key to unlock the door, he opens it and leads them inside. The room they find themselves in, considering the ostentatiousness of what they've seen so far, is rather plain. A simple wooden table in the center of the room with chairs set around it upon a bare wooden floor.

"Now, if you will take a seat," the man replies, "we can discuss whatever it is that brought you here."

Jiron takes his seat but feels slightly put off by the amicable nature of their host. "Who are you?" he asks.

"Where are my manners?" he asks. "You can all me Ohan."

"Ohan?" asks Stig. "I don't think I've ever heard that name before."

Ohan gives him a grin and says, "Not too surprising. In my life I've only encountered one other person who had the privilege to be called such. And that was quite a ways from here as a matter of fact."

"Indeed," says Jiron.

"You seem awfully...uh..." stammers Reilin.

"Nice?" he asks. When Reilin nods he shrugs and says, "To be honest I'm just bored. My job is to take care of the members here and to keep the House in order. Aside from Kozal, you are the only ones I've seen in days. And frankly, he isn't much of a conversationalist."

Jiron is beginning to warm up to the man. Giving him a grin he says, "I could see that."

"Oh, he's not a bad sort once you get to know him," he replies. "Just likes to read. Never saw an ex-swordsman read like he does. Anyway, we are getting away from what it is that brought you here."

"We are looking for a man by the name of Azku," Jiron explains.

"Azku you say?" he asks.

"Do you know him?" asks Stig.

"I know several men by the name of Azku," he replies. "Two happen to be members that stop by here from time to time."

"The one we wish to contact was in Inziala about a month ago," explains Jiron. "Said he was stopping by here when he left."

"Hmmm," Ohan says as he visibly turns inward to think about what Jiron just said. Finally after a full minute of contemplation, he nods and says, "Yes. I think I know the one you are looking for."

Excited, Jiron says, "Can you tell us where he is?"

Shaking his head, Ohan says, "Sorry, that would be against the rules I'm afraid."

"Can you at least tell us if he's here in town?" Stig asks.

"I am not sure to tell you the truth," he replies, "haven't seen him in a couple days. Although many of the members don't always drop by here on a daily basis."

Jiron looks at the man, frustrated by his lack of help despite his friendly and accommodating nature. "Is there any way in which you can be of help?" he finally asks.

"Oh yes," he replies. "You could leave him a message that I will be more than happy to deliver to him as soon as he puts in an appearance."

"Which could be a long time?" asks Jiron.

"I'm afraid so," Ohan answers.

Stig looks to Jiron and says, "It's better than nothing."

Jiron thinks for a moment and then says, "If that's the best you can do, so be it. Tell this Azku that we are staying at the Soaring Eagle and that this regards a certain incident that happened back in Inziala. Tell him the woman in question is with child and we desire to settle this matter forthwith."

Ohan's eyes widen at that. "Is the parentage of the child in doubt?" he asks.

"As for that," replies Jiron. "It might be best if I take it up with Azku."

Nodding, Ohan says, "That may be the wisest course."

"So do I," replies Jiron. Standing up, he says, "We thank you for your time and if you should see him, also tell Azku that we are leaving on the morrow. It would be best for all parties to have this settled before that time."

"Should I see him, I will most assuredly let him know," he states.

"Excellent," says Jiron. Indicating for the other two to stand, he gestures for Ohan to escort them out.

"I must say," he begins as they leave the room, "you gentlemen certainly have laid waste to the monotony which is the life of a Caretaker. Thank you very much for coming."

"Any time," Stig says.

Out in the main room, Kozal is still at the table reading. His eyes flick up and remain on them until they enter the hallway with the suits of armor. Stig definitely does not like the man's attitude.

Once they've reached the door leading outside, Ohan opens it for them and bids them good day. Jiron and the others leave the Order of the Scarlet Sword and pass back into the plaza. He stops abruptly when he notices something he hadn't before.

"What?" asks Stig.

Indicating the statue atop the fountain, he says, "Look at the way it's facing." When the others look, they see what he means. The statue is facing directly toward the door leading into the Order of the Scarlet Sword.

"So?" asks Reilin. "It has to face somewhere."

"I don't know," he replies. "It just struck me as odd that a statue of a soldier is facing the entryway to a guild of soldiers."

"Think there could be some connection?" asks Stig.

"Maybe. But right now I'm not really concerned about it." Turning toward the other two he says, "All I care about right now is talking to Azku."

"He may not even be in the city," says Reilin.

"Perhaps," states Jiron. "Although after the message I left, if he is we will know soon." Stepping out, he leads them back to the Soaring Eagle to wait for Azku's appearance.

Chapter Eighteen

Back at the inn they tell James and the others about what transpired at the Order of the Scarlet Sword. At the description of the red banner that hung by the door, Scar interrupts by saying, "I think there was one in the City of Light." All conversation ceases as every eye turns toward him. "If you described the banner hanging out front correctly, then there was one just like it on Copper Street."

"Wasn't that within the merchant's district?" asks Stig.

"That's right," replies Scar. "I met a patron in that area for some reason, I forget exactly why, but I do remember seeing a banner just like the one you mentioned hanging on a building there." He can see the doubt in some of their eyes. "I'm telling the truth."

"I believe you," says Shorty. "I saw it too."

"What can it mean then?" asks Reilin.

James soon finds everyone's eyes upon him for some sort of explanation. "Don't look at me," he says. "I don't know."

"But you can guess," says Jiron. "You always have some idea about everything."

"Do I?" he asks surprised. When everyone nods their head, he shrugs. "Guess it's due to my over active imagination. Always made me a good Dungeon Master." When he sees them looking confused by the term, he waves away the question that was on their tongues. "It doesn't matter."

"Well?" asks Jiron.

"Maybe it's a guild that transcends nationality," he replies. "From what you said, it's comprised of fighters and those who have dealings with them such as weapon smiths and those scholars who deal with the theory of fighting." Looking to Jiron he asks, "The man said that a Commander of Ten was a member?"

Jiron nods. "Yes, that's what he said."

James remembers going up against one of those on his trip to recover Miko from the Empire. The one he faced was exceptionally skilled with the sword not to mention the added ability to use magic. "It seems odd that such a one would be a party to something that consists of elements outside of the Empire."

"When this Azku gets here," Jiron says, "we'll ask him."

The others agree and for the next several hours they toss around different ideas of what the Order might mean, what it does, that sort of thing.

Darkness settles in with a vengeance and they finally decide Azku is not going to make an appearance this evening. James sends them all to their rooms and then climbs into bed. He no sooner blows out the candle than there's a knock on the door.

Jiron is out of bed in a flash and runs to the door. Flinging it open, he sees one of the inn's boys standing outside. The boy hands him a letter and says something in the Empire's tongue then turns around to head back downstairs.

"Reilin!" Jiron calls out.

A nearby door opens up and Reilin sticks his head out. "What?" he asks.

Indicating the departing boy, Jiron holds up the recently delivered letter and says, "Ask him where this came from."

Moving from the doorway, Reilin hurries toward the boy and hollers for him to stop. The boy pauses at the top of the stairs and turns back to see what Reilin wants. Reilin and the boy exchange a few words before the boy turns back to the stairs and heads down.

Returning to where Jiron waits in the doorway, he says, "One of the street kids delivered this and said it was for you."

"Me?" asks Jiron, looking at the letter.

"Yes," he replies. "The kid didn't give any further explanation other than that a man had asked him to deliver it right away."

"Must be from Azku," says James.

Jiron hands the letter to James and says, "Can you read it?"

Taking the letter, James opens it and finds it is written in the northern tongue. "Yes I can," he replies.

"What does it say?" Jiron asks.

"It says…

Red Lantern Bridge. One hour. Come alone.

"Red Lantern Bridge?" asks Stig. The others have gathered in the hallway to see what's going on.

To Reilin, Jiron says, "Go downstairs and see if you can find out where we can find Red Lantern Bridge."

Nodding, Reilin says, "Right." He then turns and hurries to the head of the stairs. In a second he's disappeared down the stairwell.

James indicates for everyone to come into his room while they wait for his return.

"Looks like you got his attention," says Brother Willim.

"If it is him," says Miko. "We have been misdirected before."

"I agree," James says. "There's no way to know if this is from him or not."

"I realize that," states Jiron. "I'm not stupid." He puts his arm around Aleya and they wait for Reilin's return.

A few minutes later, the door opens and Reilin walks in. "I found out where it is," he announces.

"Where?" Jiron asks.

"It's in the heart of the city," he explains. "A tributary from the river winds its way through underground tunnels until it emerges in a large park area the locals have constructed. The waterway runs for two hundred feet before returning to the underground tunnels on its way back to the river. Several foot bridges span it and one of them has two red lanterns that are lit at either end during the night. That's where its name came from."

"Where is it?" he asks.

Reilin explains. "If you follow the street running in front of the inn down to the right for six blocks then take a left, that street will take you all the way to the park. From there, just look for the red lanterns."

"Very good," Jiron says as he stands up. "I'll be back," he tells the others.

Aleya grabs him by the shirt and says, "It might be a trap."

"I know," he says. "I'll be careful."

"We're going with you," says James.

"The note said to come alone," he objects. "If I bring all of you, he may not show himself."

"Don't worry," assures James. "We will be at a discreet distance and I'll use my mirror to keep an eye on what's going on. If trouble arises, we will rush to your aid."

He considers the plan for a second then nods. "Just don't be too close," he says.

"We won't I assure you," James tells him.

"Alright then, let's go," he says.

Aleya jumps up and rushes to her room where she returns with her bow and quiver of arrows slung across her back. "A bit conspicuous don't you think?" asks Brother Willim when he sees her.

She puts on her cloak to hide her weapon but now simply looks like a severely hunchbacked woman. "Any better?" she asks.

"No," he replies shaking his head. "Best to just leave it off."

Taking off her cloak, she then removes her bow and quiver. Wrapping them within the cloak, she tucks the bundle under her arm and then looks to Brother Willim. "Better?" she asks.

Nodding with a grin, he says, "Much." In his hand he carries his staff, the only weapon the Priests of Asran are allowed to utilize.

Now that everyone is ready, Jiron makes for the stairs and then down to the common room. He angles for a side door that leads into the alley between the Soaring Eagle and the chandlery shop that is next door.

Once in the alley, he turns to James and says, "Stay a good deal behind me. He could be observing us right now."

"Understood," he says as he places his hand on Jiron's shoulder. "Good luck."

"Thanks." Turning toward the street which passes before the inn, he moves quickly. Reaching the street, he turns to the right and is gone."

"How long do you think we should wait?" asks Stig.

"A couple minutes or so," replies James. Taking out his mirror, he soon has Jiron in sight as he walks down the street. Giving him some time to put distance between them, he waits until he reaches the street that he's supposed to turn down. Once he sees Jiron turn onto the other street, he glances up and says, "Okay, let's go."

Moving to the end of the alley, Scar and Potbelly take the lead while James stays in the middle of the group. Miko takes his arm to help guide him as he's trying to keep Jiron in view with his mirror.

"Not too fast," he says. "We don't want to catch him before he gets there. Remember, the meeting is for an hour from now, we still have some time." Scar and Potbelly slow down to a more moderate pace.

Keeping a constant eye on the mirror, he sees Jiron reaching what must be the park. The street he's walking upon opens out onto a large area with trees, grass and many walkways. Benches are spaced periodically along the walkways. Some even now have people taking their ease upon them, primarily couples.

When James' group turns onto the street leading to the park, he glances up and looks around. To Scar and Potbelly he says, "Try to find an out of the way place where we can hold up until he needs us."

Another street down they come to a closed open air eatery. The place looks like it hasn't been open for some time. Adjacent to it is an area deep in shadow with tables and chairs where patrons could dine on the food they purchase. Scar leads them to the table furthest from the street where the shadows are the deepest.

"Best we're going to find," he says.

"This will do nicely," says James. Then to the pair he says, "Keep watch."

Nodding, they move back to separate locations near the street where shadows help to conceal them from those passing by.

James takes a seat and lays the mirror upon the table. Everyone else gathers around to see how Jiron makes out.

After leaving the others behind in the alley by the inn, he got to thinking about what if Azku doesn't speak his language. He almost turned around to take Reilin with him but then remembered that the note the boy had delivered was written in northern. Plus, it did say come alone. He hopes Ohan back at the Order of the Scarlet Sword mentioned that few of them spoke the Empire's tongue.

He counts off the streets he passes and when he comes to the sixth intersection, takes the street branching off to the left. It takes him some time to traverse the length of the street to the park, but the street finally ends and the park unfolds before him.

If it wasn't for the distraction of his worry about Tinok, he might've been able to enjoy it more. Several cobblestone paths wind through the trees and grass, benches are spaced in such a way that those who decide to rest for awhile, may do so in private. Quite an unusual sight to find here in the desert.

Just past where the street ends is a large open area from which the paths through the park begin. A lone musician is setting up to play there in the open area. He puts a bowl down on the cobblestones, takes the guitar-like instrument in hand and soon has a lively melody coursing through the park.

Jiron ignores him and scans the park for any sign of red lanterns. Not seeing anything immediately, he decides to take the center path through the park. At some point it has to intersect or come close to the branching of the river that is supposed to flow through here. Then it will be easy enough to follow the water until he comes across the bridge.

Stepping quickly, he enters the park. Lights begin to flare into being as two men move from lamp pole to lamp pole, lighting the lanterns hanging there. The sight of them lighting the lanterns gives him the thought that perhaps the lanterns on the bridge haven't been lit yet. Whether they have or not, he still feels confident that he can find them.

The path he's on doesn't go in a straight line, rather it winds first this way then that in a leisurely progression through the trees. When at last the smell of water comes to him, he stops and tries to ascertain which direction it's coming from. Before he can determine which way, the sound of water running over rocks can be heard coming from his right.

Moving off the path, he cuts through a small copse of trees. When he exits the other side, the small branch of the river appears before him. He looks first one way then the other and spies a bridge spanning the water off to his left. No red lights come from the area, but then none of the other lanterns in the area have been lit yet.

He can see one of the lantern lighters making his way along the cobblestone path leading to the bridge. Light after light flares to life as the man works his way closer, lighting each lantern in turn. When the man at last lights the lantern hanging from the pole just before the bridge, Jiron holds his breath. If those lanterns there on the bridge don't burn red, he's going to have some words with Reilin.

The man approaches the bridge and brings his long stick with a burning candle on the top toward the lantern. Jiron watches from the trees as the candle enters the lantern. Then a burst of red light appears and he sighs in relief. This is the place.

He's not exactly sure, but he thinks he may have a half hour left before the time of the meeting. Scanning the park, he finds one of the benches that's close to the bridge. Fortunately it's currently not occupied. Facing the bridge as it is, it will afford him a good view of whoever crosses it. Sitting down, he settles in to wait.

"What's he doing?" Stig asks.

"Waiting, of course," explains Miko. "There's still some time before the hour is up."

"Suppose no one shows?" asks Aleya. Already she has taken her bow and quiver of arrows from out of her cloak. The quiver is slung over her shoulder while her bow is in hand, strung and ready just in case.

"Go back to the Cracked Ladle I guess," James replies with a shrug. "We'll worry about the 'what ifs' should it prove necessary." He always hated it when someone did the 'what ifs'. It never ended and eventually he got on them about it and made them stop.

As it looks like nothing is going to happen right away, they relax. All that is but James who must maintain the image in the mirror. He's not about to take the chance that something may happen should he but looks away for an instant.

A few couples have made their way across the bridge during the time Jiron spent observing it, as well as half a dozen kids. At one point while he was waiting, a man came and sat down on the bench next to him then started talking to him. The man was dressed well and seemed a friendly sort. Of course the fact that he was speaking the Empire's tongue posed a difficult problem.

Feigning a sore throat and that he couldn't talk, Jiron coughed a few times and the man eventually got the idea. Getting up, he says something that was probably close to 'Hope you get better' and then walked off.

As the man walked away, Jiron wondered if that could have been the man he was supposed to meet. He doubts it, the man didn't seem to be other than what he appeared, someone out for an evening stroll before bedtime.

The time comes when Jiron figures it must be close to the appointed hour. Coming to his feet, he leaves the bench behind and makes his way over to the bridge. Still looking around, he doesn't see anyone nearby. Stepping out onto the bridge, he walks until he's reached about mid-span then stops. Turning to face one side, he leans his forearms on the rail and waits.

"He's on the bridge," James tells them. He scrolls the image around the area to see if he can discover anyone approaching.

Aleya comes over and looks at the image in the mirror. "He's awfully exposed there," she says worriedly. "One arrow and it's all over."

"Let's hope it doesn't come to that," says Brother Willim.

"Yes," mumbles James, "let's." Scrolling the image further, he suddenly sees half a dozen men moving down a path that runs along the edge of the water toward the bridge. "Might have something here," he announces. The others move in close to watch.

The path the six men are on comes to a forking. Either they can continue on the path which continues straight, or take the other path that crosses another of the bridges over the water to the other side. The men come to a stop for a moment. Then three of the men move to take the path over the bridge. Once on the other side they quickly leave the path and split up. They then begin making their way through the park toward the bridge upon which Jiron is waiting. Two of the three remaining men also leave the path on their side of the water and work their way toward where Jiron waits.

Stig says, "They're surrounding him."

"We can't just sit here!" exclaims Aleya. "He needs us."

Shaking his head, James says, "Not yet."

"What do you mean not yet?" asks Aleya. "They are *surrounding* him! We can't just sit and wait for them to kill him."

"We aren't even sure they mean him any harm yet," offers Brother Willim. "If we move prematurely, it may spoil whatever chance Jiron has of finding out what he needs to know."

"But..." she begins then trails off when she realizes the rest are willing to wait. Moving closer to James, she watches the events unfolding in the mirror. The five men that have moved off the path are making a circuitous route around to the far side of the bridge. Not directly, rather moving back and forth like they are hunting for someone.

"Could they be looking to see if he's brought someone else?" Reilin asks.

Nodding, James says, "That's entirely possible." The man who had remained on the path remains at the spot where the group split up, as if he's waiting for something. Returning the image to the men among the trees, he sees them coming to meet on the opposite sides of the river further downstream from the bridge. They pause there for but a moment before returning along almost the exact same route they took the first time.

Once they've come back to the man on the path, they confer for a moment then the five men move back into the trees. Before they disappear into the shadows, James sees two of them remove crossbows they had hidden beneath their cloaks. The sixth man begins walking quickly toward the bridge where Jiron waits.

Aleya gasps when she sees the crossbows but the others tell her they have to wait.

Jiron has grown impatient. It must be past the time already and still no one has made any attempt to contact him. He starts to think that perhaps there is another Red Lantern Bridge in this city and that he's at the wrong one. Making up his mind to wait for a count of a hundred heartbeats, then if the man still hasn't made an appearance, he'll leave.

At sixty-six heartbeats, the trod of someone upon the cobblestones is heard coming toward the bridge. Jiron turns his eyes to the sound and can see the silhouette of a man passing through the light from one of the lampposts.

As the man enters the last lighted area before the bridge, Jiron can make out some of his features.

He's definitely a man of the Empire, there can be no doubt of that. Other than that, it's hard to determine anything else about him. Turning onto the bridge, the man comes forward and stops six feet from Jiron.

"Are you the one whom I was to meet here?" Jiron asks.

"I am," the man replies.

Pulling forth the necklace, Jiron says, "I am interested in knowing where you came by this." He holds it up so the heart with two diamonds is clearly visible.

The man's eyes betray the anger he's keeping in check. "Is this why you wanted to meet with me?" he asks.

"Yes," replies Jiron. "It's of the utmost importance that I know where you got it."

"Then what you told Ohan was…" he says, his words trailing off.

"A ruse," finishes Jiron. "Yes, I'm sorry about that. But I desperately need to talk to you."

The man's face turns red in anger. "We are finished here," he says and abruptly turns around to walk away.

Jiron moves forward and places his hand on the man's shoulder. "I need to know where you got this!" he insists.

From out of the trees, a crossbow bolt flies and embeds itself in the bridge's railing not two inches from where Jiron stands. "Let go or the next one won't miss," the man says.

Jiron glances to the direction from which the bolt was fired but the light from the lanterns at either end of the footbridge prevents him from seeing very far into the darkness. He releases the man's shoulder and takes a step backward. The man then continues his way to the end of the bridge.

"Did you see that?" asks Aleya. "They shot a crossbow bolt at him." She looks to James who in turn glances to Scar.

"Go get him and bring him back here," he says and then returns his attention to the mirror. As the others except Miko and Brother Willim rush to Jiron's aid, he keeps the bridge's image in the mirror. Jiron stands there with his arms slightly out from his body as he watches the man walk away. James was sure the bolt was more of a warning than anything else. Otherwise the two men with crossbows would have both fired.

Before the man moves out of the light at the end of the bridge, he sees Jiron moving his arms. It takes him but a moment to realize that he's signaling him to follow the man with his mirror.

"I don't think this went well," he says to Miko. Scrolling the image, he follows the man as he moves down the cobblestone path. Once he's far enough away to be out of visual sight of the bridge, the five other men that had accompanied him to the park appear and leave with him.

Brother Willim and Miko sit on either side of him as together they watch the six men move through the park. James wants to know what happened to Jiron but doesn't dare take the image off the man for fear of losing him. He half expected Jiron to launch an attack on the man but after several minutes go by, he returns to the deserted open air eatery with the others.

"You got him?" he asks when he sees James still watching the mirror.

James nods his head in reply, never taking his eyes off the man. "What did you find out?" he asks.

"He definitely knows something," he explains. "But once he learned that what I told Ohan at the Order of the Scarlet Sword wasn't entirely accurate, he left."

"I don't know if the others told you yet or not," James says, "but there were five others with him stationed out in the trees surrounding the bridge."

"Yeah, I kind of figured something like that when the bolt hit the bridge," he replies.

James motions him over and Miko gets up from his seat to allow Jiron a closer view of the mirror. Scar and Potbelly resume their positions by the road to keep an eye on anyone passing by. However at this hour of the night, the number of people on the streets is dwindling rapidly.

They continue watching the men work their way through town. At one point, three of the men depart and head off on another side street. At the next intersection, another one leaves as well. The remaining man stays with him the remainder of the way until he arrives at a very nice townhouse. Four stories tall, the building is quite impressive.

The two men climb the three steps to the door where the man reaches in his cloak and removes a key. Placing it in the lock, he opens the door and enters. The other man follows him in and closes it behind them.

James cancels the spell and sits back. He rubs his neck as it grew stiff from bending over the mirror for so long. "Glad that's over," he says. Casting a look to where Jiron sits next to him he asks, "I suppose it wasn't just idle curiosity that prompted you to have me follow him was it?"

Jiron shakes his head. "No."

"You intend to go after him?" he asks.

"I have to find out where he got the necklace," Jiron replies. "One way or another."

"I thought you would feel that way," James says with a sigh. Getting to his feet, he pulls forth his cloth. Having watched the man in the mirror for as long as he has, he's able to get a fix on his location. Letting the magic flow, the cloth soon points the way to the townhouse the man entered. "Let's go," he says and heads out.

Chapter Nineteen

James leads them through the streets until the townhouse the man entered comes into view down the street ahead of them. "That's it," he says. They then move a little further down the street before positioning themselves across the street next to the corner of another townhouse. Here they can remain hidden in the shadows and still keep an eye on the place.

"Scar, Potbelly," Jiron says as he turns to face them. "You two make your way around back. If someone tries to leave, detain them." He waits for them to nod and move out before he turns to James and the others. "The rest of you stay here and keep an eye on the front. I'm going to have a quick look around."

"Be careful," urges Aleya. He gives her a hug and a kiss before moving off.

James stands there in the shadows as Jiron races across the street and disappears into the alley adjacent to the townhouse. They wait for several anxious minutes before Jiron appears rounding the far side.

Keeping close to the wall, he moves quickly along the side of the building in their direction. When he passes the alley where he originally left the street, he pauses and looks both ways. Seeing that the street is deserted, he darts across to where James and the others are waiting.

"There are two other doors beside the front," he says when he arrives. "One in the alley on this side and one in the back. Scar and Potbelly have the back one covered."

"How do you plan on getting in there?" Brother Willim asks. For a priest, he sure seems to be taking a more active interest in this sort of thing than one would expect.

"On the far side of the building, there's an open window on the second floor," he explains. "The window is dark so it's safe to say the room should be empty."

"Alright," James says, "Let's go." As he starts to move toward the building, Jiron stops him by placing a hand on his chest.

"No," he says. "You and the rest stay here. I'm taking Stig with me." When he sees James beginning to object, he cuts him off by saying, "He's better suited for this than you are and I doubt if we'll have need of magic in there."

"He's right," Miko says. "You're great with magic and strategy, but you are horrible at sneaking or remaining quiet."

"I don't think so," objects James. Then he catches Aleya nodding too. "I can't be that bad," he says.

"You're not...bad," she says. "It's just that Stig is much better." Then she turns her attention to him and says, "In fact, I know someone else who would be much better."

"Who?" asks Jiron.

"Me," she replies. "I can sneak up on a deer and tickle it behind the ears before it even knows I'm there."

James sees the objection starting to form in Jiron's mind. Giving him a grin, he says, "If you say I can't go because I'm too loud, then you should at least take the one best suited for this."

"But there could be fighting," he says. "I need someone who can guard my back."

The rest of them grow quiet as a dark look comes over Aleya's face. That's when he realizes his mistake. "Are you saying I can't handle myself?" she asks with barely controlled anger. "Are you saying I am some addlebrained woman who should just stay home and wait for her man to return?"

"That's not what I'm saying at all," he counters. He glances over to James for help but only gets silence.

"Then what are you saying?" she asks, daring him to slight her again.

Sighing, he turns and looks at her and says, "Stig is from the pits. His prowess at fighting is greater than yours." He can see her bristle at this and hurriedly continues. "I don't say this to lessen your own ability, but he survived in the pits against some of the meanest fighters I've ever seen." Placing a hand on her shoulder, he softens his voice. "I know you are skilled, but we don't know what's inside there and I need someone who can walk silent yet hold their own should things turn bad."

Not liking this one bit, she can see the logic in what he's saying. "Take Stig then," she says. "See what I care." Then she turns her back on him and stalks off further into the shadows.

Jiron casts a hurt look to James who says, "She'll be okay. Go do what you have to and take care of this when you get back."

"Alright," he says. Looking into the darkness where Aleya disappeared for a moment, he then turns to Stig and says, "Leave your shield."

"Right," he says. Taking it off his arm, he hands it to Miko. "Take care of this for me will you?"

"Sure," he replies as he takes the shield.

"If you hear a commotion," Jiron says, "come running."

"You can count on it," James assures him. "Good luck."

Jiron flicks a final look to the shadows and then nods for Stig to follow. After a quick glance to make sure the coast is clear, they race across the street. Once there, they stay against the side of the buildings until they reach the alley on the far side of the townhouse.

Moving into the alley, Stig follows Jiron as he quickly makes his way down until he's almost at the end of the building. Coming to a halt, he looks up at the open window Jiron indicates.

"Wait here," Jiron says. Then moving to the wall, he examines it with his hand for a minute. Then using the cracks and imperfection in the stone wall, he begins to climb. He never thought that the climbing he and Tinok had done years ago would prove to be so beneficial. How it came about was that one day Tinok bet him he couldn't climb the defensive wall surrounding the City of Light. That first time he tried it, he lost the bet. Time and again he came back to the wall and kept trying, he hates it when something, anything defeats him. It took him the better part of a year, but when he brought Tinok back to the very same wall and bet him again, he won the bet. After that, he taught Tinok the skills he had acquired and before you knew it, they were like spiders on the wall.

Inching his way upward, he's soon past the ground floor and within a foot of the open window. Down on the ground, Stig watches absolutely amazed. He wouldn't have thought anyone could have climbed a sheer wall such as he's seeing Jiron do now.

Finally, his hand comes to the window ledge and takes a firm hold. Then he brings his other hand to the ledge and pulls himself up and in through the window. The room he finds himself in is quite dark and wishes he would have thought to have James make him one of his orbs. Too late now. He removes the rope coiled about his middle and tosses a length of it out the window down to Stig below. Bracing himself and taking a secure hold of the rope, he feels Stig test it to see if he's ready. Then the tension on the rope increases dramatically as Stig begins to use the rope to climb up.

Holding firm with his feet braced against the wall under the window, Jiron maintains a tight grip on the rope. In no time at all, Stig's hand appears at the window. He grasps the window ledge and lets go of the rope as he begins lifting himself inside. Jiron releases the rope and moves to help him in.

Once Stig is safely within the room, Jiron coils the rope again around his midsection. Moving silently, they make their way cautiously through the dark room until they come to the door. Jiron places his ear against the wood of the door and when he fails to hear anything, opens it a crack.

No light comes through from the other side as the door opens. Swinging it in further, Jiron looks out into a hallway passing to the left and right. Sticking his head out, he looks down both ways, only to find that both are dark. Several of the doors are open allowing the light from the moon shining overhead to spill in.

"Doesn't look as if anyone's on this floor," he whispers to Stig.

"Might be upstairs," Stig suggests.

Jiron nods agreement. "Let's find the stairs up and then work our way down." Moving out into the hallway, he turns to the left as one direction is as good as another. Stepping softly, neither one makes any more sound than the odd creaking of a floorboard. But even that is minimized by them placing the sides of their feet right against the wall.

They pass two doorways, briefly checking them out, before they reach the stairwell that appears to run all the way from the ground floor to the top. The stairs descending down to the bottom floor are dark, while light comes from up above. "Wait here," Jiron says to Stig who nods that he understands.

Stepping on the flight of stairs going up, Jiron quickly and silently ascends to the third floor. Muffled voices reach him before he gains the top causing him to slow. When it doesn't look as if they are approaching, he continues the rest of the way. At the top of the stairs, he hears the voices more clearly. It sounds as if there are at least five different men and all are talking in the Empire's tongue.

Candles burn up and down the hallway on the third floor in wall mounted holders. Peering around the corner, he sees the hallway extends to the left and right. The voices are coming through one of the closed doors down on the right.

Then all of a sudden, one of the doors to the right opens and a man in armor walks out. In the brief glance Jiron had of him before he ducks his head back, he could tell this was not the man he met on the bridge. The man's footsteps are leading further down the hallway away from where Jiron waits.

Peering back around the corner, he sees the man walk to the far end of the hallway where he turns to the left and disappears. Jiron then glances back down to where Stig waits and signals for him to come up.

When he joins him on the top couple of steps, Jiron indicates the hallway extending to the right and says, "I think there's a meeting going on in a room down there. At least four men are in there, another just left."

"Do you think Azku is in there?" Stig asks.

"I would think so," he replies.

"Do we take him now?" he asks.

Shaking his head, he says, "No. First we have to be sure he's in there."

"How do you plan to do that?" Stig asks.

Not for the first time he wishes he could do some of the things James can. A magic mirror to show him who is in there would definitely come in handy right about now.

The door to the room the men are in again opens up and another man steps out. This man is dressed in fine attire with a sword hanging at his hip. Moving in the same direction the previous man went, he has soon left the hallway.

"Maybe the meeting is breaking up," suggests Stig.

"Could be," he agrees. Then his eyes notice that the door the two men had come out of is ajar. "Look!" he says excitedly as he directs Stig's attention to it. "Be right back," he says and steps quickly into the hallway and moves down to the door.

The men remaining within the room sound as if they are still in the midst of some conversation. Jiron moves to the door and peers through the slight crack. Inside he sees another man in armor, his helm resting on the table before him sitting across from the man he saw at the bridge. Just when he places his hand against the door to push it open a little bit wider to see better, the voice of the third man comes from right on the other side of the door. Jiron jumps back just as the door swings inward.

Plastering himself against the wall, he sets a hand onto the hilt of his knife and watches the doorway which is only a foot and a half away. Standing there exposed in the hallway, he's sure that he'll be seen.

The man's voice comes to them again as he backs out of the room and continues talking to those still in there. With his attention directed back into the room, he fails to notice Jiron there only a foot behind him. The man says a few more words then closes the door. Without a glance in Jiron's direction, he moves to walk down the hallway in the same direction as had the other two men.

Jiron remains absolutely still until the man is halfway to where the previous two men turned out of the corridor before backing away from the doorway. He makes the stairs where Stig is waiting just before the man turns and leaves the corridor.

"Man that was close!" whispers Stig.

Turning to him Jiron finds him wearing a wide grin. "I thought for sure it was all over," he admits.

Trying to stifle a laugh that's trying to break through, Stig says, "I never saw anyone jump like you did when that door opened."

"Okay," Jiron says, "enough." He gives Stig a stern gaze which does nothing to help control the mirth that's threatening to take control. "He's in there with one other individual."

Getting himself under control, Stig says, "You sure?"

"Absolutely," he replies.

"Then the odds are even," he states. Pulling his mace from the loop that secures it to his belt he adds, "What are we waiting for."

Jiron nods. "Don't kill anyone," he warns. "We want information, not enemies." Then just before they step out of the stairwell and into the hallway, the door to the room opens yet again.

The waiting is always the worst part of anything. Standing in the darkness, James watches the townhouse. It's been fifteen minutes since Jiron and Stig disappeared around the far side. Only the fact that they haven't returned and that it's remained quiet gives him any indication that things are going well. If things hadn't, it wouldn't be nearly so peaceful.

Taking out his mirror, he checks on Jiron's progress and finds him and Stig at the top of some stairwell looking around the corner down a hallway. "Things are going okay so far," he says. *No one has died yet.*

"James!" whispers Miko urgently.

Looking to where he's pointing, he sees a man in armor along with another man in fine clothing leaving the townhouse through the front door.

"Is either one of them the guy?" asks Reilin.

Shaking his head, James says, "No. He must still be inside." They watch as the two men turn and follow the street in their direction. Everyone remains stock still as the two men walk past. Hidden in the shadows as they are, the two men fail to see them and soon disappear in the distance.

"Good," grunts Shorty.

Turning toward him James gives him a questioning look.

"Just that now there are less to deal with if things go bad," he explains.

Nodding his head in agreement, James turns back to watch the townhouse once more.

A couple minutes later the front door opens again and another man leaves. This one is obviously from the north. Dressed in finer than average clothes with a sword hanging at his waist, the man turns in their direction just as the other two had. As he makes his way closer to where they are hidden in the shadows, James gasps.

"What?" asks Miko.

"I know him," he says then waves for Miko to be quiet as the man is quite close now and might hear them. It's been a long time since he's seen that face. Back in the city of Cardri it was.

When the man has moved past and disappeared down the street, James says, "His name is Orrin."

"Orrin?" asks Miko.

"Yeah," nods James. "Do you remember when we were being held in that root cellar and I used some boards to kill the men holding us so we could escape?" When Miko nods he continues. "And do you also remember that I went to meet someone who had sent one of those boards to me at our room?"

"That was after you rescued Perrilin right?" he asks.

"That's right," he says with a nod. Pointing to the departed figure, he says, "That was the man who met me, but he works for another of more importance. They never told me who they were, just wanted to know about Lord Colerain."

"How does he figure in all of this?" asks Brother Willim.

"I don't know," replies James. Then to Shorty he says, "Follow him and see where he goes." When Shorty nods he adds, "Then meet us back at the inn."

"Right," he says then hurries off down the street after the man named Orrin.

Things are getting more and more interesting.

The two men leave the room and turn down the hallway away from Jiron and Stig just as the others had. When they leave the hallway where the previous men did, Jiron says to Stig, "Come on."

Entering the hallway, he runs on silent feet following the path the men took. When he reaches the point where all five of the men turned out of the hallway, he comes to a well lit spiral stairway leading down.

Jiron pauses a moment to listen and can hear their voices from way down below. Nodding for Stig to follow, he takes the stairs as quickly as he can while still remaining silent. When he reaches the point where he's sure the second floor should be, the stairs continue down. This stairwell must be a straight shot all the way down to the ground floor.

Continuing down, he soon sees where the stairwell ends. Slowing to a crawl, Jiron approaches the opening. The stairs come out at a large room designed for entertaining guests. A large fireplace sits in one wall, dark and cold. Two tables with six chairs each sit at either end of the room. Bookshelves line two of the walls with numerous volumes upon them.

To Jiron's right, another door stands open and the men's voices can be heard coming from the other side. Crossing the room quickly, Jiron peers through the door and sees the two men walking down a finely decorated hallway to a door at the end. When the men get there, the one he met at the bridge opens it for the other. The two men shake hands and the man in armor says a few parting words then passes through the doorway and into the street.

Closing the door, the man turns around and begins to head back toward the room in which Jiron and Stig currently occupy. "He's coming!" Jiron tells Stig.

Stig nods and takes position behind where the door will swing open and Jiron flattens himself against the wall on the other side. With knife in hand, he waits for the man to enter. They can hear his steps approaching.

All of a sudden, a blood curdling scream knifes through the silence of the house. A servant had come from out of the stairwell leading to the third floor and saw them there.

"Get the servant!" Jiron hollers as he throws open the door. With sword drawn, the man from the bridge almost runs into him on his way into the room, so unexpectedly did the door open.

Coming to a stop, the man takes in Jiron in front of him and Stig having his servant girl in hand. Stepping back a foot to give his sword room to maneuver, he finally takes a good look at Jiron. "You!" he exclaims in disbelief. Raising his sword he prepares for attack.

"Wait a minute!" yells Jiron. He lowers his knife and raises his hands. "We're not here to rob or hurt you."

"Then what are you here for?" he asks, clearly not believing him.

Pulling forth the necklace, he holds it up for the man to see. "I want to know where you got this!" he demands.

"You broke into my home, scared my servant half to death, just to ask me that?" he asks incredulously.

"I told you at the bridge this was important," explains Jiron.

The man's eyes shift from Jiron, to the necklace, then back again.

"I need to know where you got this," Jiron says again, "and I'm running out of time!"

Azku puts away his sword as there is clearly no immediate danger. "Let her go," he says.

Jiron never takes his eyes off of him as he says to Stig, "Go ahead."

Stig releases the woman who runs past Jiron and clasps the man in a tight embrace, her sobs are muffled from where she has her face buried in his shoulder.

Patting her on the head, the man says to her in a soothing voice, "It's okay. Go on upstairs and I'll take care of this." He places his finger under her chin and raises her face so her eyes look into his. "It'll be okay."

She gives Jiron and Stig a fearful glance before moving down the hallway away from them. The man watches her as she walks swiftly away and enters a doorway further down. Turning a face red with anger back to his two uninvited guests, he says, "I suppose I won't get rid of you until I either kill you or talk with you."

"I would prefer to talk," replies Jiron.

The man indicates with a nod of his head for them to return to the room at the foot of the winding stairway. Jiron still has his knife in hand as he backs up into the room. "You are Azku, yes?" he asks.

"That's right," the man replies.

"The same Azku that gave a young lady this necklace in Inziala?" he asks. When Azku gestures for him to take a seat on one of the chairs, he does. Stig remains standing next to him as Azku sits in the chair facing him.

Sighing, Azku nods. The anger that was so hot when he first encountered them in his house begins to cool.

"Why did you spurn her when you found out about the child?" Stig asks.

Azku glances at him then back to Jiron. "I thought you wanted to know about the necklace?" he asks, completely ignoring Stig's question.

"I do," Jiron replies.

"Why?" Azku asks. "Why go to all this trouble?"

Bringing out the necklace, he says, "The last time I saw this was the night my best friend's fiancée died. This was a gift to her from him shortly before. The following morning, my friend departed and I haven't seen or heard from him since."

"He left?" he asks.

Nodding, Jiron says, "I don't know why he left, maybe he was too overcome with grief. The necklace was in his possession when he took off."

"I see," the man says. "So you hope that I can be of some help in finding him?"

"That's right," Jiron states.

The man looks at him, the anger he initially felt continues to melt away. Not completely, he's still upset about being accosted in his own home. "What will you do with the information should I have any you can use?" he finally asks after a moment's thought.

"I don't follow," Jiron tells him.

"I'm not stupid," he says. "If a necklace of such emotional importance is not with your friend, I would suspect it wouldn't have been relinquished willingly." He pauses a moment to see if his words have any effect. When Jiron fails to react he knows that Jiron has come to the same conclusion.

"Can you help me?" Jiron asks.

"Perhaps," he replies. "I acquired the necklace through a business associate some time ago for the woman I loved. That was before I realized the woman was...soiled." His eyes tighten with remembered pain from the night when he had to spurn her.

Coming to sit on the edge of the chair, Jiron asks, "Who?"

"It would be problematic should anything befall this man," Azku states as he sees the burning intensity behind Jiron's eyes. "Would giving you his name be a death sentence should you find that your friend is already dead?"

Jiron shakes his head. "No," he replies. "All I want to do is find out what happened to him."

Azku studies him for a full minute before asking, "Would you be willing to give your solemn word to leave him as you find him?"

"Yes," replies Jiron. "I give my word that I and those with me shall cause no harm to the person you name."

"As strange as it sounds, I believe you," he says. "But before I tell you his name, I must warn you."

"I assure you," Jiron tells him, "I and my friends are more than capable of handling ourselves."

Azku gives him a sardonic grin, "I'm sure you are. However, you may wish to know that due to your earlier visit to the Cracked Ladle, you and those with whom you travel may have drawn the attention of an Eye."

"An Eye?" asks Jiron. "As in an Eye of the Empire?"

"The same," he nods. "You see the Order of the Scarlet Sword counts many who are not of the Empire among its members. This gives the Eyes of the Empire cause for concern, they think we're a bunch of spies and such. Nothing however could be further from the truth."

"I would think they would move against such an organization," Jiron says. "From what I've heard of them, they tend to be fairly ruthless when they feel something is not right."

"Ordinarily that is true," nods Azku. "But keep in mind, some of the highest commanders in the Empire's forces are members. It's also rumored that the Emperor himself is one too, but I have yet to see creditable evidence to support it. Those in high places keep the Eyes from moving against our members." He pauses for a moment before adding, "Members from the Empire that is. Anyone who's from outside the Empire is fair game."

"So they keep our Houses under observation and anyone who enters is immediately suspect," he says. "Those they've never seen before are doubly so."

"Very well," says Jiron. "We may be targeted by an Eye. It won't be the first time."

Azku's eyes widen at that. "Really?" he asks.

"Oh yes," Jiron replies without expanding any further upon it. "Now, can you tell me who you received the necklace from?"

"In the city of Cyst to the south, you will find the person in question in the large compound on the eastern edge of town," he explains. "When you arrive, ask for Buka."

"Is Buka the one from whom you received the necklace?" Jiron asks.

Nodding, he adds, "Though I doubt if he'll be willing to help you."

"Why?"

"For one thing he hates those from the north," he explains. "For another, he's a slaver. Being from the north as you are, he's just as likely to make you a slave as look at you."

From behind him, Jiron hears Stig snort. "I'd like to see him try," he says.

"A slaver huh?" he muses.

"I know how those of you from the north view slavery," Azku states. "Are you still going to be able to hold to your word and cause him no harm?"

Jiron nods. "Yes."

"Good. If you break your oath to me, no power on this world will protect you from my wrath," he warns. "I'll find you no matter where you go."

"Your threats are unwarranted," Jiron assures him. "I do not break my oath."

"Good enough then," Azku states. Standing up, he says, "Now that I've answered your questions, would you be kind enough to take your leave?"

Coming to his feet, Jiron offers his hand. Hesitantly, Azku shakes it. "I thank you," he says.

Azku nods and steps aside so he and Stig can leave. Moving past him, Jiron and Stig walk through the door and into the hallway then down to the door. Azku does not accompany them.

"That went better than I thought it would," Jiron states. Opening the door he glances back down to the room and sees Azku still standing there, his eyes upon them. Then he passes through to the street outside.

Stig follows him out. "What if he lied to us?" he asks.

"Then I'll come back and kill him," Jiron replies matter-of-factly.

Outside, they check to make sure the street is quiet. Then Jiron has Stig go around back to get Scar and Potbelly and meet him across the street with the others. As Stig moves to do as requested, Jiron hurries across the street.

Before he completely crosses the street, James leaves the shadows. "Everything go alright?" he asks.

Jiron nods his head. "Yes. I found out what I wanted to know."

"Good," states James.

They wait there a few moments before Stig arrives with Scar and Potbelly. While they wait, James fills him in on seeing Orrin from Cardri leave Azku's house and informs him that he sent Shorty to follow.

"There's an Eye in the city too," Jiron says and gives him the gist of what Azku told him.

"That may complicate things," he says.

"Not if we leave town as soon as possible," states Jiron.

When Stig and the other two are seen crossing the street, Jiron suddenly notices that they are one person short. "Where's Aleya?" he asks.

"What?" replies James. "She's right…" he trials off when he realizes she is not among them. "Aleya?" he calls out in a hushed voice.

When no answer is forthcoming, Jiron hollers very loudly **"Aleya!"** Again, no reply. "Fan out and find her," he says and moves toward the area where she had stalked off just before he and Stig went to talk to Azku. Worried and fearful, Jiron's pace quickens. About to call her name again, his eyes catch sight of something on the ground. Stopping fast, his heart skips a beat when he sees her bow and quiver of arrows lying on the ground. Two of the arrows have spilled out of the quiver and lie next to it on the ground.

"Oh no," he says as he reaches down to pick them up. "Aleya!" he hollers again. Turning to the others he says in a voice filled with anguish, "He's got her."

"Who?" asks Miko.

"The Eye!" he exclaims.

Chapter Twenty

"We have to find her!" Jiron exclaims as he turns to James.

"Maybe she took off on her own," Potbelly suggests. "She was pretty mad."

"Are you insane?" asks Jiron as he rounds on him. "All alone in a hostile city where she doesn't speak the language? I don't think so."

James pulls forth his cloth, not for the first time he wishes for something better with which to work with, and says "Okay, let's find her." Sending out the magic, they watch the cloth rise and point the way.

Moving out quickly, they walk as fast as they can without drawing unwanted attention. It doesn't take them long to figure out where the cloth is indicating. On the south side of town sits one of the largest buildings in Morac.

Easily five stories tall and built like a fortress, the place is massive. No windows on the first two floors, only a very sturdy wooden door in front for an entrance. Two heavily armed men stand watch outside the door and several windows hold men with crossbows. Everyone is looking outward and scanning the area.

"Think they're expecting someone?" asks Scar.

"Yes," replies Jiron. "Us. Wait here," he tells them. Then he stays in the shadows as he makes a circuit around the building to see about another way in. He finds what could be another door, there's a large square wooden section in the rear stone wall. It could be a door but there's no handle or anything else that might be used to open it from the outside. Men are stationed at windows on the other sides as well, making it impossible for anyone to sneak up to the building without being seen.

Returning to the others, he tells them what he's discovered. "If we storm the place," Stig says after he's done, "they will probably kill her."

Jiron nods, pain in his eyes. "Then how are we to get in there?"

James gazes at the building and shakes his head. "I don't know," he admits.

"Maybe this Orrin fellow you saw leaving Azku's house might know?" suggests Potbelly. "From what you've told us, it sounds like they have their fingers in many different pots."

"Could be there's no love lost between the Order of the Scarlet Sword and the Eyes of the Empire," adds Scar. "Might be worth a shot to go see what he can do."

"If we do, it's got to be quick," states Jiron. "No telling what they could be doing to her in there."

"Very well," James says. Then to Scar and Potbelly he says, "You two stay here and keep an eye on the place. See if you can figure out a way we can breach its defenses."

"You got it," affirms Scar.

"Shorty was to meet us back at the inn once he found out where Orrin is staying," James says to the others. "Be best if we try there first."

"Okay, but let's hurry," urges Jiron.

Leaving Scar and Potbelly there to keep an eye on Aleya's captors, the rest hurry back through the streets to the inn. When the inn finally comes into sight, they find soldiers of the Empire in and around the place. They come to a quick halt and Jiron has them duck into the shadows of a nearby alley. Then just as they reach the mouth of the alley, a squad of six guards exits the inn with Shorty in their midst. Hands tied behind his back and blood running down the side of his face, it's easy to see he didn't go quietly.

The leader of the squad hollers something back into the inn and is answered by someone inside. As the squad leaves the inn, the leader of the squad directs several other soldiers to move into position around the building, blending into the shadows. Once the men are positioned such that they can see the inn yet remain out of sight, the leader has the squad move out. They turn down the street and begin moving in the direction of the building where Aleya is being held.

"If we had been any later we would have fallen into their trap," Miko says.

Jiron nods and watches as the squad comes closer.

They remain quiet and still in the shadows as the squad passes by. "We can't let them reach that building," James says once the soldiers have moved further down the street from their hiding place.

"Ambush?" questions Stig.

"You better believe it," replies Jiron. "I'll take Stig and get ahead of them. James, you and the rest follow close behind."

"Okay," James replies.

Jiron and Stig move into the alley and run to the other end where it opens onto the next street over. It runs parallel to the one the guards are taking and will allow them to get ahead of the squad without being seen. James takes the lead and enters the street behind the departing squad with Miko, Brother Willim, and Reilin right behind. A slug from his slug belt rests in his hand.

"Are you going to kill these men?" asks Brother Willim.

James glances to him and nods. "Afraid so. Our friends are in mortal danger, we don't have time to play it safe."

Brother Willim sighs and nods understanding. The death of any man is hard on the Priests of Asran.

James maintains a discreet distance and they follow the guards for a couple blocks. Then they notice that the street ahead of the squad is darker than it was when they passed through earlier. The streetlights are out. James grins and thinks, *Smart thinking Jiron.*

The squad appears not to be bothered by the fact that the street lights are no longer lit and continue to walk forward. Just before they enter the darkened area, James sends the magic forth and breaks the rope binding Shorty's hands behind his back. Shorty's pace falters a moment by the unexpected freedom and almost doesn't recover in time to prevent his captors from realizing he's no longer bound.

James can see him nod his head three times to let them know he'll be ready. "Any time now," he says under his breath and hears Miko say, "Yeah."

Then ahead of the marching guards, a shadowy figure detaches itself from the greater darkness and approaches them. The guards, oblivious to the oncoming threat, continue to march.

"Now!" he hears Jiron holler and the shadow leaps toward the lead guard.

Throwing his slug, James takes out one of the rear guards as the one Jiron engages falls lifelessly to the ground.

Stig rushes in from the side and the battle is joined. Shorty tackles the guard to his left and wrestles him to the ground. Kneeing him in the stomach, Shorty struggles for possession of the man's sword.

Another slug flies and takes out the remaining rear guard. Jiron has both knives out and is trading blows with one while Stig stuns the one he's facing with a powerful blow of his mace to the side of the man's head. Stig then follows through with another bone crushing blow to the head. Brains and bone shatter under the impact. Maces are brutal weapons in the hand of an expert.

Jiron dodges to the left to avoid a thrust by his opponent, then dodges back and sinks his knife in the man's side. Lashing out with the pommel of his other knife, he knocks the man backward and to the ground. Jiron glances around and sees Shorty getting up from the ground with the guard's bloody sword in hand. The guard lies on the ground unmoving, his life blood beginning to pool on the ground next to him.

James and the others come running and Reilin says, "Quick, get the bodies in the alley." Glancing around, it doesn't look as if anyone has taken notice of the fight. The street remains quiet.

Working quickly, they get the dead guards off the street and into the alley without anyone taking notice. "When morning comes, it won't take very long before the bodies are found," Stig says.

"We won't be here by then," Jiron tells him.

"You okay?" James asks Shorty.

"Yeah," he replies. "They jumped me when I returned. I took one of them out before they could take me."

Jiron comes to him and asks, "Did you find where Orrin is staying?"

Shorty nods. "Yes, he's staying at an inn not too far from here. Now, could someone tell me what's going on?"

"We'll explain on the way," Jiron says. "Show us where he's staying."

As Shorty heads out, the others fill him in on the events so far.

Moving quickly toward the inn where Orrin is staying, they are forced to alter course twice to avoid patrols moving along the streets. The increased patrols have to be in response to them being in town.

"There it is," Shorty says when the inn comes into view.

"Which room is his?" asks James.

"Third floor," he replies. "Second room on the right."

"Jiron, come with me," James says. "The rest of you stay here." With Jiron beside him, they hurry across the street and enter the inn. The common room still has a few night owls at the tables. The bard, if there had been one, has long since gone.

They move toward the stairs located at the rear of the room at a normal pace. When they reach the foot of the stairs, they quicken their pace, taking them two at a time until they reach the third floor. James then walks down to the second door on the right and knocks.

When the door opens up, Orrin looks out with the question he was about to ask still upon his lips. His eyes widen when he sees who it is standing at his door.

"Remember me?" James asks.

"Oh yes," he replies. Then a smile comes across his face, "You've given the Empire no end of trouble since last we met."

"Can we come in?" James asks.

Opening the door wider, Orrin gestures for them to enter.

"Thank you," James says as he and Jiron enter the room. After they're in, Orrin closes the door and walks over to the only table in the room.

"Please," he says indicating the chairs around the table, "have a seat." As they sit he adds, "Sorry I can't offer you any refreshments."

"That's alright," James assures him. "We'll survive."

"Did you follow me here?" he asks.

"Why would you say that?" Jiron asks.

"I'm sorry, do I know you?" Orrin asks.

"This is my friend Jiron," James says.

"Oh yes, the knife fighting Shynti," nods Orrin.

"You seem to know an awful lot about us," Jiron says, a frown coming to his face. He doesn't like the fact that an absolute stranger would know such things.

"Yes I do," he replies without expanding further. "As to your earlier question, I attended a brief meeting by an associate at his residence. At the meeting, I learned of your presence in the city and how you used a ruse to get him to meet with you. He wasn't too happy about that."

"I realize that," James tells him. "We followed him to his house."

"Obviously," Orrin says. "You're here aren't you?" He glances from Jiron then to James before asking, "So why are you here?"

James gives him a rundown of what's going on with Aleya, that she's being held captive, and where. He also relates how Shorty had been taken at the inn where they were staying. "What we came here for is to see if you could help us in any way to get inside that building," James concludes. Sitting back in his chair he gazes hopefully at Orrin.

Outside, Miko is waiting in growing impatience and dread. "Come on James," he mumbles to himself, "there isn't much time." Then from down the street fifty men, a mix of guards and soldiers come marching down the street.

"Damn!" says Stig. "Run!"

"But what about James and Jiron?" Miko asks.

"They'll meet us back where we left Scar and Potbelly," he explains. "Now move it!" Running for their lives, they flee down a side alley.

The soldiers move to the inn and surround it. Smashing in the front door, the soldiers and guards run inside.

Crash!

The noise from the soldiers smashing the inn's door in comes to them even here on the third floor. Orrin stands up and yells "You led them to me!" Grabbing a pack on the floor, he heads for the door.

Jiron grabs him by the shoulder and demands, "What about the building?"

"If your friend is being held within the Eye's Court, there's nothing you can do" he says. Throwing open the door, Orrin glances back at them and says. "You better leave her there and get out of Morac while you still can." Then locking eyes with James he says, "The Eyes have dealt with mages before, be careful." With that, he knocks off Jiron's hand and runs into the hallway.

James is at the window looking down at the street below. "They're everywhere," he says. Down below he can see soldiers staked out all along the street with more arriving from all directions every minute. "Hope the others got away safely."

"Stop talking and let's get out of here!" urges Jiron. Leaving the room, they begin to head for the stairs when Orrin emerges out of them at a run. Behind him they hear the pounding of feet of soldiers on their way up.

"To the roof!" he yells. "Follow me."

Just as he passes them and continues down the hallway, the first soldier emerges from the stairs. Jiron pulls his knives and says, "Follow him. I'll hold them off until you are on the roof."

"Good luck," James says as he turns and races after Orrin.

Completely nestled within his element, Jiron feels all the frustration, fear and anxiety that has been his companion for the last few weeks burst out of him in a flurry of action. The first soldier who reaches him strikes out with his sword only to have it deflected by one knife as the other sinks three inches into his side. Kicking out, Jiron knocks the man back into the others coming out of the stairs.

Rather than wait, Jiron takes the battle to them. Anger takes one, frustration another as the pent up emotions find release in combat. With every strike he makes, he loses more of the emotional turmoil and peace comes to fill its place.

Block, stab, twist, deflect, blow after blow he deflects only to strike back with devastating results. Three men now lie upon the hallway floor, their blood flowing as life leaves them. Still more emerge from the stairs, almost as if they are eager to feel the kiss of his blades. Jiron is only happy to oblige.

As the press of men steadily moves him backward down the hallway, he expects to hear James hollering to him that he's reached the roof. A little concerned that he hasn't as yet, he puts the worry aside and lets his blades dance.

Suddenly to his right, a door opens and a man with a sword strikes out at him. The unexpectedness of the blow causes him to fail to dodge in time and the man scores a shallow wound on his right shoulder.

He kicks out at the soldier he is currently engaged with and sends him backward into his fellows then turns to the civilian in the doorway. As the man strikes at him once more, Jiron easily dodges the blow. The man didn't take into account the possibility of missing and thus has thrown himself off balance.

Lashing out at the man, Jiron takes him across the throat with a knife then elbows him back into the room. Just then he hears James holler that he's made it to the roof. Leaping into the man's room, he slams shut the door and throws the bolt.

Such a flimsy bolt might deter the common thief, but there's no way it will long hold out against sustained blows. Moving over to the bed, he quickly drags it over to the door as blows begin to hammer on it from the other side. Using his boot to scoot the dead man out of the way, he settles the edge of the bed against the door.

Bam!

Hoping that will give him enough time, he moves to the window and throws it open. He sticks his head out and turns his face to the roof. "James!" he hollers.

Bam!

A moment later he hears James' voice coming from the roof above, "I'm here!"

Unwinding the rope from around his waist, Jiron yells, "I'm throwing up my rope, catch it!"

"Right!" he hollers back.

Bam!

Getting enough slack to make it up to James, he leans out and throws it up. He can feel it stop as James catches it. "Now, move down the roof ten feet to your left and brace yourself!" he hollers.

Bam! Crack!

The bolt breaks from the wall as the door jamb shatters.

"Ready!" he hears James yell and the rope's slack is taken up as James readies himself.

Jiron climbs onto the window ledge and then glances back to the door. Already open a foot, the men on the other side are gradually pushing it and the bed further into the room. Taking a firm hold of the rope, Jiron sees a soldier squeeze through the opening and charge him.

Jumping out and trusting in James, he holds onto the rope tightly. With James holding the upper end of the rope ten feet to the left, he swings out and over to land below where James is located. Now ten feet away from the window, he begins climbing up to the roof. Before he makes it up to the roof's edge, a soldier sticks his head out and sees him there hanging by the rope. He begins calling out to those below.

"Come on!" he hears James grunt from above him.

Hand over hand, Jiron climbs the rope the rest of the way to the roof. Bolts begin firing at him from the soldiers in the street below. One strikes his pack and embeds itself while the rest go wide. At the roof's edge, he reaches up and takes hold. Releasing the rope, he pulls himself up and onto the roof.

James takes hold of his shirt and helps him over the edge as bolts continue to fly from below.

Bang! Bang! Bang!

Jiron turns his attention to the source of the banging and sees that the trap door leading from the roof has several crates placed upon it. "Orrin said he brought those up here when he first arrived just in case," explains James.

"Good thinking," he says. Looking around, he doesn't see Orrin anywhere. "Where did he go?"

James indicates the far side of the inn facing the rear courtyard. "He had a rope there and was over the side right after we pushed the crates on top of the trap door," he explains.

Jiron runs over to the rope hanging over the edge and looks down. A dozen men are standing at the base of the rope. When they see him looking over the top, they begin yelling. "Not this way," he says. Taking his knife, he cuts Orrin's rope and lets it fall to the street below. Now they can't come at them from that direction.

Bang! Bang

"That's not going to hold forever," Jiron says.

"No," replies James. "I've got an idea but not sure how well it will work."

Jiron takes in the distances between the inn and the other buildings next to it. None are very close and any attempt to jump will be seen by those below. "Okay, what is it?"

James outlines what he plans to do and Jiron nods with a grin. "Bold and dangerous," he says, "I like it." He and James then hurry over to the furthest part of the roof from where the soldiers are attempting to break through the trapdoor.

Kneeling down, James summons the magic and begins tracing out a three-foot by three-foot square on the roof. As his finger moves along the surface, a line forms in its wake. He's using magic to cut out a section of the roof. When he has two sides of the square done, the edge of the square section that has already been cut begins sinking into the roof. Jiron takes out one of his knives and jams the blade in the crack to prevent it from falling in prematurely.

The only problem with his plan is if he's doing this above an area that currently has a guest or that the soldiers are in, they'll be found out quickly. If that happens, they will not get another chance.

Bang! Bang!

Jiron glances to the crates holding the trapdoor closed and sees that they still remain covering the trapdoor. Returning his gaze to James, he sees the third side is finished and the fourth is halfway done. Pulling his other knife out, he jams it into the crack on the fourth side to keep it in place until James is done.

When his finger reaches the point where he began, he stops. "Now to pull it up," James says. Removing his knife, he uses it to pry up one of the sides. When he has it high enough to get a grip on it, he and Jiron lift the section of the roof up and set it down on the roof next to the hole.

Reclaiming his knives, Jiron immediately grips the edge of the hole and lowers himself down. He finds himself above a bed in one of the rooms. A quick scan reveals no one is currently within the room, nor does it look like anyone is currently occupying it. Letting go, he drops onto the bed and hollers up to James, "Come on!"

As James begins working his way through the hole, Jiron moves to the closed door and can hear the soldiers on the other side in the hallway moving about. Very quietly, he throws the bolt on the door and then returns to the bed just as James drops onto it.

"Once more," he says to Jiron. Moving over to an open area, he again kneels down and just as he did up above, begins carving out a section of the floor. This time it takes him a lot less time and as they pull the section of the floor free, light comes through from below. James gives Jiron a worried glance.

"Nothing for it now," he says as they finish pulling the section of the floor free.

Below this room is the kitchen. The smell of baking bread rises from below where the cook is preparing food for the following morning. Jiron sticks his head down and finds the kitchen empty.

Not believing their good fortune, he is quickly through the hole and drops down to the kitchen. Many people are out in the common room, and he moves to the door leading there. Opening it a crack, he peers through and finds the room packed with people. Seems the soldiers have gathered everyone from the inn, including the staff, and is holding them there.

Closing the door, he turns just as James drops to the floor. Moving to him, he indicates the common room and whispers, "They have everyone out there."

"Now, how do we get out of this place?" James asks.

Aside from the door leading into the common room, there is the door leading to the rear courtyard or another hallway leading further back into the inn. A look through the window overlooking the courtyard reveals over a dozen soldiers out there.

With just the hallway left, Jiron pulls a knife and moves into it. It's rather narrow and extends a ways back. The first doorway they come to reveals the inn's larder. Barrels and boxes rest on the floor while shelves line the walls, full of food and other cooking supplies.

Continuing on down, they come to another door. It's opened a crack and light comes from the other side. Jiron moves to peer in through the crack and discovers a soldier of the Empire rifling through what looks to be the innkeeper's belongings. The soldier gives a satisfied exclamation as he pulls a small pouch from one of the innkeeper's drawers. He jiggles the sack and Jiron can hear the sound of the coins within.

A floorboard under Jiron's foot suddenly gives off with a creak and he steps back from the crack. Within the room, the sounds the soldier was making quiets. Cursing the creaking floorboard, Jiron slowly moves back to peer into the room.

Suddenly, the door is pulled open and the soldier looks in surprise at Jiron standing there. Without thought, Jiron lashes out with his fist and connects with the man's throat. As the man staggers backward, Jiron pulls out his knives and advances.

The man tries to cry out and alert his comrades, but the blow to his throat has frozen his vocal chords. All he can make are quiet squeaks. Pulling his sword, he brings it up barely in time to block Jiron' attack.

No time for niceties, Jiron presses the soldier hard, feinting and attacking, blocking and thrusting. On the third exchange, he gets his knife within the man's guard and pierces him just under the breastbone. As the man staggers into him, Jiron strikes him on the chin with the palm of his hand and snaps his head backward. An audible crack can be heard as the man's neck breaks.

Out in the hallway, James has kept an eye on things and so far no one has come to investigate the noise. When Jiron begins to bend over and starts removing the man's armor, James asks, "What are you doing? We don't have time for this."

"Then stop standing there and help me," he says.

James enters the room and together they quickly get the man's armor off. "Here," Jiron says as he hands him the helm. "Put it on."

Getting the idea, James puts on the helm. It's a bit loose, but should work well enough for what he believes Jiron has planned. He also takes the man's cloak while Jiron puts on the bloody armor.

Neither one of them would pass a close inspection, but in the dark and confusion outside, they just might be able to pull it off. Jiron tosses him the sword and he buckles it on. "Ready?" he asks.

"No," replies James with a grin.

Moving out of the room, Jiron takes the lead. They continue to follow the hallway to the next room which is a small greeting room where the innkeeper and family can entertain guests without having to be in the common room. A door in one wall stands closed.

Opening the door slowly, they find it opens onto the edge of the rear courtyard. A quick glance reveals no soldiers are in the immediate vicinity. "Let's do it," Jiron says as he opens the door and strides outside, James following a step behind.

Walking in a straight line to the gates of the courtyard, they pass by several soldiers, none of whom give them more than a casual glance. Upon reaching the gates, they hear a commotion and glance up at the roof. They have broken through the trapdoor and must have discovered the hole they escaped through. A soldier on the roof is yelling to those below.

Opening the courtyard gate, they walk through and find more soldiers stationed out here. But walking like they have the right to be there, plus dressed at least partially in 'appropriate armor', they move right past them without being noticed.

Keeping a steady pace, they work their way through the soldiers until they leave the last one behind. Once they have put a suitable distance between them, they break into a run. Fleeing into the night, the find a quiet spot and shed their ill-gotten armor. Then they begin working their way back to the building containing Aleya.

Chapter Twenty One

Keeping to the shadows, James and Jiron make their way quickly from street to street toward the building where Aleya is being held. Down the street ahead of them, a squad of soldiers emerges from a side street. "This way!" Jiron whispers as he ducks into a side alley.

Plastering themselves against the side of the alley, they hold still as the footsteps of the soldiers approach. The light from the lanterns that two of the soldiers are holding gradually illuminates the street just outside the alley as they draw near. When the soldiers reach the mouth of the alley, the light from the lanterns fully reveals James and Jiron where they are pressed to the side of an adjacent building.

James holds his breath and silently prays that none of them happen to look in the alley or they will surely be discovered. As fortune would have it, the soldiers continue past without one of them seeing the two fugitives hiding within the alley. Once they've moved on, he lets out his pent up breath and says, "That was close."

"Too close," agrees Jiron. Peering around the corner of the alley, he finds that other than the retreating backs of the soldiers that just marched passed, the street is empty. "Come on," he says and moves back onto the street.

Lights from several different groups are seen moving on adjacent streets. The number of men searching for them is steadily growing. It's going to be hard enough just to reach the Eye's Court as Orrin called it, let alone rescuing Aleya and getting free of the town.

They make it down several more blocks before having to again duck into the shadows as another squad makes its way past. "Can't be too far from it now," Jiron comments once the squad has moved on.

"Let's hope not," replies James.

When the street is once again clear, they leave the alley and continue on. Keeping to the dark, they are forced to weave around the circles of light given off by the lit lampposts so as not to be spotted. Then finally, the large structure appears down the street ahead of them. Even two blocks away, they can see that an additional dozen men now stand guard before the front entrance.

Keeping to the edge of the street near the buildings, they slowly make their way closer until they are but four buildings away. "Where are the others?" asks James. He was hoping to have come across Miko and the rest by now. Fear that they may have been captured or even killed begins to grow within him.

"Use your cloth and find them," Jiron tells him.

Feeling stupid for not having thought of that himself, he can only assume the events of the night must have him rattled. Taking it out, he casts the spell and is surprised to see that it indicates they are in the building he and Jiron are hiding against. "They're in here," James says as he pats the wall.

Several feet behind them lies the doorway into the building. Jiron moves back to it and tries the handle. Finding it locked, he removes one of his knives and begins working on the lock. He soon has it opened and they move inside.

"Miko!" whispers James as loudly as he dares once the door is closed behind him. They remain still and listen for a reply. When nothing comes, he again whispers, "Miko!" this time a little bit louder.

A shadow passes across the doorway leading to another room. "James?" he hears Miko ask.

"Yes," he replies. Then his orb springs to life, barely giving off any light, just enough for them to be able to see each other.

The rest are right behind Miko, even Scar and Potbelly. "Am I glad to see you two," Scar says.

"We were getting worried that you might not have made it," Potbelly adds. "But not too much, seeing as how nothing blew up or anything."

"What did you find out?" Miko asks.

"Nothing," replies James. "Orrin said for us to abandon her. That to attempt a rescue was tantamount to a death sentence."

"Are we going after her then?" Reilin asks. No one even bothers to answer him, they all know the answer.

Jiron comes before Scar and Potbelly and asks, "Did you two see anything that might help?"

Shaking his head, Scar says, "Not really. The buildings adjacent to the one holding her are three stories or less. Guards are posted on all four sides including the roof. I'm not sure how we could get in there without being seen."

"There's always the sewer," replies Miko.

An audible groan escapes James. "Only if there are no other alternatives will I do that again," he says. To Scar he asks, "How close can we get without being seen?"

"Pretty close," he replies.

"Good, then take me there so I can see what's going on," he tells him.

"I'm coming too," states Jiron.

When Scar nods, Jiron says, "The rest of you stay here." That's when he notices Miko has a tart in his hand. Surprised, he glances around and for the first time notices they are in a baker's shop. Over to one side he sees where the baker's leftovers from the day before are stacked together. He goes over and helps himself to a quarter loaf of bread and lays three coppers down on the counter next to it.

James notices it too and snags three of the four remaining tarts before Miko has a chance to finish them off. He too lays a couple coins on the counter and then takes a large bite as he follows Scar to the back of the building. "I think the baker is asleep above us," he explains. James nods understanding.

Scar takes them out the back to the street running behind the building and then quickly over to the mouth of an alley that leads back to the street the Eye's Court faces. Upon entering the alley, they move quickly to where it opens onto the street. From there, James has a good view of the face of the Eye's Court across the street as well as the alley directly across from them that runs beside it. The guards in the street are none too far away.

The alley on the other side of the street that runs along the side of the Eye's Court is wider by far than the ordinary alley. Peering around the corner he can barely see that the alley on the far side of the Eye's Court is just as wide. He realizes the buildings bordering the Eye's are further back in order to create a buffer zone that would prevent any attempt at gaining access from their rooftops.

Four men with crossbows are seen in windows on the third and fourth floor facing the front. The side facing the alley across from them has four men in similar position, two on the third floor and two on the fourth. The windows on the fifth floor are dark and closed. Another four men are stationed on the rooftop, each looking out over a different side.

Aside from being set back away from the Eye's Court, the building across from them is only three stories tall, as are all the others adjacent to it just as Scar had said. James stands there several minutes while he takes in the positions of the men in, on and around the building holding Aleya. It's definitely a tough nut to crack.

"Alright," he says and indicates they should return. "I've seen enough."

Just as they are leaving, more soldiers arrive and join those guarding the front of the building. "This just gets better and better," Scar comments as they withdraw back down the alley.

Once they've returned back to where the others are waiting, James gives them a rundown of what he saw. "So," he summarizes, "any way we go, it's going to be almost impossible to get inside without being seen."

"Can you put the guards to sleep?" Miko asks. "Like that time in Cardri when you snuck back in after rescuing Perrilin?"

"I doubt it," he replies. "Those guards were bored and not alert. The ones here are expecting us to make an attempt and will fight any attempt I make. I'm just not sure I could get them all at the same time."

"The sewers?" asks Jiron.

"We don't even know where an entrance is," he says. "There's not much time. Once they've completed searching near Orrin's inn, they'll come here.

The sooner we move, the better our chance will be to get away." He glances at the others and then settles his gaze on Brother Willim. "Is there anything you could do?"

Shaking his head, he says, "I don't think so."

"How about a diversion?" asks Potbelly.

"Yeah!" exclaims Scar. "Do something like you did in Al-Kur."

"It may come to that," he says. Then he turns to Shorty. "How far away are you accurate with your knives?" he asks.

"How far away are you talking?" he responds.

"From the rooftop of the building next to it, to the guards in the windows," he replies.

Nodding, he says, "I think so. I don't have my throwing knives, they took those when they captured me at the inn. All I have are the five knives I took from the guards we killed earlier."

"Can you do it with those?" Jiron asks.

He takes one from his belt and tests it for balance and weight. "It's not well balanced for throwing," he says. "But they'll do."

"Good," says James.

"You got an idea?" Jiron asks.

"Yes I do," he nods. "But we have to get into the building on the back side, it's furthest from the guards stationed out front. Hopefully what we do will have a better chance of remaining unobserved back there."

"Now," James says as he looks to Jiron, "how do we get across the street?"

"Follow me," he says. Taking a slice of some honeyed sweet bread, Jiron leads them out the back door. Leaving through the back door again, they follow the street leading away from the direction of the Eye's Court for about a block. Then they come to a side street that will take them back to the one running in front of the Eye's Court. Turning into it, Jiron leads them back to the street where he pauses and peers in both directions. Seeing that the guards in front of the Eye's Court aren't likely to see them crossing from so far away, he waves the others forward and they race across to the narrow alley on the other side.

From there he leads them in a roundabout way until they've reached the building directly behind the one holding Aleya. Using his knife, he picks the lock and soon has the door open.

They find themselves in the residence of a rather affluent individual. Jiron suddenly freezes and holds his hand up for the others to stop. They stand there in the darkened room a moment until the others hear the creaking of a floorboard above them. Someone is awake and moving about.

"Wait here," he says. A knife springs to his hand and he moves to the door leading from the room.

As the others wait, they watch his shadow pass from the room and enter the rest of the house. A minute goes by, then two. All of a sudden, the floorboards above them begin creaking severely. Then there's a thud and all becomes silent. Footfalls are heard moving away from where the creaking came from to the stairway, then Jiron's voice hollers out, "Come on up!"

Upstairs they find a middle aged man lying on the floor of his bedroom. "Don't worry," Jiron reassures James, "he's not dead."

Scar comes forward with a length of rope and says, "Better tie him up then. Can't have him waking up and sounding the alarm before we leave." With Potbelly's help, he picks up the man and lays him on the bed. As he ties his arms and legs securely, the others make their way up to the third floor and search for the roof access.

In one of the corner rooms, they find a ladder in a closet that leads up to a trapdoor. Jiron climbs the ladder and finds the trapdoor unlocked. Pushing it up just enough to create a crack through which to see, he looks out.

The trapdoor opens up along the rear of the roof, far enough from their objective that they will remain unseen in the dark by those stationed in the windows and on the roof of the Eye's Court. "I think we can get onto the roof without being seen," he says.

"Two at a time at half minute intervals," suggests James. "You and me first." Climbing the ladder until he's on the rung below Jiron's foot he then nods the go ahead.

Opening the trapdoor, Jiron climbs out onto the roof and then holds it open for James. Once he's out, they close the trapdoor and then move to the roof's edge, all the while keeping an eye on the men stationed in the windows and on the roof of the Eye's Court. None of the watchers so much as shift their gaze even slightly toward Jiron and James.

Then, the trapdoor opens again and out comes Miko with the pack containing the Book of Morcyth and Shorty. "Over here," whispers James and they quickly move to join them. Still, the watchers fail to notice them on top of the roof.

Time and again the trapdoor opens then closes until everyone has joined them on the roof. During that time, James has been watching the men guarding the Eye's Court. The guard stationed on this side of the roof will at times leave his post for several seconds before returning. Looks as if he's talking with the others up there when he disappears. The men in the windows are stationed at either end of the building, one each from the third and fourth floor.

He gestures for Shorty to come close and points out the two on the right. "We'll take them out first," he says. Then he indicates the man on the roof, "Once we're in position, we'll wait for him to look away before throwing. You take the one on the third floor and I'll take the one above him."

Shorty nods. "But what if there are more than just them in the rooms?" he asks.

"Then things get more complicated," replies James. "But I've been watching them since I came out of the trapdoor and they've given no indication there's anyone with them."

"Once we take them out, we'll do the other two," he says. Turning to Jiron who's been listening the whole time he continues. "After they've been taken out, it'll be up to you and Shorty to get the men on the roof before anyone has a chance to notice."

Jiron looks at him questioningly. "And just how are we to do that?" he asks.

"I'll make you a ramp," he replies. To Shorty he says, "It's just like the 'bridge' Delia used when you took out the siege equipment back at Lythylla."

Shorty nods. "That's going to be quite an incline from here," he observes. Indeed, if the ramp is going to stretch from the roof of this building which is on the third floor, up to the roof of the Eye's Court which is on the fifth, the angle is going to be severe. "If I remember right," he adds, "that bridge didn't have the greatest traction."

James considers what he says a moment then replies, "I'll take care of that. You two just get up there and take those men out when it appears."

"We'll be ready," Jiron says.

"Alright then," he states. Then to Shorty he asks, "You ready?" When he gets Shorty's nod, he begins moving across the roof closer to the men watching from the windows. A slug makes its way into his hands as they come closer. "How close do you need to be?" James asks.

"Another five feet should be sufficient," he replies.

Moving closer, James keeps a constant eye on the men in the windows. Only the fact that he and Shorty are moving in darkness while the men in the windows have light coming up to them from the alley below, prevents the men from seeing them. It's easy to see the Eye within the Eye's Court is no military man. He has torches burning all around the building to prevent anyone from sneaking up close, yet at the same time, it ruins the night vision of his men. The shadows become even darker when there's a light nearby.

Shorty taps him on the shoulder to indicate they're close enough and he stops. "When the man on the roof looks away," James whispers. With slug in hand, he watches the man up there on the roof. They haven't long to wait before he looks away. Letting the magic flow, he launches the slug and strikes the man on the fourth floor in the chest, knocking him back into the building. Shorty's knife strikes home a second later and the man on the third floor staggers. James looks on in fear as it looks like he's about to fall out the window, but then he slumps forward. Half in and half out, he lies there dead in the window.

They wait a moment to see if a cry arises, but the night remains quiet. "Now for the other two," James says as they make their way over to the section of the roof opposite the remaining two men in the windows. And then just as before, they get into position and wait for the man on the roof to again turn away. When he does, slug and knife fly.

Jiron joins them just as the two men are struck and killed.

James nods to the man on the roof. "When he looks away, I'll create the ramp and you two get up there fast," he tells them.

"You got it," Jiron says. Removing one of his knives, he crouches there ready to go.

James modifies the spell in his mind. Creating the shield that will be the bridge is a piece of cake, however to make the surface have better traction so they won't slip on the way up, that takes some doing. When he thinks he's got it right, he turns his gaze to the man on the roof. Seconds go by and still the man continues to look out. Then just as James thinks he isn't going to look away again, he does.

"Now!" James whispers as one of his softly shimmering barriers appears. Beginning just in front of them, the barrier slants upward until it touches the roof's edge of the Eye's Court.

Without hesitation, Jiron leaps up and begins racing toward the man on the roof, Shorty is right behind him. They make it a third of the way when the man turns back and sees them coming toward him. Only the shock of seeing them where it is impossible for them to be prevents him from immediately sounding the alarm. Just as he comes to his senses, a knife flies and takes him in the upper chest, right at the base of the neck.

Jiron makes the roof as the man falls, and disappears as he moves to engage the other three men up there. When Shorty reaches the edge, James sees him throw another knife then disappears further onto the roof.

Motioning for the others to follow, James hits the barrier ramp running. When he reaches the section of the ramp that extends past the roof's edge and over the alley below, he gets a touch of vertigo as he looks below. Three stories down, the ground almost seems to beckon him. He can see the guards down there stationed at intervals all along the edge of the building. If one were to look up, the element of surprise would be gone.

Miko nudges him back into motion. Startled, he hadn't realized he had come to a stop. Resuming his run, he catches up to the others who have already made it to the top. Jiron and Shorty have already dispatched the guards stationed up here and Shorty is in the process of reclaiming his knives, plus adding the ones of the four dead men as well. Once everyone has reached the top, James cancels the ramp.

"Over here!" Stig hollers quietly from where he's found the trapdoor leading into the building.

Everyone quickly moves to join him and Jiron says, "We have to be fast. It won't take them much longer before they discover what happened." Turning to James he asks, "Do you know where she is yet?"

Shaking his head, James says, "I haven't had time to find her." Removing his mirror, he concentrates on her and soon her image appears in the mirror. Looking the worse for wear, she's sitting in a small room with light coming in through a window in the door. Though alone and looking afraid, she's at least not being tortured.

Then James slowly moves the image upward and she suddenly disappears as the view moves to the level above her. The area is dark and nothing but indistinct shadows show in the mirror. Moving upward yet again, the image suddenly changes and they see the roof. "She's on the fourth floor," he tells the others.

"Where on the fourth floor?" Jiron asks.

Taking out his cloth, he casts his finding spell and the cloth moves to point down and to the left. Moving in the direction indicated, he walks that way until the cloth bends and points straight down. "She's directly below," he says as he puts the cloth away.

Jiron gets her position in relation to the trapdoor set in his mind and nods. "Alright," he says, "let's go get her." Moving quickly to the trapdoor, he nods for Stig to open it.

Chapter Twenty Two

When Stig throws open the trapdoor, a strong odor wafts out. Rather unpleasant but bearable, he asks, "What is that?"

Brother Willim comes forward and smells it. "I think it comes from the berac plant," he says. Glancing to James he adds, "The leaves when burned produce a smoke that will prevent a mage from using his powers."

"Orrin did say this Eye knew how to deal with mages," Jiron states. "Guess he doesn't want you in there."

"What are you going to do?" asks Shorty.

"It's too late," he says, "I've already inhaled it." Even now he can feel his mind growing numb. Holding out his hand, he creates a small sphere the size of a marble before his magic fails altogether. Similar in nature to the one that he made in a similar situation back in Cardri, only this one will be slightly more versatile. It won't be limited to just three commands, he's worked on expanding its capabilities ever since the incident on the boat. Now, it should prove much more effective.

"Don't worry about me," he says to Jiron. "Aleya has to be our first concern."

Nodding, Jiron moves to the opening and starts climbing down the ladder. The hallway is dark with just a small amount of light with which to see. Once off the ladder, he moves quickly in search of the stairs down and finds them at the other end of the hallway. Scar and Potbelly have already made it down and are now beside him. The others are still making their way down from the roof.

"Go on!" Stig hollers as he makes it down the ladder from the roof. "We'll catch up."

Jiron nods then turns back to the stairs. With Scar and Potbelly right behind, he descends the stairway slowly. Light from the fourth floor illuminates the stairwell, and voices can be heard in conversation. He motions for Scar and Potbelly to wait as he continues down to where the stairs reach the fourth floor. There's a small landing from which the fourth floor hallway extends further into the building before the stairs continue their way down to the third floor.

Keeping his shoulder against the edge of the stairwell, he takes the steps slowly until he's on the second step from the bottom. He listens to the two men talking, one breaks out in laughter at something the other has said.

According to where James' cloth indicated Aleya to be, she should be in a room near the end of this hallway. He turns his head back to where the others are waiting, already Stig and James have joined Scar and Potbelly on the stairs. Behind them, he can see Miko coming to join them. Gesturing for them to come down and join him, he holds up two finger indicating that there are two men in the hallway. He then moves his hand across his throat. Scar nods understanding.

With knife in hand, he turns back to the hallway and suddenly charges around the corner. Behind him, the others race after.

When he turns the corner, he sees two guards standing in the middle of the hallway ten feet down. Running into them he knifes one while kneeing the other in the stomach. Scar and Potbelly soon join him and the guards lie dead on the floor.

"Stay right where you are," a voice comes to them from further down the hallway.

Jiron looks to find a black man standing before four guards who have crossbows aimed at them. "Pretty clever to make it this far," the black man says. He shouts something in the Empire's language and footfalls can be heard as many men begin to climb the stairs from below. The doors on the side of the hallway open up and more soldiers appear with swords bared.

"Discard you weapons," he says. "This is over." A smug smile comes over him as he sees victory at hand.

For a moment the world becomes silent as the two sides stare at one another. Then, the silence is pieced by the sound of something rolling along the floor of the hallway. The black man looks down as a small round spherical object the size of a marble rolls past Jiron's feet on its way toward him.

"What's this?" he asks as the round object approaches.

From where he stands in the hallway, James watches the object roll nearer to the black man. When it comes to within a foot of him, he says, "Leech times a hundred!"

The round object flashes, then the black man and the four crossbowmen drop to the floor as the object sucks them dry.

Jiron lashes out with his knife at the man in the doorway nearest him and sinks it to the hilt in the man's chest. At the rear, Stig kicks out at the man on the top of the stairs and sends him and all but one of the others tumbling back down the stairs to the third floor. Drawing his mace, he engages the remaining man on the stairs.

Then pandemonium erupts as the soldiers in the side rooms move to attack. Scar and Potbelly stand side by side as they stem the tide coming from one of the rooms, Reilin faces off with another and Miko has drawn his sword as he protects Brother William and James.

Brother Willim throws something in the air and it bursts into a massive cloud of gnats which engulfs three men. Each breath they take draws hundreds of the creatures into their mouths, throat and lungs. Fits of coughing leave them unable to either attack or defend themselves.

"Get me to my sphere," James says to Miko.

"You got it," he says. Moving next to Jiron, Miko lays into the soldiers with deadly speed few on this world can match. Behind him he hears James say, "Cancel," and the sphere becomes quiet once again. The men at the end of the hallway lay still, what life they had having been absorbed by the sphere.

"Jiron!" Aleya's voice cries out from behind the door where she's being held.

Sending the remaining soldier before him to the floor, Jiron moves down the hallway toward her voice. "Which one are you in?" he hollers.

"Right here!" she says, her voice coming through the door next to him.

Coming to a halt, he tries the door and finds it locked. Using his knife, he works on the lock and hears a click as the lock's tumblers shift. Opening the door, he almost falls backward from the impact of Aleya's embrace.

James moves past the couple and reaches his sphere. He has to move the black Eye's arm in order to pick it up. "Black Eye," he mumbles to himself. In other circumstances he would be able to appreciate the humor in that more. The sphere is glowing a dark crimson with stored power, it almost feels like it's vibrating. "Now to get out of here," he says.

Stig and Shorty are holding the top of the stairs, the sound of the fighting coming to them. Brother Willim exits from one of the rooms and says, "Those in the streets have been alerted."

"Great," James says. The fumes from the drug have really messed with his abilities. He tries to summon the magic but it will not come. "How many are down there?" he asks.

"Several score," he replies. "Most I would think are here in the building..."

"And on the way up the stairs," finishes James with a nod. "Very well then. Shield." With that, a shimmering barrier springs up around him and he begins walking to the top of the stairs. Bodies of those who had been stationed in the adjoining rooms litter the hallway. The fighting is now isolated to the stairwell where Jiron has taken Shorty's place next to Stig. Together, they make a deadly wall that none can breach.

When he comes to stand behind Jiron and Stig, he grasps the sphere in his hand and holds it out past Jiron and Stig. "Incinerate!" he says. A burst of flame explodes outwards, engulfing those unfortunate enough to be standing on the stairs. As the men begin to burn and cry out in pain, he tosses the sphere down the stairs. After making sure it isn't too close to where he, Jiron, and Stig stand he says, "Leech times a hundred." Continuing its forward motion, it rolls down the stairs, leeching from everyone it nears.

The cries still as the burning men no longer have the strength for it and James advances among them, stepping carefully. At the landing of the third floor, he finds bodies stacked one atop the other. There had been many soldiers standing there waiting their turn to attack. James has to move them with his foot in order to find a secure spot for his feet. "Cancel," he says to make his sphere dormant.

Behind him he hears Aleya's voice exclaim, "What do you mean you don't have my bow?"

"I was a bit more concerned with finding you" replies Jiron.

"My father gave me that bow," she says in a rather accusing manner.

"You would think someone who was a prisoner a moment ago would have a little more appreciation," he retorts. Then he appears at James' side.

To Jiron he says, "Somewhere around here is my sphere." Looking at the pile of bodies he shakes his head. From the stairs leading up from the second floor, footsteps are heard as more men move to attack. "I need time to find it," he says.

Jiron nods. "Scar! Potbelly! We got company," he hollers behind him. Pulling his knives he makes his way through the pile of bodies and moves further down the stairs. He can hear Aleya say, "Sure would be handy to have my bow right about now." As the first man appears around the turn in the stairwell, he puts her out of his mind and moves still further down to engage them. Scar and Potbelly arrive just as more appear and soon all three are battling with the enemy. Between the unevenness of the stairs and the bodies piled on them, the footing is quite treacherous.

"Give me a hand," James says to the others as he tries to ignore the clash of metal on metal. Pulling a limp body up, he realizes that the man isn't dead. "Be careful, some of them aren't dead," he announces. Then he looks under the body and doesn't see his sphere. Laying the man on top of another, he begins pulling up another in search of his sphere.

All but the three fighting in the stairwell begin moving bodies as they hunt for his sphere. "Here it is!" Brother Willim exclaims. Three steps down from the third floor landing, he finds it lying on a step under one of the dead men.

"Don't touch it!" yells James when he sees the priest reaching down to pick it up. "Might not be a good thing to do." Coming over to where the glowing sphere lies, he picks it up and then begins making his way down where Jiron, Scar and Potbelly are holding off the soldiers.

Jiron and Potbelly stand next to each other as they hold off the attackers. Scar with his double swords is forced to stay behind them as there isn't enough room for all three of them to fight side by side. They've actually been able to push the Empire soldiers down several steps and have reached where the stairs make a turn back on themselves as it continues down to the second floor.

"Need some room," he says to Scar as he taps him on the shoulder.

Scar nods and moves out of his way.

Just as before, James moves to take position just behind Jiron and Potbelly. Holding the sphere in his hand, he says "Watch out," to the pair as he extends his hand forward. Knowing what is about to happen, they quickly disengage and take a step back. The two men they were fighting think they are fleeing and with a yell, charge forward just as James yells, "Incinerate!"

The force of the blast knocks them backward as the fire surging out of the sphere engulfs them. The narrowness of the stairwell focuses the power and the flame roars forward. Screams and yells of men in pain come to them from further down the stairs. Then James tosses the sphere so it will roll down the stairs and says, "Leech times a hundred."

Men on fire that had but a moment before been shrieking in pain, suddenly grow quiet as they flop to the floor. The smell of burnt flesh and hair is nauseating.

Potbelly is about to move forward when James stops him. "Not yet," he says. The last thing he wants is for Potbelly to enter the leech radius of the sphere. He didn't make it very wide for safety's sake, but should you move one inch into it, you'll feel the full effect.

"Cancel," he says and then indicates they can move forward.

Jiron is the first one down the stairs followed closely by Scar and Potbelly. They make it to the second floor landing and continue down to where the stair turns back on itself. The bodies of the men slain by the leeching of the sphere end halfway down to where the stairs turns back on its way down to the ground floor. Just as Jiron moves to turn to where the stairwell continues down, three crossbow bolts barely miss him as they slam into the wall inches away. Backpedaling quickly, he moves back around the corner.

"They're not coming up this time," he tells Scar.

"Looks like they finally learned their lesson," Scar replies.

Jiron glances back toward the second floor landing where James and the others are searching for his sphere. When at last they find it, James picks it up and joins him at the turn in the stairwell. Jiron then apprises him of the situation.

James moves to the turn and peers around to look down at the assembled men on the lower level. He gets a flight of crossbow bolts fired at him for his trouble. He then opens the palm of his hand and looks at the deeply glowing sphere. If he tries leeching again, it might reach critical mass and explode. Going to have to release some of the bottled up power before he does.

To Stig and Shorty he gestures down the second floor hallway and says, "See if there's another way out. Also check to see if the windows on the other sides of the building are being watched."

"You got it," Shorty replies and they quickly move down the hallway checking the rooms.

"I doubt if there is one," Jiron says, "or they would have come at us from that way too."

"I know," James tells him. "I was sort of hoping that they were all down below and we could sneak out a window or something without them knowing."

"Doubt it," he replies.

"Me too," admits James. Then he shrugs and says, "But you never know."

"That's true," agrees Jiron. "Though keep in mind, the longer we wait, the more soldiers will arrive."

Shaking his head, James says, "I don't think there are that many more here in Morac." When Jiron looks to him, he adds, "They weren't expecting an attack so there would have been no reason to have a large garrison here." Indicating the men lying dead on the stairs both here and above, he then nods toward those waiting down below and says, "Frankly, I'd be surprised if there were many more than what's already showed up."

"You got a point there," admits Jiron.

Down below, it has grown fairly quiet. Jiron moves to where the stairs turn and takes a peek around the corner. He darts back as several bolts fly by and embed themselves in the wall.

"Still down there I take it?" asks Reilin. Jiron simply gives him a look as if to say 'That was a stupid question'.

Stig and Shorty arrive shortly after that and report that the other sides are being watched, but only by a few. "There are only three in the back," Stig tells them.

"The sides have a few more than that," adds Shorty, "but not that much more."

"Can we take the three out in the back quickly?" he asks.

"Probably could if I had my bow," states Aleya.

Jiron rounds on her. "Enough already," he exclaims. "I said I am sorry and this constant distraction from the matter at hand is not helping anyone!"

She returns his look with a stern one of her own then nods her head.

He turns back to Shorty and asks, "Can we?"

"Possibly," he says. "I can take one, maybe two before they realize it. But the third?"

They all look to James. Shaking his head, he holds up the sphere and says, "This is all I have until the drug wears off."

"That's not going to start to happen until we get out of here," Brother Willim adds. "Even then it will take hours."

"Where are the men situated back there?" Jiron asks.

Suddenly, they hear a creak from the lower stairway. Shorty picks up one of the knives from the dead lying at the second floor landing and moves to where the stairs turn back to the first floor. Moving quickly, he dodges around the corner, throws the knife then dives back just as half a dozen bolts fly through where he had just been.

From below, they hear a man cry out from where the knife found its mark. "We don't have a whole lot of time," Shorty says. Again the creaking comes as men from below once more begin to work their way up.

Scar and Potbelly says, "You guys go take them out and we'll hold them off here."

James and Jiron glance to each other and nod simultaneously. "Let's go," Jiron says then turns to Shorty. "Show me where the guards are."

"This way," Shorty says as he begins running down the hallway.

Jiron follows with James right on his heels. Shorty turns into an open doorway and before James passes through, the sound of Scar and Potbelly engaging the enemy comes down the hallway. Leaving the hallway, James enters what looks like an office of some kind. A desk with papers resting in neat stacks dominates the room.

"Over here," Shorty says from where he's looking out the window.

James crosses the room until he's next to him. Looking out, he sees the three men not more than ten feet away. They have their swords out and look very alert. The window through which James is looking is closed. They'll have to open it before they will be able to effectively strike out at the three men. He moves to the window to begin opening it when Jiron stops him and shakes his head. "What?" he asks.

Instead of replying, Jiron shoulders him out of the way and begins to open the window himself. A little hurt that Jiron didn't think he could do it, James backs up and watches him lift the window.

Inch by inch the window rises and when it is open seven inches, it lets out with a squeal. Jiron immediately stops and moves away from the window. Peering out from the corner of it, he sees one of the three men looking up in their direction. After a moment of staring their way, the man returns to looking down the alley.

Sighing in relief, Jiron returns to the window and manages to open it fully. From the hallway, the sound of the fighting is growing closer, Scar and Potbelly must be having to give ground.

Jiron turns from the window and glances to Shorty. He then nods his head in the direction of the men on the ground. Shorty nods as he pulls two knives from his belt.

"Wait," whispers Brother Willim as he lays a hand on Shorty's arm. A subtle glow surrounds Brother Willim and from outside, the sound of a growling dog is heard.

Glancing out the window, Jiron sees the three men facing away from them and toward a rather large dog that is growling most menacingly at them. He looks back to Brother Willim who says, "Slip out the window while they are distracted."

Jiron nods and begins moving through the window. Glancing to the men, he sees them with their swords at the ready and one of them is advancing upon the dog. Swinging out the window, he lowers his body until he's hanging completely from the window sill. Then he lets go and drops silently to the ground.

Pulling both knives, he stands there and waits for Shorty to appear. Not taking his eyes from the men, he hears Shorty land next to him. With a quick glance to Shorty to make sure he's set, Jiron advances behind the men. As he starts to move, the dog begins barking intently, then turns and takes off down the alley.

The soldiers begin talking among themselves as they relax. Then one falls to the ground and before the other two realize what's happening, Shorty's other knife flies through the air and takes out a second. The third one barely gets his guard up before Jiron is upon him.

One knife feints to the man's face which causes him to reflexively bring his sword up to block the blow, which leaves him open for the other. Sinking his blade in the man's stomach, Jiron quickly pulls it out and knees him in the groin. Falling to the ground, the man groans as Jiron lashes out with his foot to the side of his head and knocks him out.

Indicating the end of the alley, he says to Shorty, "Keep a lookout." With Shorty running to the alley's mouth, Jiron returns to the window. He says, "Come on," and begins helping the others down beginning with Aleya.

Back in the room, when James saw Jiron and Shorty take out the guards he says to Miko, "Help everyone out and then you get out too."

"What about you?" he asks.

"I've got to go help Scar and Potbelly," he replies. Without another word, he makes a run for the door.

Out in the hallway he discovers Scar and Potbelly are no longer on the stairs. Instead they are now halfway down the hallway and are slowly being pushed further back. Running up behind them he says, "Time to go."

Scar's two longswords have been devastating, as has Potbelly's sword and knife. The hallway between where they now fight and the stairs is littered with the bodies and body parts of those they've slain.

"Get out of here," Scar hollers to him. "We're not going to be able to hold them off much longer."

James comes and stands between them, almost getting sliced by one of Scar's sword in the process. Holding out the sphere, he stretches his arm between them and says, "Sealing barrier." All of a sudden a barrier flashes into being sealing the hallway off between them and the enemies trying to kill them.

"Get back to the others," James hollers. "I'll take care of this."

Trusting in him, Scar and Potbelly turn and double time it to the room where the others are going through the window.

James gazes at the men on the other side of the barrier who are trying to break through. He opens his hand and looks at the sphere resting in his palm. Sighing, he says, "Delay five. Cancel. Leach times hundred. Delay twenty. Spoilsport." Turning his palm over, he drops the sphere onto the floor of the hallway.

Turning around, he races back to the room. Just as he reaches the door, he glances back and sees the barrier wink out and the men beginning to fall to the floor as the sphere leeches them dry.

Moving into the room at a run, he sees Scar beginning to pass through the window. Potbelly and Miko are still in the room. He didn't give them enough time! "Move!" he cries. "We got seconds before this place blows."

"What?" asks Miko.

"Go! Go! Go!" he yells and practically pushes Scar out the window. Losing his grip, he falls to the ground. "Jump or we're all dead!" he yells to the other two.

Seeing the fear in his eyes, Miko dives through the window and is followed a half second later by Potbelly. Hitting the ground hard, Miko breaks his arm and Potbelly his leg. James flies through the window a second later.

"What...?" begins Jiron as James hits the ground and scrapes off a large area of skin from his side. "No time to explain," he yells as he gets to his feet. "We have to get out of here now!"

"Over the top?" asks Jiron. James nods. Grabbing Potbelly on either side, he and Scar carry him to the end of the alley. Brother Willim helps Miko by carrying the pack containing the Book of Morcyth.

Reilin and Shorty, as well as Aleya are at the end of the alley. When they see the others coming fast, Reilin says, "It's clear."

"Run!" James hollers to them. His tone of voice tells them this is not a time for dithering. Racing from the alley, Reilin leads them down the street away from the Eye's Court. They don't get far when...

Ka-Boom!!

...the building explodes outwards.

The concussion wave rolls over them and knocks them to the ground. A cloud of fire erupts out of the building as the sphere explodes with power leeched from dozens of men. Debris sails through the air, some of the larger pieces slam into other buildings.

Getting up, they are pelted with stones, some hitting them with bone crushing force. Aleya is hit and falls to the ground. James is there and aids her in regaining her feet. Her left arm hangs limply at her side.

"We've got to get out of here!" Shorty hollers.

"No!" James yells. "Find a place to hole up. We're in no condition to escape."

Nodding, he moves ahead and goes in search of a suitable location. A minute later he hollers, "Over here!"

They follow the sound of his voice and see him standing beside an open door waving for them to hurry.

Moving as fast as the injured can go, they hurry over and pass through the door. Just as the door shuts...

Wham!

...a large chunk of the Eye's Court slams into the upper stories of the building they just entered. The building shakes and shimmies but remains erect. Looking around, they see that Reilin has led them into an abandoned building. It could possibly have been a dye merchant's shop at one time, but in the dark it's hard to be sure.

They move from the room just inside the front door to a room further in the back. Potbelly moans as Scar and Jiron set him on the floor against the wall. All of a sudden, light floods the room as Miko removes the Star from his pouch and begins healing the injuries of the others. He starts with his own arm then goes to Potbelly. Brother Willim moves his broken arm into proper position then the glow from the Star surrounds it as it begins knitting the bones back together.

Jiron comes to James and says, "You cut that a bit close didn't you?"

"Sorry," he replies. "The drug that infused that place muddled my mind. When I set it to go off, I set it for too short a time. When I realized my mistake, it was too late."

"Well, fortunately Miko can take care of the injuries," he says. That's when he takes notice of the way Aleya's arm is hanging limp at her side. Leaving James' side, he rushes over to her.

"What happened to you?" he asks.

"Got hit by something," she replies.

"Miko!" he yells as he turns toward where he's still working on his arm.

"Leave him be," she says. "He'll get to me when he can."

"I'm sorry," he tells her and gives her a hug, all the while being careful of her injured arm.

"Don't be," she tells him. "There's too much going on for us to be fighting over a little thing like a bow." Then with her good arm, she takes hold of his chin and pulls his face closer for a kiss.

"What a mess," Shorty says from the window.

"Bad?" Reilin asks.

"That building's gone," he explains. "The streets are full of people and a couple fires have broken out in different areas."

"Anyone coming in this direction?" James asks.

Shaking his head, Shorty says, "No. Looks like they are all congregating over by what's left of that building."

"Might be a good idea to wait until things quiet down before we leave," suggests Scar.

"As long as no one disturbs us," adds Reilin.

Miko and Brother Willim begin healing the rest once Miko's arm is again whole. Shorty continues to watch the goings on outside from the window. They decide to get what rest they can before making the attempt to leave Morac.

Once Miko finishes with him, James sits against one of the walls and closes his eyes. After that blast, everyone in the Empire is going to know exactly where he is. They can't afford to stay here very long, but they could all use a short rest. It doesn't take him long to pass into unconsciousness.

Chapter Twenty Three

Waking up, James finds his head much clearer. He tries to summon his orb and succeeds then cancels it. He's much relieved now that the effect of the drug he was exposed to in the Eye's Court has worn off.

Rays of light enter through cracks in the boards covering the windows. In the dim light he sees Jiron standing at the window gazing through to the street outside. Other than Jiron and himself, no one else is awake.

As he gets up, his feet make a scuffing noise across the floor. Jiron glances over at the sound and sees him rising. Giving him a nod and a slight grin, Jiron returns his gaze back to the street outside.

James carefully makes his way through the sleeping forms and comes to his side. "What's going on out there?" he whispers.

"Seems most of the town has come by at one time or another to see what happened," he explains. "At first there were but a few guards and soldiers out there sifting through the rubble. Then about an hour ago, a force of over a hundred showed up, cordoned off the whole area and made a sweep of the surrounding buildings."

Seeing the worried look in his eyes, Jiron says, "One soldier came by and looked in through the window but moved on his way. Can't believe he didn't see you guys there on the floor sleeping."

"Luck must be with us," James observes.

"Must be," he says. "I'm not sure exactly what is going on, but the commander in charge of the men divided them up in squads of ten and sent them through the town. It won't be long before they figure out what happened and who was here."

"If they haven't already," adds James. He thinks for a moment then asks, "How far away is the inn from here do you think?"

"It isn't close, that's for sure," Jiron replies. "You're not thinking about going back and retrieving the horses are you?"

"You got a better idea?" he asks. "Without them, we won't get far."

"I agree," he acknowledges. "But there's no reason we have to have ours, any will do." He then turns back to the window and points through two of the boards to a building across the street. Four soldiers stand guard by the entrance. "They put their horses in there. There are over a score."

James takes in the building, the guards, and the fact that it's across an open street. "Pretty ambitious aren't you?" he asks. "They'll see us."

"Just a thought," he says. "Always like to know our options."

"What's out the back?" James asks him.

"Not much," replies Reilin. Having heard them talking, he decided to get up and see what's going on. "The back door opens onto an alley that runs for a ways. Last night while on guard duty I checked it out."

"Could we make our way out through the alley and return to the inn to get our horses?" James asks.

Shrugging, Reilin says, "I don't know. I didn't explore that far."

Turning to James, Jiron says, "You keep an eye on what's going on out there and I'll find out."

"Be careful," James says as Jiron begins moving toward the back door. As soon as Jiron disappears into the back, James returns his attention to the goings on outside. Not much is happening other than people working through the rubble in the hopes of finding survivors.

One by one the others wake up. Miko is the last to awaken and sits up just as Jiron returns.

"Well?" James asks as Jiron comes from the back.

Giving him a grin, he says, "The alley out back runs along the backside of a courtyard of another inn. And guess how many horses are in the stable?"

"Enough for all of us?" James asks.

Nodding, Jiron says, "That's right."

"We should leave now," Scar suggests, "while everyone's busy out there sifting through the rubble."

"My thought exactly," agrees Jiron.

"The gates out of the city are going to be watched," warns Reilin. "They'll not let us simply leave."

"I doubt if that will change even if we were to wait for a week," states James. "We go now." To Jiron he says, "Take Stig and Shorty with you and get the horses ready."

"Right," he says and indicates for the two men to follow him. Just before he leaves the room, Jiron pauses and turns back to face James. "When you follow, it's to the left out the back door."

"Got it," he says. Then Jiron leaves the room.

Moving over to Brother Willim, James asks, "How are you holding up?"

"Actually doing quite well," he replies.

"That's good," James says. "There's something that's been bothering me."

"What?" the priest of Asran asks.

"Back there in the building, the drug in the air affected my ability to summon magic," he says. "Yet you were able to. Why?"

"My magic comes from a different source than yours," Brother Willim explains. "Where you must direct and channel the power, I have merely to ask." He can see James is somewhat understanding what he's saying. "Can't really explain it better than that."

"I think I understand," states James. "Priest magic, and that which I use, manipulates the same source of power. Only, yours comes from your god whereas I take it from within me and the world around us."

"Something like that," nods Brother Willim. "But as priests, we are unable to do some of the things you can. We are limited to what our god allows."

"Checks and balances," James says. "No matter what, there's always something that will limit even the most powerful of people."

"Never heard it put quite that way before," he says. "But you're right."

Jiron leads Stig and Shorty out the back and down to the inn's courtyard. Pausing at the entrance, he makes sure the area is clear. Not seeing anyone, he waves for the other two to follow him and they make a dash for the stables.

Once inside, they find that the horses' saddle and tack are stored on shelves in the room at the rear of the stable. They go and each get a saddle with associated gear and begin to saddle the horses. Stig and Shorty finish cinching the last belt tight on their horses at the same time and go together to retrieve another saddle for the next horse.

While they are in the back gathering the appropriate equipment, a man walks into the stable and stops once he sees Jiron saddling the horse. Jiron freezes when the man begins talking to him. When Jiron fails to reply, the man pulls his sword and backs out of the inn.

Hoping to catch him before he can raise the alarm, Jiron chases him out into the courtyard. Just outside the stable he sees the man he was chasing with another dozen men. Unable to stop in time, he dodges to the side and barely evades a blade aimed at his head.

He hits the ground and rolls twice before coming back to his feet. Now, six of the men are between him and the stables. The other six are fanned out in the courtyard moving to surround him. Two of the six by the stables are moving to engage him. He strikes out at one, causing the man to jump back to avoid being struck and parries the thrust of the other. Then out of the corner of his eye he sees over twenty soldiers enter the courtyard from the entrance on the far side.

Deciding there are too many with which to deal with effectively, he back steps quickly toward the alley entrance that he originally entered the courtyard by. A sword strikes out at him and he deflects it to the side just as the other man attacks him with an overhand hack. Twisting, he manages to avoid the blow.

Stig appears in the stable's door with Shorty right behind him. Jiron sees them there set to enter the fray. "No!" he shouts at the top of his lungs. There're too many for them to fight their way through.

His cry, which had been directed at Stig and Shorty, causes the men before him to hesitate. Making use of the momentary lull, he turns and runs into the alley.

Stig and Shorty, realizing that there's nothing they can do, duck back inside the stable. The men and the soldiers race past the stable door and pursue Jiron into the alley.

"Come on man!" Stig hollers as he runs over to one of the horses. Mounting, he waits a second for Shorty to do the same. Then just as they are about to leave the stable...

Crumph! Crumph! Crumph!

...and they know that James has joined the fray.

James and the others leave the building they spent the night in and are making their way down the alley toward where Jiron said the inn was located. Then the clash of weapons comes to them and they hear Jiron yell "No!"

"They're in trouble!" Aleya shouts and they rush forward. They don't get more than two steps before Jiron races into the alley at a dead run. A second later a swarm of screaming men emerges behind him.

"Go!" he yells as he sprints toward them.

Now that sneaking out of the city is no longer an option, James lets the magic go...

Crumph! Crumph! Crumph!

...and the ground erupts under the charging men, throwing them into the air.

Then from neighboring streets, the sounds of horns blare forth as they tell the world where he is. Then from both ends of the alley, the soldiers which had arrived earlier that morning begin pouring in. "Back inside!" James yells and turns around.

Before he can get moving, Jiron races past him and bolts into the building they had just exited. "Move!" James yells as he and the others run for the doorway.

Miko is the last to pass through and slams the door shut. Throwing the bar, he puts his shoulder against the door as the soldiers on the other side begin beating against it.

"It's clear on this side," Jiron says from the window. "They've all rushed to the sound of the horns."

"What happened to Stig and Shorty?" James asks.

"They were still in the stable when all hell broke loose," he says. "I think they're still alive." Then he nods to the building across the street where the soldier's horses are being kept. "Shall we?"

Bang! Bang! Bang!

"It's not going to hold for long," Miko yells.

James nods to Jiron, "Let's go." Then to Miko he yells, "Hold it as long as you can."

Reilin moves to add his strength to Miko's and places his shoulder against the door. "Just hurry!" he yells to him.

Bang!

"You stay here and when we have the horses ready, you all come at once," James tells Brother Willim.

Nodding, he says, "Good luck."

Aleya comes forward and says, "I'm coming too."

Jiron pauses as if he's going to object then nods. "Okay," he says. Throwing open the door, he runs across the street to the doorway through which the horses are kept. James and Aleya follow.

When the people on the street see them emerge from the building, they begin to holler, scream and flee. Three soldiers appear from out of nowhere and James takes one out with a slug and prepares to launch another. "You two get the horses," he tells them, "I'll hold them off." Letting the second slug fly, he pulls another from his belt. Jiron and Aleya rush in through the door as he sends the third slug flying.

A shimmer appears around him as his shield springs to life. Standing there in the street, the shimmering shield surrounding him, he scans both directions.

Ping!

A crossbow bolt ricochets off the barrier. Turning in the directions the bolt originated from, he sees men beginning to boil out of an alley further down. Not able to make it through the door Miko and Reilin are holding shut, some have decided to make an end run and try to take them from behind.

Ping!

Another bolt strikes the barrier as more crossbowmen join the fray.

Crumph! Crumph! Crumph!

Explosions rip the street as the leading edge of the charging men is thrown into the air. Now from the other direction, more soldiers enter the street. Turning to them he again lets loose with the power.

Crumph! Crumph!

Men are thrown in the air as the ground beneath their feet explodes outwards. Moving to the doorway Jiron and Aleya passed through, he yells, "Hurry up in there!" Glancing inside, he sees two dead soldiers who must have been inside when Jiron entered. The wounds on their body are indicative of those made by a knife.

"Just a few more!" Aleya hollers back as she throws another saddle onto a horse.

Returning his attention to the street and the soldiers approaching from both directions, he moves away from the building and makes his way to the middle of the road. Both forces of men have now slowed to a crawl as they've come to realize they face a mage. Going through some of their minds is the possibility this may be the very same mage they've heard tales about.

Then suddenly from out of the doorway wherein Miko and Reilin are holding the door shut, Brother Willim and the others emerge at a run. "The door gave way!" he shouts to James.

Nodding, James indicates the doorway wherein Aleya and Jiron work to saddle the horses. "In there," he says.

The two forces that had been advancing slowly, suddenly break into an all out run toward him, possibly in response to Brother Willim and the others fleeing across the street. Bolts fly toward them. A green glow manifests around Brother Willim as he uses his staff in a blurring defense and knocks the bolts aside.

With a thought, James creates two spheres of power, similar to that which he used in the Eye's Court. Throwing one to the right and one to the left, he hollers, "Leech by a hundred." As soon as the last word leaves his lips, the two spheres flash and soldiers drop. When he realizes the leeching radius isn't wide enough to completely block off the street, he says, "Radius by four."

Now men are falling all over and the two spheres are glowing a dangerous crimson. Running for the doorway where the others went, he dives through just as one sphere reaches critical mass and explodes. A second later, the other one goes.

Two massive fireballs erupt into the sky. Those buildings closest in proximity are rocked on their foundations, two actually collapse. James is knocked to the floor by the concussion wave.

The building James and the others are in rocks from the force of the blast. One wall shivers and cracks. They fear it's going to give way and bring the entire building down on top of their heads but it only settles several inches before coming to a rest once more.

"James!" Jiron hollers.

Looking through the dust in the air, he sees Jiron in the saddle. Next to him is a horse saddled and ready. Getting up off the floor, he races for the horse and practically leaps into the saddle. "This way," Jiron says and leads him further into the building which as it turns out is a very large stable. They pass many stalls containing additional horses as they head to the large opening at the other end.

Moving quickly, they soon rejoin the others. Four more dead soldiers lay across the ground near the exit. Reilin, Scar and Potbelly are wiping their blades on the clothes of the dead men. When they see Jiron and James coming, they quickly mount.

"Let's get out of here," Jiron says and bolts down the street toward the nearest gate.

"What happened to Stig and Shorty?" asks Potbelly.

"I don't know," replies Jiron. "They were alive when we got separated."

"They're smart and resourceful," adds Scar. "They'll make it." Racing away from the scene of destruction behind them, they make their way through the streets.

Just then, the gates of the city appear before them. Jiron brings them to a halt when they discover the gates are closed and are guarded by over a score of men. "Should we try another one?" he asks.

Shaking his head, James says, "Another won't be any better. I'm sure they have them all covered." Moving forward, James says, "The rest of you wait here." The shimmering of his shield suddenly surrounds him and his horse as he approaches the men guarding the gate.

On the way, he opens his palm and creates another of his spheres. Then, he stops there in the middle of the road for a moment and stares at the sphere in his hand. Realizing that such blatant misuse of power is becoming all too easy for him, he closes his hand. There has to be another way. Death and more death, is that all there is?

Then as hard as he can, throws it far from him. "Cancel!" he says with finality and the sphere winks out. Then he glances to the men arrayed before him and resumes his advance.

Before he comes close, the officer in charge of the gate calls out what sounds like a command. Paying it no heed, James continues onward. As he draws closer, bolts begin to pepper the outside of his shield from the squad of a half dozen crossbowmen positioned to the rear of the soldiers.

James continues to press forward until he comes to within a dozen yards of the leading edge of soldiers. By this time, the order had been given for the crossbowmen to cease their hail of bolts seeing as how they were unable to penetrate the shield.

"Does anyone understand me?" James asks.

A soldier bearing an insignia which must mark him as the leader of these men replies, "I can."

"I want you to open the gates and allow us to pass through unmolested," he tells him.

"I cannot allow you to leave," the officer replies.

James can see the expression of fear in the man's eyes. The officer had to have seen the earlier explosions and understands what might be the consequences of barring his way. "I'm trying to save the lives of you and your men," he says. "I'm heartily sick of causing the death of others."

"If I should step aside and allow you to leave," the officer states, "our lives would be forfeit in any event."

James sighs and shakes his head sadly. "So be it then," he says. Turning around, he returns back to where the others are waiting. Once he returns, he moves next to Brother Willim and whispers something in his ear. When he's done speaking, he looks for Brother Willim's response.

Nodding, Brother Willim says, "It can be done."

"Then please do so," he replies.

The green glow that always accompanies the priest whenever he calls forth his god's power now springs to life around him. Raising his hands, he calls for aid.

It takes but a moment before a commotion develops near the gate. The lines of soldiers that had stood so uniformly are now deteriorating into chaos as ants boil out of the ground. Not the red fire ants as before, but still annoying and painful as they crawl inside the men's armor and begin biting.

"Thank you Brother Willim," says James. To the rest he says, "Give me a minute before following." Moving forward to the gates again, he gets his horse up to a fast trot. At the edge of the carpet of ants, he sees the ants move aside as if allowing him to pass. Glancing back, he sees the glow still surrounding Brother Willim as he works to control the swarm of ants.

Still encased in his barrier, he nudges his horse forward. With every step his horse takes, the ants move aside and away. Not having to worry about the ants climbing his horse's legs, he winds his way through the men writhing on the ground, some almost completely coated in ants, on his way to the gate.

He passes by the officer with whom he spoke to earlier. Lying on the ground, the man's hands work to try and remove the ants. But for every ten he brushes off, a hundred take their place. For a moment their eyes lock. "I told you I don't like to kill," he tells him.

Continuing his forward motion, he reaches the gate. He comes close enough so that he can place his hand upon its surface. Summoning the magic, he sends it out in one massive surge that blasts the gates open.

The thunder of hooves comes to him as the others race for the gates. He moves back to the officer and says, "I could have killed you and your men, but didn't. Remember that." The officer looks to him but doesn't make any sort of response.

"Come on man," Jiron says to him as he reaches the swarm. Using the same path as had James, he and the others race through and leave the city.

James kicks his horse into motion and follows after. Outside the gates, they take the southeast road, the one that leads to the city of Cyst. The city where Azku said the man could be found from whom he bought Cassie's necklace.

Pushing their horses into a gallop, they don't make it far from the city before they see a dozen riders exiting through the broken gates in pursuit. "Hey!" exclaims Scar. "Two of them are Stig and Shorty!" Coming to a quick stop, they turn to find that Stig and Shorty are not part of the other force of riders, rather they are being chased by them.

James turns back toward the oncoming riders. When Jiron and the others move to join him, he says, "I'll take care of this," as a dazzling shield springs into being around him. Brighter by far than any other he's ever created, it almost rivals the sun in brilliance as sparks pop and crackles across its surface.

Crumph! Crumph!

Two explosions on either side of the road throw dirt and sand upon the riders. Coming to a quick halt, the riders seem as if they are contemplating the wisdom of continuing. To help make up their minds, James suddenly kicks his horse in the flanks and races forward.

Stig and Shorty fly past as he moves toward the riders. The expressions on many of their faces are ones of fear. To go after fleeing riders is one thing, but to go head to head with a mage of such power is quite another. Their minds finally made up, they turn tail and race back to Morac.

James cancels his spectacular shield once they are fully on their way and then turns his horse back to return to the others.

"Yeah," Shorty says as he talks to Jiron, "after those soldiers chased you out of the inn's courtyard, we took two of the horses and exited the other way. We figured the rest of you could handle things well enough without us so worked our way toward one of the gates."

"That's right," adds Stig. "Then when we heard the explosion that must have taken out the gate, we raced toward where you were and arrived just after you left. That's when those riders back there showed up and gave chase."

"Glad to have you back," James tells them. "It might be wise to put as much distance between us and here as fast as we can. I expect pursuit to materialize pretty soon."

"Then let's not sit here and talk," says Jiron. "Cyst awaits." Turning to follow the road once more to the southeast, he quickly gets his horse up to a fast gallop with the others right behind.

Once Morac has disappeared in the distance behind them, Jiron angles them off the road in an almost due easterly direction. Moving deeper into the desert and away from the road, he doesn't turn them to the south until the road and the travelers upon it are no longer in sight. Then he turns to run parallel to the road on its way southeast to Cyst.

Throughout the day, James begins sinking into depression. By the time darkness falls and they've moved even further into the desert to make camp, he's withdrawn into himself and only makes one word answers when spoken to.

The others allow him time to himself, those who have ridden with him for some time now know that this is something that comes over him once in a while. Brother Willim however is unable to let him wallow in whatever misery has him in its grip. Once their meal is ready, he takes two bowls of stew and goes over to where James is sitting.

Holding out the bowl, Brother Willim says, "Here."

James takes it and gives him a short, "Thank you."

"Mind if I sit down?" he asks.

James shrugs and says, "No."

Taking a seat on the ground facing him, Brother Willim dips his spoon into the so-called stew and begins eating. He watches James for a moment before saying, "I can tell there's something gnawing away at you." James glances up to meet his gaze but makes no comment. "It might ease your mind if you tell me about it."

Locking eyes with the priest, James says, "Confession good for the soul?"

Brother Willim gives him a brief grin. "Never heard it put that way before, but yes. There are times when keeping your troubles bottled inside can do more harm than good. A tree cannot grow tall if there's a disease eating it away from the inside."

James takes another bite and sighs. "The weight of the dead is heavy," he begins. Glancing again at Brother Willim, he sees the concern and worry for him in his eyes. "Before I came here, I had never been near the dead and dying. Oh sure, I watched the news but had never connected to it emotionally. They say that my people are growing numb to that sort of thing. Heck, we're inundated with it all the time from every direction. Newspapers, TV, radio, every day you hear about how this person was found dead, or that person killed for political or religious reasons. But it never really hits you."

"But now, I personally have been responsible for hundreds, if not thousands of deaths," he states.

Brother Willim can see the pain behind his eyes. "I understand the weight you carry," he says understandingly. "Events, unfortunately, have not given you many options."

In a voice that's barely above a whisper, he says, "But that's not the worst of it." He glances up to the priest, holds out his hand and creates one of his spheres. "You've seen me use this?" he asks.

Brother Willim nods gravely. "Yes," he replies.

He rolls it around in his hand as he explains. "This is the most evil thing I have ever done," he admits.

"Evil?" says Brother Willim. "I wouldn't so name yourself, or your deeds."

"You don't understand." Holding the sphere between his forefinger and thumb he brings it up in front of the brother's face. "With this, I suck the life from people and use it to kill. First it leeches power from everything nearby, then I am able to utilize that power in various ways. Barriers, fire, explosions, you name it and I can do it."

Nodding his head, Brother Willim remains silent as James continues.

"Isn't that wrong?" he asks as his eyes turn to gaze at the sphere between his fingers. "To steal the life that the gods have given them?" He then goes quiet as the sphere disappears and he looks to Brother Willim for a response.

"Our lord Asran teaches us that to take the life of any living thing is wrong," he says. "Whether it be birds, fish, insects…" and then he pauses a moment before adding, "or man. But we do need to survive, and so we kill animals to feed ourselves, clothe ourselves and so forth."

"But men are not animals," he insists.

"No, that is true," he admits. "But let me ask you this. If a man was intent on taking your life, would you have any compunction whatsoever about removing one of your slugs from your belt and killing him with it? If that was the only way in which to preserve your life?"

"Yes, though I wouldn't want to," he replies.

"And later, would you agonize over it like you are doing now?" he asks.

"Not so much, no," he admits.

"Whether you take the life of someone with a sword, knife, or even a slug, is no better or worse than what you are doing with your sphere," he says.

"Then why do I feel this way?" he asks.

"You feel this way because you are a good man," he explains. "Each person has within them the knowledge of right and wrong. Some say it is learned from those around them as they grow up, others believe that it comes from the gods."

James nods. "I understand what you're talking about," he says. "My people call it a moral compass."

"You are feeling this way because you are going against yours. You feel this is wrong, so your 'moral compass' is working to keep you from continuing down this path." He pauses a moment to see what affect his words are having. When James makes no comment he adds, "Are you finding it easier to do the things you feel are wrong?"

"When I first discovered that the power within everyone could be taken and used, I was appalled and told myself that I would never do it," he explains. "Or rather not to do it unless absolutely necessary. Now though, I seem to be doing it on a regular basis." He turns pained eyes toward Brother Willim and says, "Now it's almost as if it's becoming a habit. I no longer even try to come up with another way."

"The easiest path is often the most dangerous," Brother Willim states. "The more you do what you know is wrong, the easier it will become the next time. And the next time."

"What can I do?" James asks.

"The solution to your problem is simple," he says. "Stop doing what you know is wrong."

"But, that could cost us our lives if I don't," he replies.

Brother Willim gives him a look of sadness. "As long you can come up with reasons why you must do things against your 'moral compass', you will. We humans can reason anything to sound like a good idea. If taking the life of people in this manner is abhorrent to you, then don't. Or resign yourself to continuing as you have."

"What will happen to me if I continue?" he asks.

"I think you know," he says.

They sit there in silence for a while while each finishes their meal. James thinks about what Brother Willim had said and knows the truth of it. After they've finished their meal, he says to him, "Thank you."

Brother Willim gives him a smile and says, "That's my job. I am a priest you know. Just think on what we talked about, follow your conscience, and you'll feel better."

"I will," says James.

The rest of the night goes well for him as he rejoins the others. By the time he lays down on his blanket, he feel much better and has promised himself not to sink further toward the 'dark side'.

Chapter Twenty Four

Out in the desert as they are, nothing disturbs them throughout the night. When the sun begins to lighten the world with the coming of dawn, they break camp and resume their trek to Cyst. Everyone can tell that James is feeling much better than he did the night before. Many credit it to the talk Brother Willim had with him before he went to bed.

Shortly after getting underway, a cloud of dust can be seen rising from the direction of the road. James removes his mirror from his pouch and checks it out to find a force of several hundred riders moving fast on their way up to Morac.

"Word of our presence is spreading," says Potbelly when James tells the others.

"Could be their heading that way has nothing at all to do with us," counters Miko.

"Possibly," says James, "but I doubt that. We better be on our guard from here on out." Throughout the rest of the morning and most of the afternoon, he uses his mirror to scan for probable hostiles in the area. A couple times he has them detour around patrols of soldiers.

"Can you find Cyst?" Jiron asks some time after midday.

Scrolling the mirror to follow the road, a city soon appears. "There is a city up ahead," he announces. "It's rather large but doesn't have a protective wall surrounding it like others have."

"Is there a large compound on its eastern side?" asks Jiron. "Azku said that a slaver named Buka could be found in such a place."

Nodding, he says, "Yes there is." He moves the image in for a closer look and adds, "It's definitely a slaver compound. There's an auction going on even as we speak." A string of young women, girls really, are being auctioned off one at a time, just as Jiron's sister Tersa had before they rescued her.

"How far away is it?" he asks.

"Not more than a couple of hours," he replies. "There's not much of a military presence there either."

"That's good to hear," remarks Scar.

"So if things go wrong, again, we shouldn't have more than the city watch to deal with," Potbelly adds.

"Well let's try not to have things go bad this time," James asserts. He makes one last scan for roving patrols then puts away his mirror. "It's clear all the way there."

"Excellent," states Jiron.

For the next two hours or so, they ride quickly across the desert always keeping the road just out of sight. Then, from out of the horizon before them, the skyline of the city appears.

"You know, it might be better if we didn't all go in together," Scar says. "They'll be on the lookout for a large group, not just a couple of people."

"Good thinking," says Jiron. Slowing down, he brings them to a halt and has them gather round. "James, Reilin and I will enter the city while the rest of you stay out here," he says. From the way Scar is groaning, he was hoping to be one of the ones to go. "As you said Scar, three will be less noticeable than all of us together. I need Reilin, he's the only one here who can talk to the people and find out where this guy is. James is along just in case."

"With any luck, we won't be too long," he continues. "Stay out here, if you have to move to avoid detection, then do so. With James' mirror we'll be able to find you should you not be here when we return."

"Good luck," Aleya says. For once she's not insisting to accompany him, much to his relief.

He moves his horse over close to hers and leans over to give her a kiss. "What about the rest of us?" Scar asks with a grin. The others break out laughing. Ignoring him, he says to her, "Be back in a bit."

"I'll hold you to that," she says and returns a kiss of her own.

"See," says Potbelly to Scar, "if he gave you a kiss, you would have to give him one in return."

"I hadn't thought of that," jokes Scar and several of the others break out in laughter once again.

"Come on," Jiron says as he turns to head toward the city. "We're wasting daylight." When he sees that James and Reilin are both ready to go, he nudges his horse into motion and soon all three are moving at a fast trot toward the road. Behind them, the others begin making their way over to a stand of stunted trees that will afford them some protection from the sun while they wait for their return.

To Reilin Jiron says, "Should you need to talk to someone, we are looking to purchase slaves."

Nodding, Reilin replies, "Okay. What for?"

Shrugging, Jiron says, "I don't know, how about for some brothel up north."

"That'll work," he says.

They soon reach the road then turn to the southeast and to the city rising out of the desert. When they came out of the desert, the other travelers upon the road look at them quizzically but otherwise pay them no mind. Keeping a steady, but not too out of the ordinary pace, they make their way toward the city through the many wagons, riders and people on foot that clog the road.

Before they reach the edge of the city proper, other buildings begin sprouting up. Inns, chandler shops, and other businesses catering to travelers line both sides of the road. They even pass by one such structure, a two story building badly in need of repair, that has several women outside attempting to entice those on the road to come inside. The way the women are dressed leaves no doubt as to what service the traveler will receive should they take them up on the offer.

Before they completely pass through the outlying buildings and enter the city, the compound in question comes into view. A large wall surrounds it and a string of slaves are being led through the gate.

"I think this is it," states Jiron.

Lowering his voice so as not to be overheard, Reilin asks, "How are we to get in there?"

"Buy a slave," James says. "It's really not that hard." He gives Jiron a glance and they both grin at the memory of their last experience. Aside from buying many of those who are currently traveling with them, Jiron had fought a blood duel with a Parvati to free his sister.

Absentmindedly, Jiron rubs the necklace that hangs beneath his shirt that marks him as a Shynti, a designation given by Parvatis to only the most fearsome of fighters. He had acquired his shortly after winning the blood duel. The fact that he is so named has proven useful on a couple different occasions.

They work their way through town, Reilin fending off the few salutations that they receive. After turning onto the street that will take them straight to the slaver compound, James' stomach cramps when he smells the most delectable odor coming from one of the open air eateries.

"Hold up a minute," he says. "Let's get a bite to eat first."

Jiron glances to the position of the sun in the sky and nods. "There are still a few hours of sunlight left," he says. "Why not?"

The mouthwatering aroma which stopped James is coming from an open pit where a whole pig is roasting on a spit. Sections have already been carved off its carcass for their patrons. "Here," James says to Reilin as he hands him a couple silvers. "We'll wait here." He and Jiron stay just outside the entrance as Reilin takes the coins and goes inside.

He returns shortly with three half loaves of bread. The insides have been scooped out and spicy pork meat with a sizzling sauce now fills the cavity. James takes his and looks at it questioningly, not sure the best way to eat it without making a mess. Then he notices two men sitting at one of the tables who are eating the same thing. Watching them, he sees one man tear off a piece of the bread, and uses it to grab one of the thin slices of pork. Then he shoves the whole thing in his mouth.

Trying it, James tears off a two inch strip of bread and snags a piece of the pork. Placing it in his mouth, his eyes soon water as the spices on the meat set his tongue afire. Looking around, he sees the counter where the place sells mugs of ale. Moving over to it, he grabs one that has already been filled and completely downs it. Several of the men sitting at the various tables have noticed his reaction and a smattering of laughter breaks out. Once the fire has been reduced to a dull throbbing, James realizes that it tastes really good. Placing some coins on the counter, he takes another mug and rejoins the others.

"Spicy?" asks Jiron.

"You could say that," he replies as he wipes away the tears forming once again. Tearing off another strip of bread, he takes more care this time and manages to reduce the effect of the spice.

When they've finished eating, they resume moving toward the slaver compound. People on the streets pay them little heed since they are still wearing their native attire and doing nothing to stand out. As they approach the slaver compound, the main gate through which the people are moving comes into view. Two slavers stand to either side of it looking rather bored. Occasionally, one of the people would stop and ask them a question before passing through.

Indicating the two slavers at the gate, Reilin asks, "Should I see if they can tell us if Buka is here?"

"Go ahead," James says.

So when they approach the gates and are near the guards, Reilin steps up to the two men and asks, "Could you tell me where I could find a slaver by the name of Buka?"

The two slavers perk up at that. "Buka?" one asks. "Why would one such as you wish to see Buka?" The other slaver moves in beside the first slaver.

"I…" he stammers then says, "I…that is we…have a mutual friend."

"You do, do you?" the second slaver asks. "I hardly doubt that."

"Who is this mutual friend?" the first slaver asks. "Maybe he's my friend too?"

The second slaver grins. "Yes, who is this friend?" he asks.

Reilin glances to James and Jiron. Unable to follow the conversation, they are no help. "That is none of your business," he asserts. "Are you going to help me or not?"

Shrugging, the first slaver says to the second, "It matters not I suppose."

"True," the second agrees. Turning his attention back to Reilin he says, "Buka is here."

"Where can I find him?" he asks.

"He's inside," the first one replies. "Not sure where exactly, but he's in there somewhere." The second one nods as well.

"Thank you," Reilin says then moves to rejoin James and Jiron. He glances back and sees the two slavers still watching him, an amused expression on their faces.

"Well?" asks Jiron.

"He's in there but they didn't know where," he explains.

"If only we knew what he looked like," James says. "That would simplify things quite a bit."

"True," agrees Jiron. Taking the lead again, he moves through the gates and into the slaver compound.

They enter a large courtyard after passing through the gate and find the auction still in progress. Over to their left on one of the long, raised platforms, a slaver is conducting the auction. A beautiful young woman stands naked next to him, obviously the one whom the people are currently bidding on. Behind the auctioneer stand another five waiting their turn.

Watching the girls being auctioned brings back the feelings in Jiron that he had when his sister Tersa was on a slave block. Before that time he had never given slavery much thought. But after that experience, he came to agree with James that slavery must be stopped and if possible, every slaver put to the sword. Or the knife as the case may be.

"We're not going to find him out here," James says. The few slavers in the courtyard are up near where the auctioning is taking place.

"I think you're right," agrees Jiron. "Unless he's one of the ones taking part in the auction."

They look around and find an unguarded door leading into one of the main buildings of the slaver complex. Moving ever so nonchalantly, they make their way across the crowded courtyard and toward the closed door. Before they reach it, Reilin places his hand on Jiron's shoulder and says, "We got trouble." He then directs Jiron's and James' gaze to the main entrance through which they entered. Guards are entering and beginning to fan out.

"Come on," Jiron says as he quickens his pace to the door.

"How did they find us?" asks James.

"I don't know and I'm not about to hang around to find out," Jiron states. The last few yards to the door he practically sprints forward. He finds the door unlocked, opens it and rushes inside with James and Reilin right behind. Just as he closes the door behind them, a ruckus is heard coming from the courtyard. One woman screams and several men yell.

"Hold the door," Jiron tells Reilin and then moves to an adjacent window overlooking the courtyard. He and James look out as Reilin braces the door with his shoulder. Out in the courtyard, the guards have two men in custody and are escorting them out the main entrance.

"They weren't after us," observes James. Then to Reilin he says, "You can relax."

Reilin nods and moves away from the door.

They find themselves in a room with storage shelves on one side and a table with several chairs on the other. Two doors exit the room other than the one through which they entered. Jiron checks the one on the right while James listens at the one on the left.

"Quiet," Jiron says after a moment's listening.

"Here too," states James.

Jiron opens his door slowly and looks out at a hallway extending away further into the building. Several doorways line both sides. The hallway is currently empty.

When James looks through his door, he finds a storage room full of chains and other paraphernalia that slavers might find useful. Turning back to the others he says, "Just a storage room."

Jiron nods and indicates they should go through his door. "Lead on," James whispers. Opening the door, Jiron moves out into the hallway. Passing slowly and silently, he listens for any noise which may indicate that someone is approaching.

As he reaches each door, he puts his ear to it and listens for a moment. When he fails to hear anything, he continues on to the next. At the third door where he stops and listens, he hears the sound of conversation coming from the other side. Motioning for the others to stop, he then moves back to join them.

"There are at least two people in that room," he says pointing to the door. Then to Reilin he says, "See if you can figure out what they are saying."

Nodding, Reilin moves to the door and places his ear against it. He listens for a moment then returns. "They are talking about another slaver," he says. "Nothing of any importance."

Just then, the door through which they originally entered opens and voices are heard coming from the other side. All three of them turn to look and find that a slaver is there with his back to them, paused in the doorway as he speaks to another.

Panicking, James grasps the handle of one of the other doors and throws it open. Jiron and Reilin both follow him in before he shuts it. A second after the door shuts, they can hear the other door close and the man's footsteps approaching down the hallway.

Jiron pulls his knife and waits next to the door in case the man should enter. But the footsteps pass by the front of their door and continue further on down the hallway. Then they hear another door open and close. Putting his ear to the door, Jiron listens and finds the hallway quiet.

"I think it's clear now," he says.

"Should we even be in here?" James asks.

"We have to find Buka," insists Jiron.

"I understand that," James tells him. "But do you think he's going to be very helpful to those he finds sneaking around?"

"We're here now," Reilin adds. "Let's just find him and get the information we need. Then get out of here."

Jiron is about to open the door to leave when they hear a door opening and footsteps approaching. They sound like they are coming from the direction the earlier footsteps went. They can hear two men talking as they pass by. Jiron looks to Reilin but he shakes his head. "Nothing important," he whispers.

As soon as the two men are gone, Jiron opens the door slowly and peers out to find the hallway again clear of people. Moving out of the room, he continues down the hallway in the direction they were originally heading.

At the end of the hallway is another closed door, they continue on down toward it. Jiron still pauses at the other doors they pass and listens to see if anyone is there. When they finally reach the end door, he reaches for the handle when it suddenly opens up.

Three slavers stand there in shocked surprise at seeing them there. "What are you doing in here?" one asks.

Jiron is about to pull one of his knives when Reilin places a restraining hand upon his. Moving forward, Reilin asks, "Isn't this the way to view the slaves?"

Shaking his head, the slaver replies, "No."

"We're sorry," Reilin says, "we must have gotten turned around. Could you direct us to where we can?"

The slaver looks at him quizzically, and seems to be contemplating whether or not to believe him. Then he makes up his mind and nods, "This way." Indicating for them to follow, the slaver turns around and begins walking down the hallway.

"Come on," Reilin says and motions for James and Jiron to follow. He can see the questions in their minds but are unable to ask. "It's okay," he says to put their minds at ease.

Trusting in him, they nod and the three of them follow the slaver. He leads them along the corridor and then pauses at a door on his right. Opening it up, they find that they are being led outside the building and into the courtyard. He indicates a doorway over on the far side and says, "Go through there and you can view the slaves waiting for auction."

"Thank you," Reilin says and then walks briskly away from the three slavers.

"What was that about?" asks James when they are again among the crowd.

"I told him that we wished to view the slaves and had gotten turned around," he explains. Glancing back, he finds the door that they just passed through closed and the three slavers gone.

Not to be deterred, Jiron looks around and sees two slavers talking to each other as they stand against one of the walls near the platform. From their age and dress, he figures them to be more than the run of the mill slaver. Deciding on a more direct approach, he grabs Reilin's arm and points to the two slavers. "Go ask them," he says. "See if they can help us."

"Alright," he says. Crossing over toward them, he gets to within fifteen feet when the two men notice his approach. They stop their conversation and turn to meet him. "Excuse me," Reilin says as he comes to a stop a couple feet away.

"Yes?" one of the men asks.

"My friends and I are looking for a slaver by the name of Buka," he explains. "Would either of you know where we might be able to find him?"

When he says the name 'Buka', both men's expressions turn dark. "Buka doesn't see anyone," the older of the two men tells him. "Let alone you people from the north."

"But this is of some importance," Reilin insists.

The younger of the two visibly frowns. "What?" he asks.

"That would be better left unsaid until we could speak with Buka," Reilin replies.

Snorting, the older man looks with derision at him. "If you wish to buy a slave, then buy a slave or go away," he says. "But Buka doesn't talk to anyone."

"We would be willing to compensate you for your help," offers Reilin.

"There's no amount you could give me that would make me help you," the older slaver states. "Your kind is only suited for the block. Only the propriety of the auction has made me endure your presence even this long. Go away before my patience wears any thinner."

Reilin looks from the older to the younger and sees the veiled threat should he persist. Without a word, he turns around and walks back to Jiron and James. "They're not going to help us," he tells them. Then he summarizes the gist of the conversation.

"Sounds like a couple of bigots to me," James says. "And you're right, men like that are unlikely to prove helpful.

"I'm not going to give up," insists Jiron.

"No one is saying that we are," James assures him.

From the platform where the women were being auctioned, the auctioneer begins speaking loudly. They turn to look and see that he's standing there alone, the girls that had been there having already been sold.

"He's saying the auction is closed for the day," conveys Reilin. "There will be another in two days."

"Two days!" exclaims Jiron loudly.

"Shhh!" says James. "Keep your voice down." Looking angry and upset, Jiron glares at him.

"Everyone is leaving," Reilin states. "We need to go or risk having attention drawn to ourselves." Indeed, the people are all moving toward the main entrance to the slaver compound. "We can't stay here." Glancing back to the two older slavers he just talked to, he sees that they continue to talk in quiet conversation near the wall and are watching them.

"He's right," James tells his friend. "We must go."

Seeing no other alternative, Jiron nods and the three of them join the crowd in its exodus from the slaver compound. Once through the gate, they move down the street for several blocks then come to a stop. Moving near the edge of a butcher's shop, they try to come up with another idea.

While they are throwing ideas back and forth, a small boy no more than eight crosses the street and stops before James. He looks up at him with a crooked grin.

"Go along with you boy," Reilin says when it doesn't look as if he's going to do anything.

The boy suddenly raises his hand and holds it out to James, the crooked grin remaining on his face. Clutched in his hand is a piece of paper. "Is that for me?" James asks. When the boy doesn't reply, Reilin translates.

Nodding his head, the boy's grin becomes larger.

James reaches out and takes hold of the paper. As soon as he has hold of it, the boy lets go and turns to leave. Reilin grabs him by the shoulder and asks, "Who gave this to you?" Bursting into a flurry of motion, the boy wriggles from his grasp and disappears into the crowd.

"Who would know that I am here?" he asks, fear growing inside him.

"Maybe it's Azku," suggests Reilin. "Other than us, he's the only one who knew we would be heading in this direction."

"Perhaps," James says as he looks at the paper.

"Better see what it says," Jiron tells him.

"Yeah," agrees James. "You're right." Uncrinkling the paper, he sees there is writing on it.

Common room of the Wallowing Swine. Hour after dusk.

"Great," says James, "another enigmatic message given by persons unknown." He sighs, "Can't people just come right up to you and say things themselves?"

"This is often the way with those who wish to remain unobserved while doing things that could bring them embarrassment, or trouble," explains Jiron.

"I suppose," he says. Looking up at the position of the sun, he figures dusk to still be a couple hours away. "Let's find where this Wallowing Swine is and then get something else to eat before we meet with Mr. Mysterious."

Jiron chuckles, "Mr. Mysterious."

James gives him a grin and shrugs. "Let's go. I'm still hungry."

Reilin asks directions and eventually they find themselves in the seedier part of town. When they at last stand outside of the Wallowing Swine, James looks at the place and shakes his head. "Why can't they arrange for us to meet at one of the better places?" he wonders.

Overall the place has the general look of disrepair, nothing major, just looks like the owner hasn't put much effort into it. The outside walls are cracked and one of the steps leading up to the front door is missing. Rolling his eyes, he can hardly wait to see what the inside is like.

"Still an hour to dusk," he announces to the others. "Let's get something to eat." They move off and head back to the better part of town.

Chapter Twenty Five

They return before the appointed time and find that the common room of the Wallowing Swine is already becoming full. James is amazed at the number of people here. All the choice tables are taken and they are forced to sit near the center of the room. Jiron would rather not sit so exposed, but there's nothing to do about it.

Once they've taken their seats, a girl comes by and takes their order. Soon, all three are sipping mugs of ale. While James sips his, he unobtrusively takes in the other patrons to see if he can possibly determine which one sent them the note.

"They have a better clientele than I would have expected," observes Reilin.

James understands what he's talking about. The outside of this tavern gave the impression of a dive, yet counted among the patrons are men and women in fine clothes. Gentlemen and ladies mixed in with the riff raff, altogether an unusual sight.

"I wonder what brings them to a place like this?" Jiron asks.

"The food maybe?" suggests Reilin.

"Hardly," he replies. "No noble I've ever heard of would be seen mixing with some that are in this room." Indeed, those sitting at one table look as though they're a bunch of thugs fresh out of the gutter. And next to them are a gentleman and a lady who have to be some form of nobility, or at the very least, wealthy.

As time passes, James begins to get impatient. Whoever had sent him the note has yet to make an appearance. His attempt at ferreting the person out by studying the other patrons has yielded nothing more than returned looks of annoyance. None of the others have given their table more than a cursory look.

Then a hushed murmur begins from the back of the room and James turns to see what it's all about. One of the wandering minstrels that are so prevalent in this world is making his way from the back. Blonde hair and dark skin, he carries his instrument to the stage that's set against the wall. Calls of 'Kir' and other salutations are given to this man, both from those who are the dregs of society and those who are well off.

"I think this minstrel may be the reason why everyone is here," observes Jiron.

From the way everyone has perked up and treating the man, James can only agree with him. "I think you're right," he says.

The minstrel sets his instrument on a stand that is already in place on the stage. Then he brings the stool that was against the wall forward and sets it next to the stand. Taking his seat upon the stool, he faces the crowd which has grown very quiet. James glances around and can see that every eye in the place is on him.

From within his cloak the minstrel produces a cracked wooden bowl that looks like it's been with him for a very long time and sets it down on the edge of the platform. Before he straightens back up, several coins are flipped from the crowd, landing in and around the bowl.

Taking up his instrument, Kir, at least that is what James assumes his name is considering the number of times people have said it to him, gets set to play. The room has fallen absolutely quiet, you could hear your own heartbeat in the stillness if you had a mind to.

Then he strums the strings of his instrument and begins to sing. With the first note, James can see why this place is so packed. The quality of the music is far superior than anything he's heard in a long time. The music is perfectly pitched and his voice seems to move inside you and pull at your emotional strings. When the music is happy, you are glad. When it moves to a more somber tone, you sink with it.

During the time the minstrel, or rather the bard as the quality of his music warrants him to be called, sings the first song not one person says anything. Silence reigns until the last note fades away, then the common room of the Wallowing Swine erupts into thunderous applause. James, Jiron and Reilin join in with great enthusiasm.

Then the bard begins a rollicking tune and the patrons resume their conversations, albeit at a much lower volume than what it was before Kir made his appearance. "I can see why the people pack this place," James comments to Jiron.

Nodding, Jiron says, "He's about the best bard I've yet heard."

The night continues to deepen and still no one has made any attempt to approach them. They empty mug after mug while they wait for whoever it was that gave them the note. An hour into his set, Kir gets up and tells his audience that he'll be taking a short break. He places his instrument on its stand and then makes his way to the back where he enters the kitchen. A smattering of applause follows him until he disappears through the kitchen door.

While he's gone, people gravitate to the stage and place coins within his bowl. James gets up as well and places a silver in among the other coins. To his surprise, he finds a couple golds already there.

Back at the table, he says to the others, "This Kir does pretty well for himself."

"Wonder why someone with that much talent hasn't been snatched up by some noble before now?" questions Reilin.

"Who knows?" replies James. "Could be he likes life on the road."

"Some do I hear," agrees Jiron.

The buzz in the tavern has grown loud during Kir's break and only subsides when he finally makes his appearance from the back. Taking his place back on the stage, he takes his instrument in hand and then pauses a moment while the crowd quiets down. He gazes around at the men and women who have come here to hear him play. His eyes stop on this table and that as they make their way from one side to the next. Then he gives them a smile and starts in on a song.

After he sings the first line, James realizes there's something familiar about this song. Though he cannot understand the words, he comes to the startling realization that he knows it. It's a song from back home that he taught Perrilin shortly after he came to this world. Perrilin had bet him a silver that he couldn't sing him a complete song that he didn't know. He taught Perrilin 'Home on the Range' and won the silver.

Kir's gaze continues to sweep the audience as he sings, yet more often than not, it settles directly on James. When he notices James looking at him, he gives him an almost imperceptible nod then moves his gaze to the next.

Perrilin? Here? Now that he's made the connection, he can see that this Kir is indeed the bard Perrilin he met long ago, despite the fact that his hair is now blonder and skin more dark. *He must have been the one that sent the note! But why?*

He keeps this realization to himself. Past experiences when dealing with Perrilin now gives him pause about informing Jiron and Reilin. Who knows who else may be listening? On one occasion he saved Perrilin from a group of men who were torturing him. Those men had been led by a man named Korgan, who James mentally refers to as Ol' One Eye. He calls him that due to the scar James had given him across the face that blinded one eye when he rescued Perrilin from their clutches.

As it turned out, this Korgan was an agent of Lord Cytok who is the left hand of the Empire's Emperor, a very important and influential person. James owes this Korgan big. Not only was he responsible for the opening of the gates at the City of Light and allowing the Empire in, but he has been trouble for James on several other occasions as well.

Whatever Perrilin is up to, he obviously doesn't want his true identity revealed. Being a spy, as that is what he has to be in one form or another, here in the Empire would be a death sentence should he be found out. So James keeps his thoughts to himself, sits back and enjoys the music.

Hour after hour they sit there and listen to Perrilin sing. He can see the other two growing more and more impatient when no one comes to them and makes themselves known. "Maybe something happened to him," James says.

Brian S. Pratt   241

"If whoever it is doesn't show, at least we've had a good night's entertainment."

"I don't like this one bit," Jiron says as he lowers his voice. He isn't able to completely enjoy the music and songs, worry for his friend Tinok and impatient that they may very well be wasting their time here gnaws at him.

"What about the others?" asks Reilin. "What do you think they are thinking since we haven't returned?"

"I'm sure they are alright," Jiron replies. "They won't get worried unless they see things blow up." James nods his head and gives him a grin.

"Let's at least stay here until Kir finishes for the night," James says. "Then we can go."

Sighing, Jiron says, "Very well. But I hope this isn't a complete waste of time."

James looks to Kir, a.k.a. Perrilin, there on the stage and replies, "I don't think it will be."

At one point when Perrilin takes one of his breaks, James gets up and says, "I need to use the bathroom." He then moves toward the back door while at the same time working to intercept Perrilin on his way to the kitchen.

"Why does he want a bath?" he hears Reilin asks Jiron.

Then he hears Jiron chuckle. "He doesn't," he explains. "You'll soon find that he uses many expressions that say one thing and mean something entirely different. This one means he has to…" The rest of what Jiron says to Reilin is lost in the buzz of the common room as he moves closer to Perrilin.

Perrilin notices him moving toward him and as their paths cross, he gives him a slight shake of the head and mumbles, "Afterward, outside." Without even pausing he continues to the back and passes through the door into the kitchen.

Likewise, James continues on to his supposed destination and leaves the common room. He then makes his way to the outhouse out back. Nasty things outhouses, this is one of the things about this world he will never get used to. Back home, the odd time when he had to use similar facilities, such as when he was camping, had been a novelty. Now it's just plain disgusting.

When he finally returns to the common room, Perrilin has yet to make his appearance again. As he takes his seat, Jiron leans forward and indicates two fellows sitting off to one side. "Do they look familiar to you?" he asks.

Looking to where he's pointing, he sees the two men in question. "Yes, they do," he replies. They are the two slavers Reilin had talked with just before they left the slaver's compound. They take notice of the fact that they are being watched and their expressions turn dark.

"Hope they try something," Jiron says.

"Here?" Reilin asks. "I doubt it."

"Why would they?" asks James. "They may hate us and would like nothing better to make us slaves, but even men such as them are constrained by society's laws."

"I have found that some men don't care a whole lot about 'society's laws'," Jiron states.

"So have I," agrees Reilin.

Just then, Perrilin makes his appearance from the kitchen and works his way through to the stage. When he reaches the stage, he picks up his instrument and gazes at the audience. He calls for any requests and the crowd shouts back the names of their favorite pieces.

Settling on one, he takes his seat and begins a long love ballad filled with tragedy, death, but ultimately ends in happiness. When he's done, he calls for another request and continues to play requests for another hour or so. Despite the lateness of the hour, the common room remains full. None apparently wish to miss out on even one song that Kir might play.

Then there comes a time when he begins strumming his instrument and announces that this will be his last song of the evening. Several people shout out protests, more an imploring for him to continue than anything else. But he shakes his head and says that this must be his last song. Then he launches into a lively one that the crowd must know well for many begin thumping the table. At the chorus, some of the crowd joins in and before the song comes to an end, the whole common room is singing the chorus.

At the end of the song, the common room erupts into a wild display as people rise and give him a thunderous applause. Coins fly to the stage, hardly any landing in the vicinity of the bowl, and Perrilin bows to them twice.

As he begins to pick up the coins, the patrons start to leave. Most make it a point to come to him and exchange words or pat him on the back. It's clear that he is a favorite around here and that for many, this isn't the first time they've been here to hear him play.

"Can we go now?" asks Jiron. "Whoever your Mr. Mysterious is, he isn't going to show."

Standing up, James nods his head. Then with a final look over to where Perrilin is collecting the coins people threw, he follows Jiron outside. The mood of those who had experienced Perrilin's performance can only be called exhilarated. Outside, they hear many animated conversations between those who have seen him before and others who had not. It doesn't take Reilin to explain to the other two what's being said for them to get the gist of it.

Several coaches are already leaving, only a couple others still awaiting their passengers. One coach is especially fine with gold worked in intricate detail. That coach has a compliment of half a dozen guards besides the two men on the driver's seat.

"Come on," says Jiron. "Let's get back to the others before they begin worrying, if they aren't already." Striding down the street, it doesn't take him long before he realizes James is beginning to fall behind him and Reilin. Slowing down, he sees him casting frequent glances back to the tavern. Finally, he comes to a stop when the tavern is just within sight.

"Let's stop here a moment," he tells the others. Then he has them move to the side of the street and stand in the lee of a building where the shadows are the thickest.

"Why?" Jiron asks.

Motioning for the other two to come close, he keeps a constant eye on the front door of the Wallowing Swine as he explains. "The person who wrote the note was in the tavern," he tells them.

"Who?" asks Reilin.

"I didn't see anyone," says Jiron.

In a very quiet voice, so quiet the other two can barely hear him, he whispers, "It was Kir."

"The bard?" asks Reilin.

"Yes," nods James.

"How do you know?" Jiron asks.

"I just do," he replies. "He wants us to meet him here in the street."

"Someday you'll have to tell me how you found all this out," Jiron says.

"Shhh!" James tells them for he just saw Perrilin come out of the front door of the tavern. He points over to where a group of people are standing just outside the front door talking to him. The manner in which they are speaking to him leads them to believe they are congratulating him on a superb performance. They watch as he shakes the hands of several of the men then turns and begins walking down the street in their direction. The people with whom he had been talking give him a final farewell then move off in the opposite direction.

As he approaches, Jiron begins to move out in the street when James grabs him and whispers, "Not yet." He waits until Perrilin is close then begins to softly whistle Home on the Range.

Perrilin must have heard him for he alters his course slightly and moves more directly to where they are. When he gets close, he gives a quick glance up and down the street then moves into the shadows where they are waiting. James begins to speak but Perrilin cuts him off with a shake of his head and signals for them to be quiet by putting his finger against his lips.

They hold still a moment, unsure what is going on. Then a motion down the street draws their attention and they see two men working their way from the direction of the Wallowing Swine. From the way Perrilin is watching them, James can tell there's something going on here of which he is ignorant.

As the two men walk down the street, they casually look this way and that. All the while they continue to maintain a steady pace. When they finally move past the spot where they're hiding and disappear down the road, Perrilin says, "They've been keeping an eye on me lately."

"Does this have anything to do with Korgan?" asks James.

Eyes widening at the name, Perrilin asks in return, "What makes you say that?"

"Just the fact that ever since I rescued you from him in Cardri," he explains, "he's had it out for me."

Perrilin looks to him and the other two and nods, "In a way."

Jiron moves closer and asks, "Why did you have us meet you?"

Perrilin glances to him and recognizes him from the time before. "Jiron right?" he says.

"Yes," he replies, surprised at how this man knows him.

James sees the confusion on his face and clarifies it for him. "This is Perrilin."

"Perrilin?" he asks, still not sure if he should believe him. "You don't look anything like the Perrilin I know."

"That's the whole idea," he says. "This isn't a good place to talk." Glancing up and down the street again, he says, "Follow me and then we can discuss a few things."

Jiron looks at Perrilin, still not convinced but trusts in James' judgment. When Perrilin steps out into the street, he follows along with James and Reilin right beside him. Perrilin quickly leads them further down the street away from the Wallowing Swine and turns left at the next crossroads.

Down this way the number of lit street lights gradually diminishes until all they have is moonlight overhead. They continue to follow him for several more minutes when he all of a sudden moves off the street and toward the doorway of the building on his right. Going up to the door, he knocks twice hard then one time softly.

From the other side, the sound of a bolt sliding open can be heard. Then the door opens a crack and a man peers through the opening. "Kir!" he exclaims throwing the door open wide.

"I may have been followed," he says and the man nods. Then as soon as they are inside the small room, the man closes the door and bolts it. Perrilin tells the man, "Have your people take a look around out there just to be sure."

"Don't worry," he says as he eyes James, Jiron and Reilin suspiciously, "it'll be done."

"These are friends," Perrilin tells him.

The man gives them a quick nod then moves into the next room.

"Who is that?" Jiron asks. "And who is following you?"

"Not here," he says and then motions for them to follow. He leads them through the door that the other man had passed through and into the room on the other side. A woman and two children sit on a bed pushed against one wall and eye them as they pass through. Neither they nor Perrilin say anything. From a table near the bed, Perrilin picks up one of the candles burning there and takes it with him.

Once they've passed through into the hallway, he leads them down to a doorway on the left. Opening it up, he indicates for them to precede him inside. The doorway is twice as thick as the average door and made of solid wood. As James and the others move inside and Perrilin shuts the door, he notices that all noise from outside of the room is gone.

"Quiet room?" he asks.

Perrilin nods as he takes a seat at one of the chairs sitting around a lone table. The others take seats as well. "We found that such a room comes in handy when you wish not to be overheard," he explains.

"Is it magical?" asks Reilin.

Shaking his head, Perrilin says, "No. Just built very thickly."

"Now what is going on around here?" Jiron asks.

"Let's just say that some of my associates and me don't exactly have the good will of the powers that be," he says.

"What do you mean?" Jiron asks, obviously not satisfied with the answer.

Perrilin gestures to the Empire type clothes Jiron is wearing and says, "As someone who himself is trying to not draw attention, I'm sure you'll understand if I decline to say more."

"Your business is your own," says James. "Though I would like to know why you gave us the note."

"Earlier I saw you going into the slaver compound," he tells them. "And then later when I saw you leave, you had the look of someone with a great deal on their minds. So I had a boy I knew give you the note and hoped you would take the chance and come."

"Why?" asks Jiron. "Sounds as if you have enough troubles without getting yourself involved with ours."

Perrilin gazes at him a moment and says, "There was a time when I was in trouble and someone came to my aid. Can I do less to repay the debt I owe?"

"You don't owe me any debt," James tells him. "Your help in introducing me to Ellinwyrd was payment enough."

"Nevertheless," he replies, "I still feel onus to help you now."

"Maybe he can help," suggests Reilin.

Jiron looks to James who nods. "It can't hurt and I definitely trust him," James says. Then turning to Perrilin, he adds, "We need to talk with the slaver named Buka."

Perrilin grows quiet at that. "Why?" he finally asks. "Do you plan to kill him?"

Shaking his head, James says, "No. All we want is some information." He then goes briefly into the final dream he had of Cassie and Tinok, what she said about the fate hanging over him, and of the trail they've followed thus far in search of their friend. When he finishes, he has Jiron take out the necklace and show it to him. "This is all we have to go on," he concludes. "The last person we talked to said that he got it from Buka a slaver here in Cyst. Now, we need to find out what Buka knows."

"Do you know him?" Jiron asks.

"Oh yes," he says with a nod. "He is the Guildmaster of the slavers in this area. A very powerful person whom it isn't wise to cross."

"Can you think of a way for us to talk to him?" James asks.

"It isn't as simple as you are making it out," he says. "No one simply goes up and talks to Buka. Very few around here have even seen him."

"We heard he is presently within the slaver compound here in Cyst," states Jiron.

"That well may be true," nods Perrilin. "From what I've heard, he doesn't leave here often."

"Can you be of any help?" asks Jiron. "If what James was told in the dream is true, then Tinok has less than two weeks to live."

Shaking his head, he says, "I don't have any connections within the slaver guild I'm afraid."

"Do you know what he looks like?" James asks.

"Yes," he replies. "But I don't know how that is going to be of any help."

Jiron looks to James. "Is it?" he asks.

"Maybe," he replies. Removing his mirror from its pouch, he says, "I've never done it quite this way before."

"Done what?" Perrilin asks suspiciously, his gaze upon the mirror.

"Try to find someone," he explains as he sets the mirror on the table between them.

"With magic?" he asks.

"How else?" James says.

"Is it going to hurt?" Perrilin asks.

Shaking his head, James replies, "No. What I want you to do is to visualize Buka in your mind, close your eyes if you need to."

Perrilin nods his head and closes his eyes. When he has Buka's image clearly depicted, he asks, "Okay, now what?"

"Nothing," replies James. "Just keep the image in your mind as clear as you can until I tell you to stop."

"Alright," he says, eyes still closed.

James then turns his attention to the mirror on the table and concentrates. The magic begins to build as he formulates what he wishes it to do. And that is, to find the person Perrilin is concentrating on.

"Is this going to work?" Reilin asks Jiron.

"Shhh!" Jiron says irritably. "Don't disturb him."

James lets the magic flow and it almost seems as if a thread of it attaches itself to Perrilin's forehead. Of course it doesn't actually do that, it just feels that way. Then all of a sudden, the image in the mirror coalesces and they see a large man gone to fat sitting on a bed in a room with two naked young women.

"Is that him?" James asks.

Perrilin opens his eyes and nods. "Yeah, that's him," he says.

"I can see why he doesn't get out much," Reilin states. Jiron nods his head in agreement.

"You can stop thinking about him now," James tells Perrilin, "I've got him."

"Now what?" he asks as he gazes at the people in the mirror.

James begins scrolling the image in small increments and then moves the image upward until the room disappears and an aerial view of the slaver compound comes into view.

Jiron pays extra close attention to the image, committing to memory the exact location of the room in which Buka is in. Finally he says, "I've got it."

"You sure?" James asks.

"Oh yeah," he replies. "I can find that room now."

Canceling the image, he replaces the mirror back in his pouch.

Reilin gets a sly grin on his face and says, "From the looks of things, I'd say he'll be in there for awhile."

"Looks that way," agrees James.

Perrilin glances from Jiron to James then back again. "You aren't thinking about going in there are you?" he asks.

"Can you think of a better way to find out what we want to know?" responds Jiron. Then he turns to James and says, "Shall we?"

"Yes," he replies as he stands up. To Perrilin he says, "I appreciate your help in this."

Perrilin rises and looks to them for a moment. Then says, "You're welcome. Just be careful."

"We will," James assures him. "Now, can you lead us out?"

He nods and moves around the table to the door. Opening it, he steps into the hallway and leads them back the way they came. A young man is now within the room with the woman and two children. When Perrilin enters the young man stands up and says, "It's all clear."

"Thank you," he replies.

The young man moves ahead of them to the door they originally entered the building through and throws the bolt open. Then he swings the door open for them and stands there holding it as they pass through. Once they are out and on the street, the young man closes the door and plunges them into darkness.

Perrilin stops and turns to them. "It would be best if we parted ways here," he says. "Never know who may be out and about."

James nods and extends his hand. "Thank you for your help," he again says.

Taking the hand, Perrilin grins. "Until we meet again," he says. Then he turns and quickly walks down the street.

"Now let's go find this guy," Jiron says.

"Not yet," James tells him. "Let's find the others first and then we'll pay Mr. Baku a visit."

Jiron nods and then heads down the street in the general direction toward where they left the others. As they go, James wonders if Buka will even remember Tinok, not to mention what happened to him. He's not sure what Jiron plans to do in that event, but he would hate to be in Buka's place should that be the case.

Chapter Twenty Six

They work their way through the city until the outskirts come into view. Moving quickly, they reach the last of the outlying buildings before the road once more enters the desert.

James brings them to a halt and then after scanning the area for a second, leads them to a spot near the building's edge where light is spilling from a window. Moving near the light, he pulls forth his mirror and brings Miko's moon illuminated image into view. Expanding it slightly he finds the others still together, most of them are sleeping.

"Good," he says as he puts his mirror back into his pouch, "they're alright." Then he removes the strip of cloth he uses to search with and soon is on his way into the night. Following the direction indicated by the cloth, they hurry across the moonlit landscape.

When Cyst is five minutes behind them, a shadow moves to intercept them which turns out to be Scar and Potbelly materializes out of the night a moment later. James' orb springs to life on his palm. "Everybody up," he says as he enters the camp.

"We know where this Buka is," Jiron says as he bends over to give Miko a shake to bring him back to consciousness. "If things go bad, we may need to get out of here in a hurry."

"What?" asks a bleary eyed Miko as he sits up and looks around.

"Where is he?" Brother Willim asks.

"In the slaver compound," Reilin says. He moves over to where the horses are tethered and begins to put the saddle on his.

"You're going to storm the place I take it?" Aleya asks.

"Not exactly, no," Jiron assures her. "Just slip over the wall and have a little conversation with him."

"Just like that?" She eyes him disapprovingly.

"No other way I'm afraid," he explains. "From what we learned this night, he isn't going to be too helpful as it is."

She lays a hand on his shoulder. "Didn't you tell me that you gave your word not to harm him? That you would leave him as you found him?"

"Yes, I did," he acknowledges.

Raising her voice she exclaims, "Then how are you going to convince him to tell you what he knows?"

"We'll figure a way," James says as he comes up behind them.

She looks from one to the other and shakes her head.

"Not much night left," Stig says as he joins them. "An hour, maybe two."

"Then we best be on our way," replies Jiron. With a last look to Aleya, he walks past her and over to where his horse waits for him. Taking the saddle from the ground, he begins readying his horse.

Several minutes pass before they are all in the saddle and ready to ride. James extinguishes his orb and Jiron takes the lead. Heading back toward Cyst, he angles toward the wall encompassing the slaver compound. Many buildings have sprouted around its walls, and Jiron brings them to a halt before they draw too close to them.

Turning to the others, he says, "The rest of you wait out here while James and I go in and talk to Buka." He and James then dismount.

"Aren't you going to need me?" asks Reilin.

Shaking his head, Jiron replies, "Not this time. As Guildmaster of the Slaver Guild, I would expect him to be able to speak our language." He hands the reins of his horse to Shorty.

"So would I," agrees Scar.

As James and Jiron make ready to return to Cyst, Potbelly says under his breath, "I'm tired of always staying behind."

"You got that right," Scar says with a nod.

Jiron glances to James and rolls his eyes, otherwise ignoring the pair. "Shall we?" he asks.

"Better get this over with before the sun rises," he says. Off to the east, the sky remains dark. The onset of dawn still has yet to makes its initial appearance. Moving quickly, they leave the others behind and are soon making their way through the outlying buildings.

In no time at all, the wall of the slaver compound appears ahead of them out of the night. Lights are seen within the compound and they make it to the wall without being noticed. This early in the morning, very few people are awake.

The wall is twelve feet high. Jiron makes a running jump and leaps toward its top. Barely reaching the upper lip, he grabs hold and makes sure his grip is secure before he pulls himself up to look over the other side.

Hanging there, he looks over and finds no one in the immediate vicinity on the other side of the wall. Pulling himself up the rest of the way, he stays as flat against the top to avoid being outlined against the light any more than is absolutely necessary. There's no ramp or walkway on the other side either, just a similar drop to the ground as on the outside.

Once he's gained the top, he swings over and lands on the other side. He then plasters himself against the base of the wall to see if anyone may have noticed his entry. When no one comes to investigate, he unwinds the rope from around his middle and throws a section over the wall to James. He takes a secure hold when he feels James taking up the slack. Then the rope grows taught as James begins climbing the other side.

The rope goes taught, then becomes loose. Grows taught again then goes loose. When he feels James try for the third time to scale the wall, Jiron sighs and says quietly, "Tie a loop at the end and I'll pull you over." He feels two quick tugs on the rope and shakes his head. He had forgotten how inept James is at things like this. When it comes to magic, he's almost unparalleled in what he can do. But physical stuff such as scaling a wall? Forget it.

"All set," he hears from the other side as the rope is tugged twice in quick succession. He begins taking in the slack, and when the rope becomes taught starts pulling James toward the top. It's a hard pull with James' weight on the other side. Hand over hand and inch by inch he gradually brings him closer to the top of the compound's wall.

As he comes near the top, James reaches up and takes hold with his right hand. As soon as he has a secure grip with one hand, he lets go of the rope with the other and helps Jiron by pulling himself up. "Okay, I made it," he says as he climbs onto the top. Taking his foot out of the loop, he tosses down the rope.

On the ground, Jiron begins coiling the rope once more around his middle under his jerkin. He keeps one eye on James' progress in getting down from the top, and the other on the immediate vicinity. So far, no one has made an appearance.

He no sooner gets the rope securely in place than James drops down to the ground next to him. "Ready?" he asks. James gives him a nod and then they set out toward the building wherein they saw Buka with the mirror.

The room in question is within one of the larger buildings in the compound and not too far from where they crossed over the wall. They keep in the shadows of the wall as they steadily work their way closer. Two men's voices suddenly come out of the dark ahead causing them to freeze and plaster themselves against the wall.

Standing still, they listen as the men's footsteps approach closer. As they come nearer, Jiron is able to discern the two dark outlines of the men. It doesn't look as if the direction they are walking will bring them very close to where James and Jiron are hiding. The dark outlines gradually change to more distinct forms until the two men pass them not more than five feet away. Too wrapped up in their own conversation, the men never even glance toward the two motionless figures in the shadows. Finally, the men move further down and enter through a doorway in one of the buildings.

Detaching himself from the wall, Jiron whispers, "That was close."

James nods in agreement as they resume their progress. Keeping between the wall and an adjacent building, they hurry along. Coming to the end of the building, they pause for a moment. A ten foot open area separates where they stand and the building wherein they believe Buka to be.

Jiron scans the area quickly. When he's sure no one is nearby, he runs across the open area to the nearest door with James right on his heels. At the

door, he again pauses to make sure their dash to the door went unobs(
Satisfied that they continue to remain unnoticed, he tries the door and finds it
unlocked.

Light comes from within as he opens the door a crack. Peering inside, he
finds the door opens onto a well lit hallway. With lit candles spaced in wall
sconces every ten feet or so, there's little chance of remaining hidden should
someone make an appearance.

"We better hurry," urges James. The sky to the east is beginning to
lighten with the coming of dawn. If they want to have any hope of making it
out safely, they best be done in short order.

Jiron nods understanding and opens the door. Doors line both sides of the
hallway, two on the left and three on the right, another door sits closed at the
end. "It's through the one at the end," Jiron whispers to him. Entering the
building, he ignores the other doors and heads directly for the one at the end.
Upon reaching it, he places his ear to the door.

After listening for a moment, he turns back to James. "I don't hear
anything," he informs him. Placing his hand on the door's handle, he slowly
opens the door to find another hallway on the other side. Like the one they
just passed through, it too is well illuminated by candlelight.

Here there are only two doors other than the ones at either end of the
hallway. One on the left is close to the doorway they are standing in, and
another on the right about midway down the hallway. "He's through the one
on the right," Jiron says. "Remember, I gave my word that no harm should
befall him."

"I remember," James assures him.

Pulling one of his knives, Jiron moves down the hall and toward the door.
James follows, closing the door between the two hallways behind him. At the
door, Jiron places his ear to it and can hear muted voices coming from the
other side. One is definitely a man's, and the other a woman's.

Receiving a nod from James telling him he's ready, Jiron takes the door's
handle in hand and slowly turns it. When he's turned it as far as it will go, he
leans back slightly then hits the door with his shoulder as he bursts into the
room.

Just as they saw in the mirror, Buka is there with two women. One is
feeding him small bites of food while the other looks to have been massaging
his feet. Both women jump back with fear on their faces when they see Jiron
there with knife in hand.

"Remain quiet and I won't hurt anyone," Jiron tells them. Behind him he
hears the door close after James enters the room. When the girls look like
they fail to understand him, he puts his finger to his lips and says, "Shhh."

They get the idea and remain quiet.

Buka on the other hand, is staring at Jiron with barely controlled anger.
"How dare you come barging into my private room in this manner," he
demands. Getting ready to yell for help, he's silenced when Jiron darts across
the room and places the edge of his knife to his throat.

"Would be best for you to remain silent," Jiron tells him. Eyeing him in a threateningly way, he waits to see if he will remain so. Buka glares at him but remains quiet. To James he says, "Get the girls into the corner."

James nods and then motions for the girls to move out of the way and into the corner of the room away from the door. He allows them to sit before returning his attention to Jiron and Buka.

"Now," begins Jiron. "I have some questions for you and if you answer them, we'll leave and no one will be hurt."

Buka's eyes flick from Jiron to James then back again. "Seems I am at your mercy, for now," he states. Neither fear nor anger is present in his voice, though his eyes tell of dire consequences in store for them later.

"We are looking for someone," he says. "And the trail has led us to you." Moving the knife away from Buka's throat, he still keeps it near just in case.

Buka grins an evil grin at him. "What makes you think I know anything about this person?" he asks. "And why would I tell you anything?"

Jiron pulls forth the necklace and holds it before him. "Do you remember this?" he asks. "We met an acquaintance of yours who told us he got this from you."

"So?" he asks.

"I want to know where the person is you took this from?" demands Jiron.

Then suddenly he breaks into laughter, hardly the response they were expecting. "What? Are you planning on rescuing him?" Again the laughter rolls forth.

"So you know it was a 'him'!" exclaims Jiron triumphantly.

He nods his head and the laughter continues to roll out of him.

Jiron glances to James and sees the confusion mirrored on his friend's face that he himself is experiencing.

As the laughter subsides, Buka regains his composure and says, "I haven't laughed like that for some time."

"Why is it funny?" asks James.

Buka turns his attention to him and replies, "You don't think I'm going to tell you anything do you?" Then he sits up on the edge of his bed. "Damn northerners."

"This northerner is going to kill you if you don't tell me what I want to know!" Jiron demands as he moves in closer.

Buka looks up at him and shakes his head. "I don't think so," he tells him.

"I will!" insists Jiron.

Buka comes to his feet and says, "Then do it!" Staring him in the eye, Buka dares him to kill him. When Jiron fails to follow through on the threat, he snorts. "I thought not."

Bam!

Jiron's fist connects with Buka's nose and knocks him back to the bed. "We aren't leaving here without the information," he states.

"I ain't telling you anything," Buka says. Rubbing his nose, he makes sure it isn't broken then looks up at Jiron standing over him. Then he gets a thoughtful look and says, "Unless you do me a favor first."

Looking doubtful, Jiron casts a quick glance to James then returns it to Buka. "What kind of favor?" he asks.

"One that's been needing to be done for some time," he replies. "If you do this for me, I'll tell you exactly where you can find the one who had that necklace."

"How do we know we can trust him?" James asks Jiron.

"You don't," Buka replies to James. Then to Jiron he says, "Fair trade, a favor for the information."

"What's the favor," he says.

"There's a person in Cyst that has caused me problems from time to time," he explains. "I want you to take care of him for me."

"We aren't going to murder anyone for you," Jiron tells him. "Even if it means not finding out the information."

Shaking his head, Buka says, "It isn't his murder that I want."

"What is it you want?" James asks.

"His right hand," he replies. "I want you to bring me his right hand and I'll tell you what you wish to know."

James expects Jiron to reject the offer right away and is amazed that he's even contemplating the request. "You can't be thinking of doing it are you?" he asks.

Jiron glances to him for a moment before asking, "Why haven't you taken care of this before now?"

"He has many friends here," he explains. "If I were to move against him, the situation would become more troublesome. Should you do it, I won't have to worry about such things. After all, if you succeed, things work out well. If you don't, you're just northerners they'll execute for the attempt."

"Who is it?" he asks. James is absolutely astounded that he even asked.

"His name is Kir," Buka replies. "He's a bard that is currently playing at the Wallowing Swine. Bring me his right hand and I'll tell you what you want to know."

Kir! He means Perrilin!

"Very well," Jiron says with a stiff nod.

"But…" begins James when Jiron stops him with a wave.

"In case you have any thoughts about giving me a hand of someone else," Buka tells them, "you must take it from him tonight during his performance at the Wallowing Swine. I'll have someone in the audience to witness that it happens. Afterward, come to the compound's gate and the guards will let you through. Then, and only then, will I tell you what you wish to know."

Jiron and Buka lock eyes. Then he replaces his knife back in its sheath and nods. "We'll be back," he says.

"Make sure you are not followed when you come to the gates," Buka says. "I wouldn't want to be distracted by an angry mob." When he sees Jiron nod, he adds, "I trust you two can find your way out on your own?"

Just then, the door to his room opens and a middle aged slaver walks in. His eyes widen when he sees Jiron and James there in the room. His hand grabs his sword and has it halfway out when Buka stops him.

"These gentlemen were just leaving," he says.

The man glances to Buka and realizes there is no immediate threat. Sliding his sword back into its scabbard, he backs out into the hallway as James and Jiron leave the room. He watches as they walk down the hallway back the way they came until Buka calls him into the room.

"I want you to put a couple of our men on them," he tells the man. Then he gives him a brief rundown of what they want and what they said they would do for it. "Make sure there is someone at the Wallowing Swine tonight just in case they actually go through with it."

"Do you think they will?" the slaver asks.

Shrugging, Buka replies, "Maybe. If they do I doubt if they'll make it back here."

"Why do you say that?" he asks.

Grinning an evil grin, Buka says, "The crowd at the Wallowing Swine loves Kir. They'll tear those two apart." Then he and the other slaver break out into laughter.

James and Jiron follow the same route back out as they did when they came in. Still working to keep from being seen, they reach the wall and this time, once Jiron is on the other side, he automatically makes the loop for James' foot before tossing the rope over. When he feels the tension increase on the rope, he pulls him over.

As James lands on the ground next to him, James asks, "You aren't really serious about doing what he requested are you?"

Jiron looks at him and replies, "Not exactly, no." With the rope once more secured around his middle, he steps out and heads back to where they left the others. Walking quietly and quickly, they make it back to the others.

"You find out what you wanted to know?" Aleya asks. Then she can see the hard set of his jaw and that look in his eye he gets when things aren't going his way. "You didn't, did you?"

"He wants us to do him a favor first," Jiron replies.

"What does he want us to do?" Scar asks.

James glances up to him and says, "Pay a visit to an old friend." Off to the east, the sky is lightning with the coming of dawn. "Let's get a room and we'll explain everything to you." As they head back to the road leading deeper into town, he glances to Jiron's back and wonders just how far he's willing to go in order to find Tinok.

Chapter Twenty Seven

Shortly after their arrival at the Wallowing Swine and just before the evening meal is being served, the two slavers whom they saw there the night before arrive. The two men take the same table they had before and proceed to order their meal.

James and Jiron sit at a table near the stage while the others are at various tables scattered throughout the common room. James is the first to see the two men and point them out to Jiron. "Think they're the witnesses Buka said would be here?" James asks.

"I would think so," replies Jiron. He glances over to where Aleya and Potbelly are sitting at the table closest to the entrance. She sees his look and returns one of her own. Slightly strained and worried, she gives him a brief smile and nod.

Perrilin is scheduled to begin his performance in an hour so they settle in and eat a light meal of roast lamb and bread. As they eat, the crowd coming to hear Perrilin play begins to arrive. Many of the faces are familiar from the night before. The buzz of conversation within the Wallowing Swine gradually grows as more and more of the tables begin to be filled.

By the time Perrilin makes his appearance, all the tables are filled. The proprietor has even placed stools and chairs against the walls to accommodate the number of people who showed up. "Would have to be a crowd tonight wouldn't it," Jiron states.

"Yes," replies James.

Finally, the noise at the rear of the common room increases as Perrilin makes his way from the back to the stage where he places his instrument on its stand. Again, he puts the time-worn wooden bowl on the stage then returns to the back. The crowd murmurs in delighted anticipation as they know this means that he is about to come and perform.

Several minutes later, Perrilin exits from the back and applause follows him all the way to the stage. Taking up his instrument, he turns back toward the crowd and an expectant hush descends onto the common room. Then he strums the strings and launches into a rollicking ballad full of daring-do and love.

He's into the third stanza when he sees James and gives him a brief grin and a nod. James returns it. Glancing around the common room, he sees how much the people are enjoying the music, and it saddens him how they'll react to what they're about to do.

The two slavers keep casting glances to him and Jiron. Whether the looks are telling them to get on with it or whether simply because they don't like them, it's hard to tell. Whatever the reason, James decidedly doesn't care for it.

For two and a half hours they sit there in the common room while Perrilin performs. When he leaves on his second break and heads to the kitchen, James locks eyes with the others positioned in the room and nods his head. They return the nod knowing the time has come.

"You ready?" he asks Jiron.

"Yes," he replies with a glance to the door leading into the kitchen. "When he's on his way back."

"Right," agrees James.

Just then, one of the two slavers gets to his feet and begins walking toward their table. "Not now," whispers James to himself. Jiron hears him and sees the man coming toward them.

Then the murmur in the back of the room suddenly swells as Perrilin exits from the kitchen. He pauses a moment to exchange words with a man at one of the tables.

The slaver is almost to them when he's bumped into from the side. Ale splashes all across his front as the man who bumped into him loses control of his cup. "Sorry about that," Reilin says in a manner that suggests he's entirely too drunk to be walking around. Using his hands, he tries to brush off the liquid that is beginning to soak into the slaver's clothes.

By this time, Perrilin has finished his conversation and is heading toward the stage.

"Fool!" the slaver says as he knocks Reilin's hands away.

"I'm truly sorry about this, sir," Reilin says then places his left arm around the man's neck and begins laughing. Those nearby who have been observing him and the slaver chuckle at the sight.

When Perrilin moves adjacent to their table, James and Jiron get to their feet. James gives Perrilin a greeting and holds out his right hand.

"Get off me you idiot!" the slaver yells and pushes Reilin away.

Stumbling backward, Reilin hits the edge of a table with his leg and crashes into a man and woman.

Perrilin stops and takes James' hand to shake it with a glance over to where Reilin is now laying across the two people's laps. Then from behind him, Scar jumps up and grabs him around the chest just as James grips his hand hard and stretches his arm across the table.

Jiron produces a hatchet from out of his cloak that acquired earlier for just this moment and raises it high. Bringing it down hard, he severs the hand from the arm.

Perrilin cries out as blood spurts forth from the bloody stump and the room becomes still from shock.

Then a woman screams and the room bursts into action. Scar lets go of Perrilin who falls to the floor clutching the bleeding stump and moaning in pain. He knocks the slaver whom Reilin spilt ale on to the floor as he clears a way for Jiron and James to make their escape. They make it halfway to the door before three men move to block the exit.

Cries and shouts erupt as the people surge forward toward them.

Leading the way, Scar pulls forth his double swords and begins striking out at the men barring his way. One man manages to draw forth his sword but Scar batters it aside and plunges the point of his sword into the man's shoulder.

Then Jiron is there beside him and the other two men are quickly thrust aside. With the way to the door clear, he yells, "Come on!" With the other two behind him, he bolts for the door. Before he can reach it, another man, rather large and angry, moves to block his escape.

Barely slowing even a little, Jiron strikes the man with the pommel of his knife just before Scar hits him with his shoulder and knocks him out of the way. Moving out into the street, they race into the night. Behind them, they hear another woman scream as she swoons into unconsciousness and just happens to fall into the men rushing after them.

Aleya's body hits the first man who was trying to catch them, which knocks him into the second one and suddenly the doorway is jammed with bodies writhing on the floor. By the time they are able to untangle themselves, their prey has disappeared into the night.

Splitting into search parties, the men begin combing the streets to find the two who did this to Kir. The most beloved and skilled bard they have ever had the pleasure to experience. Blood is on their minds, and if they should come across the men who did this, there is little confusion as to what they will do.

Back in the Wallowing Swine, Reilin, who by this time has become miraculously sober again, shouts for all to hear, "We have to get him to a healer!"

Three men come and pick up the moaning and blood soaked Perrilin. Then Reilin shouts again, "This way!" and begins leading them out the back door. He and the three men who are carrying Perrilin race out the back and into the courtyard there. Several of those who were there to see Perrilin perform follow them out.

Then, racing across the courtyard, they leave through the courtyard's gate and enter the street. Turning right and away from the tavern, Reilin leads Potbelly, Stig and Shorty who are carrying Perrilin, as well as the crowd following them, quickly down the street.

Ducking into a side alley, James puts the severed hand into an empty pouch and ties it shut. Then the sound of running feet comes and they plaster themselves against the alley wall. Holding still, they wait for the group of men to race past before returning to the street.

"Scar," Jiron says, "Go after the others and make sure they make it to the rendezvous."

He gives him a nod then runs back down the road to the tavern. "Now," begins Jiron as he points to the blood soaked pouch, "let's get rid of that and get out of here." He then turns down the street in the direction leading to the slaver's compound. Breaking into a run, they race along the street all the while keeping eyes and ears alert for anyone in the vicinity.

"The whole city will be searching for us before long," James says. Forced to hide in the shadows as two guards make their way down the street, they wait and watch as the men come forward. By the way they're just walking along, it's unlikely they have yet to learn about the events at the Wallowing Swine. Whether they have or haven't, he and Jiron aren't likely to run the risk that they have.

After the two guards turn the corner and disappear, they return to the street. "It's not far from here," announces Jiron. And sure enough, the gate to the slaver compound appears before them shortly. It's closed and stationed out in front of it are two slaver guards.

Jiron brings them to a halt before the guards at the gate have seen them. "If they don't let us in," he says to James in a whisper, "we're going in anyway."

"What about your promise to Azku?" he asks. "If we should do anything to hurt or destroy this place or its people, you will be breaking your word."

Jiron looks at him and replies, "If he breaks his word, then what I agreed to is no longer binding."

James gives him a look like he still thinks it should. "Whether someone else keeps their word or not, doesn't affect your own honor. Only your choices. You swore to leave Baku as you find him, and you should."

An argumentative look crosses Jiron's face as he stares back at him, "We'll see." Moving out from the shadows, he heads toward the gate with James right behind.

The guards are quick to notice them coming in their direction. They stay where they are and make no movement or gesture as they arrive. "Come back in the morning," one says when Jiron comes to a stop several feet away.

"We have a package for Buka," Jiron says.

"What kind of package?" asks the second guard.

"The kind that I'll have to kill you if I tell you," replies James.

The first guard whispers something to the second who nods and turns back to them. "You two match the description of two we were to keep an eye out for." He looks them up and down, taking in the blood staining both their clothes. Then he nods to the first guard.

Removing a ring of keys, the first guard moves to the gate and unlocks it. Pulling it open, he says, "Was told to tell you to meet him in the same place as you had before."

James gives them a nod, "Thanks."

Without a word, the second guard waves them on through.

Passing through the gate, James and Jiron enter the slaver courtyard as the gate swings closed behind them. The sound of the turning of the lock tells them the guards have locked it again. Lanterns are hung at intervals around the courtyard, filling it with abundant light. From one of the buildings nearby the cry of a slave is heard.

Something about this just doesn't feel right to Jiron. Maybe it's the events of the night that has him rattled, whatever the reason he has a hand resting on one of his knives. "Be on your guard," he whispers to James.

"Think he'll try something?" James asks.

"I don't know," he replies. As they cross the courtyard, he realizes the place is deserted. For this time of night there should be someone out on one errand or another. A noise from the darkness causes him to stop in the middle of the courtyard and peer in that direction.

"What?" asks James.

"I don't know," he replies. When the noise doesn't repeat itself, he says, "May just be my imagination." Resuming their trek across the courtyard, they come to the building wherein they met Buka the night before.

As they are expected, Jiron makes no attempt at stealth and opens the door. Entering the hallway, he passes through it to the door separating the two halves of the building. At the next door, he opens it and continues into the next hallway. Moving down, he comes to the door wherein Buka had been the last time. This time however, he knocks upon the door.

"Come in," is heard from the other side. Opening the door, they find Buka sitting at the table with three other men there with him. One of the men they recognize as having been a guest at the Wallowing Swine this evening. The other two slavers they saw there, the ones James was sure had to be the ones Buka sent to observe the taking of the hand, are not.

"You have it?" Buka asks.

James removes the blood soaked pouch and tosses it onto the table in front of the slaver Guildmaster. Buka nods to the man sitting to his right who then takes the pouch and opens it. Upending it over the table, the hand drops out and lands before Buka. A trail of blood oozes its way across the tabletop from the severed hand.

"We have kept out part of the bargain," Jiron says.

Nodding, Buka replies, "So it would seem."

"Now, tell us where the owner of the necklace can be found," demands Jiron.

"Calm down, young man," Buka tells him. "I always keep my word. Can't rise to a position such as I have if you don't." He nods to two of the other slavers there with him and they take the hand and leave. Once the two men have left the room and the door once again is closed, Buka gives them a look and starts to laugh.

Startled by the unexpected reaction, Jiron asks, "What's so funny?"

Bringing his laughter under control, Buka says, "The knowledge of where your friend is will do you no good."

"Why is that?" James asks.

"For one thing," replies Buka, "you can't get to him even if you know where he is."

"Where is he?" demands Jiron.

"Five days ago, he and several other slaves were taken to Ith-Zirul." He pauses a moment to see what affect his words are having. When neither of them reacts to the name, he shakes his head and chuckles.

"Why is that so funny?" asks Jiron.

"Because," he says with a grin, "none who go there ever come out."

"Where can we find it?" Jiron asks.

"Ah," Baku says as he holds up a hand, "I only agreed to tell you where you could find your friend, and I have."

"But we need to know!" demands Jiron.

Baku's face darkens as all signs of amusement leave him. "Our bargain is concluded," he states, tone getting an edge to it. "I suggest you leave now."

James can see the storm building behind Jiron's eyes. Laying a hand on his arm, he says, "We should go." When Jiron hesitates, he adds, "At least we know the name of the place. Trust me, we'll find it."

With a slight nod, he allows James to lead him to the door. Never once taking his eyes from Buka, he hears the door open behind him. "Come on," James tells him. Passing out into the hallway, his eyes continue to bore into those of Buka until James closes the door.

"Some day, he and I will meet again," prophesizes Jiron. "And when we do, only one of us will walk away."

"Should that day come I wish you all the luck," says James. "Right now though, we have to get back to the others."

Jiron nods and together they hustle back out the way they came in. Once out of the building they head across the courtyard to the gate. Jiron is internally fuming over what Buka told them, rather what he didn't tell them. They have a name of where he is, but not where the place is located.

All of a sudden from up ahead of them, they hear the creak that signals the opening of the gate. Jiron comes to a stop when he sees the two slavers from the Wallowing Swine passing through.

"You!" one of the slavers exclaims when he recognizes them. Drawing his sword, he advances upon Jiron and James. "You shall die for what you did this evening."

"Never again will the music of Kir be heard in this world," the other yells as he, too, draws his sword.

Jiron gives them a grin and draws forth both knives. "If it's a fight you want, I'll oblige you," he says. With that he again moves forward, wanting nothing more than to vent the anger and frustration Buka instilled within him on these two.

As Jiron moves toward the two men, James removes one of his remaining slugs from his belt in the event Jiron should need his help. Just before Jiron reaches them, James catches movement out of the corner of his eye. Turning his gaze in the direction of the movement, he suddenly realizes there are men within the darkness on the far side of the lanterns. Then, he hears a voice speak a command, one that he's heard dozens of times before in battle with the Empire.

Just as the twang of a dozen crossbows breaks the stillness of the courtyard, he creates a barrier. A fraction of a second later, the flight of bolts strikes the barrier and ricochets off. That's when he realizes he unconsciously made the barrier large enough to encompass not only himself and Jiron, but the two slavers as well.

Jiron, oblivious to what is transpiring around them, is only concerned with the two slavers. For their part, all they want is to kill the men who took the hand of one they held in awe.

As one slaver thrusts at Jiron, the other brings his sword at an angle to slice into Jiron's side. Deflecting the thrust to the side with one knife, he brings the other in to catch the oncoming blade on the knife's crossguard. Thrusting the sword upward, he moves inside the man's guard and knees him in the stomach. Knocked backward by the blow, the slaver staggers two feet before regaining his balance.

Turning his attention to the other slaver, Jiron knows he only has a moment before the man he kneed returns to the fight. He strikes out at the first slaver's head with a knife which causes him to bring his sword up to block the blow, then comes in with the other and opens a three inch cut along his side.

Now bleeding, the slaver gives an inarticulate cry and brings his sword in for a thrust at Jiron's midsection. Dancing to the side, Jiron deflects the attack and brings his other knife in for a blow to the man's neck. Unable to avoid the blow, the slaver cries out as the blade rips into his the left side of his neck, practically severing his head from his torso. Falling to the ground, the slaver flops around a second before becoming still.

Just then, the other slaver rejoins the fight and strikes at him with an overhand hack which he barely sidesteps in time. Backing up, Jiron readies another attack when he finally takes notice of the barrier. Glancing outside of it, he sees over two dozen slavers ringing them, about half having crossbows. "Don't worry about them," he hears James say. "Finish this guy then we'll deal with the others." Jiron gives him a nod and advances on the remaining slaver.

With his partner lying on the ground dead, the second slaver cries out as he launches into a series of blows designed to bully his way through Jiron's defenses. But Jiron has seen many such attacks before, and by others more skilled than the man before him. Moving his knives quickly and deftly, he deflects the blows and waits for the opening he's sure will appear.

He begins to deflect the man's sword in a pattern he's used many times to create an opening. Each time the sword comes at him, he deflects it in such a way that the man becomes slightly more unbalanced. Until finally, the opening appears and Jiron strikes out with a barely seen attack and sinks his blade in the man's chest.

Stepping backward, Jiron watches as the man looks in confusion at the hilt sticking out of his chest. Then his sword falls from his fingers as he drops to his knees and topples over. Moving forward, Jiron reclaims his knife and wipes both blades off on the man's clothes. Standing up again, he looks around once more at the ring of slavers surrounding them.

"What now?" he asks James. He can see the bolts lying on the ground on the other side of the barrier from the futile attempt to attack them.

With the threat from the two slavers within the barrier nullified, James turns toward those on the outside. "We're leaving," he tells them. To Jiron he says, "Follow me."

Jiron nods and replies, "Lead on."

Altering his course, James no longer moves toward the gates, rather he heads to the back wall of the slaver compound. One slaver gets in their way and threatens them with his sword. Before the edge of the barrier reaches the man, James says, "Move."

The slaver either doesn't understand or ignores the command for he advances forward. Raising his sword to strike, he's suddenly struck by the barrier before he can complete the maneuver. The unexpected blow knocks him off balance and he hits the ground as James and Jiron continue on by.

"Look," Jiron says as he points to the door leading into the building wherein Buka met them. The Guildmaster stands there in the doorway and glares at them as they move closer.

"I see him," replies James. When he draws closer, James says to Buka, "We're leaving. Anyone you send after us will die."

"You aren't going to get away with this," the Guildmaster states, the implied threat quite apparent.

"Better men than you have tried to kill us," Jiron tells him, "yet here we are."

Buka didn't get to be Guildmaster by being stupid or acting foolishly. Having seen the bolts being deflected by the barrier and the subsequent knocking aside of the slaver, he knows there's nothing he can do to prevent them from leaving. Signaling for his men to back off, they keep a good distance between themselves and the two men protected by the barrier.

James continues moving forward toward the wall. Beside him, Jiron keeps an eye on those following along behind them as they approach the wall. "They're still following," he says.

"I know," replies James. Coming to the wall, James summons the magic and directs a blast toward it.

Bam!

The wall explodes outward and when the dust clears, they find a ten foot section of the wall gone. James turns back to the slavers and warns them again, "Follow me at your peril."

Stepping forward, James and Jiron carefully make their way through the rubble. Once past, they continue in as straight a direction to the edge of town as they can. Before they've gone more than half a dozen yards from the hole in the wall, three slavers rush through after them.

Crumph!

The ground under them explodes upward and throws them into the air. When the men come back down and strike the ground, they fail to move. "Any more?" James asks.

"Doesn't look like it," Jiron replies.

"Good," nods James. Resuming their progress, they continue away from the wall. As long as they have the wall in sight, no more slavers attempt to make it through.

Chapter Twenty Eight

The coldness of the stone sucks the very warmth from his body. Not for the first time has he questioned the logic which made him leave his friends behind. At the time, all he could think of was vengeance. Those that took his love away from him had to be made to pay and he knew that as long as he continued to travel with James, that was unlikely to happen.

For a long time, every day was torment for him. Each morning a renewal of his loss and every evening a lonely time spent mourning what no longer could be. At first he sought out and executed ranking members of the Empire's forces. His first victim was some officer in a small town not too far from where he left the others behind.

He had ridden into town, eyes red and swollen from his grief. When he saw the officer appear out of a doorway, his vision turned even redder. Not caring about who would see him he leaped from his horse and approached the man. The officer noticed his approach and turned to greet him, but instead was only greeted by the point of one of Tinok's knives. A quick thrust and it was over, the officer never even had a chance to defend himself. It was murder, pure and simple.

He bent over and carved a heart with two dots upon the man's forehead. To this day he still doesn't know why he did that, but ever since, it became his calling card. Whenever he killed another of the Empire's officers and nobles, a similar design was carved into their foreheads as well.

The first year he spent as a loner, moving from town to town, staying on the fringe of society. Not being able to speak the language was a definite handicap at first. But after awhile he began to pick up on it.

That's when he began to hear rumors and stories of a great mage who was wreaking havoc among the Empire's cities and citizens. Each time he heard the tale, the story would grow. A grin would come to him, for he knew that his friends were still alive. And better yet, hurting the Empire.

At the end of winter and before spring began, he started accumulating people of like mind. First one, then another learned of him and sought him out. Each wanting to work to hurt the Empire. Some were common thugs and murderers who saw him as a chance to strike back at the government that had hurt them so bad. Others were more along the lines of those who wanted a change. They were tired of the way the Emperor and his army controlled everything. How the average person had little chance to improve their lot and so forth.

So by the time summer came along, he had a band following him numbering two score. He had thought that by this time he would have been captured and killed. Only reason he can think of why they didn't spend more resources in trying to capture him was that there was another they wanted more. James was playing merry hell with them and they wanted him bad. What forces were sent looking for him were either easily avoided or destroyed.

Then came the news that Black Hawk, infamous leader of men that he was, had resurfaced. Not only that, but with a band of men was actually pushing the Empire's forces back. He wouldn't have credited the story except along with the news of Black Hawk came the tale of how the mage had joined with him.

That was when he began to go after bigger targets. Armories, workshops, things like that. No longer satisfied with skirting the fringe and taking officers unawares, his force began planning attacks and sowing dissent. Which only brought more people to him. At one point his force numbered over three hundred men.

But then came the day when he made his mistake.

He was leading his band to a small town where they planned to make a raid for supplies. Stealing food and other necessities has been the way he kept his force supplied. What money they may come across tends to be spent on other things, like women.

The town was a nexus for local herders and growers, those that were able to coax something to grow in this type of climate. Earlier, he had sent a man ahead to scout the town who returned with news that the storehouses were filled to capacity. Needing food badly, he turned his force and headed straight toward it. What he didn't realize was that he was riding into a trap.

Though he didn't know it at the time, a smart young officer had been put in charge of hunting him down. And after several months of pursuit, this officer had learned his habits well. So well in fact that he had the storehouses at this town stocked, spread the word of the food stored here, and waited in the hopes Tinok would take the bait. Which of course is exactly what he did.

When his force rode in and began laying siege to the town's guards, soldiers boiled out of the neighboring buildings. Out numbered, Tinok's force was quickly decimated. Only a handful managed to escape. One of those lucky few was Tinok himself.

Now on the run with a much larger force hot on their heels, they fled. Despite the cunning he had developed during his time as a marauder, he was unsuccessful in losing them. Then the inevitable happened, their horses became fatigued and were unable to outrun their pursuers.

Tinok decided to make a last stand at an old stone farmhouse they stumbled across. From the relative safety of inside its stone walls, he and the four others who had made it that far with him watched from the windows as the enemy soldiers surrounded them.

The officer in charge gave them the opportunity to give up peacefully, but that was something none of them was willing to do. Replying in a less than humble attitude, Tinok cast aspersions on the officer's family tree and told him what he could do with his offer of surrender.

On three sides of the farmhouse were windows where they could keep an eye on what the enemy was doing. The fourth was solid stone containing neither door nor window. He and the others kept a constant vigil.

Tinok watched as the soldiers began massing a large pile of wood a hundred feet from the front door. They quickly had the pile of sticks and dried bushes stacked quite high. An hour, maybe two passed after the pile was completed and the enemy sat there and waited. Then, about the time it was growing dark, four riders appeared with bulging satchels tied behind their saddles.

When the riders stopped and began opening the satchels and removing the contents, Tinok began to understand what they were about to do. For inside the satchels were small bladders that the Empire used in transporting lantern oil. He looked on in growing fear as the pile of wood was lit.

Again, the officer in charge came to stand before them and said for them to surrender or be burned out.

Tinok glanced at the others. They all understood what was about to happen, and Tinok's chest swells with pride as his men to the man refused to surrender. Tinok shouted defiantly out to the officer saying they would rather burn than surrender. The officer replied that he is more than happy to comply.

Before the onslaught of fire, the officer positioned half a dozen crossbowmen outside of each window and door. He knew that at some point they would have to come out. Once they were in position, he called for the riders. They came with torches and used the now flaming pile to light them. Other riders came and were handed a single bladder of oil each. Then, the onslaught began.

Three riders with bladders rode fast for the farmhouse and threw the oil filled bladders at the windows. Tinok and the others tried desperately to prevent the bladders from coming through, but when they did, a flight of bolts flew through the windows at them. One of his men cried out as a bolt struck him in the neck. Two of the three bladders successfully made it through and smashed open on the floor of the farmhouse.

Right behind the riders with the oil came the riders with the torches. Just as the ones before them did, they threw their burning brands through the window. Two of the torches were successfully blocked, but one made it through and landed onto the oil covered floor.

Whoosh!

The oil on the floor ignited and fire spread across the floor just as another set of riders came with more bladders of oil. Distracted by the burning oil within the farmhouse, they were unable to prevent the others from coming through. Two of the bladders broke open on impact, increasing the already fierce fire burning across the floor. The third remained intact upon impact. Sitting in the fire as it was, it didn't take long before it exploded.

The oil contained within the exploding bladder flew in all directions. One of the men with Tinok was unfortunate enough to be in close proximity to it. He screamed in agony as the burning oil hit him and began to burn.

Coughing and rasping, he and the two remaining men decided to go out fighting. Kicking open the door, Tinok raced out with knives in hand. Behind him the other two had their swords drawn as they charged the soldiers to sell their lives as best they could.

No sooner did the door slam open than six crossbows released their deadly projectiles at the escaping men. One went down with two bolts in him, the other gets hit in the leg and continued on. None of the bolts hit Tinok and he saw the crossbowmen twenty feet before him. With a cry, he sprinted for them.

Regular soldiers quickly moved to protect the crossbowmen and he was soon surrounded with armored men. He managed to drop one of them with a lucky strike before he was struck on the back of his head and knocked unconscious.

He and his man that was struck in the leg with one of the crossbow bolts were tied and thrown across the backs of two horses. For a week they were taken across the desert until they arrived at what they learnt was the city of Cyst. All of their belongings but their clothes were taken, including the necklace he had given Cassie shortly before she was killed. That more than anything else took the fight from him. His mind burned for revenge, but his heart just felt like ashes.

He was sure slavery would not be his fate, rather the hangman's noose. After what he and his men did, there could be no other fate for them. The first day he and Esix, the sole remaining member of his band, waited in apprehension for someone to come and tell them what was going to happen to them. But no one did.

They remained in one of the slave pens in Cyst for a week, maybe two. Time lost meaning after the first several days as one merged into the next. Each day they waited for the hammer to drop, yet their waiting was in vain for no one came to them. Until one day a man in armor came and took them. No word was given as they were escorted from the pen.

Neither one of them understood the significance of the man in armor at the time, simply that everyone including the slavers treated him with utmost respect. Tinok thought that some of them held back barely controlled fear while in his presence. He too could feel something about the man, whether from the man himself or due to the reaction of the others, he wasn't sure.

As he waited for other slaves and prisoners to be gathered, Tinok noticed an insignia on the man's armor. Three dots with lines running between them yet not touching them. Later he was to come to know that the insignia marked the man as one of the dreaded warrior priest's of Dmon-Li. Terrible fighters who wield the power of their god with terrible strength.

He, Esix, and fourteen others were loaded onto two wagons and taken west. Before the end of the first day, a wall of fog appeared from out of the distance ahead of them. It grew larger the nearer they came to it and it didn't take Tinok long to realize the fog was to be their destination.

The other slaves in the wagon with him grew nervous and fearful when they came to the realization as had Tinok that they were heading for the fog. He heard one of them call the fog the Mists of Sorrow, and from others he learned that it held a fell reputation.

Tinok watched the fog grow ever closer. Then all of a sudden it was all around them. One minute it was over a hundred yards away, and the next it was encompassing them. A man sitting next to him began having hysterics and was struck on the back of the head. Knocked out, the man's screams and pleas were silenced as he fell against Tinok who was on the verge or losing it himself. Not wanting to be struck like the man next to him had been, Tinok kept a tight reign on the fear fighting to take control.

The fog now surrounding them dampened all sound. Even that of their horses' hooves upon the ground was barely heard. Cold and clammy, it felt like it was trying to suck the warmth from you. It didn't take long before the cold seeped its way to his very core. Teeth chattering, he wrapped his arms around himself in an attempt to keep warm. The others in the wagon with him did the same.

He's not sure when it happened, but at one point the shadow of some beast passed through the mist not too far away. It was the size of a horse yet ran along the ground like a dog. There for a moment before disappearing back into the fog.

"What was that?" Esix asked him.

"I don't know," he replied. Glancing to the warrior priest leading them, he's at least somewhat comforted by the knowledge that their captor isn't reacting to the beast's presence. Which meant there was no immediate threat from it. "Could be something like a watchdog," he guessed.

"Maybe," agreed Esix.

If it was a guard dog of some kind, the possibility of escape from wherever they are going began to seem unlikely. Tinok kept scanning the fog surrounding them while they continued to roll through and saw the beast several more times. At least he hoped it was the same beast. One they may be able to deal with should they get away. More than that and it's a fool's hope of ever getting out of here.

They rolled on through the night without more than minimal breaks to feed and water the horses. Tinok dozed on and off until he and the others in the wagons were taken out to answer the call of nature. None strayed too far from the wagons, the thought of facing what is out there kept them from even thinking of trying to escape. Once done, they were reloaded back onto the wagons and they resumed their progress through the fog.

Through the night and most of the next morning they were taken further into the fog. Finally, a dark shadow began to form ahead of them in the fog until they drew close enough and discovered the dark shadow was in actuality a large stone building.

How large the building may be couldn't be seen due to the denseness of the fog. A large black wall was all they saw before it disappeared into the fog. Made of massive stone blocks, it looked very strong and impregnable. To the surprise of Tinok and the others, the warrior priest led them directly to the imposing stone wall.

The warrior priest stopped and dismounted when he reached the wall. Coming forward, he stopped and stood motionless before the black wall. With neither movement nor speech, he stood there like a statue until a grinding noise came from within the wall. Suddenly, a section began receding backward into the wall and then slid to the side. It revealed an opening wide enough for a wagon to pass comfortably and tall enough for a mounted rider.

Returning to his horse, the warrior priest mounted then began leading them into the dark edifice. One man in the wagon behind Tinok's began screaming incoherently and tried to break free from his bonds. Yanking at the chain connecting his manacles to the eye ring in the bed of the wagon, he tugged at it furiously.

One of the riders escorting the wagons rode to the side of the wagon and struck the man on the back of the head with a club. The impact knocked him into the bed of the wagon and stilled his cries. Tinok continued glancing to the wagon but didn't see the man get up. Fearing he may be dead, he looked to the other prisoners. Fear was in the eyes of every man in the wagon.

"What is this place?" Esix asked.

Tinok just shook his head.

Then their wagon rolled into the opening. If they thought it was cold out in the mist, within the opening it was absolutely frigid. Dark and cold, the tunnel extended into blackness. As they moved further away from the opening, the light from outside began to fade. When the last rider was within the tunnel, Tinok again heard the grinding noise of the block returning to its place within the wall. The light completely faded away as it moved once more into position.

They rode in complete darkness for several minutes, the clip-clop of the horse's hooves and the creaking of the wagon wheels were the only sound. Then the wagons came to a halt and a light appeared to dispel the darkness. Not a bright light, just enough to be able to see that they were in a large room.

The warrior priest dismounts and disappeared into one of the archways leading from the room. Tinok and the others remained seated in the wagon, unsure what to do or what their fate may be.

All of a sudden, a small creature appeared in the air before Tinok. It's scaly, somewhat man-like form was bent over as if from carrying too much weight. Red eyes aglow with an inner light stared from its gnarled head at Tinok as it hovered there before him.

Tinok returned its gaze as others in the wagon began taking note of the creature. Several men made the sign to ward off evil which had little effect. Reaching up his hand to touch it he almost grabbed the creature before it vanished, and then it reappeared before another man at the other end of the wagon.

More of the creatures began popping in and staring at the men in the wagons. Then from the archway the warrior priest exited through, footsteps could be heard. A moment later, the warrior priest appeared and with a gesture to the guards that had accompanied them, he had them begin unloading the prisoners.

Their chains were unlocked from the wagon's eye rings, then were taken out of the wagons and lined up on the cold stone. The iciness of the floor sent shivers up into Tinok. Once all the men were gathered, they were made to follow the warrior priest. Moving through the archway, he led them through another dark tunnel.

The same faint light which was present in the room behind them seemed to follow their progress. The light was rather unnerving as there was no discernable source for it. It just was. Dozens of the creatures that had appeared before them in the wagons now began popping in and out. They took a look for a short time then disappeared.

At the end of the tunnel, they came to a room with four pens used to hold men and were divided among them. Tinok and Esix were put together in the same one. All this time, neither the warrior priest nor the guards accompanying him have spoken a word.

Once all the men were within the pens, the warrior priest gave them a final once over before he left. The guards followed him out and soon Tinok and the others are left alone in the pens.

How long ago that was, Tinok is no longer sure. The small creatures have been a constant menace as they continue popping in and out. Food is brought to them by hooded men, who despite their attempts to engage in conversation, remain quiet. Both Tinok and Esix have tried to get a good look within the hoods but there isn't sufficient light with which to see.

Thinking back on his life, he now regrets his decision to leave Jiron and the others. Fate has led him awry it seems. How he wishes to be able to see the face of his friend one last time before the end. For he feels that his end is approaching.

Chapter Twenty Nine

At the rendezvous near the western edge of town, they find Miko and Brother Willim with the horses. The others have yet to make it back from the Wallowing Swine. "They haven't returned yet?" asks James.

Shaking his head, Brother Willim says, "Not yet."

"Damn!" curses Jiron. "We don't have time to stand here and wait for them."

"I know," agrees Miko. When James looks to him he adds, "We heard the explosions."

"I think everyone in town heard them," comments Brother Willim.

"So what do we do?" Jiron asks James.

"We wait," he replies. "That's all we can do."

Brother Willim asks Jiron, "Did you find out what you came here for?"

Nodding, Jiron says, "Buka said that he was taken to some place called Ith-Zirul. Ever heard of it?"

Brother Willim's face blanches slightly at the name. Nodding his head, a grim expression comes over him. "If that is where your friend has been taken, then all hope is lost," he says.

"Why?" Jiron asks.

"That's what Buka said too," says James at the same time. "What does it mean?"

Taking a deep breath, Brother Willim explains. "Ith-Zirul is the High Temple of Dmon-Li."

"Dmon-Li!" exclaims James.

"It is said none other than those who worship Dmon-Li ever leave Ith-Zirul," he says. "And if your friend is indeed within the walls of that cursed place, it would explain some things."

"Such as?" asks Jiron. The hope that he experienced when he first heard of the location of his friend is slowly dying the more he learns of where he is.

"For one thing, it would explain why you can't use magic to find him," he explains. "The temple would be warded against such things. Also, you said the image was fuzzy when you saw him. That no matter how much magic you used, it never became better."

"That's right," states James.

"You see," Brother Willim says, "the High Temple of Dmon-Li is hidden within the Mists of Sorrow."

James nods his head as more connections are made. "During our journey to find Miko when he was captured by the Empire," he begins, "we passed by a wall of fog that one of our number said was the Mists of Sorrow." Turning to Jiron he asks, "Remember?"

Nodding, Jiron says, "Yes, I remember."

"When Delia and I went to examine it in the morning, it was so close to our camp that we saw a shadow pass through its fringe. At the time I didn't know what it was, and frankly hadn't thought about it until now. It was one of those hell hounds that have been set against us on several occasions."

"You mean the Mists is guarded by those things?" Jiron asks.

"It would seem so," he says.

"The Mists is just the first hurdle," Brother Willim says. "After that there is trying to find the entrance. From what my brethren have been able to gather over the centuries, the temple is massive. We could be in the Mist for a long time before ever coming to the door. All the while, you can rest assured they will be throwing everything they have at us."

"And should we make it through the Mists and enter the temple," James says, "we still have to find Tinok." To Brother Willim he asks, "Will my magic be able to locate him once we're within its walls?"

"I just don't know," he says. "It would depend on the type of wards they have in place."

Then all of a sudden their attention is drawn to rapidly approaching footsteps coming from further into town. From the sound of it there must be more than a couple people coming toward them.

Jiron places a hand on the hilt of one of his knives and moves toward the sound while the others remain quietly with the horses. As whoever is approaching draws closer, he can hear one of them asks, "Where the heck are they?"

He relaxes when he realizes the voice belongs to Scar. "Over here!" he calls out softly. The footsteps come to a stop and he can now see their silhouettes in the moonlight. Moving toward them, he again says, "Over here." Then to James he hollers, "It's them."

"Jiron?" asks Reilin.

"Yeah," he says, "and it's about time you guys showed up."

As they move to join him, Potbelly says, "We had a few people follow us out of the tavern. Took us a bit to shake them."

"Is he alright?" Jiron asks.

"He's fine and everyone is accounted for," Stig assures him.

From out of the darkness appears the blonde haired Kir with a grin. "I wasn't sure if we were going to pull it off for awhile," Perrilin says. The front of his outfit and most of his right sleeve is coated in blood.

As Jiron leads them back to where James and the others are waiting with the horses, he says, "For a minute I thought we had actually cut off your hand. You're quite convincing."

"Thank you," he says with a slight bow. "I've had plenty of practice faking my own death." Then they arrive where the others are waiting and he looks to James as he adds, "But that thing with the pig's bladder and intestine was pure genius."

James gives him a smile and says, "Saw it on a show once about movie magic. Of course they used other material, but we made do with what was available to us."

After they had left the slaver compound and rejoined the others, they went to an inn and dropped off the horses as well as everyone but James, Jiron and Reilin. They then asked around and found out where Kir was staying. He was quite surprised when they showed up at his door.

When told of the task Buka had set for them, that is to take his right hand, he decided that Kir had outlived his usefulness. Then together they worked out a plan that would enable them to fool Buka and allow Perrilin to make good his escape. After all, those who knew Perrilin the bard was masquerading as Kir, would hear about him losing his hand in front of the crowd at the Wallowing Swine. That alone will allow him to create a new identity without immediate suspicion.

So the following morning, they went to a local butcher shop and purchased a medium sized pig's bladder, three feet of intestine, and a lot of pig's blood. They sewed the end of the intestine to the bladder and filled the bladder with the blood.

Next was a visit to a communal grave where they throw dead slaves. Seems a single grave is too much work for just a single slave. So they dig a pit and when it becomes filled with dead slaves, they fill it back in. Needless to say, the pit is usually far outside of town due to the odor. But Perrilin knew that any place with a slaver compound would have one and they soon located it. The rest was easy.

During the break when they agreed he would be attacked, in the back of the kitchen, Perrilin placed the pig bladder under his left arm and strung the intestine under his shirt all the way to his right hand. Then a hand and portion of the forearm of a dead slave were extended from the end of his right sleeve.

When he was grabbed and Jiron cut the hand from the forearm, he squeezed the pig's bladder and the pig's blood sprayed out the end of the section of intestine. All in all it looked like his 'stump' was spraying blood. Then it was a simple matter for Reilin and the others to get him out of there, hide the evidence, and rejoin James.

"What will they do when they come looking for you?" asks Stig. "After all, some of the people there really cared about you."

"They'll find me gone," he replies. "I'm sure they'll hunt through the temples and when they still can't find me, the rumors will start."

They mount their horses and head out into the night away from town. As they leave the buildings behind them, James fills the others in on what they learned from Buka and the ramifications that go along with it. "So, we have less than ten days remaining," James summarizes. "We know where he is. All that's left is to go get him."

"Oh, that's all?" asks Aleya mockingly. "You can't be thinking about breaking into this temple. It's madness!"

"Now, it won't be that bad," Jiron tells her.

She turns a withering glare upon him and is about to launch into how stupid the plan is when Miko says in a calm but sure voice, "We must." Her glare now turns to him. Cutting her off yet again, he says, "No matter what the cost, we must try to stop what is going to happen. Even if it means all of us die in the attempt."

James brings them to a halt and turns to Miko. "What do you mean we have to 'stop what is going to happen'?"

"Just what I said," he replies. "This goes far beyond Tinok, Cassie, even you James."

"You'll have to explain that to me," Scar says.

"Something's been gnawing at me ever since you told us your last vision when you learned it was Cassie in your dreams," he explains. "And it finally, as you say, clicked together. I don't believe the dream was given to you for Tinok's benefit. Rather, it was a way to get you to go to that temple in the middle of the Mists."

Turning to Brother Willim he says, "Your dreams of late have ended with the sundering of a black, mist shrouded tree. From which a creature issues forth and destroys the garden. Am I right in saying the garden represents the world?"

Brother Willim nods his head. "I have always thought so."

"A black tree shrouded in mist and now a black temple residing within a blanket of mist." Glancing from between Brother Willim and James he concludes, "It's too much of a coincidence with everything that's been happening."

Nodding, Brother Willim says, "I agree. I came to that conclusion a short time ago."

"Therefore, something is going to happen within the High Temple of Dmon-Li when the moon turns black. Whatever it is, should it be successful, will destroy the world."

They grow silent as each ponders what he just said. "Could it be possible?" Aleya asks. Gone is her stern glare to Jiron. Now a more thoughtful, perhaps even fearful expression has taken its place.

"Yes," replies James. He remembers that other place he was in long ago, the one with the burnt trees and shadows that Igor had rescued him from. "Oh yes, I believe it can happen. That it probably has happened to other worlds, other places."

Miko turns to face James. "Is this why I was made High Priest?" he asks.

"More than likely," he replies with a nod. "As High Priest, you would bring more to the table than just being plain old Miko."

"How far away is this temple?" asks Scar.

They turn to Perrilin who says, "The Mists of Sorrow lay a little over a day to the southwest, but their position fluctuates at times. Once within them, I'm not sure how much further the temple will be."

"Then I suggest we ride for another couple hours and then rest until dawn," Jiron says. "In the morning ride until we reach the Mists then rest until the following morning. It would be best if we were at our peak when entering the Mists."

James nods. "I agree," he says.

Moving on, they ride to the southwest as planned and stop after putting many miles behind them. They post a watch throughout the night while they sleep. Once the sun begins to rise once more, they're back in the saddle and again moving southwest.

The terrain grows steadily more unforgiving the further they go. Cracked land and stunted trees for as far as the eye can see. After leaving their campsite, Brother Willim is the first to notice the lack of living things in the area. "I can't sense any birds or beasts nearby," he announces at one point. "I've never before been to an area such as this."

"What could it mean?" asks Reilin.

"Nothing good I assure you," the priest replies.

The day progresses hot and dry. Worries rise as they push deeper into what Scar has begun to call the land of the dead, a not too far off description considering the lack of life they've encountered.

Three hours before sundown, the Mists of Sorrow appears on the horizon. Just as he remembers it, a wall of fog in an area where no fog should be able to exist. As they ride forward, the wall of fog steadily grows until they come to within a mile of it. There they stop and make camp for the night.

"We'll stay here through the night," James tells the others as they set about making camp. "We should be safe enough here."

Jiron looks at the wall of fog with Aleya standing next to him. "I hope so," he mutters. He turns to her and says, "I wish you weren't here."

"I know you do," she says. "But there's no other place I would rather be."

Putting his arm around her, he gives her an affectionate squeeze. Then they return to the others and help with preparations for the meal. A filling meal of the last of their dried beef and a few old tubers Brother Willim dug from the ground satisfies their hunger if not their taste buds. How the tubers came to be here is anyone's guess, could be they manage to grow in the wintertime.

Once the meal is over and they are sitting around a campfire, they decided to risk one seeing as how nothing is out here, they settle in for the night. As hard as it may be, they try to put what may happen on the morrow out of their minds as they spend one last time together like they use to back at The Ranch. Stories and songs, most of which are by Perrilin, go a long way in taking away their worries and fears. But when the time comes to sleep, once again each one begins to dwell on what will happen. For some, sleep takes a long time to come.

"Where is it?" asks Stig.

The lightning of the sky with the coming of dawn revealed that the fog was nowhere in sight. "I told you it moves," Brother Willim says. "The edge has simply moved further away from us."

"It must be scared," jokes Shorty. "It knows we are on the way." A couple snickers are all he gets for his levity, not nearly what he was hoping for.

"Guess we'll have a little more of a ride this morning than we anticipated," James says. Climbing into the saddle, he waits for the others to mount. Then he nods to Jiron to lead the way. With Aleya riding beside him, he heads out.

The fog doesn't take too long to makes its appearance. Less than an hour after they get underway it appears on the horizon. The sight of the fog before them affects each in their own way. Most however feel a sense of dread at the sight, one of impending doom.

Steeling their nerve, they continue on toward the wall of fog. It rises to a point high above the ground and when they at last reach its boundary, it towers far above them. "Never seen fog or mist behave this way before," Perrilin states. "A sheer wall rising to the sky like this."

"This is no ordinary mist," Brother Willim states. "It differs slightly from that you would normally find in the world."

"How so?" asks James.

"Hard to explain," he replies. Gesturing to the mist before them he says, "This goes against the natural order of the world."

They pause momentarily at the mist's boundary. James gazes intently at the mist before them and tries to penetrate its murky depths. "Everyone keep a constant lookout for hell hounds," he says to the others. "With any luck, they may not be in this area."

"I wouldn't trust to that if I were you," comments Potbelly.

"I'm not," he responds. Then with a glance to Jiron, he nods that they should enter.

"Here we go," breathes Jiron as he nudges his horse to move forward.

As they enter the mist and it envelops them, it almost feels as if the mist is sucking the warmth right out of their bodies. The world turns hazy as the light from the sun above becomes diffused as it works its way down to where they are. Sound too, seems to be muffled in some way, the clip-clop of the horses' hooves no longer resonates as it had when they were not in the mist.

Onward Jiron leads them. Everyone stays in a compact group, all unconsciously remain together for safety. When after a few minutes' time nothing happens, Jiron picks up the pace.

James wants desperately to use magic to see if there is anything nearby, but realizes that if he does, those within the temple will undoubtedly pick up on it. So he resists the temptation and uses what senses are available to him; sight, smell and sound. Unfortunately, the mist allows neither one to be very effective.

Time becomes meaningless within the constant grayness of the mist. They begin jumping at imagined shadows as the monotonousness of the mist starts playing tricks on their senses. "Is there anything you can do about this?" Shorty asks Brother Willim after they've been in the mist for what must be over an hour.

"No," he replies. "It's not natural."

"Too bad," states Reilin.

Another few minutes pass by and Jiron suddenly comes to a stop and peers intently into the mists ahead of them.

James stops next to him and asks, "What is it?" Looking forward into the mist, he tries to see what Jiron had.

"I'm not sure," he replies. Not taking his eyes off the mist he adds, "Thought I saw something."

From behind them Scar pipes up and says, "Could have been your imagination. This sort of stuff can do that to a man."

"Maybe," he says in a tone which tells the others he doesn't think that's what it was.

James continues staring into the fog but fails to see anything. "I don't think there's anything out there," he says. Rarely though is Jiron wrong about something like this.

Aaaah!!!

Then suddenly Stig cries out as one of the hell hounds leaps from out of the mist and slams into his horse. The creature's claws rake the side of the horse, ripping and tearing as it bowls them both over. Stig leaps from the saddle and hits the ground hard. Rolling, he comes up and faces the creature with mace and shield ready.

The creature looks up at him and charges just as Brother Willim throws something in the air. A tangle of vines bursts into being and ensnares the creature.

Light blazes forth as Miko holds aloft the Star and speaks in a language none can understand. The mist rolls backward until a wide clearing devoid of mist surrounds them. Another of the creatures is revealed when the mist rolls back. A beam of light surges from the Star and strikes the second creature. Rearing back, the creature lets out a primal scream of pain as the light from the Star lances through it.

The first creature struggles against the vines holding it. Smoke rises as the heat of the creature chars the constricting vines. In little time, the creature breaks free and leaps. James spies the creature leaping for Stig and lets the magic flow. A barrier forms around the creature in mid leap. Stig dodges to the side as the barrier encased creature hits the ground right where he had been standing.

Increasing the magic to the barrier, James changes its nature and turns it quickly colder. Inside, the creature struggles against the barrier but is unable to break free. Then, just as he had many times before, James begins shrinking the barrier in on the creature until its life force goes out and the barrier implodes.

By this time, Miko has the second creature all but destroyed. The light from the Star is still searing into it, extinguishing its life. Soon, the creature collapses completely and erupts in a cloud of noxious black smoke, leaving a charred area upon the ground where it was destroyed.

Jiron scans the area for more of the creatures then hollers, "Everyone okay?"

"I'm fine," replies Stig. He walks over to his horse only to find what he already knew. It's dead. The side where the creature attacked it has been ripped to shreds.

To Miko, Jiron asks, "Can you continue to keep the mist at bay?"

"Not a problem," he replies.

Jiron then glances to James and says, "Seeing as how they know we're here already and all."

Nodding, James says, "Good thinking. Better pick up the pace a bit from here on out."

"Are we sure we're still going in the right direction?" asks Aleya. "I can no longer tell which way is which."

Miko points off into the mists and says, "It's that way."

"How can you tell?" asks Potbelly.

"Ever since we entered the mist, I have felt something," he explains. "I wasn't sure what it was until just now. It's the temple. It feels like a disease."

"Then you take the lead from here," Jiron says. "I haven't been sure for awhile if we were even going in the right direction."

With a nod, Miko takes the lead and they continue on.

Stig mounts behind Shorty, he being the lightest of the group. Thus their combined weight will tire his horse less than if Stig rode with another.

Aleya stares at the charred spot on the ground where the creature Miko killed fell. She swallows hard and steels her nerves as she follows along with the others. If she still had her bow and arrows, she would definitely feel better.

Miko continues to maintain their island within the mist through the magic of the Star. Able to see more than a couple feet in front of them takes the edge off the dread that had filled them since entering the Mists. It's still absolute quiet other than the noise that they and their horses make which lends an eerie feel to the whole thing.

"If that's all we are going to have to face," begins Potbelly, "we should be able to make it to the temple."

"What are the odds on that though?" counters Scar as he gazes to the wall of mist, first to one side then the other. "There's bound to be more of them out there."

"Not to mention warrior priests," adds Potbelly. "If there's any place that would have them, it would be here."

"Quiet!" insists Jiron. "Keep your eyes open and your mouths shut."

Staying quiet, the riders continue to forge their way through the mist and closer to the temple. After riding for a ways, James whispers to Miko, "How much further is it?"

"I'm not sure," he replies. "The feeling continues to grow as we draw nearer, but I'm unable to determine how close it may be."

Then the tingling of magic being worked comes to him. "Magic!" James exclaims as he comes to a stop and throws a barrier around them.

"Where?" asks Jiron as he and the others come to a stop.

"I feel it too," says Brother Willim and a green glow suddenly surrounds him.

"Is it strong?" asks Shorty.

"Very," replies James.

Coming to a stop, they remain there for a short time within James' protective barrier and still nothing materializes. Then out of the mist before them appear two forms, both heavily armored.

"Warrior priests!" cries out Brother Willim.

They raise their hands in unison and a wave of dark magic rolls toward the barrier. More felt than seen, James braces for the impact. When the dark magic strikes the barrier, James cries out as a shockwave travels back along the magic stream to him. It hits him like a lightning bolt and knocks him off his horse. The barrier winks out.

"James!" cries Stig as he vaults off his horse and comes to his aid.

The light from the Star increases tenfold as a beam lances outwards from it toward the two warrior priests. It strikes one of them, causing him to stagger. Where the beam struck the warrior priest, a sizzling hole gapes in the man's armor, but the man himself appears unaffected. Leaping from his horse, Miko holds aloft the Star as he draws his sword and moves to engage the two warrior priests.

"Miko no!" cries out Jiron. There's no way he'll be able to handle two. The last time he faced off against only one he barely survived.

Just then, another of the hell hounds darts from the mist straight toward where James is lying on the ground. Stig hears him coming. Getting up from where he had knelt at James' side, he turns and braces for the attack. Even before the hell hound closes with him he feels the heat radiating off of it. Striking out with his mace, Stig connects with the creature's shoulder and excruciating pain burns his hand as the creature's heat is absorbed by the metal of the mace. Then a split second later one of its forepaws strikes his shield and throws him a dozen yards away.

James regains his senses just as Stig is being swiped aside and sees the creature turn its attention back to him. Leaping for him, the creature opens its maw to rip out his throat and is suddenly entrapped by another of James' shields. Rolling aside, James gets out of the way before the entrapped creature hits the ground right where he had lain.

As he begins shrinking the shield onto the creature, a flash of white light draws his attention over to where Miko is battling one of the warrior priests. The other one is currently entangled in a mass of vines as Brother Willim lays into it with his staff. Jiron is there giving Miko and Brother Willim what help he can. A stab here, a slash there, he's connecting but his attacks are not being nearly effective enough.

Bam!

An explosion knocks the vines away from the warrior priest that was entrapped. Now free, he begins laying into Brother Willim with incredible ferocity and skill. Jiron, when he tries to get in a blow is knocked backward just like someone swatting a fly.

With the green glow surrounding him, Brother Willim's staff is a blur as he counters and blocks the warrior priest's attacks. But that is the limit he's able to do as he faces the full force of a warrior priest's skill. His mind is so set on blocking the blindingly fast attacks that he's unable to do aught else.

Scar and Potbelly have reached Stig's side and are helping him. Aleya and Shorty along with Reilin and Perrilin stand by the horses, feeling helpless in this battle.

James works to implode the shield encasing the hell hound when he sees another emerge from the mist and turn its gaze on those standing with the horses. He casts another shield around that one which causes such a drain that he's no longer able to quickly shrink the shield around the first one. Its progress is now down to about a tenth of the rate that it was before.

Miko fortunately is holding his own against his opponent and if anything is getting the upper hand. Along with attacks with his sword, the Star in his hand lashes out with bursts of light that strike the warrior priest with devastating results. The man's armor now shows holes in several places and a few are even beginning to ooze blood.

Then out from the mist another hell hound emerges near Miko. James sees it and before it has a chance to attack, he creates a third shield to trap it. Now the drain of magic is such that he's totally unable to shrink the barriers even a minute amount. In fact, the magic is being drained from his so quickly that he's not even sure how much longer he'll be able to maintain the three shields he's currently holding.

As if that wasn't enough, he feels a spike in the tingling sensation. The ground starts to shake and groan as cracks appear across its surface. Then with a mighty shake which almost topples everyone, the ground splits open in a dozen places. Man shaped creatures crawl from the earth. Four feet tall and the color of fresh turned earth, they immediately move to attack whoever is closest once they are free of the ground.

We can't win this! James suddenly realizes.

As Scar and Potbelly face off against five of the creatures, they hold them off of the unconscious Stig lying between them. Shorty, Reilin and Aleya are facing off with another two.

James sees one approaching him. They aren't moving very fast, sort of like the loping gait of the undead in the first Night of the Living Dead movie. Taking a slug from out of his belt, he uses as much magic as he can spare and launches it at the thing.

Striking the creature in the center of the chest, he's surprised to see a large part of its midsection dislodge and be thrust out its back. When the midsection hits the ground, it breaks apart like dirt. Taking another slug, he launches it, this time at the creature's leg. It smashes into its upper thigh and the section from its hip to its knee comes loose. Now only on one leg, it topples to the side where it hits the ground and breaks apart.

He glances over to where Scar and Potbelly are using their swords against the creatures with little affect. Their blades cut into them but do little damage. "Scar!" he yells. "Use Stig's mace! You have to bash them, not cut them."

Scar glances over to him for a brief moment and then sees the one that he took out with his slugs, lying shattered on the ground. Seeing Stig's mace on the ground at his feet, he kicks out and pushes the nearest creature back. Then in one fluid motion thrusts the sword in his right hand into the ground, bends over and picks up the mace, then strikes out at the closest creature. The mace strikes its shoulder.

He's surprised to see the shoulder, along with the arm attached to it, come off the creature. "Bash them!" he cries out to the rest. "Cuts don't hurt them!" Striking out with the broadside of his sword, he connects with the creature's head and knocks it off. "Yeah!" he yells triumphantly as he begins laying into the rest.

Potbelly begins using the broadside of his sword and they soon have turned the creatures into a pile of dirt.

"We aren't going to win this!" James yells to them. "We have to get out of here."

They turn to see him standing there, legs shaking from the exertion of maintaining three barriers. Scar nods, then he and Potbelly go to help Reilin, Shorty and Perrilin where they are having trouble with their opponents.

The warrior priest facing off with Miko is showing mass damage to his armor and exposed skin. Miko himself has several wounds running with blood which begin to heal over rapidly as the magic of the Star works to preserve his life.

Brother Willim is not so fortunate. The warrior priest he's up against shows very little damage form the battle and is still going strong. Jiron had to quit the battle with the warrior priest in order to deal with one of the earth creatures. But once he had it reduced to a pile of dirt he quickly returned to help him.

When the last of the earth creatures falls, James calls for the others to get into the saddle. That they have to get out of here. Just then a blinding flash of light erupts from the Star. Glancing that way, James sees Miko's opponent fly backward and hit the ground. Another flash of light strikes the warrior priest where he lays on the ground. His body spasms, then grows still. Looking around, Miko begins moving to help Brother Willim and Jiron when Jiron hollers to him, "Help James!"

He turns and sees him there barely holding onto the barriers encasing the hell hounds. Leaving Brother Willim and Jiron to handle the remaining warrior priest, he makes his way quickly to the nearest hell hound. Holding the Star aloft, Miko envelopes the hell hound in a white glow. Between the glow and the barrier, the creature's life force within is quickly snuffed out.

With the third barrier no longer needed, James is better able to maintain the remaining two. "Thanks," he says to Miko.

Miko gives him a nod then moves to the next one where he repeats the process.

Brother Willim and Jiron are still not able to get the better of the warrior priest they are up against. Staff and knives are no match for the skill and speed with which their opponent attacks. Even with the power of his god, Brother Willim has received numerous wounds as he's unable to keep up with his opponent's speed.

Jiron tries to help, but he isn't able to get in close enough with just his knives.

"Miko!" Scar yells urgently from where he and the others are by the horses.

Miko takes his eyes off the hell hound he's working to destroy and sees the shadow that is even now approaching James. The magic of the Star disappears from around the hell hound as he turns it onto this new threat.

James sees the shadow approaching but there's nothing he can do. When the glow surrounding the hell hound winks out, it appears again surrounding the shadow. Stopping it in its tracks, the glow begins sucking the life out of the shadow and sending it back to where it came from.

It's all up to him now. James concentrates on the barrier of the hell hound Miko had all but destroyed and begins to shrink it still further. Despite the resistance he feels from the creature within, he's able to at last implode it and destroy the creature.

The shadow encased in the glow of the Star begins shrieking as the white glow burns into its blackness. With one final ear piercing scream, it vanishes.

James now works on shrinking the barrier encasing the final hell hound. "Miko!" he hollers. When Miko turns toward him he yells, "We can't stay. Go help Brother Willim and Jiron."

Miko gives him a nod and rushes over to them with the light of the Star blazing forth. Drawing his sword, he joins the fray. Brother Willim disengages, his staff becoming still as Miko's sword begins attacking the warrior priest.

"Jiron," Brother Willim says, "Miko and I will finish here. Get to the horses." Then from the corner of his eye he sees the first warrior priest that Miko took out beginning to stir. "Now!"

Jiron too sees the warrior priest beginning to recover. Running, he reaches the horses just as the barrier around the final hell hound implodes completely, destroying the creature. "James," he yells. "Time to go!"

James nods his head and starts toward where the others are already mounted. Suddenly his legs give way and he falls to the ground. The strain of fighting to control three barriers against the struggle of the hell hounds took all he had. Weak as a kitten, he tries to get back up but his arms are too leathery.

Then Jiron is at his side and helps him to his feet. Scar is there a split second later and together they get him over to the horses. "Are you able to remain in the saddle?" Jiron asks as they reach the side of his horse.

"Yes," he replies. "Just help me up."

With Scar's help, Jiron helps him into the saddle. A bit wobbly but he should be able to maintain his balance enough to get out of here. Tied across the back of another horse he sees the still body of Stig. "Is he alive?" he asks Potbelly.

"Yeah," Potbelly replies. "But if we don't get out of here and let Miko take care of him, I'm not sure for how long."

Brother Willim is suddenly moving past James' horse toward his own. Looking back at the warrior priest, he sees him entrapped with vines. "That's not going to hold him long," Miko says as he appears and mounts his horse.

"Let's get out of here!" Jiron yells.

Taking the lead, Miko holds aloft the Star to maintain the clearing within the mist. Aleya and Shorty are riding double and Perrilin has the reins of the horse carrying Stig. James hangs on for dear life as Miko leads them back out of the mist. Bringing up the rear are Scar and Potbelly.

Then suddenly Scar cries out as his horse is struck from behind. Another hell hound has appeared and took a massive chunk out of his horse's rear flank. Jumping clear of the saddle before the horse crashes to the ground, Scar hits the ground, rolls twice and comes up facing the approaching beast with both swords out.

The beast cries out as a shimmering field encases it and stops its forward movement. "Hurry!" yells James. Spots begin to dance before his eyes and he is leaning precariously in the saddle.

Potbelly kicks his horse and gallops back to Scar He reaches down a hand and Scar takes it, swinging up behind him. Kicking his horse, Potbelly races to rejoin the others.

"Alright?" James hollers to him as they come abreast of him.

"Just bruised," Scar replies.

Then James feels the tell-tale prickling that always accompanies the working of magic. "They're coming!" he hollers. Unable to spend the time to finish off the hell hound, he simply maintains the barrier as long as possible as he races away with the others.

Sagging over the neck of his horse, it's all he can do now to simply hang on. If he had the strength he'd tie himself to the saddle, but he doubts if he can do even that little bit. As his horse runs, he begins to notice green shoots growing in the ground they're racing over. Turning his head to look behind them, he sees brier bushes growing rapidly from the ground. A glance back to the front reveals the green glow around Brother Willim as he spreads seeds upon the ground as he rides.

Unable to hold the barrier any longer, he hopes they have a big enough lead on the hell hound to enable them to get away.

"How much further?" Reilin asks.

"I don't know," replies Miko.

From his position at the rear, James continues glancing back into the mist. He prays that they'll be able to get out and away before the warrior priests or the hell hound can catch up with them.

Then all of a sudden, they're out of the Mists. From the way the sky is beginning to darken, it has to be just before dark. "Don't stop!" yells James. Looking back, their pursuers have yet to make an appearance.

The light of the Star fades and finally winks out. Miko no longer needs it to keep back the mist. Riding hard, they race across the ground away from the wall of mist. When no pursuit is forthcoming out of the mist, Jiron has them slow down and then come to a stop.

"Why aren't they pursuing?" Shorty asks.

"Who cares," Scar says. Then to Miko he adds, "You better take a look at Stig."

Miko sees him tied across the back of his horse and says, "Get him down." As Scar and Potbelly remove him and lay him upon the ground, Miko says to Jiron, "Let me know instantly if anything comes out of the mist."

"You got it," he assures him.

Miko then goes over to Stig and with the Star begins working to revive him.

Jiron dismounts and goes over to where James is all but falling out of the saddle. "Here," he says as he reaches his side. "Let me help you."

Allowing him to help him down, James is soon sitting on the ground. "Shorty, keep an eye on the mist will you?" he asks.

"Already doing that," he says. "What are we to do now?"

James looks up to see Perrilin coming over to sit next to him. "I don't know," he replies.

Perrilin looks him up and down with a worried look on his face. "You look tired," he says.

"I am," James replies. Sighing, he puts his head in his hands and closes his eyes in an attempt to stop the world from spinning.

"Are we to camp here?" Jiron asks.

"I don't think doing so within sight of the mist is a good idea," he replies. "It does move you know."

"We all need a break," Jiron says. "I wouldn't push it more than another hour or so."

"James!" Shorty exclaims as he gets to his feet and looks back the way they came.

They turn and see two figures emerging from within the mist. They stand there a moment, obviously looking toward where they have stopped, then return back into the mist.

"They mean not to follow?" asks Shorty.

"Looks that way," replies James. "At least not at the moment."

"Could be they're gathering their forces before coming after us," suggests Reilin.

"If that's the case," Jiron says, "we best not be anywhere near here when they do." Glancing over to where Miko is working on Stig, he says, "As soon as Stig is ready to travel, we leave."

The others nod their heads. James glances back to the mist and the temple hidden within. *But how are they to get inside?*

Chapter Thirty

Several minutes later, the glow surrounding Miko and Stig disappears. Miko comes to his feet and turns to the others. "He'll live," he says. "The creature's blow cracked some ribs, and being tied across his horse's back didn't do much to help the injuries either. They're fine now but he needs rest."

"Can he take a couple hours in the saddle?" Jiron asks.

When Miko looks skeptical, James adds, "We really should try to get as far away from the mist as we can before stopping for the night."

"The journey won't be good for him," he tells him. "But what must be, must be."

"Alright then," James announces. To Scar and Potbelly he says, "You two be in charge of helping Stig. The rest of us get ready to ride."

As Scar and Potbelly assist a weak and wobbly Stig onto his horse, Jiron goes over to Aleya where she's staring off toward mist. "You alright?" he asks.

Shrugging, she continues staring at the mist. "Is that what happens?" she asks.

"I'm not sure I understand what you are asking," he tells her.

"When you and James go on your adventures," she says then turns to gaze into his eyes. Pointing back to the mist she adds, "Do you get into situations like what we just went through?"

Nodding, he places his hand on her shoulder and says, "Sometimes. But not always."

"I had no idea," she admits. "Oh sure, we've been in scrapes since this summer began. But nothing like what we just went through."

He can see the fear in her eyes, worry for what the future may hold. "I understand how you feel," he tells her. "Back there, I was scared to death let me tell you. For a while I thought we were through."

"What about next time?" she asks. "Suppose we don't survive it? I've been thinking about what is going to happen should we somehow manage to find a way into the temple. I...I just don't want to lose you."

"Nor I you," he says.

"Ahem."

Looking over his shoulder, Jiron sees James and the others are already in the saddle. He turns back to her and gives her a hug and kiss. "Don't worry, we'll make it through this."

Squeezing him tight, she says, "I hope so."

Breaking off the embrace, they move to their horses and mount. "Okay," he says to the others, "let's go." Leaving the mist behind them, he heads eastward. Aleya rides beside him.

It takes them over an hour before the mist disappears completely in the distance. Then they ride for another hour just for good measure before stopping for the night. When they do, Miko attends to the rest of the company who have injuries.

Scar and Potbelly help Stig from his horse and onto his blanket where he goes to sleep almost immediately. Dinner is cold rations as they do not wish to take the risk of someone being in the area and see their fire. Before the rest of the company turns in, James and Jiron move away from the others and talk of what they should do. Brother Willim joins them.

"Any ideas?" Jiron asks.

"One, but I'm not sure if you're going to like it," he replies.

"What?" asks Brother Willim.

James pulls out the medallion he recovered from the underground temple they passed through near the fortress of Kern. In the starlight the sign of the warrior priest is barely visible.

"You still have that?" he asks.

"Oh yeah," he replies with a nod.

"What is it?" asks Brother Willim.

James hands it to him and he inspects it for a moment before handing it back. "Have you ever heard of warrior priests being able to travel great distances in the blink of an eye?" he asks.

"No," he replies. "I have never heard that before."

James replaces the medallion within his pouch and says, "We've come across a system of teleportation daises in several different locations. The last time Jiron and I used one, we ended up in the very same temple complex where I first found this medallion." He looks to Brother Willim to gauge his reaction.

"I'm not sure I'm following you," he admits.

"Okay, let me explain it this way," he says. Bending over, he pulls an old exposed plant root out of the ground and draws two circles in the dirt a foot apart. Pointing to the circles he says, "Suppose these represent two of the teleportation daises in two different temples. Say the temples are separated by a hundred miles of land and water. You with me so far?"

"Yes," nods Brother Willim. "Go on."

"Now," he begins then points to the circle on the left, "should a person bearing one of these medallions step upon this dais, he will be instantaneously transported to the other." Moving his root from the left circle, he brings it over and taps the one on the right. "I'm sure there is a way to control where the daises send you. The only problem is that I haven't figured it out yet."

"What do you propose to do then?" Brother Willim asks.

"Find someone who does," he explains.

"But wouldn't that mean someone who has access to one of the medallions?" observes Brother Willim.

"That's right," says Jiron. "And the only ones who would, would be those in the temples."

"I would even guess it to be only those in the temple hierarchy," James says. "Which would mean they would be quite powerful."

"And you're planning on forcing one of them to help you?" he asks.

James nods. "I'm not sure how yet, or where, but we're running out of time."

"Perrilin's spent time down here," Jiron says. "He may know of something that would suit our purpose."

"You're right," agrees James. "Bring him over if you would."

"Be right back," he says then gets up and heads over to where the others are beginning to fall asleep. In little more than a minute, he returns with Perrilin.

James gives him a rundown of what they plan and then asks him if there are any major temples nearby. "It needs to be a fairly large one as I'm not sure if they are all equipped with these teleportation daises."

"They're not going to help you," he tells them. "You better understand that right now." He can see the determination in their eyes and adds, "They will die before they do."

"What other choice do we have?" Jiron asks. "Our time is beginning to run out."

He glances from James to Jiron then back again. Remaining silent while he searches their eyes, he finally asks, "You seriously mean to go through with this?"

"Yes we are," Jiron states with finality.

"Very well then." He then grins as he says, "If we don't get ourselves killed in the process, this will make one unbelievable saga."

Jiron chuckles, "You got that right. It already has been."

"Now Cyst, the town we left rather abruptly had a temple, but it wasn't what you would call a main one," he explains. "Further to the south is a larger town by the name of Zixtyn. I've been there several times and the temple there trains many of Dmon-Li's new acolytes. It's not just a single temple but a complex of over a dozen large buildings and another score or more of auxiliary structures. If there's any place that would have one of those teleportation daises, it's there."

"How far is it?" Jiron asks.

"Two, maybe three days," he says. "There is another city just over a day or so to the east that has a temple, though it isn't nearly as large as the one in Zixtyn. But if it should prove not to have one, it could complicate things."

Jiron nods, "Not to mention the fact that we would waste time Tinok does not have."

"I don't think we have much choice," James tells the others. "In the morning, we'll make for Zixtyn." Getting to his feet, he gives out with a yawn and says, "Best we get to bed."

"We all could use sleep after what we went through today," agrees Brother Willim.

They then return to where the others are already mostly asleep and find their blankets. Except for Jiron who has pulled the first watch, they are quickly asleep.

Early the next morning when they rise they are alarmed to see the Mists of Sorrow visible to their west. "It's a good thing we rode as far as we did before we stopped," Reilin says.

James turns to him and then gestures to the mist, "That's why we did." To Scar he asks, "How's Stig doing?"

"Better," he replies. Scar and Potbelly are sitting with Stig and sharing a quick breakfast before they get underway.

Stig looks up and says, "I'm sore. Those creatures really pack a mean punch."

"You know," begins Scar, "if they ever get the Pits open again, we could make a fortune if we could somehow manage to get one of them and put it in there to fight."

Eyes lighting up, Potbelly exclaims, "Everyone would come to see it, and pay handsomely for the opportunity!"

Jiron turns on them and says, "Now all you have to do is go back into the mist and get one."

Scar waves away the hand, "Details, details." He and Potbelly begin working on a way in which they could make this venture a reality.

"They've got to be out of their minds," Reilin comments to James.

He grins and shrugs. "It gives them something to do."

They keep a constant watch on the Mists. It makes no move to either come closer or pull back, and nothing emerges from it. James was sure they would have kept up the pursuit, after all they had him and the others almost taken out as it was. The only explanation he's been able to come up with is that the foes they encountered had the duty to prevent anyone from passing through the mist. And once they were out didn't feel the need to continue the pursuit. Still, it doesn't feel right.

Once everyone is finished with their less than satisfying meal, they get their horses ready for travel and are soon on the road. "We'll have to head more to the east on our way to skirt around the other side of the Mists of Sorrow," Perrilin states. "There's a major trade route over there that runs from Cyst to Zixtyn."

"But won't they be looking for us after yesterday?" cautions Aleya.

"Possibly," replies James. Taking out his mirror, he holds it up and adds, "I'll be keeping a lookout for anything that we may need to stay clear of."

"Besides," adds Stig, "a major trade route will have heavy traffic traveling upon it which will enable us to blend in."

"Hadn't thought of that," admits James. "Good thinking." To Jiron he says, "You and Reilin take the lead. Head due east until we come to the road."

"You got it," he says. Then with a nudge into the sides of his horse, he takes the lead with Reilin right beside him. The others fall in behind and they make their way across the desert to the east.

It takes them three hours of riding before the trade route leading to Zixtyn comes into sight. Periodically during that time James uses his mirror to scan for hostiles in the area only to find it clear. Long before they come to the road, James finds it in his mirror. Many wagons, riders and people on foot are upon the road traveling in both directions.

After he tells the other what he saw, Perrilin nods and says, "It's one of the main roads in the Empire. It's the most direct way from the Empire's southern territories to those in the north."

"We shouldn't have much problem getting lost in the crowd then," James states.

When those traveling upon the road finally come into view, the others agree with his statement. Pressing forward, James and Reilin lead the others over to the road. As they approach, those upon the road give them curious looks. A group of riders coming in out of the desert, two of the horses having two riders upon their backs, all in all a rather odd occurrence for this area. None of those traveling upon the road do more than look however, and they soon leave them far behind.

During the rest of the day, Perrilin keeps the hood of his cloak tight about his face. It's unlikely that anyone upon the road will recognize him, but you never know. When they reach the town of Hyrryth a couple hours before sundown, he tells them that they need to stop here for the night.

"Why?" asks Jiron. His anxiousness in reaching Zixtyn is written plainly upon his face.

"I need to remove Kir and don another face," he says. "There is a shop here in Hyrryth where I can procure the needed materials."

"Very well," decides James. "Aside from that we can all use a rest." Glancing to where Stig rides with Potbelly, he can see him drooping in the saddle. Although it's true the Star healed him, such healing always takes a toll on the strength of the one healed. The magic of the Star uses in part the energy of those it heals, and only time and rest will replenish it.

Jiron acquiesces and when they reach the walls of Hyrryth, Jiron leads them through the gates and into the city.

"Best if I lead here," Perrilin says. Moving past Jiron, he takes the lead. He continues down the street leading from the gate for several blocks before turning down a smaller side street to the left. Not too far down this street he stops before a two story building with a sign depicting a skewered scorpion.

Dismounting, Perrilin says "I'll be right back." He then goes up the stairs and in through the front doors.

"Shouldn't he worry about someone inside recognizing him?" Reilin asks in a whisper to James.

"I would think so," he replies. "But I'm sure he knows what he's doing."

A few minutes later, he emerges with another man. Both are talking in hushed tones as they leave the inn. They pause a moment just outside the door and Perrilin hands the man a small pouch, which from the sound it makes when it exchanges hands is filled with coins. The man glances to James and the others then turns and begins walking down the street.

When James makes to ask Perrilin what's going on, Perrilin puts his finger to his lips and gives a slight shake of his head. Then he says, "Stable's around the back." Taking the reins of his horse, he leads the others down a side alley and then into the rear courtyard. Once they have the horses settled in for the night with a pail of oats the stableboy supplied for each, they leave the stable and make for the rear door to the inn.

Inside, they pass through the common room and then into a hallway leading to their rooms. "I was able to get six rooms," he says. "I hope that will be enough?"

"It will be fine," James assures him.

They each get settled into their rooms and then gather in James and Jiron's room. "So who was the man you left the inn with?" asks Shorty.

"Just someone whom I've dealt with before," he replies. "He went to get the items I need to remove Kir from the world."

"Been here before I take it?" Scar asks.

"My journeys have taken me many places," he tells him.

James looks at him and wonders just how far flung his network extends. Though Perrilin has never come right out and said it, he has to be a spy or something similar. After all he uses disguises, Lord Cytok who is the right hand of the Emperor wants him in a bad way, and things always seem to happen when he's around. Someday he hopes to discover who he really is and what his agenda may be.

"Mind if we go down to the common room for a drink?" Scar asks. When he sees that look come to him that usually means an argument is pending, he adds, "We promise not to get into any trouble."

"Very well," agrees James. "Just be sure you don't."

Taking Reilin with them, the pit fighters head down the hallway to the common room. James watches them go then turns to Jiron, "You're not going?" he asks.

Shaking his head, he says, "Aleya and I will head down in a little bit."

"Oh?" he asks.

Jiron gives him a grin and says, "Nothing like that."

"If you say so," James tells him.

Then with Aleya on his arm, he leaves the room and escorts her down to her room.

"They make a nice couple," Brother Willim states.

"That they do," agrees James.

A short while later the man whom Perrilin sent for the items he requires returns and gives him a package. Perrilin thanks the man and then adjourns to his room where he will begin to work on removing all traces of Kir. The man leaves once Perrilin has the package and is heading for his room.

"I think I'll stay here and read more of the Book of Morcyth," Miko says. Brother Willim offers to remain with him and he accepts.

Having nothing else to do, James takes his leave and makes his way out to the common room. Finding Scar and the others at a table off to one side, he heads over and joins them.

The food here at the Skewered Scorpion is rather good and after they have finished with their meal one of the traveling bards shows up. At first James thought this may be Perrilin in disguise, but when he began singing his first song, knew that it wasn't. The man wasn't even in the same league as Perrilin where music is concerned. Still, the bard's music was enjoyable.

Two hours after James joined them, Perrilin makes his appearance. His skin is again back to its normal color and his hair is very dark, all in all looking quite different than he did when he was Kir.

"Looking good," he says as Perrilin sits down.

"Yeah," agrees Shorty. "Hardly look like you did."

"Well, let's not talk about it if it's all the same," he says.

James nods understandingly. He then looks over to where the hallway down which their room lies opens onto the common room. Jiron and Aleya should have been out here by now. Not to mention Miko, he's never been one to miss out on food.

"Sounds like you had a tough childhood," Aleya says to him as she lies in his arms. Ever since leaving the others and coming to her room, they've lain on her bed. Doing nothing more than holding one another and talking, they've completely lost track of time.

"We did," he replies. "If it wasn't for the Pits, I don't know how Tersa and I would have survived." Then his stomach gives out with a loud growl, informing him of the lack of sustenance it holds. Glancing to the window, he sees that night has fallen outside.

A single candle burns on the room's table, just when it had been lit he can't recall. "Maybe it's time we go join the others and get something to eat."

She reaches her lips to his and gives him a soft kiss. "Sounds like a good idea to me," she says. Another moment's embrace then they get off the bed and leave the room.

The noise from the common room fills the hallway with loud raucous laughter and conversation. As they close the door to her room, Jiron notices light coming through the door to James' room. Stopping next to it, he puts an ear to the door.

"...not sure I can do this," he hears Miko say.

"Who else is there?" responds Brother Willim's voice. "Do you think you are to be the only priest Morcyth will require?"

"But, I don't know the first thing about training other priests," he states.

"Isn't it outlined in the book?" Brother Willim asks.

"Well, sort of…"

Jiron removes his ear and gives Aleya a smile. "Brother Willim is explaining things to Miko that he hadn't thought of before," he explains.

"Like what?" she asks as they resume moving toward the common room.

Jiron gives her a chuckle and says, "I don't think he understood the scope of the responsibilities a man in his position is going to have."

Upon entering the common room, they pause and look around to see where the others are sitting. After scanning the room once, Jiron's grin that he had at Miko's expense disappears. Searching the room one more time, he doesn't see James or any of the others sitting at any of the tables.

Aleya notices it too. "Maybe they returned to their rooms," she suggests.

"Let's hope so," he says. Turning around, they hurry back and enter the room where Miko and Brother Willim are discussing things.

"Is James in here?" he asks as he opens the door.

"Haven't seen him since he left to join the others in the common room," replies Miko. Then he sees the worry upon Jiron's face. "Why?" he asks with growing apprehension.

Not bothering to take the time to reply, Jiron leaves the room and begins checking the rooms of the others. One by one, he finds each of them empty.

"They're gone!" he exclaims after checking the last room. Racing back down the hall to the common room, he looks around anxiously for any clue as to what may have happened. But everything looks to be as it should be. The bard is singing, the patrons are happy and enjoying themselves. Yet where are they?

He starts to enter the common room when Aleya takes him by the arm. "Don't," she says. "Let's go back to the room and discuss it in private."

Behind her he sees Brother Willim and Miko nodding agreement. Allowing her to take him back to his room, they enter and close the door.

"They wouldn't have simply left and not told anyone," he states. Then pointing in the direction of the common room he says, "Someone out there has to know what happened."

"I am sure that is true," Brother Willim states. "But if you go out there and begin questioning people you are going to raise suspicion." When Jiron turns his gaze upon him he adds, "You don't speak the language."

"None of us do," Miko says.

"Then what are we to do?" Aleya asks.

Jiron begins pacing as he thinks about the various courses of action available to them.

"Perrilin did say that he came here often," offers Miko. "Remember when we first arrived, he entered and immediately left with someone?"

Halting his pacing, Jiron turns and asks Miko, "So?"

"So, it would stand to reason that the people who run this place also know him," he replies.

"And may prove to be helpful in finding out what happened," concludes Brother Willim.

"Very well," he says. "The rest of you stay here and I'll go find out." As he turns to leave, Brother Willim puts his hand on his shoulder and stops him.

"I don't think it would be wise for us to split up," he says.

"I agree," adds Aleya.

Nodding, he says, "Okay then, follow me." Leading the way, Jiron leaves the room and returns back down the hall to the common room. Barely slowing down, he crosses through the tables and heads straight for the kitchen area. On the way he hunts for the proprietor that he saw earlier but the man's no where to be seen.

At the door leading into the kitchen he pushes it open and barges right in. On the other side lies a large cooking area with a long table against the side wall where meals and other items are being prepared for their patrons. Not seeing the one he's looking for, he ignores the stares of the workers and walks through the kitchen to the door leading deeper into the inn.

One man moves to put himself between Jiron and the door. He holds up his hand and says something in the Empire's tongue which can only be 'You shouldn't be here' or something to that effect. Jiron pushes the man out of the way and opens the door. On the other side of the door there's a short hallway with closed doors on the right and left. The end of the hallway opens onto a room that looks like it's designed for receiving guests. Sitting at a table in that room, Jiron can see the innkeeper talking with another man whose back is to the hallway.

The innkeeper looks up in startlement as they leave the kitchen, and the man whose back is to them turns to look. It's the man who had fetched the items Perrilin needed to remove Kir. Both men stand up as they pass through the hallway.

A voice hollers to the innkeeper from the kitchen area and he replies in a reassuring tone of voice. Jiron glances back and sees the man he pushed out of the way standing in the doorway staring at him with a grimace. The innkeeper hollers to the man again and he nods then closes the door.

"Come in gentlemen," the innkeeper says in their language. Then adds, "and lady," when he sees Aleya there with them.

"We need to talk to you..." begins Jiron.

"Yes, I know," the innkeeper interrupts him. Gesturing to the vacant chairs at the table with him and the other man he says, "Please, won't you have a seat?"

The innkeeper says something to the other man. Nodding, the man gets up and leaves the room by the other door to the right of the hallway they entered through. When he sees Jiron about to ask about the man, he says, "He'll make sure we are not interrupted."

"And why would he need to do that?" Miko asks.

Waving away the question, the innkeeper says, "There is little time. I had thought they took all of you. Thank the gods they did not."

"Who?" asks Jiron. "Who took them?"

"An agent of a very powerful person here in the Empire," he replies. "One whom it is unwise to openly stand against. He knew of Kir being here and wanted him. He made us drug the ale going to his table, and when they were all unconscious, several of his men came and took them."

"They were after Kir?" asks Jiron. "I thought for sure they were..." He trails off, not finishing the thought. Turning to Miko he sees him nod, he too thought they had come for James. James simply happened to be in the wrong place.

"Where did they take them?" Brother Willim asks.

"One of our men followed them when they left and will report back when he knows," the innkeeper states. He glances from one to the other then says, "So far, the Empire remains unaware of this inn's involvement in certain activities. It would be beneficial for all concerned if they continue to remain ignorant of that fact."

"Don't worry," Jiron assures him. "Your secret is safe with us."

Suddenly, the door to the right of the hallway opens and the man who had been here when they arrived enters the room. He glances to Jiron and the others and then looks questioningly to the innkeeper.

"It's alright," he says in the northern tongue. "They're Kir's friends."

Nodding, the man says, "They've been taken to the Keep."

"Can you take us there?" Jiron asks as he comes to his feet.

"Yes," the man says, "but it is heavily guarded."

"You would stand little chance of getting in there," the innkeeper states. "It's very well fortified."

"We'll see about that," he says.

"Is there anything we can do to help?" asks the innkeeper.

Jiron glances to Aleya then nods, "Yes, there is one thing." He tells him of his need and the innkeeper tells them that he will be able to accommodate the request. They wait there for a few minutes while the other man is sent to get it.

When he returns, he hands Aleya a beautifully worked bow and a quiver of arrows. She takes it and looks in awe at the workmanship that had gone into it. Intricate designs run its length and when she strings it, the pull is strong. "This is a good bow," she says.

"It was one of several made by a friend of mine who is a master woodworker," the innkeeper says. "I trust you find it acceptable?"

"Oh yes," she says with a nod. "It's far superior to anything I've ever seen."

"Then it's yours," he tells her.

"Thank you," she says with a grin.

"Now," Jiron says. "Take us to the Keep."

"It's not as simple as that," the innkeeper says. "We are fairly certain there are still agents watching the inn."

"So?" Miko asks.

"Depending on how long they've been watching your group," he tells them, "they may recognize you when you leave."

"That could prove problematical," Brother Willim states.

"What do you suggest?" asks Aleya.

Chapter Thirty One

Malki had been placed to watch the front of the inn since he and others had come to take those people away. Though he wasn't told why they were taken, he knew they had to have been wanted by people in high places. Especially if you consider who it was that put the whole operation together. Whenever you see his face, you know that whatever is going on concerns the highest levels of the Empire.

He and the others who are staking out the inn are looking for a couple other people, and should they appear, they're to take them too.

The front door of the inn opens and he turns his attention to those coming through. Two people emerge, a couple by the looks of it. The man is leaning heavily upon the woman who is working to keep her man upright. Malki grins at the way the drunken man tries to negotiate his way down the few steps to the street.

Cursing at her man, the woman loses her hold on him as he stumbles down the remaining two steps and crashes to the street. Giving him a swift kick to the side in anger, she drags him back to his feet and together they work their way down the street.

Behind the couple comes another pair, two men this time. One has a stiff leg that looks as if it's unable to bend it at the knee. He limps and shuffles alongside the other. Upon making it down to the street, both men turn and go the opposite way that the woman and her man had gone.

Not the people he's interested in, Malki remains in the shadows and keeps a watch upon the door.

Once Miko is sure the inn is out of sight behind them, he takes Brother Willim down a side street. Moving into the shadows, he helps Brother Willim remove his staff that had been hidden beneath his tunic. It had been secreted within his trouser leg, which gave him the appearance of having a stiff leg. Having walked so far pretending that his right leg was stiff has made his left one ache.

"Is anyone following?" Brother Willim asks as he finally gets the staff free of his clothing.

Miko stares back down the street for a second then shakes his head. "I don't think so."

"I really didn't think it was going to work," he admits.

"Let's go to the rendezvous and pray that Jiron and Aleya made it there safely." Miko then takes the lead. With the pack wherein lies the Book of Morcyth slung securely across his back, they hurry to the appointed place.

It isn't far and when they arrive they find Jiron and Aleya already there. Another minute and the man who is going to lead them to the Keep appears.

"Let's go," Jiron says to the man. He's a little put out that the man has yet to offer him his name. But like James always says, 'What you don't know can't be tortured out of you'.

Taking numerous side streets they work their way across town to the Keep, only taking the main thoroughfares when they have no other choice. When the Keep finally comes into view, he takes them to a spot down a block from the main entrance. Standing in the lee of the building where the shadows are the thickest, they have a commanding view of the gate.

The gate stands in a curtain wall which surrounds the inner keep. Outside the gate stand six soldiers, three of which have crossbows. Atop the curtain wall, additional soldiers are seen walking to and fro as they keep watch. Beyond the curtain wall, the Keep itself rises high.

"Beneath the Keep is an extensive dungeon where prisoners are taken and interrogated," the man tells them. "That's where you'll find them."

"How do we get in?" Miko asks.

"That's up to you," the man says. "I managed to arrange for a diversion. It's not much but should draw the attention of the guards on the walls for several minutes."

"When will it begin?" Jiron asks.

"Once you figure out what you are going to do to get in," he says, "I'll go and get it started." He points off to an area of town back the way they came. "When it happens, it will come from that direction."

Jiron nods. Indicating the curtain wall on the opposite side from where the distraction will take place, he says, "So our best bet would be to try something in that direction."

The man nods in agreement.

Turning his attention to Aleya, Miko and Brother Willim he says, "You three stay here." Then to the man he adds, "You come with me. We're going to take a look around."

"Be careful," warns Aleya.

"I will be," he says. "Be right back." With the man in tow, he stays next to the buildings across the street from the curtain wall and makes his way to the far side. Once he reaches where the curtain wall curves and begins moving directly away from the street, he comes to a stop.

Scanning the street he makes sure it's clear, then turns his attention to the closest guard atop the wall. The guard is moving toward the corner of the wall where sits a guard tower. From the guard tower, the wall turns ninety degrees and moves directly away from the street. Another wide thoroughfare runs alongside the wall as it moves further away.

Jiron remains motionless as he watches the guard approaching the guard tower. When the guard comes to within three feet of the tower, he turns about and begins heading back the other way.

"Come on," Jiron urges then races across the street with the man right behind.

Aleya watches Jiron make his way down the street then pause a moment before darting across. Her eyes move to the guard on the wall, and is relieved when he fails to react to Jiron's crossing.

"Relax," says Miko. "Jiron's done this sort of thing many times from what James tells me."

Aleya doesn't comment, simply nods her head as she continues to stare at the place where Jiron disappeared. She waits an agonizing fifteen minutes before he reappears. Darting across the street with the man right behind, he then works his way back to where she and the others wait.

When he rejoins them, he announces, "I think there may be a way to get in."

"How?" she asks.

He looks her in the eye and says, "It's going to depend on how good you are with the bow."

"What do you want me to do?" She then listens as he lays out the gist of his plan to them. Nodding her head, she can see where her bow will play a pivotal role in what's to come. When he's finished laying it out, he asks, "Anyone see something I may have missed?"

Brother Willim shakes his head, "Not I. You seem to have it all worked out fairly well."

Jiron turns to the man and says, "Go tell them we're ready."

The man nods his head and melts into the night on his way to begin getting the distraction underway.

After he leaves, Jiron turns to Brother Willim and hesitates a moment. Then he asks, "You know there's a chance we'll not get out of there without a fight?"

Brother Willim only nods in reply.

"I need to know I'll be able to rely on you should the situation arise," he says.

Gazing at him with sadness in his eyes, he says, "You know the priests of Asran are not allowed to hurt fellow human beings. That to do so will mean dire repercussions in this life and the next."

"Brother, I understand that," replies Jiron. "But you also know that if we don't get James out of there and into Dmon-Li's High Temple before the moon turns dark, it could well mean the end of everything. Your dreams, more than any of the others, tell us that."

"I know," he states.

"You once said that to keep a garden healthy, there comes a time when a gardener must prune to save the whole," Jiron tells him. "This is the case as it stands now. You may need to prune to save the whole." He can see the pain in the Brother's eyes.

Miko comes and lays his hand on Brother Willim's shoulder. "Asran will understand," he assures him. "It's for the greater good."

Griping his staff in a grip so tight that almost causes him pain, Brother Willim nods. "I will do what I have to," he says in a voice taut with pain. But the pain he is feeling is not that of the body, but of the soul. He has vowed to never take the life of an ordinary man. As the leader of the Hand of Asran, he had been trained to defeat those of power such as the warrior priests. Never had he believed that his skill would be used against those whom he vowed to protect. The fact that they may worship another besides Asran does not matter. Giving a silent prayer to Asran to forgive him for what he may be called to do, he gives Jiron a nod. "Let's go."

Jiron gives him a comforting pat on the back and then says, "Follow me." Taking them along the front of the buildings across the street from the curtain wall, he brings them to a halt once they've reached the place where he crossed the street before. A street as wide as the one they are on runs along the wall as it turns and moves away from them.

He has them wait there until the guard atop the wall reaches the guard tower then turns back to go the other way. "Now!" he whispers as he bolts across with the others right behind.

Melding in with the shadows across the street from the wall, he takes them further down until he reaches a point where two of the guards walking upon the wall are visible at the same time.

Stopping, he indicates the guards on the wall. Then he shows them a statue of a warrior with an upraised sword that stands between them upon the edge of the wall. To Aleya he says, "That's where I want you to put your arrow, between the upraised sword and the statue's head. Can you do it?"

She gauges the distance and nods. "I believe so," she replies.

"Can you do it with a rope tied to the arrow?" When she looks at him he raises his tunic to show her the rope secured about his waist.

"I...I don't know," she admits. "I've never shot an arrow with a rope tied to it before." She then looks to his eyes and nods, "But I'll give it a try."

"Pick your best arrow," he tells her as he begins uncoiling the rope from around his middle.

She removes the quiver of arrows from her back and begins going through them one by one. The third one she comes to is slightly thicker than the others and is very straight. Holding it up, she says, "This one."

Jiron takes it and ties the end of the rope to it very, very tightly. When he's sure it won't come off in flight, he hands it back to her. "It's going to drag some due to the tension of the rope," he tells her.

"I understand," she says. Holding the arrow, she feels how the rope alters its balance and increases its weight twofold.

"Ready?" Jiron asks.

Placing the arrow to string, she looks at him and nods, "Ready."

"Take aim but don't shoot right away," he tells her. "When the two guards are both walking away from the statue at the same time, I'll say 'now' and then let it go."

"Okay," she says. She looks up at the statue on the wall, raises her bow and pulls the string back. Holding it there, she gets her aim set and waits. Three seconds later, Jiron whispers 'now' and she lets go.

The arrow and rope sail through the air and cracks into the wall a good three feet below the feet of the statue. They freeze as they look to the guards to see if they heard the noise, but neither one of them even so much as glances back.

Jiron quickly pulls in the rope until it and the arrow are back with them. The head of the arrow is cracked from its impact with the stones of the wall. "We'll try it again," he says.

Aleya nods and begins searching through the quiver for another arrow. Feeling bad that she didn't make it the first time, she vows to make it the second. Handing the next arrow to Jiron, she waits for him to secure the rope to it once more. Then once he's handed it back to her, she again places it to string and takes aim at the statue.

"Now," Jiron says and she again lets the arrow loose. And just as the first one, it impacts upon the wall in almost the same place as the first one had.

Jiron begins pulling in the rope when Miko places a hand on his shoulder. "Someone's coming," he hears him whisper in his ear. Dropping the rope, he looks where Miko is indicating and sees a guard turning the corner and begins walking down the street toward them. They move further back into the shadows and hold still.

Then his eyes go to the middle of the street where the end of the rope lies with the shattered arrow still attached to it. The way the guard is moving down the center of the street, he's going to walk right over it.

"Jiron!" Miko whispers as he points to the arrow.

"I know," he says. Never taking his eye off the approaching guard, he draws one of his knives.

Thirty feet from the arrow, the guard still fails to notice it. At twenty feet, one of the men atop the walls hails him and they wave to each other. At fifteen feet, he turns his attention back to street level as the guard atop the wall resumes walking his patrol. At ten feet the guard starts humming a tune as he continues along. At five feet, he's still oblivious to the fact that an arrow tied to a rope lies across the street. Then his foot steps on it.

The guard stops and lifts his foot. Bending over, he looks to see what it was that he stepped on. Picking up the arrow, he looks at it for a second and then rope attached to it. He sees how the rope is tied to the end of the arrow and that it extends into the shadows on the other side of the street. Pulling on the rope, he looks more closely into the shadows. Then all of a sudden, one of the shadows breaks off and rushes him.

Before the man knows what hit him, Jiron attacks and silences him before he can sound the alarm. Then with Miko's help, he drags the guard's lifeless body back into the shadows before the guards on top of the wall notice what happened.

Once he's sure the guards on the wall failed to see them, he pulls in the rope. By this time Aleya has another arrow already selected. He again secures the rope to it and hands it back to her. "We don't have much time," he tells her. "We must be ready when whatever distraction they are planning goes into effect." When she takes the arrow, he puts his hands on her shoulders and gives her a quick kiss. "I know you can do this."

Nodding, she puts the arrow to string and sights on the space between the statues head and the upraised sword. She takes a deep calming breath to center herself as her father always taught her. *He could do this*, she thinks to herself. *He could do anything with a bow.*

And so can you.

It's almost as if she can feel him there behind her as he always did when teaching her the bow. A hand on her waist, another to help steady the bow. The words he used to say when passing on his wisdom. *Steady on girl, take your time. Patience, always patience, never rush it.*

"Now!" she hears Jiron say. But she doesn't release the arrow. *Only when it's time, Aly.* Then it almost feels as if a hand raises her bow ever so slightly higher. "Now!" urges Jiron.

"Do you sense that?" Brother Willim asks Miko.

"Yes, I do," he replies. "What is it?"

"I'm not sure," Brother Willim says.

Now, Aly.

Releasing the bowstring, the arrow shoots forward. They hold their breath as they watch it arc through the air toward the statue. Then it sails perfectly between the head and sword.

"I did it father," she says quietly to herself. And she can almost feel a pat on her back, the same as her father use to give her when she successfully learned what he was trying to teach.

"Yes!" says Jiron. When all the slack in the rope is gone, it yanks against the end he's holding in his hand. Looking to the two guards, he sees they still have their backs turned. Rushing over to the wall, he begins pulling the slack back in until he feels the arrow catch in the crook of the statue between the neck and the upraised arm. Giving it a couple tugs, he ensures it's not going to slip out.

Then he holds still as the guards turn and begin approaching the area where the statue is located. Praying for them not to notice the arrow and rope, he waits. The watch they are walking takes them to within several feet of the statue. But then they both reach the end of their watch, turn and begin to walk away from the statue again.

Leaving the rope where it is, he runs back over to where the others are hidden in the shadows. "Now," he says once he's rejoined them, "we wait for the diversion." Another ten minutes go by before a commotion begins to develop. The guards on the wall turn their attention to the far side of town, and one of them points to something. Coming together, they begin talking excitedly to one another.

"Aleya, you need to take them out fast," he tells her.

Nodding, she removes two arrows from her quiver and sets one point first into the ground before her. The other, she puts to her bowstring and aims. This is something she is confident she can do with little problems.

Releasing the first arrow, it flies true and strikes one of the guards in the back. Before the other guard realizes something is happening, another takes the second guard through the spine just below the neck. The first man topples onto the top of the wall while the second one falls off and lands in the street not far from where Jiron and the others wait.

Indicating the guard, Jiron says to Miko, "Get him out of sight. When I get to the top, the rest of you climb up. Before he runs over to where the rope is hanging against the wall, Brother Willim stops him.

"I've never climbed a rope before," he admits.

"Don't worry," he assures him. "James never could either. Let the others go first then tie a loop in the end of the rope. Then we'll pull you up."

"Alright," Brother Willim says.

Moving to the wall, Jiron takes the rope and very carefully begins climbing up. He understands that he can only apply steady tension to the rope. That to suddenly jerk on it may snap the arrow in two. So hand over hand, he slowly and steadily works his way to the top. As he climbs the rope, he can hear raised voices coming from within the Keep area on the other side of the wall.

When he finally reaches the base of the statue, he grips the top of the wall with one hand and then pulls himself up. Once on top, he looks over to the far side of town and sees what the diversion is.

"Not much huh?" he mumbles to himself. *The damn fools set fire to the town.* And so it appears, for fires are burning in several different sections of the city. Men are running through the streets on their way to put them out.

He casts a quick glance to the guards on the other walls, and the gaze of each is directed to the far off fires. The grounds within the Keep area are fairly deserted, a few guards walk to and fro as they keep watch. One man, a civilian, hollers to one of the guards down there. Together they quickly make their way through the gates and toward the fires.

Sure that everyone's attention is averted, Jiron removes the arrow from the statue and unties the rope. He's just taking a firm hold of it when he feels the rope grow taut as someone down below pulls on it. Jiron gives the rope two quick tugs to let them know he's ready, then braces himself.

He receives two quick answering tugs before someone begins climbing up. In a moment Aleya appears and he offers her a hand which she takes. He then pulls her the rest of the way up onto the wall.

The first thing she notices are the fires burning throughout the city. "What do they think they're doing?" she asks.

"I don't care as long as the rest of the guards are looking away from us," he says. Gesturing to the guard she killed with her bow, he adds, "Grab his crossbow and make like you are him walking the wall."

Nodding, she says, "Right." Then moves over toward the dead guard.

Another two pulls announces Miko's turn up the rope. He has a much more difficult time at it than Aleya had, but after a few tense moments, he makes it. Jiron has him pretend to be the other guard that should be up here instead of dead down below.

He sets himself for hauling up Brother Willim while Miko moves further down the wall. When the rope jerks twice, he begins hauling him up. Pulling up a person is much more strenuous than holding while they climb. When he figures he has pulled Brother Willim up about half the distance, the rope suddenly vibrates. Sensing there may be trouble, he calls for Miko and together they rapidly pull it up.

As the end of the rope reaches the top, they find Brother Willim holding on with one hand to the loop where his foot should be. In the other hand he's gripping his staff. "What happened?" Miko asks as they haul him the rest of the way up.

"My staff slipped," he admits somewhat embarrassed. "When I moved to catch it, my foot slipped out of the loop. I almost didn't catch hold of it in time."

Miko grins and says, "That would have hurt when you hit the ground."

Nodding, Brother Willim sits on the wall and tries to calm his trembling nerves.

Jiron coils the rope in his hands as he looks over the wall and into the courtyard below. There are still few guards upon the grounds down there but none in close proximity to the section of wall they're on. A check toward those upon the walls finds them still staring at the fire burning in the city. So far, none of the guards have yet to notice that something is going on.

"Aleya," he says and when he has her attention waves for her to come over to him. "There are three guards down below," he tells her and then shows them to her. One is on the far side and is just moving beyond the Keep's wall, another is walking across the middle of the courtyard, while the third is closer and moving their way.

"Take out the man coming our way," he says.

"You got it." Removing an arrow from her quiver, she places it to string and aims at the approaching man. When she's sure she's got him, the arrow is released. Flying true, it strikes the man in the chest and knocks him backward to the ground.

"Miko!" Jiron says as he begins lowering the rope over the side of the wall to the courtyard below. "Get down there fast and get that guard out of sight." When the rope is played out and he has a firm grip, Miko begins to rappel down the other side. As soon as he's down, he says to Aleya, "You're next."

Nodding, she takes the rope and descends to the ground below.

Once she's down, he turns to Brother Willim and asks, "Can you make it down by yourself?"

He holds up his staff and says, "Not holding this I can't."

Jiron gives him an annoyed look and shakes his head. Then he grabs the staff and throws it over the side. "Now can you?"

Brother Willim looks over the side and watches his staff as it lands on the ground below. Turning back to Jiron he nods, "I think so."

"Then please hurry," he says. "Our luck won't last forever."

"Right," he says. Taking the rope, he begins to work his way down. When he reaches the halfway point, he loses his grip and begins sliding down. By the time he hits the bottom, he has a good case of rope burn on both of his hands. Praying to Asran, he uses his magic to heal the burns.

"Stop!" exclaims Aleya.

The urgency of her cry breaks his concentration and the spell stops. "What?" he asks.

"You were glowing like a candle," she explains. Looking around, she's relieved to discover no one noticed his magical aura.

"Sorry," he says. "Forgot about that."

Jiron lands on the ground next to him and whips the rope back up where it dislodges from the place he had secured it. As it falls to the ground, he begins coiling it back around his middle. He had seen the green glow surrounding the priest but had been too far away to alert him.

Miko joins them and brings Brother Willim his staff. "Here you go," he says as he hands it to him.

"Thank you," he replies. He takes the staff gingerly as his hands still throbs with pain.

"If you need to heal yourself," Jiron says, "Best to wait until we get inside."

"And how are we to do that?" he asks. "Through the front door?"

"Actually, that is exactly what I intend for us to do," he says. "Currently, the courtyard here is free of guards. One's around back and will reappear soon. The other one just disappeared in through the main entrance, which as you'll notice remains open. If we hurry, we might be able to make it."

"No guts no glory?" Miko asks with a grin.

Jiron nods with an answering grin. He recognizes another one of James' expressions. "Let's go." Running swiftly they cross the courtyard, taking advantage of what shadowy areas there are. No cry ensues by the time they reach the area before the Keep's gate. Doubling their speed, they race through the entrance.

Chapter Thirty Two

"So, you're awake are you?"

James cracks open his eyes to see who it is that's talking to him and the light in the room stabs his eyes like a red hot knife. He moans and tries to rub them but can't. His mind at first is unable to figure out why, but then comes to the realization that his wrists are manacled above his head to the wall behind him. Squinting so as to allow only a very minimal amount of light through to his eyes, he tries to see what's going on.

"Everyone else was fooled by that stunt you pulled in Cyst," the oddly familiar voice says. "But I knew it couldn't be true. I knew you would end up here. So I came and waited for you to show. I didn't expect my efforts to yield results so quickly."

Smack!

His eyes somewhat adjust to the light in the room and he's now able to tell that the voice is not addressing him. Rather, the man is talking to someone else who is tied to a chair in the center of the room. The man in the chair is facing away from where James is sitting on the floor thus he's unable to get a good look at who it is.

He slowly moves his head to scan the room. The others who had been in the common room with him at the inn are sitting in a row against the same wall as he is. Each is manacled to the wall in the same manner. Over on a table against the wall he sees their belongings haphazardly stacked, it doesn't look as if anyone's taken the time to search through them yet.

Returning his attention to Perrilin, for that is whom he finally realizes is sitting in the chair being interrogated, he sees the man interrogating him strike him again across the face. In his drugged state, it's hard for his mind to function properly and it takes him a bit, but he begins to recognize the man interrogating Perrilin. He's seen him before.

With a scar running along the side of his face across one eye, it would be hard for James to ever forget him. Korgan, or as James better knows him, Ol' One Eye. The man from whom he rescued Perrilin when he had him in a farmhouse outside of Cardri. The man who aided the Empire by poisoning the guards in charge of the gates in the City of Light. A powerful agent of Lord

Cytok. To be here in his hands bodes ill for James and the others. He has little love for the man. In fact he's one of the few people he's met that he wouldn't feel any qualms about killing.

Smack!

Korgan strikes Perrilin across the face again and then gazes at him for a second. Moving in close to Perrilin's face, he lifts one eyelid and examines the eye beneath. "Damn!" he curses. Then he says something in the northern tongue to one of the three guards there in the room with him. Abruptly turning about, he exits through the door behind him.

James feigns unconsciousness as he works in his mind what exactly is going on. From what he overheard Korgan say, he came here for Perrilin. The fact that James happens to be here as well could possibly have eluded him for the moment. James fervently hopes that he will continue to remain ignorant of it.

The last thing he remembers is eating and drinking back at the inn as they listened to the bard play. From his brief scan to the others sitting there on the wall with him, he doesn't think that they have all the others. But which ones are here he can't tell. He did see Scar and Potbelly for sure, maybe Reilin too. For all their sakes he prays that Miko and Jiron have yet to be taken. If those two are still at large, then they stand a good chance of getting out of this.

In the meantime, he keeps his eyes closed and hopes the effects of the drug wears off sometime soon.

"Now where?" whispers Aleya. Miko just shrugs.

After entering the keep, they've been searching the halls for the way to the dungeons below. Three guards and two servants lie dead behind them, hidden in closets, under beds, etc. They had the misfortune of being in the wrong place at the wrong time when the four intruders happened by.

Now the corridor they've been following ends at a meeting hall where a dozen tables are placed about the room. One of the larger tables has four men standing around it looking at a map laid out across its top. Two are soldiers, commanders by the looks of them, and two civilians. The men are talking earnestly to each other.

Jiron moves back from the end of the corridor where he had been spying on the men. Joining the others, he has them move into what seems to be an unused storage room. There he relates to the others what he saw. "We'll never find the way down in time," he says.

"You should never have killed those servants," states Brother Willim.

Jiron gives him an annoyed look and says, "If they had spoken our language, I wouldn't have. We need to find someone with whom we can talk."

Suddenly from the room where the four men are looking over the map, they hear raised voices. Jiron moves to the storage room's door and peers out to try to see what's going on. Unable to ascertain anything, he turns back to the others and says, "I better check this out."

"Be careful," Aleya tells him.

With a nod to her, he exits from the room and hurries to the end of the corridor. One of the voices within the room has grown agitated and is beginning to yell. Moving to the end, Jiron peers into the room. A fifth man has entered the room and is yelling at the other four. His face is set in an angry expression as is the others whom he's yelling at.

"I know you," Jiron whispers when he sees the face of the new arrival. "Ol' One Eye Miko called you," he says to himself. He'll know where James is located. In fact, he's likely to be the one doing the interrogating. Jiron grins at this stroke of good fortune.

The men argue for another several minutes before a soldier hurries in through another doorway. The talking comes to a halt as the five men turn their attention to the new arrival. He delivers what is most likely a quick report then waits.

The older of the two soldiers says something to the other one who then follows the soldier from the room. The remaining soldier then turns back to face Ol' One Eye. He says something to him in a calm voice that's straining to be anything but. Then Ol' One Eye's single remaining eye narrows and his lips press together hard when the soldier finishes speaking. Turning on his heel, Ol' One Eye stalks off across the room and exits through a side door.

Jiron looks at the door and knows that has to be the way to where James and the others are being held. Glancing back to the soldier and the two civilians, he sees the two civilians begin to leave through the door which the soldier had come through earlier. Once they've left, Jiron rushes back to the others.

"I think we may have a break," he says once back in the storage room. Then he briefly tells them what transpired. Miko gasps when he hears that Ol' One Eye is back in the picture.

"He'll kill James!" he blurts out.

Jiron looks at him and asks, "Have you felt any murders or deaths since we entered the keep?"

Looking surprised, Miko shakes his head, "No."

"Then they're still alive," he states. "If we hurry they may remain so." He then jerks his head in the direction of the meeting room and says, "There's one man still in the room between us and the door Ol' One Eye took. If we take the soldier out fast, we can follow Ol' One Eye right to James."

"Then let's hurry," urges Miko.

"Aleya," he says, "take him out with your bow, it'll be quicker."

"No problem," she assures him. Moving to join him, she pulls an arrow from her quiver and places it to string. Keeping the string relaxed until it's time, she hurries along beside him. Behind them come Miko and Brother Willim.

At the end of the corridor, Jiron motions for the other two to wait back a ways while he and Aleya proceed. He creeps to the end of the hallway and peers into the room. The soldier remains alone in the room. Turning back to

Aleya, he indicates the room and nods. Moving out of her way, he allows her to move into position.

She looks around the corner and sees the man standing there, bent over the map on the table. Taking a calming, centering breath, she steps away from the wall and draws back the bow at the same time. Just before she releases, the man looks up and they lock eyes. Then the arrow is launched. In a blur, the man dodges out of the way, and his hand comes up to snatch the arrow out of the air.

Once she releases the arrow, Jiron pulls his knives and moves to rush into the room just in case the arrow didn't complete the job. When he sees the man standing there with the arrow in hand, he moves forward to finish it.

"Korgan was right," the man says as he draws his sword. "The fire in the city was just a ruse so a rescue attempt could be made. I didn't believe someone would willingly burn down a whole city just to save a few lives." He then braces for Jiron's attack. "I'll have to apologize to him after I've killed you."

Before Jiron can close with him, a noxious looking black cloud forms between them. From the hallway he hears Brother Willim gasp, "Magic!" Jiron comes to a quick stop and backpedals quickly to avoid coming into contact with the black cloud. He doesn't take two steps before it begins moving quickly his way.

"Down Jiron!" Brother Willim cries out as he enters the room, aglow with power.

Trusting in the priest, Jiron jumps to the side and hits the floor. He no sooner lands on the floor than something strikes the center of the black cloud. One of Brother Willim's many seeds he carries begins to grow, and as it grows, it absorbs the black cloud. Blossoming into a black orchid, the seed draws all the cloud into it until finally dropping to the floor.

Miko appears with sword in hand and closes with the soldier. Metal clashes as the two blades meet. Both men move with incredible speed, yet Miko is the faster of the two. The time he had the Fire in his possession having given him great skill and speed.

Then Brother Willim is there beside him, his staff smashing into the soldier's armor. "Help the others Jiron," the priest yells. "We'll deal with this."

Jiron gets up off the ground and motions for Aleya to follow him as they leave the combatants behind. Passing through the door Korgan had used, they enter a smaller corridor. Moving down it quickly, Jiron begins to smell the mustiness of an enclosed area. "We're close," he tells her. The clash of swords from the battle they just left follows them as they hurry down the corridor.

Another dozen yards brings them to the top of a narrow spiral stairway descending into darkness. The odor of mustiness is strongest from that direction. "This way," he says. "Stay close to me." He sees Aleya nod then begins taking the stairs down.

Whack!

Brother Willim's staff takes the soldier again in the side of the head. Twice the soldier tried to send the noxious black cloud toward them, and twice Brother Willim countered it with magic of his own. Now, three orchids lie on the floor, all but crushed by the combatants' feet.

The soldier has been on the defensive since shortly after Miko and Brother Willim engaged him. His armor shows tears and dents from where sword and staff have left their mark.

Miko's sword is moving almost faster than the eye can see. For every two of his blows that the soldier manages to block, one makes it through his defenses.

Whack!

The soldier's sword hand is dealt a heavy blow by Brother Willim's staff which causes him to lose his grip. As his sword flies out of his hand, Miko comes in with a thrust and sinks his sword to the hilt in the man's breastbone. With a cry, the soldier staggers back and crashes into one of the tables. Smashing though its top, he dies before his body even reaches the floor.

Just then, the door opens up and the two civilians enter the room. They come to an abrupt halt when they see Miko and Brother Willim standing there over the dead body of the soldier. They immediately do an about face and race from the room hollering for help.

"That tears it," Miko says. He puts his foot on the soldier's chest as he grips his sword and pulls it from the man's body. He's had this sword a very long time. In fact, it's the one James had improved with magic just before his fateful fight with the warrior priest at the foot of the Dragon's Pass. And it has served him well since. Using a strip of cloth torn from the dead man's clothes, he cleans off the blood.

"Let's go," he says and takes the lead as they head for the door through which Jiron and Aleya had gone. Before they make it that far, the sound of feet running toward the room comes to them. Glancing back at the door the two civilians ran through, Miko sees the door burst open and guards begin pouring into the room.

"Go tell the others!" he hollers as he pushes Brother Willim through the doorway.

"What about you?" Brother Willim asks.

"I'll hold them off," he asserts. Drawing his sword again, he says, "Go!" Turning back, he sets himself to meet the assault.

"Good luck," Brother Willim says then runs through the door.

The stairs spiral around three times before ending at the mouth of a corridor. It extends away from stairs and in the distance they can see where it opens up onto a dimly lit room.

"Hope that's where we'll find them," Jiron says to Aleya as he enters the corridor.

"Should be," she replies.

Moving forward at a run, they soon are approaching the room with the light. Movement is seen on the other side. From the amount of light coming through the partially opened door, there can't be more than a single candle burning on the other side.

Jiron glances back to Aleya and finds her with arrow set to bow, ready. Reaching for the door, he pulls it back and races into the room. A single guard is sitting at the table, and before Jiron can cross over to him, an arrow flies past his ear and takes the man through the neck.

"No!" cries out Jiron as the guard falls to the ground dead.

"What?" asks Aleya.

"He could have told us where they were being held," he tells her.

"Sorry," she said.

He sighs. "Don't be," he says. "You did the right thing considering the circumstances. Just hold off a second next time." Looking around the room, they find three doors which lead deeper into the dungeon, all of which are closed.

"Which one?" she asks.

"I don't know," he replies.

Moving past him into the room, Aleya begins examining the floor before each of the doors.

"Now what are you doing?" he asks.

"Seeing if the floor may tell us which way to go," she says. Then she kneels down before the door on the right and says, "This way."

"How can you tell?" he asks coming to kneel beside her.

She points to a scuff mark on the floor. "This is more recent than anything else before the other two."

Nodding, he gives her a quick hug and kiss. "I knew I brought you along for some reason," he says with a grin.

She returns his grin and reaches for the door handle. Opening it up, they find a corridor lined with doors on both sides. Each of the doors is very stout, with a small window about two thirds of the way up, and a sturdy deadbolt lock.

The corridor grows dark at about the fifth set of doors and then remains so until coming to another light far in the distance. Jiron takes the lead and is about to enter when Aleya stops him. "How are Miko and Brother Willim to know which way we went?" she asks.

"It's the only door that's open," he tells her with the expression that she should have known that.

Giving him a weird look, she takes the dead guard and drags him by the hand until he's halfway in the doorway. Removing her arrow from the guard's body she says, "Now there won't be any confusion."

Jiron rolls his eyes as she cleans her arrow on the dead man's shirt. Muttering to himself, he sets off at a quick run toward the light at the other end of the corridor with Aleya right behind. As they pass through the dark area, a voice calls to them from behind a door on their right.

Jiron pauses and turns his attention toward the voice. A hand reaches out toward him as the voice again calls to him pleadingly in the Empire's tongue. "Sorry," Jiron says to whomever the hand belonged to then resumes his run toward the light at the end of the corridor.

"Shouldn't we have done something for that man?" Aleya asks in a hushed tone.

"Don't have time for everyone," he tells her. "Got to save the ones we came for."

She remains quiet as they reach the area of the corridor where the light from the end begins to illuminate.

Jiron slows down and starts walking on the balls of his feet in order to reduce the chance of his boots making a scraping noise. If there is anyone ahead, he doesn't want to alert them that they are there. Moving closer to what is beginning to look like a room that the corridor opens out onto, they strain to hear if someone is there. Silence is all that comes from the room ahead of them.

When Jiron is no more than five feet from the end of the corridor, he motions for Aleya to wait while he moves forward to check it out. Leaving her behind, he keeps close along the corridor's right side as he edges forward. The room is an interrogation room, or at least he thinks so. Within are several torture devices used in extracting information. One, a cage not tall enough for a man to stand erect has a decomposing corpse within it. Four torches held in wall sconces are the source of the light.

Jiron waves Aleya forward and she enters the room. Two other corridors extend from the room, one straight across from the one they just left, and another to their right. He moves to check the one across the room and gestures to Aleya that she should check the other.

The one down which Jiron checks is dark and quiet. Aleya moves to the entrance of the one to the right. Stepping a few feet into the corridor, she hears voices coming from further down. Returning to the room, she says, "There's someone down this way. I can hear voices."

Jiron crosses over to the entrance to the corridor just as someone bursts into the room from the direction they came. Startled, he pulls his knives as Brother Willim comes to a stop before him. "Miko needs help!" he exclaims.

"What?" he asks as he puts his knives back into their sheaths.

"Guards showed up," he explains. "Lots of them. He's holding them off."

"Damn!" he says. Making his mind up quickly, he says, "He'll have to hold out a few minutes longer. Follow me." With there being no longer any time for skulking about, he sprints down the corridor toward the voices. Even before he reaches the end of the corridor he recognizes Korgan's voice.

"...been too long," Korgan says.

Whack!

"Tell me what I want to know and I'll be merciful," he says.

"You'll get nothing from me," Perrilin's voice replies.

Perrilin? He would have thought for sure that Korgan would have been interrogating James first. No time to figure it out, he doubles his speed when he hears the sound of someone being struck again. As he draws close, he sees a guard standing with his back to the mouth of the corridor. Jiron pulls his knives, and when he emerges from the corridor, sinks one of them into the guard's back. He strikes the man with such force his knife sinks to the hilt and wedges in between two vertebrae. As the man lurches forward from the blow, his knife is pulled from his hand.

"Jiron!" he hears Stig shout happily.

In a flash he scans the room. Sees Korgan standing startled before Perrilin who's tied to a chair, three other guards in the room beside the one he just killed, and his friends shackled to the wall.

Reaching down, he pulls the dead guard's sword from its sheath and turns to face Korgan. One of the guards pulls his sword and rushes Jiron, but is thrown backward onto a table by the force of Aleya's arrow striking him in the chest.

"Stay where you are!" cries Korgan. Moving closer to Perrilin, he lays the edge of a knife menacingly alongside the bard's throat.

Jiron stands there and contemplates his next course of action.

Thwock!

Another arrow flies from the corridor and takes Korgan in the shoulder above the arm that's holding the knife. Perrilin cries out as the knife rakes across his throat when his captor is struck.

"Kill them all!" Korgan cries as he staggers back from the blow.

At his command, the two remaining guards rush Jiron.

"See to Perrilin!" Jiron hollers as Brother Willim enters the room. As his knife blocks the blow from one guard, he yells to Aleya, "Find the keys!" Bringing the sword in from the side, he causes the second guard to dart backward.

Brother Willim rushes past where Jiron is battling with the two guards and comes to Perrilin. Blood gushes from the severed jugular and he knows the bard has little time left.

"No you don't!" cries Korgan. Right hand hanging limp at his side, blood flowing from where the arrow is sticking out of his shoulder, he brings up his sword in his left hand. Moving forward, he attacks Brother Willim to keep him from saving Perrilin's life.

"Don't kill him!" James cries out to Brother Willim.

Aleya searches the body of the first man Jiron killed upon entering the room for the keys. Not finding them, she moves to the guard she killed with the arrow. There on his belt is a ring of keys. Taking them, she moves to where James and the others are chained to the wall and begins releasing them.

Brother Willim takes his staff in hand and is suddenly surrounded by a green glow. With speed augmented by the power of his god, he strikes out with his staff. One blow to knock aside the sword coming toward him. A second blow to the hand holding the sword, a crack can be heard as bones break. As Korgan's sword falls to the floor, a third blow takes him alongside the head.

The blow to the head leaves Korgan dazed. Staggering backward, his legs give out and he falls to the ground.

Dropping his staff to the ground, Brother Willim returns his attention to Perrilin. The glow surrounding him suddenly intensifies as he works to stop the flow of blood. The death cry of the last guard Jiron is fighting fails to interrupt his concentration. In short order, the blood stops flowing as his magic heals the severed artery and the skin begins to heal over.

"Is he okay?" asks James as he comes to stand beside him.

Nodding, Brother Willim tells him, "Yes." The glow surrounding him has disappeared and he turns his attention to James. "We have to hurry and get out of here. Miko is upstairs holding off the guards."

"What?" exclaims James. Then he puts a hand on Brother Willim's shoulder as he loses his equilibrium for a moment.

"Are you okay?" Brother Willim asks.

"They drugged us," he explains.

"What are we going to do with him?" Jiron asks as he comes to stand over Korgan. Coming back to his senses, the man tries to get up but Jiron kicks him in the face to keep him on the floor.

Brother Willim turns his attention to James and moves his hand to James' eye. "Let me take a look," he says.

Standing still while Brother Willim examines him, James says to Jiron, "I've got some questions for him. Leave him here with me, Brother Willim and Aleya. The rest of you get up there and help Miko."

"Can you handle him?" Jiron asks James.

"He won't go anywhere," Aleya says.

Jiron turns to her and sees her standing there with arrow to string and aimed directly at Korgan. "Alright then." Then to the pit fighters and Reilin he says, "Let's go."

"Just a second," Brother Willim says to them as he reaches into his cloak. Removing a small pouch, he reaches in and hands each of those who was drugged two small leaves.

"What's this?" Scar asks as he takes his.

"They will alleviate the effects of the drug in you body," he says.

Scar puts them in his mouth and starts to chew. "Yuck," he says and almost spits them back out.

"Don't," cautions Brother Willim. "You must swallow them. They will work fairly fast once in your system to counteract the drug."

"Thanks," he says with a bitter look on his face. Then he and the others move to the table with their belongings and retrieve their weapons and other equipment.

"Come on," urges Jiron once the others have their things in place. Then leading the others out, he races back into the corridor and hopes they will be in time to help Miko.

"Here," says Brother Willim as he hands James three of the tiny leaves.

"Why do I get three?" he asks, taking them.

"The third will help to restore your magical ability," he says. "Just two will make you okay, three should remove all traces of the drug."

Putting them in his mouth, James can see why Scar reacted the way he had. They taste awful. He then glances over to where Korgan sits on the ground. Blood still oozes from where the arrow protrudes from his shoulder.

"Remember me?" James asks him. "It's been awhile."

"Yeah, it has," he agrees. "Should have killed you when I had the chance."

"True," nods James.

"I won't make the same mistake a second time," Korgan vows.

"If there is one," states James. Walking over to the table with their belongings, he removes his pouches and begins securing them once more to the belt around his waist.

"What are you going to do now?" Korgan asks. "There's no way you'll be allowed to leave here."

"We'll see," comments James. Once the pouches are properly secured, he glances back to see Brother Willim helping Perrilin from the chair. A bit groggy and weak in the knees, he at least can stand on his own. Satisfied that he's not going to die on them, he turns his attention back to Korgan.

"I've got a couple questions for you," he tells him.

Korgan laughs. "What makes you think I'll tell you anything?"

Ignoring his statement, he reaches into one of his pouches and pulls out the medallion bearing the sign of the warrior priest. He holds it up before him and asks, "What makes this so special?"

Other than looking to see what he holds in his hand, Korgan fails to react in any other way.

James stares into Korgan's eyes as he says, "I know it has something to do with the way Dmon-Li's temples are interconnected." When he sees his eyes widen ever so slightly at that, he knows that Korgan understands what he's talking about.

"I'd like to know how?" he asks.

"How what?" Korgan replies.

Indicating the medallion, he says, "How this figures into it."

Korgan grins. "Is that what you wish to know?" he asks.

James nods. "Yes it is," he affirms.

He breaks into a laughter which is cut short by the pain in his shoulder. Finally ending in a coughing fit, he brings it under control. "Sorry," he tells him. "No matter how much you torture me, there's nothing I can tell you about that."

James turns and looks questioningly to Brother Willim who has been watching. When he receives a nod telling him that Korgan is most likely telling the truth, he turns back to Korgan. "Then why were you so interested in it that time you had us in the City of Light?" he asks.

"No harm in telling you that," he says. "It's common knowledge that anyone other than a priest of Dmon-Li who is caught in possession of an item bearing their mark, is to be held and handed over to them as soon as possible."

James nods. That would make sense seeing as to the nature of the medallion and how it activates their transportation daises.

"We need to get going," Brother Willim says. "They may need our help up there."

"You're right," he says. "Go ahead and start helping Perrilin up. Aleya and I will finish down here."

Glancing to where Korgan sits on the floor, Brother Willim asks, "You're not going to kill him are you?"

"No," replies James. "I promise you when we leave this room, he will still be alive."

Brother Willim nods. Then with one of Perrilin's arms across his shoulders for support, they leave the room and begin working their way down the corridor.

The room remains quiet for several seconds after Brother Willim and Perrilin leave. Then Aleya breaks the silence by asking, "You aren't really going to leave him alive are you?"

Nodding, he says, "I gave my word." When he sees her about to protest, he repeats, "I gave my word."

"Then shouldn't we get out of here?" she asks.

"You know I'll kill you the instant we meet again," Korgan warns him. "The fact that you spared my life will do little to persuade me not to."

James nods. "I know." Then to Aleya he asks, "Do you still have the keys?"

Nodding, she gestures to where they hang on her belt.

"Good. Let's go." Moving out, he exits the room. Aleya follows him into the corridor, never taking her eyes off of Korgan until she's out of the room.

"I think it's a bad idea leaving him alive," she tells him.

James remains silent as he walks down the corridor. At one point he holds out his hand and his orb appears on his palm. Canceling it, he nods to himself, very glad the leaves worked and that his magic is again at his command.

They pass through the interrogation room with the four torches and then move quickly down the corridor with the cell doors lining both sides.

When they reach the room with the lone guard that Aleya had killed with her arrow, James holds out his hand and says, "Let me have the keys."

Giving them to him she says, "Here you go."

Looking at the other exits he asks, "Which one?"

Pointing to the one that she and Jiron had entered, she says, "There." They cross the room and pass through the door to the corridor on the other side. James then closes the door behind him and uses the keys to lock it. Then he closes his eyes and concentrates for a full minute. When Aleya starts to say something, he holds up his hand and stops her.

As soon as his eyes pop open again, she asks, "What did you do?"

"Just a little something so Korgan won't be alone," he says.

Sitting on the floor, shoulder throbbing with pain, Korgan listens as their footsteps disappear in the distance. Once they disappear altogether, he works his way to his feet as best he can.

"Stupid of him to leave me alive," he says to himself. Moving to the doorway they had passed through, he leaves the room as well and makes his way down the corridor. Upon reaching the interrogation room with the four burning torches in wall sconces, he immediately moves into the corridor with the cell doors lining both sides.

He can hear the door at the other end shut and the turning of the lock. None too worried about being locked down here, he knows that someone will be coming soon to check on things.

When he's reached about halfway to the door, he comes to a stop when a noise disturbs the quiet. A clanking noise. Trying to figure out what it is, he's soon to realize that it is the locks of all the cell doors unlocking by themselves. Then all of a sudden two of the cell doors between him and the door at the end swing open. The prisoners held within leave their cells and enter the corridor. One of them turns in his direction and sees him there.

"Korgan!" the man exclaims in glee.

Seeing the prisoner moving toward him, Korgan begins to return back down the corridor. A glance behind him shows the prisoner has quickened his pace and is closing the distance rapidly. He breaks into a run as he races back to the room with the four burning torches. Every step sends pain radiating out from where the arrow is embedded in his shoulder. His hand that's broken throbs very badly as well. Upon reaching the room, he enters and quickly throws his good shoulder against the door and slams it shut.

Bam!

The prisoner hits the door on the other side. "Korgan!" the man yells, "I'm going to kill you!"

Bam!

Again the man throws his weight into the door and manages to push it open an inch before Korgan gets it closed again. His arm extending from the shoulder with the arrow in it is numb and hangs limp at his side. Gritting his teeth he puts his other hand, the broken one, on the bolt in the door.

Bam!

The prisoner hits the door and knocks it open once more. Shoving hard, Korgan throws all his weight against the door and gets it closed. Then with an excruciating cry of pain, he pushes the bolt closed with his broken hand. The bones grind together as his muscles and tendons push and pull in his effort to lock the door. When at last the bolt sinks into its place, he gasps from the pain and sinks down to the floor.

Then a noise draws his attention to the other passages leading from the room as more prisoners begin moving into the room. Seeing him there, the prisoners grab various interrogation instruments and move toward him. His cries echo throughout the dungeon for a short time until finally becoming still.

Chapter Thirty Three

When James and Aleya reach the bottom of the spiral staircase, the sound of fighting can be heard coming down from above. Taking the steps quickly, they reach the corridor at the top. Emerging into the corridor, James looks toward the fighting and sees Brother Willim and Perrilin still several yards within the corridor.

"James!" Brother Willim calls to him. Waving him forward, he says, "They're holding their own for now."

"Anyone hurt?" he asks coming to a stop next to the pair.

Shaking his head, Brother Willim says, "Not so bad as to be life threatening. I think a couple of them have sustained injuries."

"How are you doing?" he asks Perrilin.

"Better," he croaks. His hand rubs the spot where Korgan's knife had cut him. "I don't think the knife touched my vocal cords."

James can understand why that would be a concern for him, being a bard and all. His voice is his life. Just then Aleya rushes past with bow in hand and moves to the end of the corridor. She puts arrow to string and they hear the thrum of the string as she lets it fly.

"You better get out there," Perrilin tells him. "We need to be gone before more reinforcements arrive."

Nodding, James says, "Good idea." Turning toward the fighting, he leaves them behind and rushes to the meeting room. Even before he arrives, he can see the dead bodies of Empire soldiers that litter the room. Tables are either lying on their edge or shattered. All in all the entire room is like a scene right out of a horror movie.

As he reaches the end of the corridor where it opens onto the meeting room, Aleya lets loose with another arrow and immediately reaches for a third. Placing it to the bowstring, she glances to James and says, "It's almost over."

She takes aim again as he enters the room. Three enemy soldiers are still standing. Jiron, Scar and Stig are faced off with them. Over to their left he sees Potbelly working to dislodge his sword that had been caught between the ribs of a fallen foe. Reilin stands near Miko as he bends over Shorty, the glow from the Star enveloping both of them. Coming over to them, he looks questioningly at Reilin.

"He took a slice along the side," Reilin tells him. "Miko didn't think it was all that serious."

He nods. Then his attention is drawn back to where the battle still rages as the man facing Jiron cries out. He looks back just as Jiron yanks his knife out from the man's armpit and shoves him away. Scar's two swords dance in a weaving pattern before one of them suddenly darts forward and takes his opponent through the chest. His opponent stumbles into the soldier facing Stig and disrupts the man's defense allowing Stig's mace to connect with the side of his helm.

Dazed, the man is unable to defend against Scar who moves in and strikes his head from his shoulders. A calm settles over the room as the last opponent falls dead to the floor.

James quickly takes in the room. Over a score of soldiers lie strewn about the room, all but a few are dead. Those that are still alive won't be for much longer, their wounds are too grievous and James doesn't plan to wait around for Miko to heal them.

"Miko," he hollers. "We have to go."

The glow surrounding him and Shorty winks out and he turns his head to gaze to his friend. "All done," he says.

"Good." Then to Reilin he says, "You help Brother Willim with Perrilin. Stig, you help Shorty along."

Shorty gets to his feet and announces, "I don't need any help. The wound wasn't that bad."

"Okay then," James says with a nod. He turns to Jiron and says, "Get us out of here."

"You got it." Moving out, he takes the lead with Scar and Potbelly bringing up the rear. He follows the most direct path to the gate leading out of the Keep. The halls of the Keep are eerily deserted and he comments on that fact to the others.

"It's the fire," Perrilin explains. "Word came when it first started for every able bodied man and woman to go fight it." He grins as he adds, "Korgan was a bit put out that the Lord of Hyrryth ordered all his men away. He argued that the fire was a ruse friends of mine had made so they could rescue me. But no one believed him."

"I believe the guards you killed back there in the other room were all that was left here in the Keep," he says.

"There were two civilians that fled when the fighting broke out," Miko tells him. "They were in that meeting room going over a map with a couple soldiers. One of the soldiers we killed looked important."

Nodding, Perrilin replies, "He was. That is if the body of the Commander of Ten I saw back there is the one you're talking about. He was the Commander in charge of this region of the Empire. His loss will be a severe blow."

Jiron comes to a junction of hallways and takes a moment to figure out the best way. Then he turns down to the right and they continue on.

"That's not the first one we've faced," James tells him.

"Really?" he asks.

"Yes." He then briefly goes into the details of how Jiron had returned to Mountainside for his backpack that held incriminating evidence, his subsequent capture and eventual liberation at an oasis.

"That is truly something," says Perrilin. "It's said they are fearsome fighters and can wield magic."

"True on both counts," Miko says. "But the one we faced here in the keep only used one spell."

"Maybe they only have one to use," suggests James. "That was all the one at the oasis had used."

"Could be," agrees Scar.

Jiron comes to another junction of hallways and motions for everyone to halt and remain silent. Moving to the corner, he peers around the edge to the right. A dozen guards stand at the entrance to the Keep. Half are facing in while the others are facing out. Returning to where they wait, he tells them of the forces blocking the exit from the Keep.

"Any crossbowmen?" asks Reilin.

Shaking his head, he says, "No, just guards."

"We can take that many," Potbelly says.

Jiron nods his head then turns to Aleya. "How many arrows do you have left?" he asks.

She checks her quiver and says, "Eight."

"Move out in the hallway and start taking them out," he says "They'll charge if they see only a lone archer. Just keep firing at them until they are close then let us know and we'll move to engage them."

"You got it darling," she says and gives him a kiss.

Turning slightly red faced at the expression of affection, he says, "Okay, go ahead."

To his embarrassment and the amusement of the others, she actually pats him on the bottom as she moves to the middle of where the two hallways meet. Pulling an arrow as she enters the junction, she puts it to string then turns and faces the guards at the entrance.

She aims for one of the guards who is furthest away from her and then takes a calming breath. Down by the entrance, she can see the guards take note of her standing there but fail to really pay her that much attention. Then she lets the arrow fly and has another to string before the first one strikes home.

When her arrow hits the man and knocks him backward with a cry, the guards turn as one toward her. She lets fly her next arrow and another man hits the ground as the rest charge. "Here they come," she announces as she looses her third arrow. By the time her fifth arrow is in the body of a dead soldier on the ground, the charging men are too close to allow her another shot. Turning, she bolts down the corridor past where Jiron and the others are waiting.

"I got five," she says as she races past.

"As long as you saved a few for the rest of us," Scar replies. Drawing forth both swords, he and Jiron move to meet the oncoming soldiers. When the first one rounds the corner, he's met by the point of Scar's sword.

One of Shorty's knives takes out the next one and then Jiron engages yet another. With knives weaving in and out, he works his way inside the man's guard and drops him to the ground.

Potbelly, Stig and Reilin come next and the battle is joined. The skill of the guards is nothing compared to the skill honed in the fight pits by the men they're facing. When Stig crushes the skull of the last man, Jiron hollers, "Let's get out of here!"

Leaving the dead lying in the hallway, they race for the entrance to the Keep. No other guards make an appearance as they cross the remainder of the hallway and pass out into the night. The smell of burning wood fills the air and off to their right above the curtain wall they see the glow of the fires that rage within the city.

Ping!

A crossbow bolt strikes Stig's shield and ricochets away. Aleya turns her attention to the walls above them and sees three crossbowmen cranking up their crossbows for another shot. Immediately putting arrow to string, she aims and lets fly. The arrow sails true and sinks its head into the chest of a crossbowman. The man staggers a moment as his crossbow falls from his hands. Then he plummets off the wall down to the courtyard below.

"Get the gate!" Stig yells to the others as he moves to put his shield between Aleya and the crossbowmen. No sooner does he have his shield in place than two bolts are deflected by its hardened surface.

"Thanks," she says as she readies another arrow. Then, "Lower your shield so I can get a shot off." When his shield drops half a foot, she aims, fires and watches as her arrow strikes yet another of the crossbowmen.

Stig raises his shield to protect her while she readies for her final shot. Taking her last arrow from her quiver, she puts it to string then aims for the remaining crossbowman. Stig glances back to where the others are racing for the gatehouse to release the gate lock. One guard lies on the ground dead while Jiron engages with another. Scar and Potbelly race past the two locked in battle and make a dash for the stairs leading to the gatehouse.

"Now Stig," she says bringing his attention back to their situation.

Lowering his shield, he hears her release her arrow and then watches as the third crossbowmen falls from the wall. "Good shot," he says.

"Thanks for your help," she says. Then she rushes across the courtyard to the fallen crossbowmen to retrieve her arrows. Stig goes with her just in case she needs protection again.

Scar and Potbelly reach the gatehouse and in no time the grinding of the gears which unlock the gate can be heard. Emerging back out of the guardhouse, Potbelly yells, "It's open!"

James sees Jiron finish off his opponent and says to Brother Willim, "Let's get out of here." He heads to the gate with Reilin and Brother Willim helping Perrilin following close behind. Jiron reaches the gate first and pulls it open. Expecting there might be an attack, he quickly scans the area and is relieved to find the street on the other side empty.

Glancing back within the courtyard, he sees Scar and Potbelly moving to join him. Then he notices where Stig stands near Aleya while she works to remove one of her arrows from out of a dead crossbowman. "Aleya!" he hollers.

She turns her head to glance at him, then returns to working out the arrow.

"We don't have time for that!" he shouts.

"He's right," Stig says to her. "One more arrow won't make all that much difference."

"It may," she says. Inserting her knife between the man's ribs wherein the arrow is embedded, she spread them apart enough to allow the arrow to come free. Wiping it off on the shirt of the crossbowman, she stands up and puts it in her quiver. "Okay, let's go." With Stig following behind her, she races across to where the others are waiting. She managed to retrieve two of the three arrows.

Jiron gives her a stern glare as they approach and she returns one equally as severe. Deciding this is not the time or place to argue with her, he leads them down the street away from the gate in the curtain wall.

"Perrilin needs to rest," states Brother Willim.

"Can you lead us back to the inn?" James asks. "The people there will take care of him. He's in no shape to continue with us."

Jiron stops and glances to where Perrilin is sagging between Brother Willim and Reilin. "Very well," he says. Moving out, he takes a right at the next intersection and begins taking them along the same path they took when they followed the other guy to the keep.

Smoke permeates the air. Thick, but not so bad as to be unbreathable, just annoying. The people out on the streets seem to be rushing in no apparent direction. Some are heading toward the fire while others appear to be fleeing it.

When at last the inn appears in sight, Jiron brings them to a halt. "What are we stopping for?" Shorty asks.

"Remember when we left, there were men watching the place," he says. "Don't want them to know we came back." Then he motions for Scar and Potbelly to work their way around to the right while he and Stig work their way around to the left. The others he has remain where they are.

He and Stig stay in the shadows as they slowly work their way to the far side of the inn. Taking it slowly, they search for anyone who may be hidden.

But by the time they meet up with Scar and Potbelly on the other side, neither pair had found anyone. "Guess they all went to help with the fire," Stig suggests.

"Possibly," Jiron agrees. Then he heads back down the street toward where James and the others are waiting. As soon as they come into view, he waves for them to join him.

"Anybody?" asks James.

"Not that we saw," Jiron explains.

"Have them keep an eye out while we take Perrilin inside," James tells him. "And send someone around back to get the horses ready." Then he indicates for Brother Willim and Reilin to follow him with Perrilin. As they head for the door, Jiron has the others fan out and take position around the inn. He sends Shorty to the stable.

Before they reach the door, it opens and the innkeeper steps out. "You got him?" he asks incredulously.

James nods. "He's hurt pretty badly though."

Glancing up and down the street, the innkeeper waves for them to enter. "Bring him inside," he says.

As they enter the dimly lit common room, James notices two other men there. One of them is the man who led them to the Keep. "I didn't think you were going to burn down the town," he says to the man.

"It worked didn't it?" he replies with a grin. "Don't worry, we were very selective in what we torched. Business concerns and homes of those with whom we are at odds with."

They bring Perrilin over to a chair and a serving woman appears with a mug of ale for him. "Thank you," he tells her as he takes the mug. Then to the innkeeper, Perrilin says, "They must leave town quickly. Send someone to help get their horses ready and give each an ample supply of food for the road."

The innkeeper nods and then has the second man go and see about getting it done. "Shouldn't take too long to get it ready," the innkeeper tells James.

"What about Korgan?" asks the man who led them to the Keep.

Perrilin turns his gaze to James who says, "I doubt if he survived."

"Did you see him die?" the innkeeper asks.

Shaking his head, he replies, "No I did not. But with his injuries I highly doubt if you'll be seeing him again." Not to mention the fact that he let all the prisoners loose down there. It's altogether likely one or two will have it in for Korgan.

"Good," the innkeeper states with satisfaction.

Perrilin lays his hand on James' arm. "I want to express my thanks for rescuing me yet again," he says.

"Just stop making it a habit of having to be rescued," he says. "I may not be around the next time."

Perrilin nods his head and grins, "I'll try."

One of the serving women comes from the kitchen with several bulging travel packs. "Here," the innkeeper says when she places them on the table before James. "Take this with our gratitude."

"I will," he replies. "Thank you."

A few minutes later the man who went to get the horses ready returns and says, "They're ready."

To Reilin James says, "Go tell Jiron to bring the others around back."

Nodding, Reilin hurries out the front door.

Coming to his feet, James holds his hand out to Perrilin. "Good luck," he says.

"You too James," he says, taking the hand and giving it a firm shake.

Reilin returns with Stig who together take the food packs out back to secure onto the horses.

"You better get out of here," Perrilin urges. "It won't be long before the search will be on."

"Right," he says. "Until next time." Then with Brother Willim in tow, he crosses the common room and leaves the inn by the back door. Jiron and the others are already in the courtyard waiting with the horses. Two additional horses are present, replacements for the ones lost in the Mists.

Jiron sees him exit and says, "Everything's set."

"Good. Let's get going." James then moves to one of the horses and mounts.

The man who had led them to the Keep comes to stand beside his horse. "A man of ours reported that the gates leading from the city to the south were open less than an hour ago," he says. "If you're lucky, they still will be."

"Then let's not waste time talking," Jiron says. He nudges his horse into motion and heads for the gate leading from the inn's courtyard.

"Safe journeys," the man says.

"Thank you for everything," James replies then turns to follow Jiron.

They are soon out on the street and moving quickly toward the southern gate. Smoke continues to thicken as fires rage in several areas of the city. In the haze and darkness, visibility is reduced to almost nothing. If it weren't for the lighted street lamps hanging at the intersections, they would never have been able to find their way to the gates.

When they finally turn down the street that runs directly to the southern gate, Jiron gets his horse up to a fast trot. There are no fires in this area and the only people on the streets are the more disreputable of the city's citizens. Not so much beggars as prostitutes and what James takes for thieves and drunkards. They pay them little mind other than a woman calling to them as they pass.

"There's the gate," Jiron says as its gaping maw appears out of the smoky darkness ahead.

"Anyone around?" Scar asks.

"Doesn't look like it," he says. "Stay alert."

They ride up to the gate at a quick pace. Each scans the area ahead and to the sides of the street for the presence of any hostiles lying in wait. The wall above the gate appears clear as does the area before it.

James all of a sudden gets the feeling they're being watched. Could be just nerves and lack of sleep, but he feels like there's someone out there. He pulls one of his few remaining slugs from his belt and holds it ready. Ahead of him, Jiron has pulled ahead and is just about to pass through the gate. The area remains quiet.

Kicking their horses into a faster pace, they bolt through the gate and hit the road on the other side. No bolts fly from the dark, nor do soldiers manifest and try to stop them.

"Did we kill them all back at the Keep?" asks Reilin.

"That, or they're busy fighting the fires," James replies. Glancing back at the city, he can see the glows from where the different fires still burn.

Jiron sets a furious pace as they leave Hyrryth behind. The sliver of a moon overhead shows that time is all but up. A few more days at the most and the Shroud of Killian will again blind the giant's eye.

They ride for an hour until all sight of the city and the fire's glow disappear behind them. Then they pull off the road for a ways and make camp. They leave the horses saddled in the event a quick getaway is required. Jiron takes the first watch and begins walking around the camp's perimeter to help keep himself awake. The others work to get their bedrolls rolled out on the ground and positioned in the dark. A few hours sleep before they plan to hit the road again.

James feels a hand shaking him awake as a voice says, "James, wake up. It's morning and Jiron wants to get moving."

Groaning, James rolls over and says, "Doesn't he ever sleep?"

"I don't think so," replies Miko. Despite not looking at him, James can hear the grin in his voice. "Get up before he comes over here and wakes you up."

"I'd like to see him try," James says with eyes still closed.

Miko's hand again shakes him. "Come on, everyone else is already awake."

James lifts his head and cracks open his bloodshot eyes. Looking around, he verifies the truth of Miko's claim. Taking a deep breath, he releases it and says, "Alright. Give me a second."

"I'll have some food ready for you when you get up," Miko tells him.

"Thanks." He hears Miko get to his feet and walk away. He almost falls back asleep before he even realizes it. Right in the middle of a dream about nothing in particular, a boot begins nudging him. Opening his eyes he sees Jiron standing there.

"Can't a guy get any rest around here?" he asks.

"No," he says. "Tinok's time is almost gone. We no longer have the luxury of resting and taking our ease."

Sighing, James says, "I know." Sitting up, he looks to Jiron and can see the worry in his face. It troubles him to see that. With sleep now an impossible goal, he gets up and makes ready to travel. After finishing off a quick meal Miko hands him, they mount and begin making for the road.

Back at the road they join the traffic already upon it and turn south. "It's at least two days until we reach Zixtyn," Jiron announces. "Let's pray we have no further delays." Kicking the sides of his horse, he's soon up to a gallop. Then they begin putting miles behind them.

Chapter Thirty Four

Two days of hard riding bring them at last to the walls of Zixtyn. The way it sprawls across a wide area makes it one of the largest towns they have yet come across. Which is odd seeing as how no major waterway runs through it. Usually people tend to settle where there's water, like a river or lake. But here there's nothing. No river, no lake, yet here they are.

"This place is huge," comments Scar when it first comes into sight. "You wouldn't think such a large population could survive together out here."

"I know," agrees James.

Off to the west of the city sits a large, tall edifice which can only be a temple. Dark and foreboding, it almost seems to draw light into itself rather than reflect it outwards. Surrounding the temple are many buildings of various sizes which have to be the place where the training of Dmon-Li's priests takes place.

"That's it," says Brother Willim. "That's what we have to get inside."

"Oh, man," utters Reilin.

A wall surrounds the complex but isn't designed to keep people out. It's more to mark off the area as part of the temple complex. There are many ways in which to pass through, many gates and openings.

"There's not much light left," Jiron announces. "Best if we find an inn and do a little reconnoitering in the morning."

James turns and looks at him askance. "In the morning?"

Nodding, he replies, "Yes. We still have at least two days left. Now that we're close we can't afford to act prematurely or rashly. In the morning I'll take Reilin and Shorty and scout the area."

"Good idea," agrees James.

It takes another half hour before they reach the outlying buildings. Not so much due to distance as people. Many people crowd the streets and they are forced to slow to a crawl in order to make it through.

Several inns appear along the road as they pass through the outskirts, most of which look to be dives or even worse. They decide to continue further into Zixtyn until they come across a decent one.

There are guards moving along the street but they don't pay James and the others any more attention than they do to everyone else. They're there more to keep order than looking for men wanted by the Empire.

Jiron leans next to James and whispers, "Word about what happened up north hasn't reached here yet."

James nods and whispers back, "Doesn't look like it." Then all of a sudden the tingling sensation runs across his skin. Magic is close. He starts looking around to find its source when Brother Willim takes notice of what he's doing. Moving his horse closer he says, "It's the temple. They're performing magic there."

Calming down, James turns to look at him. "It is a school," Brother Willim explains. "They are just practicing."

"I hope you're right," he says. Still unnerved by the constant tingling, he continues to scan the area for any mages. And come to think of it, this is the first time he's felt the presence of another doing magic other than those he's traveling with, since that battle with the mages. Could it be possible he took them all out with the explosion? He doubts it, but why else would no mages be present? Nor warrior priests for that matter, just that one time in the Mists of Sorrow when they were attacked. Definitely curious.

Pressing on into town, they reach an area where five streets converge onto a large plaza area. In the center of the plaza is a large stone structure easily three stories tall. On one side, teen feet from the ground, a long wooded pole extends outward for about fifteen feet. Then it connects to another series of wooden beams that form a lattice work above where four mules are turning a wheel.

At the base of the tower on the opposite side from where the mules turn the wheel, water issues forth to fill a large trough area. Women, slaves, and small children are there filling large jugs with water.

"So this is where their water comes from," James observes. "They pump it from beneath the ground."

"It would take many such buildings to satisfy the thirst of so many people," Brother Willim adds.

"There well may be more," James replies.

Three smaller troughs catch the overflow from the larger. All three have children playing in them. One man has paused next to one of the smaller troughs and is allowing his horse to drink.

As their horses are in need of water, they move to another of the smaller troughs and let them drink their fill. While there, James takes a closer look at the water pump. Always one interested in ancient technology, he admires what they've accomplished. Though with his technologically advanced knowledge, he can see where they could improve on the design.

Slaves, both male and female, come and go as they fill water jugs. The sight of them fills James with disgust. How one human being can ever consider another as property is beyond his understanding. Off to one side, a small child dressed in a slave loincloth is being strapped by an older man.

James feels a hand on his shoulder and that's when he realizes he was on his way over to rescue the child. Glancing over his shoulder, he sees Jiron there.

"We can't," he says.

James can see the pain in his eyes too. Ever since traveling with James, he's grown much more conscious to the plight of those around him, especially kids. Steeling himself, James turns his back and tries to shut out the crying of the child. "Let's get out of here," he tells Jiron.

"Sure," he says. Then he returns to the others and they start to get back in the saddle.

James walks woodenly to his horse and mounts. Unable to help himself, he glances back to where the child was being beaten and finds him lying unmoving on the ground. The man has stopped strapping the boy and says something to the child as he nudges him with his toe. Still the child remains unmoving.

He watches in horror as the man works the toe of his boot under the body and flips it over. The boy's head lolls to one side. That's when it finally hit home that the man must have killed the boy. His vision turns red as anger suffuses him. A slug makes its way into his hand and he cocks back his arm to deliver judgment on the man for the death of the child. Just as he's about to throw, an arm grabs his and stops him. Turning, he sees Miko there.

"The child's not dead," he says quietly. "Though he will be if we do nothing."

Turning back to the boy, he sees the man nudge him one more time with his foot then turn and walk away. None of the other people on the street even so much as bat an eye at what this man has done to a child. Probably because the child is a slave and who really cares about the fate of a slave.

Leaping from his horse, James runs across the plaza toward the child. Picking him up, he can tell that he's only unconscious. Blood from the boy's wounds where the man's strap had cut into him smears his arms and clothes but he doesn't care.

Standing up, he turns back only to find Jiron standing there. "Find us an inn, fast!" he insists.

Jiron looks about ready to protest. Then he sees the seriousness in James' face and nods. Moving over to Reilin, he points toward the main thoroughfare and tells him to find the first inn and get them some rooms. Moving quickly, he hurries to get it done.

James starts carrying the boy toward the street where Reilin disappeared in search of an inn. Miko is beside him and has a hand on the boy's chest. "He's going to make it," he assures him.

Hardly even hearing him, all he can think of was that he turned his back on this child and it almost cost him his life. Never again.

The others are following along behind, Scar and Potbelly are leading James and Miko's horses. When Reilin appears in the street ahead of them, he holds up several keys indicating he's procured rooms for them. Having him lead the way, James follows with the boy.

Jiron has the others take the horses around back to the stable as he and Brother Willim accompanies James and Miko inside. The inn is rather nice, probably costs way too much, but he fails to notice. All his thoughts are now on the boy.

Reilin takes them through the front door and skirts around the common room. The proprietor sees them carrying the boy in but doesn't say anything when he sees the slave cloth around his loins. Up the stairs and down the hall, he takes them to the third door on the right and opens it for James.

Moving into the room, James takes the boy to one of the two beds and lays him down. Beside him, the glow from the Star appears as Miko begins healing the boy. James backs away and gives him some room when Jiron comes, grabs his shoulder and turns him around. He can see Jiron is not very happy about this.

"What do you think we're going to do with that boy?" he asks. "You know where we're going." He gazes into James's eyes for a second then says, "Unless you are planning on letting him go and become a slave again."

Shaking his head, James states, "No, he'll not be a slave again."

"So are we taking him with us?" Jiron asks. "He can't be more than eight or nine at the most, maybe younger. He'll slow us down."

"Jiron," Aleya says as she enters the room behind him, "he's coming with us whether you like it or not."

Tuning on her, he says, "We are going into battle. There's no way that child belongs there."

"I know," Aleya states. "But what choice do we have. I will not turn my back on him now that he's our responsibility."

Jiron gazes to her and then back to James. "This is madness!"

"Could be," agrees James.

Just then the light from the Star winks out and Miko gets up from where he was kneeling next to the boy. He looks to them then says, "He's fine now, just needs some sleep."

"Good," James says. Then to Aleya he says, "It might be best if you were to be the one to stay in here with him. He might not react badly with a woman."

She grins at him. "Of course," he replies. Leaving her brother there, she crosses over to the other bed and throws her pack onto it. Then she sits on the bed next to the boy. "We'll be fine. You might want to get him some regular clothes though. These slave rags have to go."

"We'll get some for him," James says then turns his attention to Jiron. "When you're out, pick up some clothes for the lad."

"Fine!" he says. Not entirely happy about the whole thing, he grabs Reilin and tells him that they have shopping to do. With Reilin in tow he stalks out of the room and they can hear his feet upon the floorboards of the hallway all the way to the stairs.

A second later Scar and the others join them from stabling the horses. "What's wrong with Jiron?" he asks.

"Yeah," adds Potbelly. "He almost walked right into us on the stairs."

Once out onto the streets, Jiron begins calming down.

"What's wrong?" asks Reilin.

"He is always doing something like that," he replies. Bringing his voice down to a whisper he adds, "Knowing we are about to infiltrate the temple, here he is saddling us with some kid."

"I can see your point," agrees Reilin.

"It's not that I don't feel for the boy, it's just that so much is riding on what we're about to do." Jiron then walks along in silence until they come across a clothier. He waits outside while Reilin goes within and purchases clothing the boy is going to require.

When Reilin leaves the clothier's shop, he has several packages in his arms.

"How much do you think he's going to need?" Jiron asks, surprised that he bought so much. "You must have enough there for several kids."

Shrugging, Reilin gives him a grin. "I didn't know the kid's size so bought several sets just in case," he explains. "It's James' money anyway."

"Great." Taking a couple of the packages from him, Jiron then turns and heads back to the inn.

A block down from the inn, they see a large group of people gathering in the middle of the road. Several guards are there in the center of the group trying to get the crowd to move back.

"I better see what's going on," Jiron tells him. Handing the packages back to Reilin he says, "Take these to James and let him know I'll be along shortly."

"Okay," he says with arms now full of packages.

Jiron moves forward while Reilin angles to the side to avoid the crowd ahead of them. At the crowd's edge, Jiron is unable to see what it is everyone is staring at. From the mood of the crowd, it isn't good. He begins working his way through to the center by gently nudging and elbowing people aside.

When he at last reaches the middle, he sees a dead man lying on the ground. One of the guards is examining the body and when he gets up, Jiron realizes he recognizes the man. He was the one who had been strapping the boy. Blood soaks the front of the man's clothes from where his throat had been slit from ear to ear. Having seen enough, he starts working his way back out of the crowd. Once free of the crowd, he hurries back to the inn.

At the room he finds the boy awake and eating some of their food. His eyes are wide as he gazes from face to face. Snuggled in next to Aleya who is softly stroking his hair, the boy shoves what's left of a piece of cheese into his mouth. The packages Reilin brought are sitting on Aleya's bed as yet unopened.

"How is he?" he asks as he enters the room.

"Fine for the most part," Aleya says softly. "His name's Aku."

"So what was going on outside?" James asks. "Reilin said there was a crowd in the street?"

"There was," he replies. "You know that man who was beating Aku?" When Jiron indicates he does, he adds, "He's been murdered. Looks like someone slit his throat."

"Good," states James. "He deserved it."

"More than you would know," Reilin tells him. "From what little I've managed to get out of him, he has been abused for quite some time. Any little infraction and he would get a beating. He even said there was another boy when he first arrived at his master's house that had died by his master's hand."

"And no one did anything," James says in disgust.

"Slaves are property, like a chair," Reilin explains. "No one thinks twice about what a person does to their slave. Except maybe if it was a public nuisance or indecent, then they would. But it wouldn't be because of what they did to the slave, rather how the situation affected those nearby."

"I hate this place," states James with great feeling. "I usually don't like saying hate, but in this case I feel it's justified."

"Just calm down," Jiron says. "We still have to get in that temple and we need you focused."

James nods. "I know," he says then sighs. "Can't let it get to me." He glances over to the boy and sees him take a proffered piece of dried meat and begin chewing on it. At least he was able to help one small child.

"Supper is just beginning down below," Scar says. "Maybe we should adjourn down there and leave Aleya alone with the boy?"

"Might be a good idea," agrees James. Then to Reilin he says, "Tell Aku to stay here in the room with Aleya. That we'll take him with us when we leave."

Once Reilin informs the boy, he grins, nods and replies. "He'll stay," Reilin translates for them. "In fact he's rather happy about the whole situation."

"I would be too if I were in his place," comments Shorty.

"Come on," Potbelly urges. "I'm hungry."

"You're always hungry," Scar says as the pair leaves the room "Remember the time when you..."

James grins to Jiron as Scar's voice moves down the hallway. He motions to the rest of them and they follow Scar and Potbelly down to the common room.

Jiron is the last to leave. "You going to be okay in here?" he asks.

"We'll be fine," she says. "Go have fun."

"I will," he tells her. Then he closes the door and hurries to catch the others.

They only spend an hour down below before Jiron announces that he's heading back up to check in on Aleya. Leaving her alone with the boy in the room has been worrying him. Ever since the incident at the Eye's Court, he hasn't wanted to let her out his sight for any length of time. He doesn't know what he would do if something were to happen to her.

James decides to call it a night too and accompanies him upstairs. The others remain in the common room for a little while longer.

Back in the room they find Aleya and the boy asleep on the bed. The way she's holding him protectively gives Jiron a warm feeling inside. He stands there with James a moment just staring at them before she cracks an eye open and waves him inside.

"I'll take her room," James says. "You two can stay here with Aku."

"Thanks," Jiron says appreciatively as he enters the room.

James closes the door and grins. They're not even married yet and already it looks like they may have an addition to the family. The thought of Jiron as a father figure to the boy makes him chuckle. He reaches the room that was supposed to be hers and opens the door.

"Excuse me," a voice says behind him, practically making him jump in startlement.

Turning around, he sees a young man wearing slave cloth. He's standing not more than three feet away. "You speak my language?" James asks him.

Nodding, the slave says, "Oh yes. My master has many dealings with your people and found it useful for me and others to be able to understand what they are talking about when he's not around."

James could definitely see the benefit in that. "What can I do for you?" he asks.

The slave moves closer and says quietly with head bowed in respect, "I wish to know how the boy fares?"

"You mean Aku?" James asks.

"Yes sir," he replies.

"Why?" James looks more closely at the young man before him. Couldn't be more than seventeen or eighteen, he wonders what interest a small boy could hold for him.

"He's my brother," the slave admits.

James glances down the hallway and sees another slave at the head of the stairs watching them. He opens his door and says, "Why don't we talk inside."

Nodding, the slave moves to follow him into the room. "Is he okay?" he asks.

Once the door closes, James lights the candle on the table with magic. Either the slave didn't notice or he chose not to comment on it. Sitting down, he indicates for the young man to take the seat across from him. Almost without pause, the young man moves and takes the seat.

"He's fine," James tells him. He can almost see the young man visibly relax. "He was hurt pretty bad but we got him cleaned up."

The slave lifts his face to meet his eyes, something he's rarely seen a slave do to a free person. "What are you going to do with him, if I may ask?" he asks.

"We had planned on taking him with us," James explains. "I didn't want to save him only to have him become a slave again. Also, one of us has taken a liking to him."

"I'm glad," the young man says.

James leans back in his chair and stares at him a moment. "I don't know if you heard but his last owner, the one that practically beat him to death, was murdered."

The young man doesn't even flinch at the news.

"I take it you know something about it then?" James asks. When he fails to respond, James says, "He deserved what he got if you ask me." Still unresponsive, he asks, "You killed him didn't you?"

"Yes!" exclaims the young man. "He was a swine who treated poor Aku terribly."

"Good for you," James tells him. At that the young man lifts his head and gives him a slight grin. "Now, what do you intend to do? Are you here to get your brother back?"

Shaking his head, he says, "Hardly. Leaving with you would be the best thing that could happen to him. You and your friends seem a decent enough sort." He then meets James' gaze again and says, "If there's anyway that I can be of service to you, don't hesitate to ask. For all that you've done and hopefully will do for Aku."

James considers his offer. He sits there for a minute or two before saying, "Perhaps there is a way you can be of help."

"Anything," he says.

"Can you help us get into the temple here in Zixtyn?" he asks.

The young man blinks twice but otherwise doesn't react. Then he says, "You aren't serious are you?"

"Completely," replies James.

"Why?" he asks.

"That's our business," he says. "Can you?" James can see thoughts racing through his mind as he thinks about it.

"I may know someone who might be able to help," he finally says. "I won't know if he will until later tomorrow morning though."

"Will he keep this secret?" James asks.

"Oh yes," he replies. "This man holds no love for the temple or those who work for their god." Glancing to James again he asks, "Are you planning mischief?"

James nods. "In a way," he says. "I won't say more than that."

"If that's your goal, I'm sure he'll do what he can to aid you in your endeavor," the young man tells him. He suddenly gets to his feet. "I have to go. I'll come back sometime late tomorrow morning with word."

James comes to his feet as well. "Would you like to see Aku before you go?" he asks. Gesturing to the room down the hall he says, "He's asleep."

Shaking his head, the young man says, "It would be best if I didn't. You see he doesn't know of me. I've been keeping an eye on him all his life but haven't had contact with him."

"Why?" he asks.

The slave grins and says, "Like you say, 'It's my business'."

"As you wish," concedes James.

The young man goes to the door and leaves without another word. James stares at the door and wonders if he did the right thing in trusting that information to a complete stranger. Only after the young man left does he realize that he doesn't know for sure if the young man told the truth when he said he was Aku's brother. Praying that he did the right thing, he turns in for the night.

Chapter Thirty Five

The following morning when they all but Aleya and Aku gather in James' room, he tells them of the visitor he had the night before. Their response was less than favorable.

"Are you out of your mind?" Scar asks.

"What were you thinking?" demands Jiron.

Raising his hands, he quiets their protests. "Calm down all of you," he says. "If it was a mistake, the city guard would have already been here. Since they aren't I can only assume that nothing will come of it from that quarter."

"Do you think that this slave is going to help us enter the temple?" Stig asks. "Seems a rather untrustworthy individual to trust our lives to."

"Right now we don't know what may come of it," he replies. Turning his gaze to Jiron he says, "I think we should continue with what we had planned. You take Reilin and Shorty to reconnoiter the place, see if there's a way in." He sees Jiron nods then adds to the others, "As far as Aku is concerned, I don't think it would be wise to mention his 'brother' to him. Seeing as he knows nothing about him anyway."

"You may be right," Brother Willim says.

"Now I judge it to be about two days to the dark of the moon, so we have that amount of time to find a way into the temple. After that it will just be a matter of getting to the teleportation dais."

"Still sure you can figure that thing out?" Jiron asks.

"To be honest, I don't know," he replies. "But I don't see any other way to reach Tinok in time."

"Go to sleep," suggests Stig. "Maybe the gods will send you another dream to help you along."

Brother Willim shakes his head. "You can't look for these things," he explains. "They come when they do."

James nods his head. "I think we've received all the help we're going to," he says. "We know where we have to go and how to get there. We just need to do it." To Jiron he says, "Perhaps you should get going."

Jiron nods and gets to his feet. "Reilin, Shorty, let's go," he says before turning for the door. With them in tow, he opens the door. Pausing, he glances back to James and says, "If that guy should show up again, don't commit to anything until I get back."

"I don't plan to," he replies.

Jiron meets his gaze meaningfully then turns and leaves. Reilin and Shorty follow him out and then close the door behind. Those in the room hear their footsteps move down toward Aleya's room and stop there for a moment, probably to let her know what's going on. Then they hear a door close and their footsteps continuing down the hallway.

James turns to the others and says, "Now we wait."

Knock! Knock!

After the others left, James had laid down on the bed. Fatigue from the previous two days of travel gets the better of him and he soon drifted off to sleep. The knocking on the door snaps him out of it.

Getting up off the bed, he crosses to the door and cracks it open. Out in the hallway is the slave he talked with the night before. In his hand is a wadded piece of cloth. Opening the door wider, he gestures for him to enter. Once the young man crosses into his room, he sticks his head out and sees the same slave at the head of the stairs as had been there the night before.

Then the door across the hall opens and Scar sticks his head out, probably having heard the knocking. He sees the slave in his room and looks questioningly to James. James gives him a sign saying it's okay, then jerks his head toward the slave at the head of the stairs. Scar glances that way and sees him standing there. He turns back to James and nods.

Closing the door, James moves to the table and takes the same seat he sat in the night before. The slave does the same. "Did you talk with the person you mentioned last night?" he asks.

The slave nods. "Yes I did."

"And?"

"And he thinks you're a fool for seeking to enter the temple," he explains. "But said that he might be willing to help you if you were to come and meet him."

"Why?" he asks.

He shrugs. "I don't know. If you want his help, you are going to have to come and meet with him."

James sits back and considers it. He recalls what Ceadric had said about the Empire offering a hundred thousand gold piece reward for his death. Could this be a ploy to cash in on it? "I suppose I would have to come with you alone? Couldn't take someone with me could I?"

"No," the slave states. "He said for you to come alone." He then tosses the wadded piece of cloth he holds in his hand onto the table. "He also said for you to be wearing this."

James picks up the cloth and sees it's one of the loincloths the slaves wear. "Just this?" he asks, none too happy about parading around in such a thing.

The young man can't help but grin at the expression on James' face. "Yes, just that."

"I can't," he says, replacing it back on the table.

"You must if you are to meet with him," he insists.

"I understand that," James assures him. Then he stands up and removes his own shirt. Underneath he's very white and pale. Having never been one to walk around bare-chested, he never built up a tan. "I could never fool anyone in thinking I was a slave. Do I look like someone who's spent time out in the sun in nothing but a slave's loincloth?"

"No, you don't," he says. "This is going to complicate things."

"Yes it will." Putting his shirt back on, James takes his seat again.

Just then there's another knock on the door. The young man sitting across from him gets an alarmed look on his face. "Relax," James tells him. Getting up, he crosses over to the door and opens it.

Out in the hallway he sees Scar and Potbelly standing there with the slave who had been at the top of the stairs held between them.

"What is this?" demands the young man sitting at the table in James' room.

James gestures for them to enter and once they've left the hallway, closes the door. Turning back to the young man, he says, "I don't like being spied on."

"He wasn't spying on you," the young man assures him. "He was making sure I was okay."

"Same thing if you ask me," Scar says.

"Let him go," James says and the other slave is released. The slave then moves to the side of the young man and they stand together staring defiantly at James and the others.

"Don't really act much like slaves do they?" Potbelly observes.

"No," agrees Scar. "Very few slaves I've run across would dare to cross eyes with a free man. Let alone ask demanding questions of one."

"Go get Brother Willim," James tells them.

Potbelly turns and leaves the room. The two pairs continue to stare at one another until he returns with Brother Willim and Miko in tow.

James sums up the situation for them, the fact that someone may be able to help, but that he has to come dressed as a slave.

"No!" exclaims Miko. "Absolutely not."

Scar just laughs. "Can't imagine you going around in one of those," he says.

The look on the young man's face is growing darker by the minute. James takes note of the fact and says, "I'm not saying no." Miko turns to look at him incredulously. "Calm down," he says. Then to Brother Willim he says, "But the problem is that I am not exactly what you would call tan." Pulling up his shirt, he shows them his pale skin. "I would stand out among all the other slaves."

Brother Willim nods his head. "Yes, I can see that you would," he agrees.

"What I need is something to give me the appearance of having been out under the sun," he explains. "You being into plants and all, I thought you might be the best one to help me."

"There are saps and other things which could be combined to give you the required appearance," he says. "Though I don't know if they are available in this area."

The young man's expression softens somewhat when he realizes James is at least considering doing as requested. "If you were to supply me with a list, I could see about acquiring the needed items," he offers.

"This is a bad idea," Miko insists.

James turns to the young man and asks, "Do you really think your friend will be able to get us inside the temple?"

"If anyone can, he would be the one," the slave replies.

"Very well." Then to Brother Willim he says, "Tell him what you need." Once Brother Willim has told him of several different ingredients that will work, and the slave successfully recites them back to him, James gives him coins to pay for the items.

"How long will it take you to combine the ingredients once you have them?" he asks Brother Willim.

"Not long, maybe a half hour at the most to get it just right," he explains.

"So you intend to meet with him?" asks the young man.

James turns back to him and says, "As of right now, maybe. Another member of our party is not here," he explains. "When he returns I'll know for sure whether I will or not."

"Very well," he says. "I'll be back." Then he and the other slave move toward the door. Scar opens the door for them and they leave. Closing the door, he turns back to James, glance at the slave rag still on the table and grins.

"What?" James asks.

"Aren't you even going to try it on?" he asks. Several of the others in the room start snickering at that.

Jiron, Reilin, and Shorty return a couple hours later. When apprised of what the young man said, Jiron of course was adamantly against it. "No, no, no, NO!" he exclaims. "You can't even be thinking about taking this course of action."

"I haven't committed to it as yet," he replies. "What did you find out?"

"The place really doesn't have much of a guard," he explains. "The area among the outer buildings of the temple complex affords many places in which to hide."

"How about the temple itself?" Scar asks.

"That may be a little tougher nut to crack," Jiron says. "Several braziers sit by the temple doors which I'm sure at night are lit. There will be no way to sneak in once they have been. Anyone in the vicinity will undoubtedly see us heading to the doors."

"Were there non-priests present on the temple grounds?" James asks. "Maybe we could disguise ourselves as a disciple or something."

"That wouldn't work either," interjects Brother Willim. "Temples to Dmon-Li are not known for the attendance by the faithful. If a group this size were to approach, they would become interested in us. Not saying suspicious, at least not at first, but it would definitely be seen as something out of the ordinary."

"So if I understand this correctly," James says as he glances between Jiron and Brother Willim, "any frontal assault will draw attention."

Brother Willim nods and Jiron says, "Most likely."

"Is there a back way in?" asks Stig.

"If there was we didn't see it," replies Shorty. "The temple is pretty big too. It may take us some time to locate this dais thing you want to get to once we're inside."

"Perhaps this slave's plan is the best course to follow right now," suggests Reilin. When the others give him glares, he sticks to his guns and says, "At least go and see what this guy can do for us."

"I'd want you to follow and keep an eye on me," James tells Jiron.

"Oh, you can bet I'll be doing that," he says. Picking up the slave rag off the table he says, "Shouldn't you be getting into this thing then?"

James looks in disgust at it and shakes his head. "Not until I have too."

Another hour goes by and the young man has yet to return. When it's but a couple hours before dusk, he again appears at James' door. This time he's alone, the other slave that was with him the previous two times is absent. Tucked under one arm is a package which he hands to Brother Willim upon entering.

"I found everything you requested," he says. "Took some doing, though.

Bother Willim takes the package and nods. "I can imagine." He then opens it up on the table and begins removing the contents.

Turning to James, he asks, "Are you planning on meeting with the one whom I spoke of?"

"Yes," he replies. "It doesn't look as if I have much choice."

"Then when you're ready I will escort you to him," he says.

Picking up the slave cloth, James asks rather unhappily, "Are you sure this is the only way?"

"If you wish to meet with him, yes."

Sighing, James says, "Very well." While Brother Willim is beginning to crush some leaves in a bowl, he takes the slave cloth. "I'll be in the next room when you're ready."

Brother Willim nods. "Be there when I am done."

James then leaves the room and goes to the next one over. Once he's inside and alone, he holds up the cloth and a shiver runs through him. *Nothing for it,* he tells himself and begins removing his clothes. Naked, he picks up the cloth and begins working to secure it around his loins. Not nearly as easy as he first thought, it takes him three attempts before it's on well enough that it won't fall off when he paces back and forth.

Knock! Knock! Knock!

"Yes?" he hollers through the door.

"It's me," he hears Miko says.

"Come in," James tells him.

When the door opens, Miko comes in and sees him standing there in naught but the slave cloth. "Man oh man," he says with a mischievous grin.

"What?" James asks.

"First of all," he explains, "you have it on wrong. Here let me help you fix it." Closing the door he moves forward and removes the slave cloth. Then he shows him the proper way to wear it. "The way you had it on, it would have fallen off in no time." Tucking the last piece within the part circling his waist, Miko nods and stands up.

"I feel naked," James says.

"That feeling will get worse once you're out in public," he says. "Trust me, I know."

James only nods.

They stay in the room for a half hour and Miko coaches James in the nuances of being a slave. Keeping your eyes lowered, never talking back, all the things he learned during his time as a slave.

By the time Brother Willim makes his appearance, James has the basics down and should be able to pass himself off as one. Entering with his bowl in hand, he pauses a moment when he sees James there. White skin contrasting badly with the tanned areas of his body that had been exposed to sunlight, he almost glows in the dark.

James can see how Brother Willim is trying to fight back a grin that's threatening to break out. "Go ahead and laugh if you want to," he tells him.

Unable to restrain it, the grin breaks forth. "Sorry," he says as he comes forward and begins applying the mixture to his pale skin with a cloth. In fact, he applies a coating to every square inch of his skin, including that which is under the loincloth. "With this on, you'll be able to blend in with the other slaves."

James stands there and endures it. The mixture itself doesn't have all that bad of an odor, sort of smells like the forest on a hot summer day. It takes Brother Willim ten minutes to adequately apply the mixture, and when he's done he steps back to look.

"That will do nicely," Miko says. "You look just like a slave off the streets."

"Do I?" he asks.

"Yep," replies Miko. "Now, let's go back to the others."

James gets a slight panicked look at the though of others seeing him like this, but what else can he do? Face slightly red, he follows Miko out of the room and then over to the room where the others wait. He hesitates just a moment before entering behind him.

Every eye is on him and he feels very self-conscious. "Well?" he asks.

"Remarkable," Aleya says. "If I didn't know it was you, I wouldn't have recognized you." The others nod their agreement.

"Are you ready?" the young man asks.

"No," he replies. "But let's just get this over with."

The young man moves toward the door and James steps aside to let him pass. "Be back as soon as I can," he tells them.

"Good luck," offers Shorty.

As he leaves the room and closes the door behind him, James turns to follow the young man.

"Just keep your eyes down and follow me," he says.

"What if someone tries to speak to me or stop me?" he asks.

"One person isn't likely to accost or bother another person's slave without their approval beforehand," the slave explains. "That would be a severe breach of etiquette. In fact, depending on whose slave it is, there could be more serious repercussions."

Descending the stairs, James hears the noise from the common room. In his loincloth, he feels very exposed. If it wasn't for the mixture Brother Willim put on him to darken his complexion, he's sure his skin would be beet red in embarrassment. Stepping off the bottom step, he follows the slave as he skirts the edge of the common room and leaves through the back door. He was sure that everyone in there was staring at him, but having kept his eyes lowered in proper slave fashion, he couldn't tell.

Out in the street, he soon realizes just how tender his feet are. Walking barefoot as the other slaves are, he tries to ignore the rocks and other hard items that seem to find their way under his feet with every step.

"How far is this place we're going to?" he asks.

"Not very far," he replies. "Just down a couple more streets."

As he continues to follow the young man, he glances to the people on the street. Almost unbelievably, not one of them is even giving him a second look. He could be a bug crawling on the ground for all they care. Growing in confidence that he's not going to be found out, he begins to relax. He even grows accustomed, to a point, in wearing nothing but a loincloth.

If this had been the middle part of the day, the sun would have burnt him to a crisp. But seeing as how dusk isn't very far away, it kind of feels good to have this much skin exposed.

After the slave leads him down one of the side streets, he begins to notice that they are moving into the poorer section of town. The streets are not nearly as kept up as they had been where they came from. Also, the people on the street begin to get a more bedraggled appearance.

Up ahead and to their right lies a narrow alley. Barely wide enough for two men to walk side by side, it's wedged in between what looks to be a tannery and a rendering shop where they separate fat from animal remains. The smell coming from both places is appalling. To his disgust, the slave turns and leads him to that narrow alley. Having no choice, he follows.

"Stay close," the young man says as he enters the alley.

Holding his breath against the stench of the two businesses he's passing between, James steps into the opening. Several times during the course of moving deeper into the alley, his bare feet squish into something soft and feeling very nasty. In the faint light which illuminates the alley, he's not sure if it's human excrement he's stepping in or something else equally offensive. He tries to control his rising gorge as he hurries to catch up with the young man.

The alley grows lighter as they approach the other end. James actually tries to hurry the young man along a bit in order to get out into what he hopes is fresher air. As they reach the end and step from the alley, he takes a deep breath of air that is only slightly better than what he had to endure in the narrow passage. He glances down at his feet but he's unable to determine what exactly he stepped in.

They've come out into an area completely blocked in by the backs of buildings which are only one or two stories tall. Maybe forty feet by thirty, it looks like what may have been a plaza at one time before some of the abutting buildings were built over it. Oddly enough, no windows are present in any of the buildings encompassing this area. Only the alley from which they passed through and a single door in one of the walls are the only apparent ways out of here. It's to the door that the young man is leading him. Other than themselves, this place is deserted.

"This way," the slave says to him.

Stepping in behind, James crosses the vacant area. The slave pauses at the door until James catches up with him then says, "On the other side of this door, say nothing. Even should someone come to you and begin talking, say nothing. Understand?"

"Why?" James asks.

"Just do it," he replies. When he gets a nod from James, he opens the door.

James follows him through and is surprised to find a tall stack of broken pieces of crates, boxes and old furniture no more than two feet before the door. In fact, the stack is higher and wider than the doorway. They are forced to practically squeeze out from the doorway due to the lack of room between the door and the stack. Then the young man closes the door and James is again surprised to discover that the door melds into the wall perfectly, concealing the fact that the door is even there. Whatever this place is, this entrance probably isn't known by too many people.

Without a word, the slave moves to step out from behind the stack and enters a courtyard bustling with activity. Slaves under the watchful eye of men are hauling crates and other items from a warehouse and stacking them on four wagons. The young man moves over to where two small boxes are stacked not too far from where they entered from. He picks one up and motions for James to do the same. Then he makes a circuitous route around the courtyard and finally brings James to the wagons being loaded.

Placing his box within one of the wagons, he nods for James to do the same. Then they turn about and enter the warehouse out of which the rest of the slaves are hauling boxes. Once inside the warehouse, they encounter a man who is directing the slaves in picking up boxes and crates to be placed on the wagons.

No sooner do they enter the warehouse than the man in charge directs them to pick up a rather large one that takes two. Not hesitating, the young man does as directed and James joins him in lifting the crate. He glances questioningly to the young man and only receives a shake of his head in response.

Crash!

One of the slaves further back in the warehouse has dropped his box and is now lying on the ground holding his leg. The way he's holding his leg and crying out, James thinks that it may be broken.

Then from out of nowhere two slaves come and immediately take the crate from them and continue hauling it out to the waiting wagons. Startled by their sudden appearance, James doesn't immediately realize the young man has turned and is walking quickly toward a stack of boxes sitting at the rear of the warehouse. Seeing him moving away from him, James quickly moves to follow. He casts a quick glance to the man in charge of the slaves and sees how his attention is now fully on the slave lying with the broken leg. From the set of the man's face, he feels sorry for the fate of the slave.

Half a minute later, they squeeze through a gap between the stacks of boxes. Sidestepping, James passes through and comes to a small cleared space between the stacks of boxes and the rear wall of the warehouse.

Moving to a set of three boxes, two set side by side and the third on top of the other two, the young man says, "Give me a hand."

James comes forward and the young man has him grip the stack of three boxes in two specific spots. Then together, they lift the edge of the boxes up. The edge comes up to reveal that the three boxes are secured to the top of a trapdoor. Once the trapdoor is raised sufficiently, the young man has James pass through first. There's a drop of three feet and then a series of steps leading down into darkness.

James hops down onto the steps and holds the trapdoor open while the young man hops down beside him. Together they lower the trapdoor and are plunged into darkness. James has an urge to create an orb, but resists it. The last thing he wants to do is to let whoever is down here know what he's capable of. Keeping that information secret has proved beneficial on several different occasions.

Once the sound of the young man moving down the steps comes to him, he slowly follows. Step by step, he descends ten steps before coming to a narrow passage. Keeping a hand on one wall as a guide, he walks forward, all the while allowing the sound of the young man's footsteps to lead him.

"Where...?" he begins when the young man's voice says cuts him off with "Keep quiet!" So keeping quiet, he continues to follow him. At one point, the passage they are in makes a sharp turn to the right. James didn't realize it quickly enough and wound up stubbing his toe on the wall in front of him.

"Shhh!" the young man whispers when James began cursing his throbbing toe.

After that, he kept one hand out in front of him as well as the one to the side. A good thing he did for it saved his toes another stubbing when the passage abruptly curved back to the left. A faint light can now be seen coming from further down this new passage. It steadily grows brighter as they move toward it until James recognizes that the light is making its way through the cracks around a door.

He quickens his pace when he sees the young man is already at the doorway. Light floods the passage as the door is opened and he has to squint for a few seconds until his eyes get readjusted to the light. Moving out of the passage, James enters what appears to be an ordinary cellar beneath some building.

Two other men are in the room, both dressed as slaves. One of them is the same slave as Scar and Potbelly had nabbed keeping an eye on them in the hallway outside their room.

"Go on in," the slave says to the young man.

Without a word, the young man steps toward the opening on the far side of the cellar. An archway separates the room they are in with the one lying on the far side. Many candles are lit within the next room and as James passes through the archway, he sees a middle aged man lying on a series of cushions upon a rug on the floor.

"I brought him," the young man says to the other.

"Leave us," the man on the cushions says.

Bowing to him, the young man backs out through the archway.

Indicating a cushion sitting on the floor near him, the man says, "Please be seated."

"Thank you," replies James. Moving to the cushion, he settles down on top of it.

"It's not often I have guests here," the man tells him. Lifting up a plate bearing slightly squishy sliced fruit that's turning brown, he offers it to James.

Really not wanting any of the old fruit, yet not wishing to offend his host, he takes one. Placing it in his mouth, he chews it and can taste the slight rancidity of spoiled fruit. "Thank you," he says as he tries to swallow without spewing it back up again.

The man smiles and nods. "A pleasure to meet one such as you," he says.

James arcs an eye questioningly at him. "Oh, I know who you are," he explains. "James I believe your name is. And a mage of some power."

James eyes him suspiciously and remains silent.

"Oh you needn't try to hide the fact," he says. "But who you are doesn't really matter now does it? You wanted some information I believe?"

"Who are you?" James asks.

"Ah, that is a question many would like to know," he replies. "Suffice it to say that I am the Slavemaster."

"Slavemaster?" asks James.

"More of a title than a profession really," he says.

"I see," says James.

Without expanding any further on who he is, the Slavemaster says, "I understand you are planning on entering the temple here in Zixtyn."

"That's right," he says. James is more at ease now. Seeing as how the man knows him and has yet to either dispatch him or turn him in, he doesn't feel there is any immediate threat.

"Why?" the Slavemaster asks. "You'll have to pardon my curiosity, but you are the first person I've ever met who actually wanted to go into one. Other than Dmon-Li's priesthood that is."

James gazes at the Slavemaster and gauges just how much to tell him. "Can you help us gain entry?" he asks.

"Possibly," he replies. "You see, I'm the only one that I know of who was ever a slave within the temple and escaped. But that was some time ago, when I was a younger man."

"The one here in Zixtyn?" James asks hopefully.

The Slavemaster shrugs, obviously unwilling to give him that much information about himself. "So why do you wish to gain entry into the temple here in Zixtyn? I assure you, what you tell me will not find its way out of here."

Deciding to trust to fate, he says, "A friend has been taken to Ith-Zirul. We know there's a way that the temples, or at least some of them, are connected through magical transportation devices."

The Slavemaster shakes his head, "Friend, what you plan is nothing short of folly."

"Be that as it may, that is what we plan to do," he insists. "Can you help us?"

"Even should you gain the temple and reach the transportation device, you wouldn't be able to use it," he asserts.

"Then you know of it?" asks James hopefully.

"Yes," he says. "I know of it."

"Can you tell me how it works?" he asks.

"You mean to tell me that you planned to break into the temple and didn't even know how it worked?" he asks incredulously.

"I have an idea," replies James defensively.

"You need more than that if you expect to get to Ith-Zirul," the Slavemaster tells him. "They won't work for just anyone, you need a key."

"I have one of those already," explains James.

"Oh?" he asks. "How would you have gained such an item?"

James then gives him a very brief rundown of finding the medallion in the temple outside of Kern. "I know it activates the dais," he states. "I'm just not sure how to make it take me to where I want it to."

"Fascinating," the Slavemaster says after several seconds of digesting what James had told him. "As to how to make it work, I don't know that part of it." When James gets a disappointed look, he raises his hand and says, "That's not to say what I do know won't help."

"Such as?" prompts James.

"You see, each of these keys is set to take you to two different places on their own," he explains. "I'm sure there's a way in which to have them take you to specific temples, but I have never been privy to that information."

"Now, if you are in the home temple of the key, which in this case would be the temple near Kern where you found it, then the teleportation dais will take you automatically to Ith-Zirul. And if you are at Ith-Zirul it will return you to the key's home temple."

"But what if you are at another temple?" he asks.

"I believe it will take you automatically to Ith-Zirul," he says. "And then from there would return you to the key's home temple."

James remains silent after the Slavemaster finishes speaking. He remembers the time under the sand at Baerustin when during their fight, he and Jiron had stumbled upon the teleportation dais there and ended up at another place. That other place was cold and had strange little creatures with claws sharper than razors. He recalls the voice in his head that said, *'You have come, mage.'* They must have been in the High Temple! Only they didn't realize it at the time. When he and Jiron had fled the place and returned to the dais, it had taken them to the temple near Kern. It all makes sense now.

"Now all there is to do is for us to reach the dais within the temple here in Zixtyn," James says.

The Slavemaster nods. "That won't be as easy as you think," he says. "For one thing, the dais is in a secret room in the lowest level of the temple. None but those in the inner circle are allowed there. It's unlikely you would reach it before being discovered."

"Could you give me some idea the best way to get to it?" James asks. "Despite the risks we must make the attempt."

"Yes," he says. "I can have a diagram made for you that would show the quickest route to the room you have to reach."

"That would be great," James says.

"You might wish to make the attempt two nights from now however," the Slavemaster says.

James looks at him curiously. "Why?"

"In two nights is the dark of the moon," he explains. "Every temple performs special rites to Dmon-Li when the moon is black. It's considered holy to them."

"Killian's shroud blinds the giant's eye," he murmurs.

The Slavemaster hears him and nods. "Yes that's what some call that time of the month." When he sees that James is lost in thought, he adds, "The priests will all be in attendance in the sanctum before the altar. However that's not to say the halls of the temple will be empty. They have over a score of temple guards that will be roaming the grounds, even within the temple itself. You'll have to somehow get through them without alerting the rest of the temple to your presence. I've heard stories of your prowess, but I doubt even you would prevail against a temple's worth of priests all working in conjunction to kill you."

"Probably not," agrees James.

Just then, the young man enters through the archway and whispers something in the Slavemaster's ear. Nodding the Slavemaster says something to the young man who then leaves the room. "Seems your friends have followed you," he says.

"Did they?" James asks innocently.

The Slavemaster isn't fooled. "Don't worry," he says. "They've been taken care of."

"What does that mean?" asks James.

"They won't be bothering us here," replies the Slavemaster.

"What did you do to them?" demands James.

"Oh, nothing harmful I assure you," he says.

James meets his gaze for a moment and then gets to his feet. "I should be going now," he says.

"As you will," says the Slavemaster. "I'll have someone drop by sometime tomorrow with a diagram I'll draw up to help you reach the teleportation dais."

"Thank you," he says. Now worried about what may have happened to his friends, James wants nothing more than to get out of there.

The young man makes his appearance and the Slavemaster says to him, "Escort him back out."

Giving the Slavemaster a slight bow, the young man turns to James and says, "If you'll follow me?"

James gives the Slavemaster a brief bow then turns to follow the young man from the room. They leave through the same doorway and are again in the darkened passage. They proceed for a ways then James feels the young man's hand on his shoulder as he directs him to stop and enter a narrow opening. It's on the opposite side of the passage than the one he trailed his hand along on the way in.

Moving through this new passage which is barely wide enough to accommodate them, they continue for a ways until the passage turns to the right. Then the young man takes him another hundred paces and brings him to a stop.

"Give me your hand," the young man says.

James holds out his hand and feels the young man take it. Moving it to the side of the passage, he places James' hand in a recess in the wall. "You must climb this until you get to the top," the young man says. "There you'll find a small wooden panel to your left. Push it open and crawl through."

"What's on the other side?" James asks.

"A chandler's shop," is the reply. "The shopkeeper has already left for the day. Do not touch anything and be careful when you leave not to let anyone see you."

"Aren't you coming with me?" he asks.

"No, you go by yourself from here," he says. "Good luck."

"Thanks," replies James. Then he hears the footsteps of the young man moving away in the dark.

Turning back to the wall, he feels around and finds a series of recesses moving from the floor up the wall. Putting his hands in the ones at eye and chest level, he then finds two for his feet. Then very carefully, he lifts one of his hands above his head and feels around until he finds the next one. One by one, he slowly makes his way up the wall in the dark.

After what seems like twenty or more different recesses have taken him over ten feet from the floor of the passage beneath him, his hand touches the stone ceiling above him. Feeling around he realizes that he's come as far up the wall as he can. Searching to his left, he finds the small wooden panel of which the young man told him. Pressing it outward, he feels it give. Pushing harder, he swings it wide. A small amount of light comes through from the other side.

The light reveals that the opening is going to be a tight squeeze for him. He then moves toward it and reaches a hand in and begins working his body through to the other side. Though it's small, he manages to wriggle through and comes out beneath a table and finds himself on the floor of the chandler's shop.

Turning back to the opening, he discovers the outside of the wooden panel has stone attached to it. When he swings the panel closed, it blends in perfectly with the stone of the wall. He then comes out from under the table and scans the shop for the way out. The door opening onto the street is to his right and he makes his way to it. Looking out, he sees the street passing in front of the shop still has people upon it. With it still being an hour until sundown, he's sure to be spotted quickly if he were to leave that way.

He makes his way through the shop and finds the back door. Opening it slowly, he discovers an alley running behind the shop. He peers out cautiously only to find there's no one in the vicinity. James then exits the building quickly and shuts the door behind him.

Once out in the alley, he turns down to the right and hurries to the end. Then, walking like he has a purpose, he enters the street and tries to figure out how to get back to the inn.

Chapter Thirty Six

"He's not in there."

Jiron quickly turns around from where he's been watching the guards outside the narrow alley that James and the young man disappeared into some time ago. He and the others had followed them to here, but after James and the slave had passed into the alley, these guards showed up and have been hanging around the entrance to the alley ever since.

When he turns around, you could imagine his surprise when he finds the slave who escorted James into the alley standing there. "What did you say?" he asks.

"Your friend isn't in there anymore," the young man replies. "He's probably back at the inn by now." He gives them a grin and then makes to move onto the street.

Jiron grabs him by the arm and stops him.

"Take your hand off me or I will scream," the young man says.

Removing his arm, Jiron asks, "Is he okay?"

"Yes," he replies. "You really should get back there to him."

"Why?" asks Miko.

The young man doesn't reply, instead he steps quickly and is soon out on the street among the people passing by.

"Let's go," Jiron says. "Something's up and we need to get back there fast." With a last glance to the guards before the alley, he moves out onto the street. Beside him walks Reilin and together they lead the others back to the inn.

Jiron is cursing in his mind the decision of James to go with the young man. He knew there was going to be trouble. Setting a brisk pace, they work their way through the early evening crowd on the street and eventually the inn appears ahead of them.

As they move to the front door, they see James in his loincloth moving toward them from down the street. "What happened?" asks James and Jiron of each other at the same time when they come together.

They both pause a moment then James asks, "Is everyone alright?"

Jiron nods then begins to ask him a question in turn when Brother Willim steps forward and says, "Maybe we should discuss this inside?"

Glancing around them, they can see they have begun to draw the attention of the other people passing on the street. After all, they are a large group standing in the middle of the road.

Nodding to the inn James says, "When I tried to go up to my room, they kicked me out. I don't know what they were saying, but it definitely wasn't nice."

"Could've been they didn't recognize you," suggests Stig.

James glances to him and says sarcastically, "You think so?"

"Shouldn't be a problem now," Shorty says. "Not with us here."

"Hope you're right," replies James. He then indicates for Reilin to take the lead.

Moving to the inn, they pass through the front door and make a beeline for the stairs leading to their rooms. James sees one of the workers who had kicked him out take note of his presence. Their eyes lock for moment but the worker fails to make any move toward him.

Once at the top of the stairs, they go down to the room where they left Aleya and Aku. When Jiron cracks the door open, he finds them both lying on the bed asleep. Aleya has her arms around the boy. It's such a tranquil picture that he closes the door and takes the others down to the next room so as not to disturb them.

After they are all in the room with the door closed, James fills them in on his meeting with the Slavemaster. When he gets to the end where the Slavemaster said that Jiron and the others won't be bothering them, Jiron suggests that he probably meant the guards who had blocked the alley entrance.

"It's a good thing they did too," James tells them. "There's no way you could have followed me through that courtyard where they were loading the wagons. You would have been seen for sure."

"Seems as if the whole thing was very well planned and executed," Scar observes.

Nodding, James says, "Yes it did. There has to be more to this Slavemaster than meets the eye." Glancing to the others he asks, "Anyone ever heard of him before?" When everyone shakes their head he adds, "He must be just a local mover and shaker."

Jiron meets his eye and says, "The question now is, do you trust him?"

"I think so," replies James. "If he can give us a diagram of some kind, it would sure help facilitate matters when we enter the temple." Then to Brother Willim he asks, "This rite he mentioned that the priests of Dmon-Li perform during the dark of the moon, ever heard of it?"

"Not specifically no," he says. "But every religion has days that are holy to them and each has specific rites that they must perform during that time. It sounds plausible."

"That's two days away," Jiron states. "Isn't that cutting it kind of close?" When everyone looks to him he adds, "I mean, Tinok could be dead by then."

"If they are performing a rite to Dmon-Li," Brother Willim says, "then that's when they will be the most distracted. Thus entering the temple would be less perilous."

"And Cassie did say he had until 'Killian's Shroud blinded the giant's eye'," James adds.

"Isn't that considered to happen at midnight?" asks Shorty.

Nodding, Brother Willim replies, "Yes. Midnight is the darkest part of the night, and thus would hold special meaning to those worshiping a god such as Dmon-Li."

James gets a thoughtful look. "Any idea when they would start the rites that night?" he asks Brother Willim.

"No," he admits. "It could be right at midnight or some time before."

"Any way to find out by then?" Stig asks.

"I don't know," Brother Willim says. "Any attempt to find out would surely raise their suspicions."

"I say we wait until the Slavemaster sends the diagram," James says. "He said it would arrive tomorrow."

Nodding, Jiron glances to him and breaks into a smile.

"What are you smiling at?" James asks. Then he looks down at himself and remembers he's in naught but a loincloth and blushes. Turning to Brother Willim he asks, "Is there anyway in which to remove the pigment you put on me?"

"Of course," he says. "Just need to scrub it vigorously in hot water and it should come right off."

"Then Reilin, go down and see about arranging for a hot bath here in the room right away," he says to him.

"Will do," Reilin replies. Heading for the door, he's stopped by Miko who puts in a request for one as well. Turning back to the others, he asks, "Anyone else?" Everyone remains silent. Shrugging, Reilin turns back to the door and is soon out in the hallway.

"I'll meet you all downstairs once I'm presentable again," James tells the others.

Getting the idea he would like them to leave, they file out of the room. James stops Jiron before he can leave and says, "It might be wise to set up a watch through the night. This close to our goal, I don't want anything taking us by surprise again."

"Good idea," he says then leaves with the others out the door.

Once James is in the room alone with Miko, he goes over to where his clothes and packs are. Digging in one of his belt pouches, he removes his mirror. Then, he uses it to try and see just what he looks like. When he finally gets a good idea, he just shakes his head and puts the mirror away. He notices Miko with a thoughtful look on his face as he remembers his time as a slave. Then they both take their ease on the beds to wait for the baths to arrive.

The following day Jiron takes most of the others and they go check out the temple. Basically seeing if there's any indication of preparations of the rite the Slavemaster told James of. Also to get a good idea of the layout of the buildings, routes the temple guards take as they patrol the grounds, those sorts of things.

James, having scrubbed himself clean the night before and looking very much his normal self, decides to remain at the inn to await the arrival of the diagram the Slavemaster promised. Miko and Brother Willim agree to wait with him. Also remaining at the inn are Aleya and the slave boy Aku. Now in regular clothes, the boy is quite happy to simply do nothing but stay in the room with Aleya. It was decided he shouldn't go out in public, no sense risking the chance that someone may recognize him and blame him for the death of his master.

Sometime after the noon meal, there's a knock at James' door. When he opens the door, one of the workers of the inn hands him a rolled message. As Reilin is out with Jiron, he is unable to question him about who dropped it off. So he nods his head to the lad and closes the door.

"Is that it?" asks Miko. He and Brother Willim are sitting at the table and have been discussing various finer points to being a priest. To James it appears as if Miko is really taking being High Priest to heart. At least he desires to be the best that he can.

James unrolls the paper, or rather papers, as there are two separate sheets. He brings them over to the table and with the other's help, spreads them out. The first one shows the layout of the temple complex. One building is circled.

Pointing to the circled building James says, "This must be the temple."

Miko nods his head and then points to what looks like the routes the temple guards take while patrolling the grounds. "With this we should have little trouble in reaching the temple," he comments.

The other sheet is a bit more detailed. It shows the inner layout of the temple. Not all of it, just the route to the room holding the teleportation dais. There are annotations at three points along the way to the dais room, but none of them can read the annotations. It's written in the Empire's language.

"Wonder what it's trying to say?" Brother Willim asks.

"I don't know," replies James. "It would have been more helpful if they were written so we could understand them."

"At least we have the map," Miko says hopefully. "With this we should be able to reach the dais quickly."

James nods his head but still looks at the three places where the annotations are the thickest. It worries him what they might be trying to say.

They study them for an hour or so before Jiron and the others return. When Jiron sees the maps, he begins comparing the one of the outer temple complex to what he had just been observing. "This looks like the routes we saw the guards taking," he says.

"Then we can assume the other is just as accurate?" asks Scar.

"I would think so," replies James.

"The patrols of the guards within the temple aren't noted," Shorty says.

"It's possible they couldn't get those," offers Stig. "Or maybe there aren't any guards roaming their halls."

"You have a point," agrees Reilin. "I mean really, who in their right mind would enter the temple uninvited?"

James glances at Jiron and grins. "Who indeed?"

Jiron grins back. "I'm going back to the temple," he announces. "I would like to make sure the routes the guards take are indeed the same as those depicted here." Picking up the diagram of the temple complex layout, he places it within his shirt.

"Be sure to take Reilin with you, just in case," suggests James.

"I'll take Shorty and Stig too," he says. Then to Stig he adds, "You better leave your shield here until we return."

Stig nods and removes his shield.

Knock! Knock!

Shorty opens the door and finds Aleya and Aku standing there in the hallway. Stepping back, he opens the door wider so they can enter.

"I got tired of sitting in the room," she tells them as she and the boy enters. "What's going on?"

They bring her up to date on what's been happening, also on Jiron's next excursion out to check on the temple guards. "See if you can scare me up some arrows too," she says. "The two I have left won't do much good if things go bad."

"I'll see what I can do," he assures her. Aku takes his seat on a chair in the corner and watches them as they talk. He remains fairly quiet for the most part, almost completely unobtrusive. But then again, that's probably something slaves have to do. He's taken to Aleya, and of all of them, seems to relax most around her. After what he's been through and the way he's been treated, it could be a while before he'll be able to fully trust anyone.

"The boy doing alright?" asks Brother Willim.

"Yes," she replies, "he's adjusting well."

Miko catches Jiron's attention before he walks through the door and says, "Bring back some tarts if you can."

"Look," he says as his gaze moves across those gathered there, "I am not going on a shopping trip. If you want something, get it yourselves."

"Alright, fine," states Miko defensively. "But if you do run across a baker, I'm sure Aku would love some."

"As well as the High Priest of Morcyth I would imagine," Stig says with a grin.

Miko returns the grin. "I'm sure he wouldn't turn any away." At that the rest of them chuckle, if not outright laugh.

Jiron shakes his head and hurries through the door before something else delays him. Reilin, Shorty and Stig follow right behind.

While they're gone to verify the accuracy of the temple complex diagram, the others adjourn to the common room for dinner and entertainment. Brother Willim and Miko opt to remain in the room and look after Aku, allowing Aleya the opportunity to have some fun.

When Jiron and the others return several hours later, they join the party in the common room. "Everything is exactly as the paper says," he tells them. Scar gets up from his chair and takes another seat to allow Jiron to sit next to Aleya. "Thanks," he tells Scar as he sits down.

"Not a problem," Scar replies.

"If that one is correct, then it's safe to say the other should be as well," Reilin says quietly.

James nods his head, "All we have to do now is wait for tomorrow night."

"Fortunately that will allow us to be at full strength when we begin," Jiron says. Signaling the server, he indicates that he and the others who just arrived with him would like an ale. In short order she arrives with four mugs and sets them on the table.

After knocking back almost half of his in one long swig, Stig leans forward and says in a hushed tone, "While we were there they brought a long string of slaves into the temple."

"I can imagine what use they'll be put to tomorrow night," says James. His imagination begins churning through different ways they might be used during the rites. Sacrifice, blood offering, or maybe just stealing their life for dark magics. The thought of the theft of their life for magic brings him back to the question his own morality. About how he had done the same when he used the sphere back in the Eye's Court. Is he really any better than they are?

Yes, he is.

What he did was out of survival. They are doing it out of choice and that is the difference. The day he no longer looks for better alternatives will be the day he can count himself as being just as they are.

The rest of the evening passes well. A traveling minstrel sets up on the platform at the end of the common room and they sit and listen to him all night. When James finally reaches the point where he can no longer keep his eyes open, he takes his leave.

Upstairs he finds Brother Willim in deep discussion of one theological idea or another. Off to one side of the room, Aku is asleep on the floor. Miko shrugs when he glances questioningly to him. "He wouldn't sleep on the bed," Miko explains. "The look on his face when we tried to get him to was one of distrust."

"I don't think he's ever been on a bed before," Brother Willim replies. "At least other than with Aleya."

"As long as he's comfortable," James says. "Try to get some rest. We'll be leaving tomorrow night." They both nod and as he closes the door, resume their discussion. Too much is on his mind as he makes his way down to his room. What will tomorrow hold? Will they be successful? And what may await them should they manage to reach the teleportation dais here in Zixtyn and make it to the High Temple?

Once within his room he undresses for bed and his eye catches sight of the barest sliver of a moon out his window. Tomorrow night will be when Killian's Shroud blinds the giant's eye. A shiver runs through him as he turns away from the window and climbs into bed.

Chapter Thirty Seven

Since they were first brought here to this dark cold place, the daily routine has been just that, routine. Three meals a day, a new slops bucket twice a day and the continual appearances by those strange little creatures who like so much to stare at them. Only once had the routine ever changed.

A man had grown sick. Tinok didn't know the man and he was being kept in the cell adjacent to his, but one day the man started coughing. Nothing serious, just a cough every now and then. Perhaps it was due to the cold, the inactivity, or something else, but the cough progressively worsened over the course of two sleep periods. With no way to tell time, Tinok has grown to judge it by the times when he sleeps.

After the second sleep period, one of the cowled figures appeared and moved to the cell containing the sick man. The cowled figure then opened the cell and entered. Moving across to where the man was lying on the cold stone floor, it stopped next to him.

A hand, rather emaciated with the skin tightly stretched around the bones beneath, emerges from the robe's sleeve. A small flask is gripped by the hand and is brought forward to the man. The poor guy is now trying in vain to scoot away but another hand emerges from the other sleeve and grabs him.

The man panics and his coughing fit increases badly as he struggles against the hand holding him still. Then a word is uttered by the cowled figure and the man suddenly grows quiet and still. Once he's completely quieted down, the hand holding the flask put it to the man's mouth and poured its contents between his lips. Unable to do otherwise, the man swallowed the liquid.

Standing up, the cowled figure turned toward the door and left. During this time, not a single prisoner within the cell the cowled figure entered tried to escape or fight. Maybe it was the feel of the place or the uncertainty that escape would even be possible, but they remained where they were.

Shortly after the door shut and the cowled figure departed, the man was able to move again. Several hours later, his cough cleared up and he felt well. Whatever that stuff was that was poured into him, it definitely cured him.

That was many sleep periods ago. And from that time to now, there was only the routine. Today however, things felt different. There was an urgency in the air that wasn't there before. A feeling that something was going to happen and that it wasn't going to be good.

Also, the little creatures that had been such constant companions since they first arrived, are absent. After their second meal of the day was brought and consumed, the man in armor again appears. Four of the cowled figures accompany him. They begin to open the cell doors and have those within come out.

"Man I don't like this," says Esix as he and Tinok, along with the others in their cell, are brought out to stand with the others.

What Tinok wouldn't give to have his knives in his hand once again. "I don't either," he replies.

They're lined up and then the warrior priest begins leading them down the passage. Going in the opposite direction than that which they did in coming here, they move along until they come to a steep stairwell leading down. The warrior priest enters the stairwell and begins descending the steps.

"Where are they taking us?" Esix asks.

"Nowhere good I'm sure," Tinok whispers back.

What dim light there had been in the cell area is all but nonexistent as they enter the stairs. With barely enough light to see the person before them, they follow cautiously as they descend down the steps.

Moving straight down, the stairs come to an area where the wall on their right suddenly ends. Unable to see any great distance, they have the feeling that where they've entered is a large underground cavern. The echoes of their footfalls give them that feeling more than anything else.

When at last they come to the end of the stairs, the warrior priest turns around and begins following the wall beneath the stairs they just came down. As they continue to follow the warrior priest, fear begins to grow in their hearts. The source of the fear isn't apparent, but Tinok can't help but stare into the darkness of the cavern. Beyond all reason, the source of the fear comes from there.

Behind him, Tinok can hear one man beginning to pant from the fear he's feeling. Another starts mumbling to himself. Trying to shut out the noises of the others, Tinok concentrates on placing one foot in front of the other as the fear he too is feeling works to take away his ability to function.

Then his fear suddenly spikes as a shadow passes close by. Darker than the darkness that surrounds them, this shadow draws every eye until it again disappears back into the darkness.

"Wh…wh…what was that?" stammers Esix, fear very evident in his tone.

Unable to formulate words, Tinok simply shakes his head.

The warrior priest at last reaches a cell that looks to have been dug out of the cavern's side. Basically a hole in the wall with a line of iron bars enclosing it. The door is opened and the prisoners are ushered inside.

Once they're all in, the door shuts and the lock clicks closed. Then the warrior priest turns and fades into the darkness as he leaves them. The four cowled figures leave with him as well. The darkness is somewhat abated by a subtle light that fills the cell area. Where the source of the light is, is anyone's guess.

The fear they've all felt since first entering the cavern still remains with them. Most of the men move as far back away from the front of their cell as they can. Tinok, to his shame, is there with them. Staring out into the darkness beyond the bars of their cell, he prays.

Night has fallen and the group gathers for one last meal before they make the attempt to gain entry into the temple. The mood is somber, even Aku has picked up that something is different than it was.

"This is truly a saga of the ages," Scar says at one point.

"What do you mean?" asks James.

"If we survive this, what a tale it will make." He glances from one to another. Then with a grin he continues. "How Scar and Potbelly saved the world."

Everyone grins, some actually laugh. "Perhaps another name might be appropriate seeing as how you two aren't even in the entire tale," says Jiron.

"I guess it would all depend on who was telling it now wouldn't it?" Potbelly asks in all seriousness. Then his face breaks into another grin as laughter rolls forth.

"Are you going to sit on the bank of that river when this is all over?" Jiron asks James.

"Man you know it," he replies. "I think each of us has had enough adventuring for awhile."

"What do you mean enough?" asks Scar. "This is the most fun we've ever had!"

"You got that right," pipes up Potbelly.

"So what do you plan to do?" asks Stig the pair. "Still going to get one of those hell hounds and put it in the Pits?"

"Why not?" Potbelly exclaims.

"Be the best money maker we've ever had," adds Scar.

Silence falls for a moment then Jiron says, "I would just like to see Tersa again. See how her teddy bears are coming along."

"Every woman in Cardri will be making them before long," Shorty says.

"Perhaps," agrees Jiron. Then he looks to Aleya who's sitting next to him, propped up against the wall behind her chair stands her bow and a quiver now full of arrows. Jiron had managed to find a fletcher here in Zixtyn and bought her a score.

"There's been something I've been meaning to do for a long time," he says as he gazes to her.

"You have?" she asks.

"Yes," he replies. "And if I don't do it now I may not have a chance to later." He takes her by the hand which begins to tremble in expectation. "Aleya, though we have only known each other such a short time..." he trials off as he has to clear his throat. He sees her nod for him to continue.

"I'm not what you could say a great catch. Not rich, never home and likely to be killed at any time, but..."

"Yes?" she asks with a catch in her throat.

"Would you be willing to be my wife?" he asks. The whole room becomes silent as everyone in the room strains to be able to hear her reply.

A single tear runs down her cheek as she nods. "Yes my dear Jiron," she says. "I would."

"Yes!" exclaims Stig and the others clap as the engaged couple share a kiss.

"A toast!" hollers Scar.

"Yes, a toast," the others say as the ale in their mugs is quickly refreshed. Once everyone's mug is filled, they turn to James who suddenly realizes he's the one they're looking to make the toast.

Getting to his feet, he turns to the couple and says, "Not very good at this, but here it goes." He sees a reassuring nod from Jiron and a smile from Aleya. "To Jiron and Aleya, may the life they embark upon be filled with joy, happiness, and lots and lots of children!" At the mention of children he sees Jiron's eye's tighten in panic but then relaxes when he realizes there's some time before he'll have to worry about one of them coming into their lives.

"To Jiron and Aleya!" the others say and raise their cups.

Then Scar comes forward with two beautiful silver cups of fine workmanship. "Jiron had informed me earlier today that he planned to do this," he explains. "So the rest of us went out and bought these as a gift."

Potbelly comes forward with a bottle of wine. Opening it, he fills each of the cups before handing them to Aleya and Jiron. "Can't have the first drink you two share after something like this be just ale."

"Thank you," Aleya says as she takes hers.

"Yes," Jiron states. "Thank you all." Taking his cup, he entwines his drinking arm around hers and they both drink at the same time. Cheers and applause erupt as they finish the wine to the last drop.

Setting their cups back on the table, they gaze into each other's eyes. Then Jiron leans forward and gives her a kiss. She returns it. Her eyes close and when he breaks off the kiss, her head lolls to the side.

"Sorry my love," he says to her as he picks up her unconscious body and carries it over to the bed. Laying her down, he turns to James and asks, "Do you think she'll ever forgive me?"

"Only time will tell," he says.

"Is everything ready?" Jiron asks Scar.

"As ready as can be," he says.

Jiron gets up off the bed and then turns to Reilin, Shorty and Stig. "If you don't see her safely back to The Ranch, I'll personally hunt each of you down and kill you."

Stig lays his hand on his shoulder. "Only our death is going to prevent us," he says, "rest assured."

Earlier that day, Jiron and James had come to the conclusion that where they are going, it would be pure folly to take Aleya and Aku along. Reilin, Stig, and Shorty agreed to escort them back to The Ranch starting at first light. He wanted Scar and Potbelly to accompany them as well, but they would not be denied their chance to have some fun. Said they were tired of always being left behind.

"Okay then," Jiron says. Coming back to his Aleya, he bends over and kisses her upon the forehead and moves a few errant strands of hair from out of her face. "How long will she be out?"

"Most of the night," Brother Willim says. "The leaves of the Acriptia plant are most affective at such things."

"We better get going," Jiron says.

James turns to Reilin and says, "Shorty is coming with us as far as the temple complex. Should things go bad, he'll return here and the rest of you get out of town before they come for you."

"It won't come to that," he says.

"Let's hope not," agrees James. "But just in case…"

"I know, get out of town," finishes Reilin.

Miko shoulders the pack containing the Book of Morcyth and Brother Willim takes his staff. When they're ready, Jiron turns to Shorty and Stig. "Thank you for doing this for me."

"You can pay us back by buying a round at the Squawking Goose," Shorty tells him.

Jiron pats him on the shoulder, "I don't know if I'll have that much money."

They laugh, a nervous, sad laugh.

"Come on," he says and heads for the door. Just before he leaves he glances back one more time to his betrothed lying on the bed. "This really is for the best," he says to himself. Then he leaves the room.

James follows right on his heels with Brother Willim and Miko coming next. After them follows Scar, Potbelly and Shorty. The rest remain within the room.

Down in the darkened street, James glances up to where the dark moon must be rising. The hackles on the back of his neck rise as a shiver runs through him. With Jiron in the lead, they make their way across town until the temple complex comes into sight. Earlier he located a deserted building where they could hide until the time came to make their play.

Once they've all entered the building and the door is closed, he moves to the window giving the best view of the entrance to the temple grounds that he plans for them to take. "How are we to know when the rite begins?" he asks.

"Those of us who can sense magic will know," Brother Willim states.

"I hope so," he says. "I don't want to cut this too close."

"We won't," James assures him. "As soon as it begins, we go."

Jiron nods and continues looking toward the complex. He sees the guard pass whose path takes him by the entrance every ten minutes. According to the way the other guard's routes lay, two minutes after this guard passes by the entrance is the best time in which to go.

Four times the guard passes by the entrance before James begins to feel an increase in the prickling sensation which comes when magic is being worked nearby. He glances to Brother Willim and sees him nods. "It's time Jiron," he tells his friend.

"Okay," he says from the window. "The guard will pass by again in a couple minutes, then we can move out." They crowd around the window and look toward the entrance in the outer wall of the temple complex. A few minutes later, the guard appears. "Let's go," Jiron says once the guard has passed by the entrance.

"Good luck," Shorty says before they head out.

Jiron turns to him and pats him on the shoulder. "You too," he replies. "See you back at The Ranch." Moving out, he leads them quickly toward the entrance to the temple grounds. This area is deserted, not even animals are present this evening. Almost as if they know something is about to happen.

Upon reaching the opening in the wall, Jiron brings them to a halt while he moves forward and enters the opening. On the far side he sees the back of the guard that had recently passed in front of the opening on his way over to between two of the smaller auxiliary buildings. Once the guard has moved between them, he waves for the others to follow and runs across the grounds. There's only about a five or six second window before another guard makes his appearance. If they haven't reached the side of the building directly across from the entrance by the time he does, they'll be spotted.

No sooner does Miko, who's the last to reach the building, presses himself against its side than the expected guard makes his appearance further to their right. Emerging from between two of the smaller buildings, he turns and walks along the face of the one to his right. Then he disappears a few seconds later as he rounds the corner and begins working his way back.

Run and wait. Once it's clear, they run again. Step by step they make it closer to the temple's entrance. They possibly could have done this without the diagram, but they would have left a wake of dead guards behind them. And with that many gone, it would have been almost impossible for someone not to notice.

Once they've made it to the corner of the building directly across from the double doors which are the temple's entrance, Jiron gathers them close. "A guard will appear in one minute from around the left side," he explains. "He'll move across the front of the temple toward the left then turn and go around to the back. Once he disappears around the corner, we have less than a minute to get to those doors and through before two other guards will appear from there," he says as he points to the building on their right, "and there," he concludes, pointing behind them.

Waiting there for the guard to appear, James feels the prickling sensation continue to gradually increase. Whatever they are doing entails quite a bit of magic.

Finally the guard makes his appearance. Six pairs of eyes watch him as he turns and crosses in front of the temple. Then, when he reaches the corner and turns to follow the other side of the temple, Jiron says, "Now."

Even before the guard completely disappears from sight, they are racing across to the doors. Taking the steps two at a time, Jiron reaches the top and pauses before the doors. He turns back and scans the temple grounds. Not seeing anyone else moving about, he takes the handle of the right door. Giving it a slight shove, he begins pushing the door open.

From within the murmur of voices comes to them. It sounds as if many men are chanting. Peering inside, he finds a large room with a vaulted ceiling. Lit torches line the walls at ten foot intervals giving off plenty of light. Besides the way they came in, there are four other exits leading from the room. Two are doors, both of which stand closed. The other two are the beginnings of hallways that extend further into the temple.

Not seeing anyone, they move inside quickly and close the doors.

James begins to pull out the diagram of the temple given to them by the Slavemaster but Jiron shakes his head. "I have it memorized," he asserts.

"You sure?" asks James.

"Definitely," replies Jiron. "We take the hallway to the right." He points to the hallway off to their right that runs along the inside of the outer temple wall.

Glancing to the diagram, James sees that Jiron is indeed correct. "Okay, let's go," he says. Moving along the side of the hall, they make for the opening of the hallway. James refers back to the diagram again and sees that the first of the areas with annotations is the room at the end of this hallway.

He shows the diagram and the annotations to Jiron as they reach the hallway. Jiron nods then scans the hallway. The right side has no openings as it's the temple's outer wall. The left wall has two openings before they reach the end. At that point the hallway opens up onto the room with the annotations. Just what the annotations mean they have yet to decipher.

Jiron has the others move just within the hallway then wait there while he hurries forward to check the two openings on the left. He moves down to the first one and finds another corridor branching off. Fortunately it's currently empty. At the second opening he finds a dark room, just an alcove really. Like the corridor before it, it's empty as well. He then returns back to the branching corridor and makes sure it's clear before signaling the others to hurry past and join him.

Then with the others following close, he moves down to the end of the hallway. The chanting they heard upon first entering the temple pervades the corridors. It doesn't sound very close, in fact it's hard to tell just where it is coming from. One thing's for sure, it isn't coming from the room ahead of them.

The room they're approaching is well lit and they can easily see within it long before they reach it. From their vantage point within the corridor, the room looks deserted. He has the others wait while he moves to the end of the corridor. Peering into the room, he finds it empty.

It's a room that stretches about forty feet away from the corridor and is close to thirty feet wide. The walls are plain and unadorned. Another corridor exits the room through the wall to their left. In the middle of the room sits a pedestal, roughly four foot high. Sitting upon the top of it is a statue of a bent and gnarled humanoid form. The statue stands two feet in height and its back is to Jiron so he's unable to get a good look at the face of it from his vantage point.

Other than the corridor wherein he's standing, the only exit from the room is the corridor to his left. There's something about this room that bothers him, then realization hits him. He waves for the others to come forward and when they join him he points to the other corridor on the left and says, "I don't think we are supposed to go that way."

James brings forth the diagram and looks at it. "You're right," he says. "According to this there should be another way directly across from where we're standing." He shows the diagram to the others.

"Then that means we know what those annotations on the diagram mean now," Miko observes. When the others look to him he clarifies, "They probably tell us how to locate and activate a secret door."

James nods his head. "I think you're right," he says.

"Okay then," Jiron says as he glances to the others. "Scar, Potbelly." Pointing to the other corridor leading from the room he says, "You two keep an eye down that corridor over there." As they cross the room to get into position, Jiron says to James, "I'll keep watch here while you find that secret door and get it open."

James nods his head. "Right."

"Ahhhh!" Miko suddenly exclaims as his knees almost buckle.

James turns to him. "What happened?" he asks concerned.

Miko turns sorrow filled eyes toward him and says, "I think they've begun killing the slaves Jiron saw them bring in here." Then again he feels a life ending prematurely.

"You going to be okay?" he asks as he sees the pain again in his face.

"No," he replies. "But what choice is there?"

To Brother Willim James says, "Stay with him." After he receives a nod from him, he moves into the room and crosses over to where according to the map the secret door has to be. On the way over he passes by the statue and notices that it is looking directly at the place the secret door must lay.

The visage of the creature is truly demonic, even down to the two small horns sprouting from its forehead. Only giving it a cursory glance, he hurries to the wall. Once there, he begins a quick search for any loose stones or sections that might activate the triggering mechanism. After several minutes of fruitless searching, he comes to the conclusion that it must be elsewhere.

Turning back to the pedestal and statue, he gives it a quick once over. He runs his hands first over the pedestal, then when he finds nothing, turns his attention to the statue.

"Someone's coming," Scar says from where he's watching the other corridor. He and Potbelly move to either side of the opening and flatten themselves against the wall.

From his vantage point in the middle of the room, James can see two of the temple guards making their way down the corridor toward the room. Moving quickly, he moves to the side of the room out of the view of the approaching guards, and quickly makes his way next to Potbelly.

Both Potbelly and Scar draw their knives and wait. The approaching footsteps grow louder as the two men draw closer. When they emerge from the corridor, Potbelly and Scar strike fast and hard. Both guards fall without a sound.

"Anyone else?" asks Jiron as he remerges from where he, Miko and Brother Willim had ducked back down the other corridor to keep from being seen.

Scar glances back down the corridor and shakes his head. "No," he replies.

"Alright," Jiron replies. Then to James he says, "Hurry it up."

Nodding, James returns to the statue. He begins trying to move the various appendages of the demonic figure. He pushes and pulls the arms, head and torso. Then one of his fingers encounters a slightly loose gnarled bump on the creature's back. "I found something," he says.

"Don't stand there talking about it," Jiron says. "Get it open."

He presses the gnarled bump but nothing happens. Another quick examination reveals two more bumps that are slightly loose, one on its stomach and another on its back. He presses all three simultaneously and is rewarded with an almost silent grinding noise as a section of the wall begins to rise into the ceiling.

James moves to the entrance and looks through. "There's another corridor extending away," he says, "exactly as the diagram shows." Brother Willim and Miko move to follow him as he steps just within the new passage.

"Nice going," Jiron praises James. Then to Scar and Potbelly he says, "Bring those two dead guards into the secret passage with you."

"Right," Scar says. Then he and Potbelly each take one and begin dragging them toward the new opening in the wall.

"Hurry it up," Jiron says to them. "We don't know how long it's going to stay open."

"Then give us a hand," Potbelly says.

Crossing the room to them, Jiron grabs hold of each of the dead bodies and helps to drag them into the secret passage. They no sooner have them inside then the secret door begins to close. When it finally settles once more to the ground, they are plunged into pitch darkness. The chanting which had been present ever since they first entered the temple is no longer audible. The chanters must be in some other part of the main temple not connected with this secret area.

In the darkness they see a glow coming from Miko. It's the glow of the Star of Morcyth from where it resides in his belt pouch. "I think it senses the presence of Dmon-Li's priests," he says.

"More likely the dark rites they're performing," suggests Brother Willim.

"Will they be able to detect it if we do magic?" James asks him.

"I don't think so," he replies. "With what they are doing, it's going to drown out anything we do, unless you're planning on something big?"

"Hardly," James says. Then his orb blossoms to life on the palm of his hand. To Jiron he says, "Lead on."

Moving down the corridor, James follows after Jiron and takes another look at the diagram. He sees that the corridor they're heading down turns to the left sharply just ahead, then just after that, turns back to the right. From there it moves forward less than ten feet until coming to an end. Then on the right side is a long, narrow room with another set of annotations.

They continue down the corridor, and true to the diagram, they follow the route until they reach the final turn where it goes back to the right. "Hold up Jiron," James says.

Coming to a stop, Jiron glances back to him.

James points to the door on the right at the end of the hallway. "Beyond that door is a long narrow room," he explains. Holding up the diagram, he adds, "And there's another set of annotations across it."

"What do you suggest?" he asks.

"Just be careful," he replies.

Giving him a nod, Jiron then moves toward the door. Placing his ear against it, he listens for any noise coming from the other side. Turning his head back to the others, he whispers, "It's quiet." Placing his hand upon the handle, he pushes and the door moves inward an inch then stops.

"If there's anyone inside," he says to James. "Your orb will give us away."

James cancels the orb and plunges them into darkness. "Good thinking," he says.

The only reply he hears is the all but silent creaking of the door as Jiron pushes it open. When no light comes through from the other side, Jiron says, "Alright James, give us some light."

When the orb appears and dispels the darkness, the light reveals the room before them to be another plain room. The walls are simply the same stone blocks that make up the rest of the temple's walls and floors. No pedestal this time. Nothing but a long, plain room. Pushing the door open all the way, he looks in while remaining in the corridor.

"Hand me the orb," he says. "Want to get a better look inside before we enter." James hands him the orb and then he extends his arm past the doorway allowing the light from the orb to illuminate most of the room. Peering around the doorway, he sees that the room extends further away than the light from the orb can reach.

"It's empty," he says after a moment's scrutiny.

"Maybe the annotations don't mean anything here," suggests Scar.

"Willing to bet your life on it?" Jiron asks as he turns his gaze on him.

"Not really, no," Scar replies.

James moves forward and takes a look. "What do you think?" Jiron asks him.

"I don't know," he says. "Looks pretty normal."

"I know," he replies. "That's what bothers me." He starts to step into the room when James places a hand on his shoulder.

"I may need to lead here," he says. A barrier envelopes him after he removes his hand from Jiron's shoulder. Something about this room has a very Indiana Jones feel to it. If it weren't for the annotations on the diagram, he probably wouldn't be feeling nearly so nervous. But they have to mean something.

Jiron steps back and makes room for him to enter. "Hope they don't sense that," he says indicating the barrier.

"So do I," replies James. Creating a second orb on his palm, he begins moving forward into the room. At first he moves cautiously. Every step he takes, expecting something to happen. But after the fourth step, the room remains quiet. At the sixth step, he gains confidence and begins moving a bit quicker.

Then it happens. He must have stepped on a pressure plate or something for a four foot iron spear shoots up out of the floor beneath him. It strikes the underside of the barrier and launches the barrier with him in it upward.

"James!" Miko exclaims from where he's watching in the doorway.

As he and the barrier come to land back down on the floor with jarring impact, another trigger is activated. Directly beneath him, a spear shoots up out of the floor. Again he and the barrier are catapulted upward, this time James is thrown on his side within the barrier. "Ahhhh!" James hollers as he's thrown further into the room.

Then every time he lands, another spear shoots upward and propels him further down the long narrow room. Head over heels, he's propelled as spear after spear launches him and his barrier further along until it finally hitting the wall at the end of the room and coming to rest.

"James!" Jiron hollers. "Are you okay?"

Sitting there in the barrier, he wonders the same thing himself. Doing a quick self check he finds nothing broken, just a few bruises from where he hit the ground hard a couple times. "Yeah!" he hollers back, "I'm fine."

Glancing to the wall at the end of the room, he discovers another door. Between where he sits and the doorway Jiron and the others are standing at is a patchwork of iron spears sticking upright out of the floor. "There's a door down here," he hollers to the others. "Make your way down. Step as closely to the spears sticking out of the floor as you can and you should be okay."

He dispels his barrier and gets to his feet as the others begin moving into the room. Following the same route the spears sped him along the first time, the others cross the room. He can hear Jiron say, "Step where I step", as he leads the others from one spear to the next.

No further spears erupt from the floor and they finally join him at the far end of the room. "Secret door, now deadly spears," comments Potbelly. "Can't wait to see what we'll discover when we reach the next set of annotations."

"Probably a demon or something," guesses Scar.

James produces the diagram and sees that another corridor extends from the other side of the door they're standing next to. At the end it looks like a spiral staircase goes either up or down then another long corridor before they reach a round room with a circle drawn in the middle. In the corridor just before the round room is where the next set of annotations is noted.

As Jiron listens at the door for any sound coming from the other side, James cancels the second orb, leaving just the orb Jiron is carrying. Not hearing anything, Jiron opens the door and they begin working their way down the hallway.

Halfway down the corridor, something causes Miko to glance backward. His heart skips a beat when he sees light now coming from the room with the spikes they had just left. "James!" he says as he points back they way they came.

The tone of his voice brings the others to a halt and they turn to see what he's pointing at. "Oh no," Brother Willim says as he sees the light within the room growing brighter.

Then all of a sudden temple guards emerge from the doorway. When they see them there, they draw their weapons and charge. There's at least a dozen or more of them coming through the doorway.

Scar pulls forth his swords and says over his shoulder, "Keep going." As Potbelly draws his sword and knife he adds, "We'll hold them off." When it looks like the others are hesitating, Scar yells, "Go!"

Then he and Potbelly move forward to engage the oncoming guards. "First one to Coryntia's realm buys," Potbelly says.

"You're on," Scar replies then the battle is upon them.

Jiron sees James beginning to pull a slug out of his slug belt. He places a hand on his arm and says, "No magic. If they think we're just thieves, they'll send guards. If you start throwing magic around, the priests will come."

"He's right," Brother Willim says.

"But they'll never survive," James says. More guards are piling up behind the ones engaging Scar and Potbelly.

"They know that," Jiron says. "We have to get to the dais!" He turns James toward him and looks him in the eyes. "Don't let their sacrifice be in vain!"

James glances back at the pair holding the corridor against what now must be over three dozen guards. Fortunately the width of the corridor prevents more than two or three coming at them at any one time. Nodding, he turns his back on them and follows Jiron as he runs down the corridor toward the stairwell. Brother Willim and Miko follow close behind.

When they reach the stairwell, they glance once more at the pair fighting in the corridor, then rush down to the lower level. The stairs wind around four times before coming out at another corridor. "It's in the room at the end," James tells the others. "But be careful when you reach the end of the corridor, that's where the final set of annotations lay."

As they head down the corridor, the sound of the fighting going on above them gradually diminishes until they are no longer able to hear it. Moving down quickly, they soon see the end of the corridor ahead of them. To their surprise, the corridor ends at a solid stone wall. Slowing down they approach the wall cautiously.

"Another secret door?" asks Miko.

"Maybe," replies James. *Could the final set of annotations tell them how to get through here?* He hopes that's what it could mean. When he sees Jiron move to approach the wall he says, "Be wary of traps."

"After that room upstairs," he replies, "you can believe I will be."

James joins him as he goes to the wall. "Looks fairly normal," Jiron says. They both begin running their hands over the wall in an attempt to find something that will allow them to gain access to the room containing the dais.

Miko and Brother Willim stand back about ten feet from the end of the corridor. Miko can feel the deaths of the guards as they fight Scar and Potbelly above them. He's pretty sure neither one of their friends has fallen yet. Elsewhere in the temple, the untimely death of slaves rips through him every so often as the priests of Dmon-Li continue their dark ritual.

His eyes wander and finally settle on a minor imperfection in the stone of the wall next to him. Not sure why it caught his eye, he moves closer for a better look. "I think I found it," he announces to the others as he runs his finger across an indentation similar in size to the medallion James has been carrying ever since finding it in the underground temple near Kern.

James immediately rushes over with his orb to see. "That's it!" he exclaims. Pulling out the medallion bearing the warrior priest's insignia, he places it against the indentation. Not exactly a perfect match, but it works.

A vibration comes to them as the end of the corridor begins to drop down in sections. When the rumbling ceases, the light of the orb reveals that the end of the corridor has dropped and created a set of steps leading down.

"Yes!" exclaims Jiron. Moving forward, he leads them down to the bottom where a short corridor connects the stairs with a room. The light from the orb shines through the doorway into the room and they see the dais sitting there before them.

Moving forward, they enter the room and find that it's round just as the diagram had depicted. "There it is," James says as they move to the dais.

"It seems odd that the room containing this dais was only reachable by going though two secret doors and a room full of spikes," comments Jiron. When James glances to him he adds, "The dais in the underground temple was right where anyone could get to it."

James shrugs. "Maybe they were built in different times," he says. "The one in the underground temple could have been constructed when they didn't feel the need to protect it."

"Could be," agrees Brother Willim. Turning to James he says, "Now what?"

"Now we get on the dais and let it take us to the High Temple," he says.

"Sounds easy enough," Miko states.

"Seeing as how I hold the medallion, it might be best if you three were to get on first," James suggests. "It wouldn't be a good idea for me to get on first and have it activate before the rest of you have a chance to join me."

"May have a point there," Jiron says. Moving forward, he hops onto the dais.

Lending Brother Willim a hand, Jiron helps him up then is followed by Miko. "What's going to happen when you get on?" Miko asks.

"If it works as I think it will," he replies, "we'll appear at the High Temple of Dmon-Li."

"Then things will get interesting," Jiron says with a grim grin.

James sighs and says, "You could say that."

"Come on," Jiron prompts when he sees him hesitating. Holding out his hand, he offers to help him up.

Taking the hand, James steps up onto the dais. A second later, they're gone.

Chapter Thirty Eight

Tinok's stomach grumbles. The time when they should have received their third meal of the day has come and gone. Still within the cell, the ever present fear remains with them. He and Esix sit against the back wall side by side. They talk of their times together, family and friends whom they're sure they'll never again see, all the while trying to banish the fear that has become an ever present, unwelcome guest.

How long they've been down here now isn't clear. The ever pervasive darkness outside their cell prevents the possibility to accurately judge the passing of time. During a time when Tinok was listening to Esix talk of an experience with a neighbor's daughter that turned into a bad situation with the girl's father, his eyes begin to detect a growing red glow some distance away from their cell.

"Look!" he says as he rises to his feet.

Esix stops talking and turns his attention toward the red glow. He, as well as the others in the cell with him, get to their feet. The red glow continuously brightens and the light coming from it casts eerie shadows about the cavern. For as the light brightens, they see that they are in fact in an underground cavern.

The ceiling vaults into darkness high above them, a few stalagmites dot the outer edge of the cavern floor. As the glow brightens still further, they come to realize that it comes from an object seeming to float in mid air two feet off the floor.

Beneath the glowing object, the floor of the cavern has been smoothed. The smoothed area encompasses a good portion of the cavern floor. It's rather hard to make out, but it appears there are six similar patterns marked out upon the floor spaced evenly in a circle around the glowing object. Each of the patterns is ringed itself by many symbols, symbols that hurt the eyes if you stare at them too long. A lone circular pattern, larger than the others, is situated not too far outside the ring of six. Twice the number of intricate symbols encompasses that one than the ones in the ring of six.

"What is going on?" Esix asks.

"Man I don't know," replies Tinok.

Then his eye catches a movement and he turns his gaze toward a shadow. But the shadow is not remaining motionless as a shadow should. Rather, it is moving across the floor and through the light the way a shadow shouldn't be able to. The sight renews the terror that Tinok had been working to banish to the back of his mind.

"There's another one!" exclaims Esix, the fear making him speak more earnestly than is his want. More than a couple of the shadows are seen moving about out there. At last they now know the source of their fear. All the while the red glow of the object continues to intensify and deepen in color.

One of the other prisoners cries out and faints when a figure appears at the bottom of the stairway. The figure walks slowly yet steadily toward the larger circle of symbols outside the ring of six. Little more than a shadow itself, the figure seems to almost suck the light from the cavern as it moves into it.

Behind the figure marches six men in armor, all can only be warrior priests. Tinok recognizes the armor of the one who had led them here through the Mists. Then come a dozen of the cowled figures.

When the dark figure that is leading them reaches the larger circle, he comes to a stop. The six warrior priests fan out behind him, and the dozen cowled figures do the same behind them.

Raising arms that can only be called skeletal, the figure begins speaking. Each syllable sends fear through the prisoners, their heads throb painfully as the words seem to cut into their minds. Tinok finds that he's put his hands over his ears in an attempt to keep the sound out, but it does no good.

At last, the figure stops speaking. Breathing a sigh of relief as the pain stops, Tinok then is filled with fear the likes of which he has never felt before, primal fear that threatens to take his very sanity. For from the darkness of the deepest part of the cavern come six monstrous monstrosities, more terrifying than anything his imagination could ever hope to match.

More of the prisoners faint dead away. Esix slumps to the ground next to him and he's unable to move to help his friend. Incapable of tearing his eyes away, he grips the bars of the cell in a grip so tight that his knuckles have turned incredibly white from the strain.

The six monstrosities move toward the circle of six surrounding the red glowing object. Each takes its place within one of the patterns surrounded by symbols. Once they are in place they come to a stop, turn to face the glowing object in the center, then become motionless.

At that point, the cowled figures suddenly start to move. Tinok watches as they turn and begin to cross the cavern toward the cell wherein he's held. Realizing they mean to come for them, he's at last able to let go the bars and moves to the very rear of the cell. All the prisoners who are still conscious do the same.

The cell door swings open even before the first cowled figure reaches it. When they enter, each one takes hold of a prisoner. Starting with the unconscious ones at first, they begin removing men from the cell. When Tinok sees Esix being taken by one, he is unable to do anything other than watch.

Having taken all the unconscious men lying on the floor, the remaining four cowled figures move on the men cringing at the rear of the cell. Pandemonium erupts as each man tries not to be the one taken. One man is shoved toward the approaching cowled figures by another. When one of the cowled figures reaches out and touches him, the man goes limp. Picking him up, the cowled figure carries him from the cell.

Fists fly as the others try to move someone else in position to be taken by the approaching figures. Tinok, to his shame, is no better. Using the skill honed in the Pits, he works to get others to go instead of him.

When the last cowled figure leaves with a man, Tinok remains within the cell along with three other men. The cell door shuts and the cowled figures carry the men toward the circle of six, places two on the ground before each of the monstrosities. Tinok moves again to the bars of the cell and looks out. He sees Esix where he lies at the feet of one of the monstrosities. A single tear rolls down his cheek.

Then pairs of the cowled figures move to stand behind the monstrosities. Once the last cowled figure is in place and has grown still, the dark one raises his arms and the glowing object seems to pulse twice. Words, painful, fearful words, begin to issue forth from the dark one. Then, Tinok looks on in horror as the monstrosities once more begin to move.

"Are we here?" asks Jiron.

No sooner had James completely stepped upon the dais then they were suddenly elsewhere. The light from the orb in his hand dispels the darkness of the room they suddenly find themselves in. The room itself is rather small, barely two feet wider than the dais. The only exit from the room is a single corridor that extends into darkness past where the light from the orb ends.

"Yes, we are," replies Brother Willim. "There's a feeling of wrongness here the likes of which I have never before felt."

The prickling associated with the working of magic is very strong upon James' skin. "They're doing the rite here too," he says in a hushed voice. Stepping down from the dais he moves to the mouth of the corridor.

"We've been here before," Jiron says to him.

"I know," replies James. They both look around for those little creatures that proved such a nuisance the last time they were here. Both are relieved that they are absent.

"See if you can locate Tinok," urges Jiron. When he sees him hesitate he says, "They'll know we're here soon enough."

"Right," nods James. Pulling forth the cloth, he casts his spell and they are elated to see it begin to move and then point to someplace below them and to the right.

"Yes!" exclaims Jiron.

"Can you see if he's still alive?" he asks.

Putting the cloth back in his pouch, he removes his mirror. Concentrating on Tinok, he tries to bring him into focus. They all gather around and watch the surface of the mirror as it begins to shift. Then it clarifies and Tinok's image appears. He's gripping what looks like iron bars as he stares out at something beyond the image in the mirror. His face is bathed in a red glow.

"Try to see what he's looking at," Brother Willim tells him.

He works to move the image away from the bars and just when something begins to appear, the mirror shatters in his hand. A drop of blood wells from his thumb where one of the glass shards impaled it.

"What happened?" asks Miko.

Eeeeek!

They turn to see one of the little creatures James and Jiron had met before hovering not more than two feet away. Its shriek sends a chill down James' spine. Jiron pulls his knives as Brother Willim exclaims, "A Hikuli!"

"You know these things?" Jiron asks him.

"Oh yes," he replies. "We've known about them for some time, only we didn't know where they were."

Eeeeek!

Screaming again, the creature disappears.

"Come on," James urges the others. "We haven't much time." The prickling sensation suddenly intensifies, whether due to the creature that just vanished or for some other reason, he can't tell. He sends forth the magic and creates a translucent floating sphere. He's used similar ones before when trying to locate someone. As it moves down the hallway, he says, "Let's go."

Jiron takes the lead with James right behind. Miko and Brother Willim follow closely.

"Do you feel it?" Brother Willim asks Miko.

"I feel something," he replies. "Never felt it before."

"This temple resonates with evil," he explains. "What you feel is the signature of evil. Remember it."

Miko glances to him and says, "I doubt if I'll ever be able to forget it."

Following the sphere, they hurry down the corridor. The coldness of where they are increases the further they go until their breath begins misting in the orb's light. And still the temperature drops. As they approach the end of the corridor, they see it open up onto a very large room. Jiron pauses a moment before entering.

"Why did you stop?" James asks as he comes to stand besides him. Then he looks to where Jiron is pointing.

Across the room from where they stand, lies a seat made entirely out of bones, some human, others not. On either side of the dark throne are two braziers burning with a purplish glow which seems to suck the warmth from them even from halfway across the room.

"It's the seat of Ozgirath," Brother Willim states, "the High Priest of Dmon-Li. We are in the Hall of Despair."

"Where is he?" Jiron asks.

"I would think he would be wherever Tinok is," he replies.

Eeeeeek!

All of a sudden the air is filled with Hikuli. They screech as they swoop down and begin raking them with their razor sharp claws. Each strike brings pain like acid.

Miko draws his sword and begins attempting to strike them out of the air, but they move so fast, that even with his speed he misses as often as not.

"The Star!" yells James as he pulls forth his medallion. "Use the Star!"

As Miko pulls forth the Star, its light shines brilliantly. For the first time in time unknown, light dispels the dark in the Hall of Despair.

The creatures pull back some distance and hover. Chittering among themselves, they shriek and hiss at the companions they are no longer able to come near.

James sees Brother Willim kneeling on the floor and is arranging a circle of leaves. "What are you doing?" he asks.

"Making a *Vyrilyzk,*" he replies. Once the leaves are in their proper position, he begins talking softly and quietly.

"What's he doing?" asks Jiron. "We have to get to Tinok."

James turns back to Brother Willim to tell him that they have to move on when he sees a small creature that looks remarkably like a garden gnome standing within the *Vyrilyzk.* "An earth spirit?" he asks in surprise. Brother Willim ignores the question. Instead he keeps his attention focused on the earth spirit and points to the Hikuli hovering in the air.

The earth spirit looks up and sees them there. The expression on the earth spirit's face changes to what can only be called hate. Disappearing for only a second, it reappears a moment later. Launching itself upward, it grabs hold of a Hikuli and the two creatures start clawing each other as the earth spirit drags the Hikuli to the ground. Then from out of the *Vyrilyzk* more earth spirits begin boiling into the room, each one launching itself at a Hikuli. The Hikuli in turn screech as they attack the earth spirits.

Brother Willim stands up and turns to the others. "Their enmity for the Hikuli is older than time," he explains. Soon the air is empty of Hikuli as scores of battle-locked creatures writhe upon the floor. Still more of the earth spirits boil forth from the *Vyrilyzk* to join the fray.

"Let's go," he says to James and Jiron. "They'll take care of them for us."

Jiron gives him a grin and a nod. Then turns to follow James' sphere where it is again moving across the Hall of Despair toward the opening of another corridor.

Ozgirath stands before the crystal that's aglow with power being channeled to it from temples both within the Empire and without. Every temple is sacrificing slaves and sending the power here to Ith-Zirul, for what he's about to do requires an incredible amount of magic.

The time for his lord to come has arrived. Ages have been spent in preparation of this moment. Plans that began centuries past have at last come to fruition. All is in ready. The six Gygnai from the home plane of Dmon-Li stand within the circles of power, two slaves who will give their lives to complete the ritual lie before each of them.

As he summons the enormous reservoir of power within himself, Ozgirath sends it forth. One by one he envelopes the Gygnai with the power and activates the magical symbols engraved in the floor about them. The symbols flare with a dark radiance as they begin absorbing power contained within the glowing crystal. When all six of Gygnai are fully intertwined in his magic, they bend down and grab the men lying before them, one in each hand. Then, they come erect again and await his command.

In the back of his mind he senses the presence of an age old enemy, but so engrossed in the ritual is he that it is soon pushed to the back of his mind and is lost. Once more bending the power to his will, he signals the Gygnai that it is time.

As the Gygnai begin absorbing the life of the slaves each holds, the symbols surrounding them begin to writhe. Then the symbols flare with a purplish radiance and the bodies of the Gygnai start to shift and waver as they in turn are absorbed by the symbols surrounding them.

The union of the life forces from this world and that of the plane which Dmon-Li calls home will now enable Ozgirath to create a gateway that will allow his lord to cross over and claim this world for his own. Enormous power is being sent to the crystal, which in turn is taken by Ozgirath. Bending the magic to his will, the High Lord of Dmon-Li invokes the final spell to create the gate.

Where the six Gygnai had stood are now six areas of shifting and pulsating darkness. With the power coming from the crystal, Ozgirath causes the areas of darkness to move toward the crystal. One by one, the darkness envelopes the crystal until it can no longer be seen. Then, the crystal ceases to be as the darkness completely consumes it.

At the point when the crystal ceases to be, the darkness latches onto the tendrils of power being sent from the temples and begins absorbing the magic directly. Coalescing into a large sphere, it slowly grows under the guidance of Ozgirath until it swells to fill the entire area within the circle of six where the Gygnai had stood in a domelike formation.

A dark redness appears deep within the blackness. As the dome absorbs the magic coming from the temples, the redness grows. Rapture fills Ozgirath as the way for his lord begins to come into being. His yellow eyes watch the redness as it consumes the blackness as more and more of it makes way for the gate.

When the redness has all but replaced the blackness, Ozgirath moves to stand before the gate. From the other side, he can feel the presence of his lord. Now, to stabilize the gate and make it permanent so his lord may cross over.

Bring them now.

At his command, four of the warrior priests who have been standing behind him motionless, turn as one and move toward the cell holding Tinok and the other three prisoners.

After leaving the Hall of Despair and the battling creatures, they follow the floating sphere along dark corridors. Several of the 'Little Brothers' accompany them. James takes note of their presence and asks, "I thought they were shy?"

"Little Brothers are normally very shy," replies Brother Willim. "But I am here and they are hoping I will lead them to more Hikuli."

James keeps glancing to them and their number constantly seems to change. First there were four, then seven, then two, and so forth. The most he saw at any one time was fourteen.

They steadily work their way deeper into the depths of the temple, all the while continuing to keep the sphere in sight ahead of them. Aside from the Hikuli they initially encountered, the corridors have been empty. James concludes that those who call this place home must be below where the magic is originating from. He maintains his orb in his hand to give them some light with which to see. Miko had replaced the Star back in his pouch once the threat of the Hikuli was past. The brilliant light the Star gave out here in Ith-Zirul was far too conspicuous and might have given them away.

Having just come down their third flight of stairs, they come across several cells that had at one time held people. "Someone was here not too long ago?" announces Jiron after he makes a quick inspection of one. "Less than a day."

"What makes you say that?" asks Miko.

Jiron indicates the slop bucket. "What's in there hasn't been in there very long," he explains. Looking around, he says, "He must have been held here."

"You sure?" Miko asks.

"Yes," he replies. "Unless you would like to come over and examine it for yourself?"

Shaking his head a bit more vigorously than intended, Miko says, "No, that won't be necessary."

"Then he can't be too much further," James says encouragingly. Already the sphere has moved further down the corridor. It hovers at the edge of the orb's light as it waits for them to follow.

Jiron again takes the lead as they hurry to catch up with the sphere. Once they've come within ten feet of it, it resumes its progress down the corridor. After following it for another twenty feet or so, a red glow begins to be seen ahead of them. Motioning for the others to come to a stop, Jiron moves ahead to check it out.

The sphere continues to proceed down the corridor toward the red glow, then it reaches the top of a stairwell and begins to descend. The stairwell is where the glow is originating.

Jiron immediately comes to a stop and hurries back to the others. "That glow is coming from a set of stairs leading down," he tells them.

"Did you hear anything?" James asks and Jiron shakes his head in reply.

"I think when we find the source of the glow, we'll find your friend," Brother Willim says. "We're very close to whatever is going on." Beside him, Miko nods in agreement.

"Then we don't need the sphere anymore?" James asks.

"I doubt it," replies Brother Willim. "And if we're close, it could give us away prematurely."

Canceling the sphere, James says, "It's gone." Then to Jiron he says, "Lead on." Giving James a nod, Jiron moves to return back to the head of the stairs.

A growing sense of fear and doom has been developing within James since before they found the cells back behind them. And when the red glow first appeared, the sensation increased. Now standing at the top of the stairs, he feels the fear become an almost palpable force.

"You okay?" asks Brother Willim.

"I don't know," he replies.

Brother Willim glances from James and Jiron and can see the fear James is feeling reflected in Jiron's eyes. "Wait a moment," he says. Then he reaches into his robe and pulls forth a small crystal vial.

"What's that for?" asks Jiron.

"It will help with the fear you are feeling," he explains.

"I'm not feeling any fear," Miko says.

"No, I wouldn't think you would be," replies Brother Willim. "You are after all a High Priest. The power of Morcyth shields you from such things." He removes the stopper and pours out a single drop of the liquid contained within the vial upon his finger. "This is Asran's Tears," he says. When James looks questioningly, he adds, "Holy water in the simplest term." He then takes the drop of holy water and rubs it across James' left eyelid. Pouring out another drop, he does the same to his right eye.

As soon as both eyes have been treated, the fear that was threatening to take the heart from him subsides to a more tolerable level. "I can still feel it," he tells Brother Willim.

Administering the holy water to Jiron's eyes, he says, "It won't remove all fear, just help you not be overcome by it." When he finishes with Jiron, he stoppers the vial and replaces it within his robe.

Next to him, a Little Brother is beginning to behave in a most excitable manner. He looks at the earth spirit and says, "We need to hurry."

"Why?" asks Jiron. Then all at once, a wave of evil rolls over them.

"It's happening," Brother Willim says as he races for the stairwell.

"What's happening?" James asks as he rushes to follow.

Jiron beats him to the stairs right after Brother Willim and they move quickly down the steps. The further they descend, the more intense the red glow becomes. Moving down the steps, they finally come to a place where the wall on their right suddenly ends and opens up onto a large cavern.

Brother Willim comes to a stop just past where the wall ends and stares down at the cavern floor. "Lord Asran!" he exclaims.

James comes to a stop next to him and looks down. His eyes are immediately drawn to a massive red, somewhat dome shaped area with traces of black running through it. Seeing it there in the center of the cavern floor, he knows beyond a shadow of a doubt that this is where the wave of evil had originated.

A dark figure, dwarfed by the size of the dome, stands before it. The unmistakable sight of two warrior priests stands behind the dark figure. Cowled figures, similar to those he encountered the last time he and Jiron were here are spaced in twos around the edge of the red dome.

"Look there!" Miko says in a hushed whisper. Pointing down below where they stand on the stairs, he indicates eight figures moving across the cavern floor toward the dark figure standing before the dome. Four of them are warrior priests, each of whom has hold of a man dressed in slave rags.

Jiron recognizes one of the men. "Tinok!" he breathes. He looks down at his lifelong friend as he is being brought forward toward the dark figure.

"Ozgirath," says Brother Willim. When James glances to him he indicates the dark figure and says, "Ozgirath, the High Priest of Dmon-Li."

Miko moves his hand to the pouch containing the Star of Morcyth but James stops him. "Not yet," he says. If he brings it out of the pouch now, its light will flood the cavern and those down below will know they're there. "Let's get closer." Already the light from the Star feels almost like it's struggling to leave the pouch.

Still unobserved by those below, they start moving the rest of the way down to the bottom. James notices that the Little Brothers are not with them. Glancing back up to the top of the stairs, he can see a large concentration of them there watching. For just a moment he thinks that they have more sense than he does, then returns his attention back to the stairs and continues down after the others.

Ozgirath waits while the last four are brought to him. Something tugs at the back of his mind but he pushes it aside. Nothing can disturb what comes next. Reaching into his robe, he pulls forth a dagger. Easily a foot and a half long, the wicked looking weapon glows darkly from the runes inscribed upon the hilt and blade.

To make the gate permanent, he must drench it with blood from this world. At the same time it must be sealed with the darkest of magic. He motions for the first of the men to be brought forward. Unable to draw from the magic being sent by the temples as that is being fed directly to the dome area, he instead draws it from the twelve cowled figures. As soon as he begins absorbing their magic, they buckle and collapse.

When the warrior priest brings the first man before him, he plunges the knife into the man's breast, spearing the heart. The man makes no sound as the knife is withdrawn. Blood begins to pump forth from the wound as the warrior priest turns and lays the man down at the gate's base. The dark magic of Ozgirath keeps the man alive as his heart continues to pump out the needed blood.

The next warrior priest brings forward the next man and again, he plunges the dagger into the man's breast. Soon, he too is lying at the base of the gate as his life's blood is leaving his body.

At the base of the stairs, the four companions watch in horror as the first two men are sacrificed. The third man is then brought forward to stand before Ozgirath. Tinok is in line to be the fourth.

"Jiron," James whispers. "You get to Tinok and get him out of here. You'll be no use in the fight that is to come."

Nodding, Jiron says, "I understand." Moving along the wall beneath the stairs, he starts edging closer to where Tinok stands in the grip of the warrior priest.

James then turns to Brother Willim and asks hurriedly, "Will the Little Brothers come and help us?"

"I can feel their fear from here," he says. "Against Hikuli is one thing. Against this...I don't know."

Out of the corner of his eye, he sees the third man fall and the warrior priest holding Tinok begins to move forward. "Whatever happens," he says, "Don't let the knife fall."

Miko and Brother Willim both understand what he's talking about and nod.

"Miko," James says, "it's time to bring forth the Star."

Miko gives him a nod as he opens the pouch containing the Star. At the same time, James pulls the medallion bearing the Star of Morcyth out from beneath his shirt. Light shines forth from both in magnificent brilliance.

Then it seems as if time stops as every eye turns toward them. The arm of Ozgirath is poised to plunge the dagger into Tinok's chest as he looks to see those who have dared to intrude upon his domain. His yellow eyes flash as he sees the Star where it shines in Miko's hand. Only for the space of a heartbeat does the world seem to stop before it once again resumes.

Kill them and take the Star!

His warrior priests draw their swords and the prickling sensation spikes as they move toward James, Miko and Brother Willim. Then just as he turns back and is about to plunge the dagger in Tinok's chest to complete the binding of the gate, Jiron comes from behind him and kicks with his foot the hand holding the dagger. The blow causes the dagger to fly free of the hand and sail through the air toward the dome. When it hits the dome's surface, there's a flash and the dagger is gone.

Noooooooooo!

Ozgirath turns his eyes onto the man who cost him his dagger. A wave of energy lashes out from him and strikes Jiron. It picks him up and throws him further back into the cavern. The warrior priest who had brought Tinok before Ozgirath still stands there holding him. Dmon-Li's High Priest moves forward and grasps the hilt of the warrior priest's sword. Pulling it from its scabbard, he raises it high to strike Tinok and add his blood to the others to complete the spell.

As the sword descends toward Tinok's breast, a shimmering field springs up around him. The sword connects with the shield and rebounds back. Anger erupts within Ozgirath. Returning the sword back to the warrior priest he says, *When the shield falls, strike. There's very little time left.*

The warrior priest nods and stands ready.

Turning to the mage who unwittingly helped him to reach this goal, he now turns the full might of his power against him. Energy crackles around him as he summons the power of his god.

When Jiron had managed to remove the dagger from the dark one's hand, James had almost shouted in glee. Then his jubilation left him quickly when he saw the five warrior priests turn their attention on him, Miko and Brother Willim.

Magic erupts from the Star as Miko begins speaking once more in the tongue none other understands. Lances of light shoot forth from the Star and strike the approaching warrior priests with devastating results. Knocked backward several feet, they quickly recover. Then a dark miasmic cloud forms before them and rushes forward.

The green glow surrounding Brother Willim intensifies as he works to counter the malignant magic being turned to bear upon them. How he wishes the other members of the Hand were with him now, he sorely needs them. Then out of desperation, he sends forth a message, **"Little Brothers! Asran needs you this day!"**

Throwing a handful of seeds toward a dark miasmic cloud billowing its way toward them, he prays to Asran to give the earth spirits courage. As the seeds blossom into green tendrils that begin absorbing the cloud, Little Brothers fill the air as they jump from the steps above and race to his aid.

Jiron shakes off the effects of the blast and regains his feet. A moment's glance shows him Tinok encased in one of James' barriers, the Little Brothers launching themselves from high up on the stairs, and James, Miko and Brother Willim fighting for their lives against five warrior priests and the dark figure whom Brother Willim named Ozgirath.

Seeing as how Tinok is in no immediate threat from the sword held in the hand of the warrior priest so long as James' shield remains in effect, he rushes toward where James and the others are under attack.

At first dozens, then scores of Little Brothers appear and swarm toward the combatants. None go near Ozgirath, instead they wash over the warrior priests like a tide. Their tiny claws scratching away at any exposed skin that isn't covered by armor. Even the armor of the warrior priests begins to show signs of their attack.

Four of the warrior priests bear the brunt of their assault. Their swords move incredibly fast as they strike out and cleave many of the Little Brothers in two. But for every one they kill, two more take its place.

Miko holds aloft the brilliantly shining Star which is keeping several shadows at bay while fending off a warrior priest with his sword. The shadows had appeared shortly after Ozgirath's dagger disappeared in the dome. The light of the Stair is preventing them from coming close. When they do, smoke seems to rise from them as if the Star's light burns them.

Whack! Whack! Whack!

Brother Willim's staff quickly strikes the warrior priest engaging Miko three times in quick succession but fails to yield any results.

Bam!

One of the warrior priests blasts a dozen Little Brothers from him and then lays about with his sword before more attach themselves to him once again. They grip the armor and use their hands, feet, and at times teeth, on any exposed flesh within their reach. Two of his fellows are already completely encased in a mass of wriggling bodies. The fourth lies still upon the ground, the armor now holding nothing more than a grisly piece of ripped flesh. That it had been a man is no longer apparent.

Ozgirath unleashes a massive surge of magic toward James which grips him in absolute agony. Every nerve ending on his body flares pain, his muscles begin to twist beneath his skin. A cry of pain is ripped from him as he drops to his knees. Responding with magic of his own, he thrusts the invading magic from him and the pain diminishes.

Grinning, Ozgirath raises his hand and blackness surrounds it. A blackness so total that is seems as if the light around it is being drawn within. Before he's able to complete the spell, a knife is thrust to the hilt in his back.

Ignoring the blade, he launches the blackness toward James then turns his attention to Jiron who is striking him with his other knife. *Fool!* Ozgirath says to Jiron. Lashing out with his arm, he connects with Jiron and sends him flying toward the dome. Striking it, he disappears.

"Jiron!" yells James when he sees him vanish. Unable to dwell more upon the fate of his friend due to the approaching bulbous cloud of black, he strikes the cloud with a wave of magic and shatters it.

"Ahhhh!"

Suddenly Miko cries out in pain. James turns in time to see the light of the Star diminish greatly as the sword from a warrior priest severs the arm holding it. Blood spurts out from the stump as he staggers backward.

Brother Willim moves in with his staff to engage the warrior priest, allowing Miko a chance to withdraw. "Get the Star!" he hollers to James.

Then a wave of darkness seems to roll over them all as Ozgirath stands there with arms upraised. James moves toward the Star and is almost upon it when he sees Miko's blood on the ground. It's moving across the ground as if of its own volition, and it's heading for the dome.

Unable to worry about the ramifications of that, he reaches where the Star is lying on the ground. Then he stands there in indecision. He knows it's his death for him to lay hands upon it, even to save it from the minions of Dmon-Li.

Brother Willim notices his hesitation and yells, "The shadows! Get the Star or all is lost!"

James turns and sees the shadows that had been held at bay by the Star moving quickly toward them. Then out of the corner of his eye, he sees Tinok where he is still encased within the barrier he put around him. "That's it!" he cries.

Casting a spell he's cast hundreds of times before, he encases the Star in one of his barriers. Bending over he picks it up. He hesitates only a fraction of a second once it's in his hand before raising it high. "Morcyth, lend me your aid!" he hollers and the Star bursts to life.

As the light of the Star blazes forth, screams rip their way through his mind as the light burns the shadows. The pain from the screams forces him to close his eyes. When he reopens them, the shadows are once again a good distance away.

He then turns to Miko and sees him on the floor awash in his own blood as he holds his severed arm to the stump. A glow forms where the two ends meet as the power of Morcyth works to reattach the limb. "Are you okay?" he asks.

Face displaying the pain he's feeling, he fails to answer other than a shake of his head.

Whack!

Brother Willim strikes the helm of the warrior priest he's facing. Bringing his staff in for another strike, the warrior priest's sword unexpectedly strikes the center of the staff and cleaves it in two. Now unable to adequately defend himself, Brother Willim is helpless to stop the next attack. "Asran!" he cries out as the warrior priest's sword penetrates his stomach.

Suddenly, the cavern is filled with the angered screams of Little Brothers. They launch themselves at the warrior priest. Now in total disregard for their own safety, they swarm the warrior priest with a viciousness one wouldn't expect from such shy creatures. The warrior priest's sword moves rapidly as he strikes one after another, but the deluge of bodies is simply overpowering.

James rushes to his side and can see the green glow already surrounding him. "Brother Willim!" he says but the brother is too deep in healing concentration to hear him.

Then all of a sudden, there's a subtle shift in the feel of the cavern. Turning his gaze to Ozgirath, he sees him radiating darkness as he faces the dome. "Oh no," James says as he sees the top of the dome beginning to sink toward the floor.

The dark ritual has been completed. The gate is now ready.

Chapter Thirty Nine

He was surprised when the knife he put in the back of the High Priest did little to hurt him. Then when Ozgirath turned and struck him, he was even more stunned by the sheer strength with which he was struck. There was very little time for him to dwell on this as he flew through the air. Then all of a sudden, he was elsewhere.

When he came to land, the first thing he felt was fear. More fear than he's ever felt in his life. Barely able to move, he looks around and realizes he's no longer in the cavern. A dark haze lays over the land, the ground cracked as if all the moisture was taken from it. The air tastes different and it's difficult for him to take a breath.

His gaze continues to turn and he knows he's not alone. There's something here with him, something of immeasurable evil and power though his eyes cannot see it. Pain erupts in his head as a malignant presence voices strange words in his mind. Putting his hands to his ears, he tries to shut them out but can't.

The dagger Jiron!

Another voice enters his mind and alleviates in part the pain the strange words give him. This voice gives reason instead of madness and curbs in part the fear he's felt since passing through. A feeling of imminent danger comes over him as the malignant voice suddenly ceases.

Take the dagger!

Again the soothing voice comes to him and in his mind's eye he pictures golden hair, a memory of long ago. Then his eyes see it. Not more than three feet away lays the dagger he knocked from Ozgirath's hand.

Yes

Lurching forward on his hands and knees, he grabs the dagger by the hilt and a searing pain courses through his hand and up into his arm. The touch of the dagger is almost more than he can bear, but he holds onto it tightly.

Flee!

The fear rises within him, as does a feeling that his imminent death is nigh. Rising to his feet, he turns around and sees a dark red area that almost perfectly matches the appearance of the dome in the cavern he just left. Only this area is flat.

Evil washes over him as he moves toward the dark red area. Falling to his knees in panic, he cringes. Then he looks up toward the dark red area and against all logic, sees the shimmering image of a woman with golden hair. He blinks his eye twice but the image of the shimmering woman remains. Beckoning to him, the image gives him strength to once more rise to his feet.

Then as he takes a step forward, a wave of force passes him and strikes the shimmering woman. A shriek is heard as she disappears. With the indomitable will that has carried him through many times of crisis, he forces first his right leg to move forward toward the red area, then the left.

Around him, it almost feels as if evil is assaulting him from all directions. The dagger in his now all but numb hand shines darkly with power. Step by small step, he forces his legs to obey him as he draws closer to the dark red area. When at last he's near enough, he gathers his courage and jumps…

My lord, the way is ready.

Ozgirath stands there in the cavern before the gate. The dome has collapsed now until only a dark red, shifting flat area remains. The gate stands ready and he awaits his lord's coming.

The gate suddenly bulges upward as sparks dance across its top. Then Jiron vaults out from the bulge and lands before Ozgirath. Behind him, the gate settles down and the sparks disappear.

Ozgirath's yellow eyes flash as Jiron appears from out of the gate with the dagger aglow in his hand.

Jiron sees Ozgirath standing there before him and doesn't hesitate in leaping forward. With a mighty cry, he plunges the dagger with both hands toward the High Priest's breast.

James sees him attacking and sends a bolt of white light from the Star to strike Ozgirath a second before Jiron does. The bolt of white light explodes when it hits him, disrupting the spell Ozgirath had planned to use in his defense.

The dagger in Jiron's hand strikes the breast of Ozgirath and sinks in to the hilt.

An inhuman cry is torn from Ozgirath as the runes on the blade flare. At the same time, James turns the full might of the Star upon him and drives him to his knees.

My lord! Your servant needs your aid!

Then the gate begins to once again bulge and the sparks appear as they dance across its surface.

"He's coming through!" yells Brother Willim. "Forget Ozgirath. You must destroy the gate."

James understands the logic of what he says and stops the beam of light going to Ozgirath. Instead he sends the magic toward the gate and works to prevent the crossing of Dmon-Li one way or another.

Jiron sees the Little Brothers racing for the stairs, fearful at what is coming through the gate. The six warrior priests are gone, now nothing but piles of blood and shredded meat remain. The shadows are still held at bay by the light of the Star. Brother Willim has Miko's head cradled in his lap and things don't look very good.

He finds Tinok lying not far away and runs over to him. The barrier which James had around him is gone. "Tinok!" he says as he comes to kneel at his side. When he doesn't respond, he puts his ear to his chest to see if he's still alive. A very faint lub-dub is heard as his heart still beats within his chest.

Giving him a gentle shake he says again, "Tinok! It's me, Jiron."

His eyes flutter open and at first he is unable to focus well enough to see. Then the sight of his friend's face comes into clarity and he smiles. "Jiron, thank god you found me," he says weakly.

"Can you stand?" Jiron asks.

"I think so," he replies. With Jiron's help he makes it to his feet. "Oh man," he says as he sees James there struggling to keep the gate closed.

Jiron turns and sees the Star shining with incredible brilliance. The bulge within the gate moves outward, then recedes. Outward, then recedes again as James struggles to keep it closed.

"I can't stop it," James says. "Even with the Star, I can't prevent him from coming through."

"What can we do?" Jiron asks.

"Get everyone out," he says. With sweat pouring down his face, he adds, "Fast."

Tinok leans on Jiron's shoulder as they hurry over to where Brother Willim cradles Miko's head. "We've got to go," urges Jiron. He sees the blood covering the front of his robes and the two halves of his staff lying on the ground nearby.

"Miko's lost too much blood," he says. "He can't make it by himself and I am not strong enough to carry him."

"Can you help Tinok?" he asks.

"I'm alright," Tinok says as he lets go of Jiron's shoulder. "My strength is coming back."

"Okay." To Brother Willim and Tinok he says, "You two help each other." Bending over, he picks up Miko. The hand that had held the dagger is still a little numb, but serviceable as life returns to it. Turning back to James he hollers, "Let's go!"

James turns his head toward them and they can see the strain etched across his face. "I can't go," he says. "If I do, he'll pass through."

"You said he's going to pass through anyway," he yells back. "We failed."

Shaking his head, James says, "If the gate is no longer here, he won't be able to pass through."

"You mean...?" he asks.

James nods and says, "I'm going to destroy it." When Jiron hesitates, he says, "I can't hold this for long." Reaching into his pouch, he removes the medallion with the warrior priest symbol and tosses it to Brother Willim. "You don't have much time."

Brother Willim snatches the medallion and puts it in an inner pocket of his robe. He nods and with he and Tinok leaning on one another, head for the stairs.

Jiron remains motionless as he stares at James.

James meets his eyes and says, "It's been fun."

A tear runs down the face of the battle hardened pit fighter.

"Go," urges James then turns his attention back to the gate.

"Come on Jiron!" Tinok hollers from the stairs.

With the unconscious body of the High Priest of Morcyth in his arms, he hurries after the other two. Moving to the stairs, he begins climbing up. He only pauses a moment when he reaches the point where the stairs leave the cavern. Looking down at his friend, he sees the light from the Star still shining forth. Completely surrounding James is a ring of shadows, not nearly as far back as they had been. "Goodbye James," he says then continues up the stairs.

"Jiron?"

Stig comes over to where Aleya is lying on the bed. Her eyes are open and she sits up abruptly when she realizes that Stig, Shorty, Reilin and Aku are the only ones in the room.

"What happened?" she asks. When the others fail to answer, she understands. "No!" she cries. Rising from the bed, she starts to head for the door.

Stig steps in front of her and says, "It's too late. They're already in the temple."

From where he stands looking out the window, Shorty says, "The whole temple area is swarming with guards and soldiers."

Aleya rushes over and looks out across the dark city. Unable to see the temple well from here, she turns to them. "How could you let them go in there alone?" she demands. They can barely meet her accusing eyes let alone answer. "How could he do this to me?" The last question is more to herself than anything else.

Gazing for a moment over to where the temple sits, she then puts her face in her hands and begins to sob. The others in the room glance to each other, none knowing what to do.

Aku gets up from his position in the corner and comes to her. He slips his hand into hers and together they stand there, with only the sound of her sobbing disturbing the silence.

"How many are there?" Potbelly asks. Deflecting a sword stroke with his knife, he follows through with his sword and guts the guard before him.

"I don't know," replies Scar. Both of his blades are red with blood from the bodies that litter the hallway from where they stand at the top of the stairs, all the way back to where they first crossed swords.

Ever since the others had left, they've held the corridor. Both now sport numerous wounds and have been forced to give ground until they now stand at the top of the stairs. Unwilling to give any more, they decided to make their stand here.

"Wonder if they made it," Potbelly says as he lashes out with his knife. The man he struck dodges back momentarily when a six inch long cut opens up on lower abdomen,

"Doubt if we'll ever know," Scar replies, then he feints with the sword in his left hand. When the temple guard raises his sword to block, he runs him through with his other.

Standing side by side, the two comrades trade blows with all who come. Only rarely do their opponents manage to get through their guard. The skill Scar and Potbelly are facing is woefully below what they're used to facing in the pits.

"We could always surrender," suggests Potbelly.

"I'd rather eat bloodworms for breakfast," replies Scar. "Besides," he begins then has to pause as his opponent's sword lunges forward in an attempt to skewer him through the middle. Unfortunately for the guard, he slips on the blood covering the floor and continues forward off balance. It's easy enough for Scar to trip him up and then nudge him toward the top of the stairs.

Potbelly sees what he did and uses his elbow to propel the guard the rest of the way. As the guard completely loses his balance, he hits the stairs and falls. Tumbling down the stairs, he hits the bottom and doesn't get back up.

"Besides," resumes Scar as he readies to meet the next in line, "no one would understand us even if we tried."

"You do have a point there," replies Potbelly.

So side by side they continue meeting all comers. Eventually, guards from the city begin to be intermingled with those of the temple. Blades sing and blood flies as man after man meet their fate at the hands of expert pit fighters.

"Move!" urges Jiron. The weight of Miko in his arms is beginning to tire him. Brother Willim and Tinok have fallen behind and he has had to wait for them to hurry up. "James isn't going to be able to hold off much longer."

"We're coming," Brother Willim hollers back. "Don't wait for us."

To himself, Jiron says, "You have the medallion, I have to wait for you." Then the other two reach him and he moves down an adjoining corridor toward the Hall of Despair. Little Brothers have been their constant companions since leaving James. Most of the time, Brother Willim has one or two who grab hold of his robe and pull him forward. Even they seem to understand the urgency of the situation.

"How much further is it?" Tinok asks. At first he didn't have much strength, but after walking for awhile, the stamina he once had has begun to return. It must have been the time held inactive here that had done it to him.

"Not much more," replies Jiron. In fact, the hallway they are in opens up onto the room containing the bone chair, the room that Brother Willim had called the Hall of Despair.

"Almost there," he says. Upon entering the Hall, he's surprised not to see bodies of Hikuli scattered across the floor. The last time they passed through here, the Little Brothers were embattled with the Hikuli that populated Ith-Zirul. The fact that the Little Brothers had come to the cavern and that no Hikuli had been seen since, seemed to say that they vanquished the little buggers.

He moves along the side wall until he reaches the entrance to the hallway leading to the dais room. "Down here and then we're home free," he announces. Moving into the hallway, he leaves the other two behind as he hurries to the end. Once he reaches the dais room, he lays Miko atop the dais then quickly returns to help the other two.

Lending an arm to both Brother Willim and Tinok, he practically drags them forward. "Easy my son," Brother Willim says when he almost loses his balance. He's still not completely over the wound to his middle the warrior priest had dealt him despite the healing he did on himself.

As they enter the room, he helps Tinok up onto the dais first, then he follows. "Now you," he says as he turns to offer Brother Willim his hand.

Brother Willim takes his hand and steps up upon the dais. The medallion in his pocket triggers the magic within the dais and they vanish.

All his life he had read in books these wondrous tales of people who had overcome the odds. Who had gone the distance despite the obstacles that lay before them. He always wondered if he had it in him to be one of those people. When he sent the others off to safety while he stayed behind, he had his answer.

But what other choice was there?

The struggle to prevent the gate from allowing the presence from the other side from getting through grows harder by the minute. Even with the power of the Star at his beck and call he doesn't have enough to prevent it for long. Having to put more and more of the Star's power into holding the gate closed, he's forced to use less in keeping the shadows away. Slowly they draw ever closer.

He has a good idea what he can do to destroy the gate, he just has to hold out long enough for the others to reach the dais and get away. If he can't, there's little hope that they will survive what's to come.

A little to his right he sees the dark form of Ozgirath as it lays upon the rune covered floor. The dagger Jiron thrust into his breast still glows with ruddy light, the dark robe remains still.

Then his eyes return to the gate as the malignant presence that James can only call pure evil tries again to bull its way through. He can sense the frustration and growing anger coming through from the other side. He can also sense lines of magical energy being channeled to the gate from elsewhere and being absorbed by it. Try as he might, nothing he does effectively interrupts the streams of power from being delivered.

When at last he deems the time is right, he creates the sphere. One that he's created twice before, each time with massive destructive power. The first time was outside the City of Light, the result of which destroyed a good portion of the Empire's invasion force. Not enough to stop them, but it hurt them bad.

The second time was not too long ago when mages came to destroy Illan's army and everyone with it. The resulting explosion that time was immense. It seared the earth for miles in every direction and weakened the boundary between the planes to such an extent that a creature not of this world was able to pass through.

Now staring at the sphere before him, he sees his death, as activating it will surely mean. There will be little chance to escape its blast once he does. Then all of a sudden, the presence from the other side makes a massive push as it tries to force its way through the gate. The gate bulges to an extent further than ever it had before. Sparks dance across its surface and just as James is sure it's going to break through, the pressure subsides.

Now James, he says to himself. *While it's regrouping for another attempt.* He focuses his eyes on the sphere and sends the command that will activate it. *For Meliana.*

No sooner does the sphere become activated than it latches onto the streams of power flowing to the gate and draws them to itself. James can also feel the power of the Star beginning to be drawn into it as well. Opening up the conduit as wide as he can, he funnels raw, primal power to the sphere.

The sphere goes from translucent to deep red in half a second as unimaginable power is absorbed into it. The magic that James had used to prevent the gate from opening is now being drawn into the sphere.

Sparks begin to appear across the surface of the gate and it bulges forward as the presence again tries to cross. Only this time, it's not meeting any opposition. As the gate opens, terror rolls over James as something begins to cross over.

Tearing his eyes from the gate, he concentrates on the sphere. Now so dark red as to be almost black, it crackles with power. Then it reaches critical mass and detonates.

Back in Zixtyn, the priests of Dmon-Li continue sacrificing slaves and directing the resulting power to Dmon-Li's altar in the nexus of the temple. Which in turn sends the power to Ith-Zirul. A backlash of energy travels back along the power stream when the sphere detonates. When it reaches the altar...

Crumph!

...the magic explodes in a tremendous conflagration of energy. The temple rocks on its foundation as the force of the explosion blasts the temple asunder.

"Jiron!" screams Aleya when the temple explodes into the night. Standing at the window, Aleya and the others see a massive fireball rising to the sky where the temple had stood.

"Damn," curses Reilin under his breath.

"Come on," Shorty says. "James said to get out of town if things went bad."

"It couldn't have been much worse than that," agrees Stig.

Aleya collapses by the window and is wracked with sobs. Stig tries to comfort her while Shorty and Reilin gather their things.

"We can't know that killed them," he says to her. "They've survived worse before."

"You think so?" she asks as she raises her head hopefully.

"Sure," he says. "But we need to get out of here before someone comes looking." To Shorty he asks, "You got everything?"

With their traveling packs in hand, he says, "Yes."

"Then head down to the stables and get the horses ready," Stig tells him.

Nodding his head, Shorty rushes downstairs.

Aleya pulls herself up off the floor and stares once again at the fire that is still arcing toward the clouds. "Please be okay," she says. Then taking a deep breath, she takes Aku by the hand and turns to Stig. "Let's go."

"What the hell was that?"

Covered in rock and dirt, Scar and Potbelly find themselves at the bottom of the stairs. The blast knocked them back and threw them down to the bottom.

"James I would imagine," Potbelly replies as he pries his leg out from under a large piece of what use to be the temple wall.

"I think I'm blind," Scar says from further up the stairs than where Potbelly had landed.

"You're not blind," replies Potbelly. "It's just dark. I think the blast collapsed the hallway up there and buried those soldiers along with the torches they were carrying." Stepping carefully, he begins feeling his way up toward Scar. "You still have that flint?"

"Yeah," replies Scar.

Then a second or two later, he hears cloth being torn, then sparks appear as Scar strikes the flint stone. A moment later, a flame appears and Potbelly sees Scar sitting on a broken section of the temple. Beside him is a strip of cloth that use to be attached to his tunic. Using his knife, Scar winds the burning cloth around the blade and holds it aloft as a torch.

"I think we're alone down here," Scar says after looking up and down the stairs for others.

"Looks that way," agrees Potbelly.

"Better see if we can get out of here," Scar says. Getting up off the broken section of temple wall, he turns toward the top of the stairs. That's when he realizes his swords are not in their scabbards. One is lying further up the stairs and the other is wedged in amongst a pile of rocks so tightly that no amount of pulling will free it.

Potbelly sees his predicament and suggests, "Take the sword from the dead guy at the bottom of the stair.

"Good idea," replies Scar and descends to the bottom where the dead guard that they shoved down the stairs lays. The man's sword doesn't fit within the scabbard around his waist so Scar removes his empty scabbard and then buckles on the dead man's. He then draws the sword quickly from the scabbard a couple times to be sure it's in the proper position. Once he's satisfied that it has an easy draw for emergencies, he bends over and tears off several strips of cloth from the dead man's shirt to use as fuel for his makeshift torch.

"Now, let's get out of here." With his knife-torch held high, he ascends back up the stairs. The stairwell is choked with rubble which makes the footing treacherous. At the top, they find little resemblance to the place they had so recently been fighting for their lives. A few bodies of temple guards are wedged in among the debris that's all but blocking the top of the stairwell.

From where Potbelly stands slightly below Scar on the stairs he asks, "Is there a way out?"

"Maybe" replies Scar. "Here take this." He then hands Potbelly his knife-torch. "Let me see if I can get us out of here." Moving toward the choked passage, he begins to feel a slight breeze which gives him hope.

Using his hands, he starts trying to push the rock away. When that fails to yield results, he begins digging out the stones chocking the passage. All of a sudden he stops and turns back to Potbelly. "Kill the light!" he exclaims quietly. "I hear someone."

Potbelly flicks the burning cloth from the blade of the knife and stomps the flame out once it's on the ground. When the passage again goes dark, they notice a faint light coming from the left side of the rock pile.

Scar moves as close to where the light is coming from as he can. After a moment of looking, he returns to Potbelly. "The blast must have broken the outer wall of the temple," he explains. "I'm pretty sure we can get out if we remove a few of the larger pieces."

"Then what are we waiting for?" Potbelly asks.

Nodding his head toward the light, he says, "The grounds out there are crawling with soldiers and priests. We'd never make it."

Potbelly then finds a large chunk of rock and sits down, Scar does the same. "Could use a rest anyway," Potbelly admits with a tired sigh. "Just have to wait until it quiets down out there before we make our break."

Leaning his head back against the wall, Scar adds, "We're still better off than we were before the blast."

"You got that right," agrees Potbelly. Then after a moment of silence he says, "You remember that time…"

Chapter Forty

Sunlight on his face is the first thing he becomes aware of. Then as consciousness continues to come back to him he hears birds chirping, feels a slight breeze blowing, and then realizes he's lying on grass.

Opening his eyes, he sees the tops of trees stretching up to a beautiful blue sky with just a trace of clouds floating high above the earth. From nearby comes the sound of water as it rolls along a streambed. Sitting up, he finds himself in a clearing next to a gently flowing stream that crosses from one side of the clearing before entering the forest on the other.

Taking a deep breath of air scented with pine, he can hardly credit what his senses are telling him. Reaching out he takes hold of a blade of grass and plucks it from the ground. Rolling it between his fingers, he tries to verify if this is real.

Then all of a sudden, the aroma of hot pepperoni pizza hits him and his stomach begins cramping. "I must be dead," he says aloud to himself.

"Hardly," is the reply from behind him.

Turning his head, he sees Igor sitting on the same log that he sat upon when James first passed through the door at the interview when all this began. Next to him on the log is a large pizza box with *Mama's Pizza* written across the top and two plastic cups filled with pop. Igor gestures to the pizza and says, "Help yourself."

Getting up off the grass, James comes over and sits on the log with the pizza between them. "How did I get here?" he asks. Never one to turn down pizza, he takes a slice and bites off a big mouthful.

"Always with the questions aren't you?" retorts Igor with a grin. "Fortunately for your curiosity, I'm in a position now where I can answer a few." He takes a slice of pizza and shoves half the slice in his mouth before biting it off.

James waits patiently for him to finish chewing. In the meantime he finishes off his first piece and takes a second. The pop in the cups turns out to be a favorite drink of his and he quickly downs a third.

Finishing off his bite, Igor says, "Take it easy. You need to make it last, there are no refills." He gives James another toothy grin. "As to your question about how you got here, I brought you here." When he sees the questions again beginning to form behind James' eyes he adds, "I snatched you the instant before that sphere of yours went off."

"Thanks," he says, "I thought I was a goner."

"Well, we owed you that much," he says.

"So can I assume that I have accomplished all that I was brought here to do?" James asks.

"Oh yes," Igor replies. "It couldn't have worked out better all things considered."

"What happened to the Star?" he asks. "Did it get destroyed in the blast?"

Shaking his head, Igor replies, "No. It would take something a bit more to destroy something like that. It's still there beneath the rubble that once was Dmon-Li's high temple."

"Once?" prompts James.

Igor grins. "The blast completely destroyed it," he explains, "as well as just about every other temple he has. It's going to take a long time for him to regain the influence that he once enjoyed on this world, if he ever does."

"What other temples?"

"Did you happen to notice streams of power being directed toward the gate that was made?" Igor asks. When James nods he says, "When your sphere exploded it sent a backlash of power along those streams resulting in rather large explosions on the other end."

"Did Jiron and the others make it out?" Picking up his third slice, he bites off a mouthful as he waits for Igor's reply.

Waving away the question, Igor hops off the log. "My time is running out and there's still one more thing to do."

James looks on curiously as Igor walks a dozen feet away. Then all of a sudden an archway appears beside the little guy. James' eyes widen as he recognizes his grandparent's home on the other side.

"A choice lies before you James," Igor tells him. "You have but to pass through this arch to be returned to the life you left behind."

James comes to his feet and approaches the arch. The feelings of homesickness that he thought were behind him come back in force. "Can I return here if I do?" he asks.

"No James," replies Igor. "I assure you, the opportunity will not present itself again in your lifetime."

Then the front door opens and his grandmother comes outside. She takes her place in her favorite chair on the porch and begins rocking. Emotions rise, as memories come of the times when he used to sit in her lap as she rocked him in that very same chair as a boy. Unbidden, a tear runs down his cheek as he watches her rock.

Igor moves over to the pizza box and grabs another slice of pizza.

"I…I don't know," James says, turning from the arch to look back to Igor.

"I must go, James," Igor says. "The archway will remain for ten minutes. Then it will vanish." Then he shoves the entire slice into his mouth.

James turns to look at his grandmother rocking on the porch once more. "But what..." he begins to say as he turns his head to look back at Igor. He leaves the question unasked when he realizes that he's alone in the clearing.

Ten minutes to decide the rest of my life?

He sits on the ground before the archway. Holding out a hand he forms his orb. *Can I give this up so readily?* But then looking back to his grandmother, he knows that he's all she and his grandfather have. Without him, they have no one.

Wracked with indecision, he continues to sit as he ponders what to do.

"James, there comes a time when..." A talk he and his grandfather had months before he answered the ad that started all this comes to mind. His grandfather had wisdom that he didn't appreciate at the time. He simply thought it was just another attempt to get him motivated in finding a job. But now that his view of the world, and life especially, has grown, he understands just what his grandfather had been trying to tell him.

Making his decision, he gets to his feet.

The following spring, life is good. Rebuilding continues to bring the City of Light back to life. Some sections of the city that were destroyed during the siege and subsequent occupation by the Empire have been rebuilt. One building in particular has been given prominence in the construction effort. Still not even a third completed, it's going to take another year or two, maybe even longer, before the High Temple of Morcyth is completed.

Its walls rise in uneven levels as the work progresses at varying speed depending on what is being built in each particular area. It actually didn't take that long to come up with a blueprint for how the temple was to be laid out. One evening Miko and a master builder went into a room at a local inn and the next morning, the plans were formed. Only divine guidance could have made that possible in such a short time.

Today however, all work has been suspended. The Madoc Patriarchal Council has declared this day a holiday, that all work must cease until the sun rises on the morrow. The city is enjoying a party the likes of which it has rarely seen and everyone has turned out.

Several buildings which had been built upon the old temple site were demolished and the rubble removed over the winter. Lord Pytherian had loaned the effort several hundred soldiers, else it would never have been done so quickly. What will one day be the temple's courtyard has been decorated in festive, spring flowers, garlands, and anything else the people could lay their hands on.

"Are they coming?" one lady shouts to the two men standing at the entrance to the temple.

"Almost," one of them yells back.

"He better hurry up or there won't be any food left," Scar says.

"You got that right," replies Potbelly. "Look at 'em, they're like a horde of locusts."

"Locusts?" asks Scar.

"Yeah," replies Potbelly, surprised he hadn't heard of the little beastie. "It's a small insect that…"

Dressed in the finest attire that could be found, they stand before where the doors to the temple will be placed once the front wall has been made ready for them. Inside, they hear the final words of Miko, as he finishes the ceremony.

"…together. From this day forward, you James, and you Meliana are one. Forever bound to walk through this life together until the end of your days." Bent over the Book of Morcyth, Miko looks almost comical in the ceremonial robes of the High Priest. He found a description of what they were to be in the Book of Morcyth and had a set made for this occasion. When he put them on, Scar and Potbelly couldn't stop laughing, which is why they had the honor to stand guard at the outer door.

He pauses a moment as he scans the pages. Silence hangs over the hall as everyone watches.

"Is that all?" asks James him quietly.

Looking up, Miko says, "Hmm?"

"Is that all?" Meliana asks.

"Oh," he says and looks up quickly at the assembled guests within the shell that will become the temple. "Uh," then he returns his eyes to the book and quickly peruses the passage on marriage. "Yes, I do believe so."

Then James turns Meliana toward him and stares at her for a brief moment. Flowers in her hair and wearing a gown of white with small blue dolphins embroidered along the hem, she's never looked lovelier. "I love you," he says.

"I love you too," she replies then their lips meet. The people in attendance erupt in cheers and clapping.

When he breaks off the kiss, James glances to where Jiron stands beside him. A big smile across his face, Jiron gives him a nod.

Aleya stands as Meliana's maid of honor, though she's no longer a maid. When both she and Jiron had finally made it back to The Ranch, they wasted no time in getting married. Now she's several months along on their first child.

James takes Meliana's arm in his and turns toward the crowd. He takes a moment to meet the gaze of those who came to share this moment with him. Lord Pytherian stands in his finest clothes, the rest of the Patriarchal Council arrayed on either side of him; Illan in his Black Hawk armor that's been shined to mirror perfection with the surviving members of Miller's band, including Fifer who's having to use a crutch due to his lost leg,; Brother Willim and the two remaining members of the Hand of Asran; Delia and Tersa stand with a much improved though still solemn Tinok as well as Shorty, Stig and Reilin; the Recruits, most of whom have their families in attendance; Roland, Ezra, Arkie, and Aku whom they have taken into their family; and finally Ceryn who was the first person he met after coming to this world.

Then he steps forward and the crowd parts, creating an aisle to the front door. James and Meliana walk down the aisle as music begins to fill the air. He glances over to Perrilin where he and several other bards strike up a festive tune. Perrilin smiles and gives him a nod which he returns.

Meliana's father is there beaming with pride. How many men's daughters have such important people in attendance at their marriage? James pauses a moment when they reach his side. "Thank you sir," he says. It took some doing in getting all this arranged in such short order. But when he asked Meliana to marry him, she went into high gear and got it all arranged.

"You do my daughter right now," her father says.

"I shall," he replies. With a grin to his bride, he says again, "Rest assured I shall." Then they resume their trek to the main entrance where Scar and Potbelly stand guard.

"...and that's why I said they're like a horde of locusts," concludes Potbelly. Noticing that the newlyweds are on their way, he nudges Scar in the side and they take their positions to either side of the entrance. Standing straight and tall, they draw their swords and hold them up with the tips touching to form an arch that the couple will pass through.

The courtyard grows quiet in expectation as the couple makes their way forward. When James and Meliana appear, the crowd cheers and applauds. The couple pauses there a moment as the cheering goes on and on. The people there know him well. His deeds have been sung in every tavern from Cardri, Madoc, and beyond. They know that no other person has been more responsible in gaining Madoc her freedom.

"Hurry up man," Scar whispers to him.

"What's the hurry?" James whispers back.

"I'm hungry!" he replies. "Been standing here a couple hours at least."

James glances at him then breaks out into laughter. Meliana can't help but do the same. Then they begin moving down the steps and make their way into the crowd with Jiron and Aleya right behind. The rest of the wedding guests follow led by Lord Pytherian and the Patriarchal Council.

"Look!" James says to Meliana with barely restrained laughter. She turns her head and sees a table filled with tarts. Next to it stands one of Miko's new priests that he's gathered to Morcyth. "He's making sure the High Priest, who since he performed the marriage is traditionally bound to be the last to leave the temple, will have some when he gets out." Unable to restrain himself any longer, he allows the laughter to roll forth.

The afternoon and evening is filled with merriment, eating and socializing. When the sun at last begins it's descent to the horizon, James and Meliana quietly slip out from the party. Not too far away is a fine inn, one of the first to be rebuilt after the Empire left. There they will spend the night before leaving for The Ranch in the morning.

Heading there arm in arm with his bride, he says, "Never has a man been happier than I am right now."

She squeezes his arm and says, "I'm glad." She then lays her head on his shoulder as he puts his arm around her.

"I just wish my grandparents could have been here to see this," he says a bit wistfully.

"I know," replies Meliana. Shortly after they were engaged, he had filled her in on everything.

When they reach the inn and are ascending the stairs to their suite on the third floor, they hear the inn's door open and footsteps running toward them. "Damn!" he says and begins hurrying his beloved along.

"What's wrong?" she asks.

"Come on!" he yells and grabs her hand as he races up the stairs. When they reach the third floor landing, they hear the person on the stairs below, rounding the second floor landing on their way up to the third.

Running down the hallway, he fumbles in his pocket for the key. Beside him, Meliana begins to grow fearful. Arriving at the door, he mumbles "Come on!" to himself as he quickly tries to find the key. Just as he plucks it from his pocket, Jiron appears on the third floor landing.

"James!" he yells.

James thrusts the key into the lock and opens the door. Practically throwing Meliana inside, he closes the door just as Jiron hits it from the outside.

"Open that door!" Jiron yells.

Placing his back against the door, James keeps it closed. "No!" he yells. "Go away."

"But it's custom!" Jiron yells through the door.

"Not for me it isn't," replies James. Then he throws the bolt and for good measure, seals the door with magic. He turns to see Meliana's face alight with amusement. "What?" he asks.

Bang! Bang! Bang!

"James! You've got to let me do this!" Jiron yells.

Ignoring Jiron's attempts to gain entry, he comes to his bride. "What's so funny?" he asks again.

"Miko told me about what happened at Rylin's wedding," she says. Then she giggles at his expense. "Go away Jiron," she yells through the door, "I think that particular tradition ends here tonight."

Jiron bangs one more time on the door before a very undignified giggle causes him to turn his attention to the stairwell. There he finds the High Priest of Morcyth with a tart in one hand, berry juice dotting his right cheek and giggling. Grinning himself, he moves down the hallway to Miko. Then together they head downstairs and leave the newlyweds to each other.

The End

Enjoy James' next adventure in:

Light in the Barren Lands

Book One of
Travail of The Dark Mage
Now available!

Check out the epically adventurous worlds of fantasy author

Brian S. Pratt

The Broken Key Trilogy

Four comrades set out to recover the segments of a key which they believe will unlock the King's Hoard, rumored to hold great wealth. Written in the style of an RPG game, with spells, scrolls, potions, Guilds, and dungeon exploration fraught with traps and other dangers.

Dungeon Crawler Adventures

For those who enjoy dungeon exploration
without all the buildup or wrapup.

Fans of his previous works, especially *The Broken Key*, will discover *Underground* to be full of excitement and surprises. First in a series of books written for the pure fun of adventuring, *Underground* takes the reader along as four strangers overcome obstacles such as ingenious traps, perilous encounters, and mysteries to boggle the mind.

Ring of the Or'tux

In many stories you hear how *'The Chosen One'* appeared to save the day. Every wonder what would happen if the one doing the choosing bungled the job?

In *Ring of the Or'tux*, that's exactly what happens. Hunter was on his way to a Three Stooges' marathon when in mid-step, he went from the lobby of a movie theater to a charred tangle of stone and timber that once had been a place of worship. From there it only gets worse for the hapless *Chosen One*. First, an attempt to flee those he initially encounters (who by the way are the ones he was sent there to save), lands him into the merciless clutches of an invading army (those whom he was supposed to defeat).

The Adventurer's Guild

Jaikus and Reneeke are ordinary lads whose dream in life is to become a member of The Adventurer's Guild. But to become a member, one must be able to lay claim to an Adventure, and not just any adventure. To qualify, an Adventure must entail the following:

1-Have some element of risk to life and limb
2-Successfully concluded. If the point of the Adventure was to recover a stolen silver candelabra, then you better have that candelabra in hand when all is said and done.
3-A reward must be given. For what good is an Adventure if you don't get paid for your troubles?

Jaikus and Reneeke soon realize that becoming members in the renowned Guild is harder than they thought. For Adventures posted as Unresolved at the Guild, are usually the ones with the most risk.

However, when they hear of a party of experienced Guild members that are about to set out and are in need of Springers, they quickly volunteer only to discover to their dismay that a Springer's job is to "Spring the trap."

If they survive, membership in the Guild is assured.

CPSIA information can be obtained at www.ICGtesting.com
Printed in the USA
LVOW061013290412

279585LV00003B/35/P